'This exploration of the Greek Cypriot community
in the 1980s is a delight. Charming'
The Bookseller

Praise for *The Mother-in-Law*:

'Vivacious Greek girl Electra and reserved Englishman Adam
are chalk and cheese on paper. Nevertheless, their bond
is unbreakable – until his mother arrives on the scene.
With sizeable pinches of love, tragedy and humour, this is
deliciously satisfying'
Cosmopolitan

'Engaging, delicately observed and believable story of a young
couple's struggle to stay together after his acid mother moves
in with them to recuperate from an accident'
Good Housekeeping

'A witty, fun yet cautionary tale of marriage'
OK! Magazine

'A whole cacophony of characters from different cultures crowd
into this warm and funny novel . . . A lovely book, rich with
snapshots of Cypriot history and culture and an excellent
observation of how different families communicate'
Candis

Also by Eve Makis

EAT, DRINK AND BE MARRIED
THE MOTHER-IN-LAW

and published by Black Swan

LAND OF THE GOLDEN APPLE

Eve Makis

BLACK SWAN

TRANSWORLD PUBLISHERS
61–63 Uxbridge Road, London W5 5SA
A Random House Group Company
www.rbooks.co.uk

LAND OF THE GOLDEN APPLE
A BLACK SWAN BOOK: 9780552773256

First publication in Great Britain
Black Swan edition published 2008

A CIP catalogue record for this book
is available from the British Library.

Addresses for Random House Group Ltd companies outside the UK
can be found at: www.randomhouse.co.uk
The Random House Group Ltd Reg. No. 954009

The Random House Group Limited supports The Forest Stewardship
Council (FSC), the leading international forest certification organisation.
All our titles that are printed on Greenpeace approved FSC certified
paper carry the FSC logo. Our paper procurement policy can
be found at www.rbooks.co.uk/environment

Typeset in 11/14pt Giovanni Book by
Kestrel Data, Exeter, Devon.
Printed in the UK by
CPI Cox & Wyman, Reading, RG1 8EX.

2 4 6 8 10 9 7 5 3 1

For TM, Emily and George

Acknowledgements

Thank you to my husband for misspending his youth and candidly sharing his stories. Thanks also to Antonia Marcou, the formidable Judith Murdoch and my editors past and present, Kate Marshall and Katie Espiner.

And in a field there stands a golden tree,
Shining with golden leaves and branches rustling
With the soft click of gold . . .

Ovid's *Metamorphoses*

1

Socrates pulled back the elastic on his sling, closed one eye and aimed at the hornet hovering menacingly above Hector's bald head. The old man dozed unawares beneath the coffee-house trellis, the ends of his white moustache fluttering as he exhaled a guttural snore. Socrates had a keen eye and good intentions but he let his stone fly at the exact moment when Hector hiccupped and the hornet floated lightly away. The stone struck the old man's head with a resounding crack. His body jerked and his eyes flew open momentarily before he collapsed head first on to the wooden table in front of him.

Earnest conversation buzzed in the coffee house. Dice and backgammon pieces rattled against wood. An upbeat *tsifteteli* blared from a small radio on the window ledge. An old man sipped grainy coffee and fiddled with his worry beads. No one seemed concerned that Hector lay sprawled on the table beside the whitewashed wall surrounding the coffee house. The old man had a reputation for dropping off anywhere and assuming peculiar poses in his sleep. Socrates rushed across the street to take a closer look and saw a bloody gash on the widower's head where the stone had pierced his skin. The unbidden spectre of his mother's angry face loomed large before his eyes. She was unlikely to believe the truth – that he had accidentally killed the man whose life he had been trying to save.

He backed slowly away and was poised to run when Hector exhaled a rasping groan. Socrates wondered if this was Hector's proverbial last breath; an involuntary exhalation of air from his lungs; his final, chilling utterance. Suddenly, the octogenarian twitched. Wearily he lifted his head and a frown took shape on his craggy, weather-beaten face. He fingered the wound and winced before opening his eyes to glare at the sling nestling in the palm of Socrates' hand. Without warning, he grabbed his assailant by the wrist, his nostrils elongating as he bared loose-fitting dentures too white for his liver-coloured face. Socrates tried in vain to pull himself free but Hector was stronger than he looked and squeezed so hard that the boy's hand, deprived of blood, began to pulsate. The widower, a builder for fifty years, was unexpectedly muscular beneath his sagging skin.

'Look! Look what this devil has done to me,' Hector cried, his dentures slipping away from his gums as he talked and spat simultaneously. 'What the hell were you doing? Did you mistake me for a bird? You nearly cracked my head open.'

Socrates saw no point in telling the truth, pleading for benevolence. No one would believe he'd meant well and anyhow his evidence had flown away, back to some grape-vine or burgeoning plum tree. In all likelihood he would be judged on his past crimes, which were many and varied and mostly premeditated.

'Giorgios, fetch me some *zivania*,' Hector called out to the coffee-shop owner while the other men scrambled to their feet and gathered round, shaking their heads.

A small tumbler soon arrived containing the strong spirit famed for its medicinal properties. Without letting go of his attacker, Hector reached into the deep pocket of his pantaloons and pulled out a rumpled, grey handkerchief. He dipped a corner into the *zivania* and dabbed his head with it, flinching when the alcohol stung his torn flesh, before knocking back the rest of the tipple and licking his lips. And then he took hold of the gnarled walking stick lying on the ground beside his chair, tightened his grip on Socrates' wrist and rose from his seat.

'I'm not letting this devil out of my sight. Not until his mother has heard about this.'

'Yes. Tell his mother,' Giorgios said, his sentiments echoed by those around them. 'Don't let him get away with it.'

'I'll march him home right now and watch his mother beat him 'til he's black as coal.'

Eleni threw her arms up in desperation, beseeching God to give her youngest son a grain, a broad bean, a modicum of sense. What had she done to deserve such a wayward twelve year old? Where had she gone wrong? Why did he insist on torturing her so mercilessly? What demon had possessed him when he assaulted the kind old man? She made Socrates apologise and dismissed his tale about the hornet as invention. He always had an excuse at the ready but this time she would not swallow it, this time she would trust her gut instinct and punish him severely.

Eleni disinfected and dressed the old man's wound, made him coffee and plied him with homemade biscuits in recompense.

Socrates did not like the way Hector ogled his mother and followed her around the kitchen. The way his gaze lingered on her backside and slunk down to her slim ankles. Wishing he had never tried to save the lecherous old man from the hornet's sting, Socrates did not leave his mother's side until Hector had sloped off, back to the coffee house, his bony cheeks flushed, his white moustache curved in a smile and peppered with biscuit crumbs. Socrates bore his mother's protracted rant with a blank expression and was sent to his room, 'to think about Hector' and 'reflect on the consequences of his wickedness'. On his way out of the kitchen he impulsively grabbed a box of matches from beside the cooker and slipped them into his pocket.

Eleni washed the dishes feeling aggrieved. Why hadn't God blessed her with a daughter to help her in the kitchen? Why were both of her sons cursed with terrible and/or life-threatening habits? Socrates had started life a cherub, the perfect son, a sweet, compliant boy who listened to his mother. Now, he loved danger. Trouble drew him like a magnet. He listened to no one. His brother Petri was no better. He was a bona fide gigolo with a penchant for foreign women, changing girlfriends more frequently than he changed his underpants. There was no hope of him ever settling down and giving Eleni the curly-haired grandchild she was desperate to swaddle. Whenever he was on leave from the army Eleni would spot him driving through the village with a different tourist girl at his side and her heart would sink into the soles of her feet and lie there, floundering heavily, like a fat catfish caught in the shallows. Eleni lay awake at night worrying that one day soon Petri would bring home the wrong kind of girl, that all her hopes and dreams would shatter as irreparably as a broken mirror.

Why was her son so blind to the beauty of home-grown girls? Had he not heard the wise old adage that it was better to choose a shoe from one's own country, even if it needing mending? What did this saying mean to Eleni? That a comfortable old shoe could be repaired, whereas an ill-fitting shoe would always pinch the toes and slide off the heel. Likewise, the wrong wife could never be made right. Eleni had always hoped her son would end up with Maria, the daughter of a neighbour, who had a good job at the airport and was a far cry from the foreigners who titillated the menfolk by flaunting their bodies and offering sex without commitment. And Maria was no old shoe. *She* was a fine silk slipper.

Born and raised in the village, Eleni sniffed social change in the air and to her it smelled as rotten as putrefying fish heads. Her safe and predictable bubble, filled with the reassuring scent of jasmine disinfectant, had blown a puncture and was rapidly deflating. Young people were leaving the village in their droves to work in the neighbouring town, enticed by the bright lights and dingy bars, by the hedonistic ambience and the availability of loose women. Eleni felt she was losing control of both her sons, that they were turning their backs on Cypriot tradition and the simple life.

*   *   *

Socrates paced his bedroom, a rectangular space too small to contain his restlessness. He had spent half the day cooped up in a stuffy classroom with the tyrannical Mr Hadjimichael, and now he was confined to his bedroom with nothing to do. A warm breeze blew through the window carrying with it a hint of honeysuckle and its pleasant associations – the scent a reminder of late-summer nights on the veranda with family and friends, surreptitiously swigging wine, eating barbecued meat, and listening to his parents sing along to the rousing love songs of Sophia Vembo and her patriotic World War II anthems mocking Benito Mussolini. Summer lay tantalisingly on the horizon and with it freedom from the classroom, its equations, Greek literature, English classes and the acid tongue of Mr Hadjimichael. An enticing landscape lay beyond his window: narrow alleyways and paved squares; and beyond them acres of green fields and chalky hills as pitted as Swiss cheese with potholes and caves.

Bored and agitated, Socrates sat on his bed and took the matchbox out of his pocket, wondering how long his mother expected him to reflect and how soon she would charge up the stairs to dole out further punishment. Perhaps she would make him sweep the back yard, or mop the parlour, or polish her silverware. He picked at the bedspread's fine hairs and pulled them off, blowing them from his fingers, watching them float lightly away. As he stroked the fluffy bedspread with one hand and rattled the matches in the other, he wondered how these fine hairs would burn. Would they ignite as easily as cotton wool and extinguish with a hiss? Were they in fact flammable or else fire-resistant? Would the burning smell be vaguely pleasant or noxious like plastic? Socrates knew a great deal about combustion, much more than Mr Hadjimichael had ever taught him in chemistry lessons with his piffling chemical reactions executed in test tubes and held at arm's length from the teacher's goggled face. Socrates loved building bonfires and feeding the flames with wood, paper, paraffin, leaves, dry grasses, pocket fluff, hair collected from the barber's shop floor, and especially aerosol cans. The blood rushed to his head as he waited for these cans to explode, fly up into the air and crash back down to earth all mangled and charred.

He climbed off the bed and lit a match, his impulsive curiosity too strong to suppress. He put the flame to a corner of the bedspread and watched the tiny fire flicker and flare and spread like a hand with a soft shushing noise. He picked up the sandal beside his bed and beat the fire out before rubbing at the singed hairs, erasing all evidence of arson. He struck a second match, savoured the sulphurous smell and set fire to another section of bedspread, the flames running along the delicate fibres and reflecting on his golden cheeks. He let the fire spread a little further this time before reaching for the sandal and beating it out, feeling strangely powerful and in full control, master of the flames. Wanting to hear the shushing sound again and watch the fire dance, he struck a third match, promising himself it would be the last. This time he gazed in wonder at the incandescent particles racing across the bedspread, watching for a second too long and acting several seconds too late.

He attacked the spreading fire with a sandal in each hand, beating the bed maniacally, striking the orange glow again and again while it spread unstoppably, finding new exits along which to unfurl its tendrils. Soon, the bed-spread was alight, and a white, choking smoke rose from its surface, making Socrates cough and gasp for breath. As he turned to run down the stairs and escape the fumes he heard a scream from outside.

'Fire! Fire! Eleni's house is on fire,' a woman called from the street below. 'Water . . . fetch water.'

Socrates recognised the high-pitched voice as that of their elderly neighbour Loulla, the camphor-scented widow who had a reputation for being mean to children.

Villagers mobilised in the street outside. Socrates heard shouts and shrill screams, small children crying, doors slamming, water gushing, the hurried sound of footsteps climbing the marble staircase. There was no time to dart across the room and hide inside the wardrobe so he dived under the metal-framed bed and huddled close to the wall as smoke began to seep through the mattress and an excitable crowd filled the room. Socrates wondered what would kill him first – the fire, the smoke or his mother. He pulled the neck of his T-shirt over his face and closed his eyes, trying to hold his breath as flames crackled above him. If fire could reduce a mighty fir to a handful of ash, what would it do to him? It would annihilate him, leaving only blackened teeth, the glass marbles in his pocket and the metal blade of his penknife . . . When water began trickling through the mattress Socrates knew he would live to see another day and set another fire and face his mother's anger. The mattress shook above him and the bed springs rattled as villagers beat down the flames with blankets and towels.

Socrates opened his eyes and saw feet dashing around the room, water splashing on to the floor. He heard the fire hiss and splutter and finally die. Villagers breathed a communal sigh of relief before they began churning out theories . . . perhaps the wind had blown a cigarette stub through the window . . . perhaps an electrical socket had fused . . . perhaps the fire had been started maliciously . . . no, no, the latter was impossible since everyone in the village loved Niko and Eleni.

'Thank God my son disobeys me,' Eleni said, surveying the smoke damage.

'Why's that?' Loulla asked. 'A son should listen to his mother.'

'I sent him upstairs for throwing a stone at Hector's head but he must have left the house.'

Hearing his name, the old man pushed through the throng and stood beside Eleni, pulling the sticking plaster from his injured head. A fire was as good an excuse as any to visit this house where he knew he would feast his eyes and his stomach.

'I bet your son had something to do with the blaze,' Loulla said. 'I bet he set fire to his bed and escaped through the window. That boy is as elusive as a rat. He's probably long gone by now, wreaking havoc elsewhere.'

Socrates felt a stab of hatred for the widow. How dare she slander him in public and plant suspicions in his mother's head! Loulla moved towards the door, saying she had to go home and lie down, and the rescue party began drifting away too. Socrates had already decided on a plan of action. He would wait for an opportunity, climb out of the window and deny all knowledge of the fire. He did not expect a girl called Stephania to bend down at that moment and tie her shoelace, to glance inadvertently under the bed, to ignore the finger he put to his lips and call out: 'Socrates is hiding under here.' In the chaotic moments that followed he vowed to make the girl pay for this betrayal.

Villagers noisily piled back into the room and got down on their knees to peer under the bed. Even Loulla splayed her arthritic legs and bent forward to glower and tut and say, 'I'm not stupid. I told you, Eleni.' What right did the widow have to feel indignant? Socrates thought. He had not damaged her bed. This was not her house. She was not his mother.

'Come out from under there, now,' Eleni screamed, trying to grab her son but unable to reach him. 'Come here, you devil.'

'Give him a beating! Smack his behind,' Loulla screeched, shaking her fist.

Socrates shrank back against the wall, refusing to come out and face public humiliation. Being stared at like some curio by dozens of reproachful eyes was degrading enough. No one seemed to care that he had nearly perished in a fire, that his throat was dry and sore and his eyes stung. The sea of bodies began to part to make way for a pair of tan brogues with clickety heels, well-worn shoes moulded to the peculiarly crooked shape of the wearer's feet. Socrates closed his eyes and covered his face, blocking out the sight of his father's shoes. He silently cursed the big mouth who had rushed across the village to the local building society where his father worked as a teller.

'What's been going on?' Niko asked his wife.

Eleni got to her feet and smoothed down her hair. 'Your son set fire to the bed.'

'And earlier today he nearly killed me with a stone,' Hector croaked. 'I have lived through three wars and fought in two of them myself yet that stone nearly saw me off.'

'He's under the bed,' Loulla said, pointing with her stick. 'If he were my son I would beat him till he broke.'

'Come out, Socrates.' Niko spoke in a commanding tone that could not be disobeyed, that was infinitely more powerful than Eleni's hysterical shrieks. Socrates crawled commando-style out from under the bed and stood before his father, feeling his legs begin to shake. Wet, bedraggled and black with soot, he lowered his head, waiting for the slap across the cheek he felt he deserved, for a booming shout to resonate in his ears.

'Give him a good hiding, Niko. Teach him a lesson he won't forget,' the widow urged, waving her stick in the air.

Niko bent forward to face his son and breathed a heavy sigh. He shook his head and tutted before crossing himself and kissing Socrates on the forehead. 'Thank God you're all right,' he said, squeezing his son in his arms, tears welling up in his eyes.

'Is that all you're going to say?' Eleni pursed her lips and crossed her arms across her chest. 'You do realise he nearly burned the house down? He's gone too far this time. He needs to be—'

'Eleni, enough!' Niko held his son by the shoulders and looked once again into his eyes. 'Son, please . . . don't ever, ever do that again. I love you and I don't want to lose you.

Do you understand? What you did was very dangerous and stupid.'

With that he turned to leave and go back to work with Loulla calling after him, 'No wonder the boy is uncontrollable. Instead of getting a well-earned slap for setting fire to his bed, he gets a kiss. What's to stop him doing the same thing again? That boy will kill us all one day, you mark my words.'

Socrates' legs trembled and a terrible sense of guilt overcame him. His father's kindness, his loving gaze and the tears in his eyes had affected him more deeply than any slap or stream of curses. He ran out of the room, down the stairs and out into the street where he burst into tears. He did not feel guilty for stealing the matches or setting fire to the bed or inconveniencing his neighbours. He had a father with a heart of gold and hated letting him down.

2

The ground, moistened by spring rain, gave off an earthy, bovine smell. A house martin sat at the entrance of a funnel-shaped nest which curled around the corner of a weathered balcony. Socrates ran beneath it, past a four-hundred-year-old marble slab bearing the insignia of Venice, a winged lion, set in the doorway of a terracotta house. He dodged a woman struggling with shopping bags laden with aubergines, small cucumbers, courgettes and several bunches of coriander. A flock of starlings colonised a roadside olive tree, its branches laden with dense clusters of cream flowers ready to mutate into oval fruit. The penetrating shouts of a mother chastising her children drifted from an open window, mingling with the shrill chatter of the hungry starlings.

Ignoring the taunts of his classmates Tino and Zaphiri who called after him, 'There goes Cholera! Don't get too close, he might be contagious,' he bolted like a frightened hare along the street. Socrates was proud of his nickname though it was used to denigrate. It gave him a dangerous, menacing air and warned people to keep their distance. It was an advantageous epithet for a boy who was slight of build, and preferable to the embarrassing comments he had had to endure for most of his early life from his mother's friends. How sweet . . . how angelic . . . what beautiful eyes . . . her friends had cooed for almost a decade. Nowadays, 'angelic' and 'Socrates' were never uttered in the same breath and the once-sweet boy was more commonly known, amongst his peers, as 'Cholera' because he was always caked in dirt and covered in lumps, scabs and bruises. He frequently crashed his bike, leaped fearlessly from high walls and scratched his legs climbing through the tight mouths of potholes. He once fell from the uppermost branches of a carob tree and broke his arm. Parading his plastered limb through the village, he had never felt happier.

Turning his head to wave at a friend, Socrates ran straight into the arms of Victora the *karagiozopaihtis*, puppet master of the shadow theatre. Victora performed in the village square three times a year and travelled the island entertaining audiences with his colourful paper puppets, that jumped and danced and beat one another before a white screen lit from behind by gas lamps. Victora was unlike any other old man that Socrates had ever come across. He was dapper, had a trimmed white beard, smelled of aftershave and always wore a beret and cravat, even in the height of summer when a shirt and tie were unbearable and temperatures rose to forty degrees. The man was as colourful as his puppets and reminded Socrates of Sir Dionysios, a well-known puppet character representing a fallen aristocrat who was overly well-mannered and always wore a top hat. Like Sir Dionysios, Victora gave the impression that he had fallen from a great height, that he had come from another place, that his clothes had seen better days, that he had fraternised with nobility.

'*Bonjour*, Socrates. Where are you going in such a rush?' Like Sir Dionysios the puppet master peppered his speech with French. 'And why are you so dirty? Come inside the house and clean yourself up.' Victora's voice was deep, hoarsened by years of shouting in the harsh, grating voice of the prankster Karagiozi, the impoverished protagonist of his simple plays. For three decades Victora had altered his voice to fit each character, switching from the nasal tones of the uppity and vain Morphonios to the barked commands of the Pasha, the highest Turkish official, representative of wealth and power.

Nodding, Socrates followed Victora into the house, feeling excited and apprehensive. Having heard his friend Marco describe the interior of Victora's strange house, Socrates had hankered after an invitation for quite some time but the opportunity to visit had never yet arisen. Now he followed Victora into a living room that was every bit as odd and eerie and marvellous as he had imagined. On the windowsill, illuminated by the light that streamed through the glass, were a row of Karagiozis in different guises – as sea captain, prophet and doctor – the respectable personae the character assumed to play his pranks and make money under false pretences. Karagiozi was prepared to turn his hand to any trade to earn a meagre living for his family, to cheat, steal and lie to make ends meet. He usually failed in his endeavours, got beaten up and returned to his humble shack poorer than when he set out.

'Relax, my young friend,' Victora said, pointing to an impractical-looking sofa covered in burgundy velvet. 'I'll go and fetch a wet cloth for your face.'

Socrates perched on the edge of a seat that sloped upwards at one end, had no backrest and was oddly positioned in the centre of the room. The velvet was thick and soft but worn in places, revealing a lattice of canvas fibres underneath. The room was filled with the memorabilia of a well-travelled man: wooden elephants, clay monkeys, painted masks, china Buddhas, a small windmill, a ship in a bottle, copper urns and silver boxes. A deep bowl on a table close by contained a heap of the biggest, most vibrantly coloured glass marbles Socrates had ever seen. He picked one up and studied the red, blue and yellow swirls running through the heavy globe of clear glass. Socrates owned hundreds of marbles, most of them frosted glass balls taken out of disused car batteries, but this was an ace, a trophy marble, one that other boys would covet. He wanted it. He had to have it. He slipped it quickly into his trouser pocket.

Dusty books with cracked spines lined the shelves of a mahogany cabinet. The walls were hung with opulent fabrics woven with metallic threads, and shadow theatre props were arranged around the room: the Sultan's sumptuous cardboard palace, Karagiozi's simple wooden house, a miniature fishing rod. Nestled among the cornucopia of strange ornaments on the sideboard was a framed black-and-white photograph of a woman in a chequered headscarf standing beside a man in black pantaloons and knee-high boots. Similar photographs of long-dead ancestors stood or hung in most village homes. Hearing Victora's footsteps

Socrates felt a pang of guilt and removed the marble from his pocket, returning it to the bowl.

Victora walked into the room holding a wet cloth. 'Why don't you put your feet up? That seat is for reclining on, you know. It's called a chaise-longue and was inspired by the traditional Roman couch.'

'I'm fine, thanks.' Socrates could not feign interest in a seat and its origins and was unaccustomed to relaxing in other people's homes.

Victora handed him the cloth and sat beside him. 'Here, wipe your face and clean your hands and tell me how you got so dirty?'

'I started a fire.'

'*Incroyable!* Where?'

'In my bedroom. It was an accident.' Socrates wiped his face and rubbed at the soot on his hands.

'At least you didn't get hurt.'

'That's what my father said.'

'Your father's a good man. And was your mother quite so forgiving?'

'I'll find out when I get home.'

The puppet master chuckled and looked into Socrates' face. 'You love fire, don't you – I can see it in your eyes.'

Socrates nodded, glancing at the marbles.

'Do you like them? All the children who come here love those marbles. Take one, if you like. Go on. They're no real use to me other than to look at and admire. Take which-ever one you want after you've wiped that black smear off your nose.'

Socrates chose the marble with red, blue and yellow swirls which he had picked up before.

'Who are they?' he asked, motioning towards the black-and-white print.

'My parents. They died before you were born. They were good people and well-loved in the village. The world feels emptier without them, I can tell you. I think about them every day and wish I had spent more time with them when they were alive. Unfortunately, we only truly appreciate what we had when it is lost to us. I can't even visit their graves as often as I would like because they're buried in my father's village which is fifty kilometres and an hour's journey away by bus.'

'Don't you drive?'

'I used to. Now, I walk or ride my bike.'

'Do you live all alone?'

The puppet master nodded.

'Don't you have a wife and children?'

Victora sighed and raised one eyebrow. 'A love of fire and an insatiable curiosity – a lethal combination. No, alas, I don't have a wife.'

Socrates had always been intrigued by the puppet master and the unusual, solitary life he led.

'Is your wife dead?'

'I never got married. Not everyone does, you know.'

'So, you never fell in love with anyone?'

'That is quite a different question. Yes, I fell in love, but only once.'

'My brother Petri falls in love all the time.'

'Good for your brother – he has the right attitude.'

'Why didn't you marry the woman you loved?'

'My Lord! I'm not used to being asked so many questions in such a short space of time. And such personal

28

questions too! If you really want to know, I wanted to marry her but her parents wouldn't have it. The era I grew up in was not the golden age, as some people of my generation like to say. Prejudice and poverty and small-mindedness were rife.'

'Why didn't they want you to marry her?'

'Didn't anybody tell you the Spanish Inquisition ended in 1820! Because, my young inquisitor, I was too poor – penniless, in fact – and so were they. Their only asset was a beautiful daughter and they wanted to sell her off to the highest bidder. So, they found her a man of means and negotiated a generous dowry . . . and destroyed their daughter's life in the process. And I left the village and travelled the world with my puppets and vowed I would never come back.'

'But you did. Why?'

'I had my reasons. Perhaps I'll tell you another time, when we know each other a little better. Now, it is my turn to find out about you.'

'What's there to find out? I haven't done anything or been anywhere interesting.'

'Then perhaps you would like to find out what you are going to do and where you are headed.'

Before Socrates had a chance to reply Victora had taken hold of his hand and started stroking his palm with bony, tremulous fingers, his eyes seeming to glaze over. '*Aman!* What roads you're fated to travel, my boy, what adventures you will have.'

Socrates felt uneasy about the puppet master holding his hand but was eager to hear what he had to say. Perhaps the rumours he had heard about Victora were true – that he could see into the future.

'You're a good boy, a kind boy, but too innocent and trusting. I can see trouble ahead, Socrates. Trouble you will unwittingly become embroiled in.'

'What kind of trouble?'

'If only it were one kind! Trouble seems to follow you as closely as your shadow.' Victora's cloudy blue eyes began to water. 'I'm sorry to tell you this but you will cry many tears, my boy. Your trust will be abused by a friend and you will hold death in your hands.'

The prophecy was exhilarating and at the same time chilling. 'Is someone going to die? Who is it?'

'I don't know who. I can only feel the approach of death, I cannot see its face. You are in grave danger, my boy, and must keep your wits about you at all times.' Then Victora leaned forward and kissed Socrates gently on the hand.

Revolted by the feel of the old man's wet lips against his skin, Socrates pulled his hand away and stood up. 'I have to go.'

'I hope I haven't frightened you, Socrates? I didn't mean to. My intention was only to help, to make you tread more carefully.'

'My friends are waiting for me.' He handed Victora back the cloth.

'Please don't be scared of me. I am a friend, someone who can be trusted. I love children. I have devoted my life to making them happy. Stay a while and I will show you my puppet collection.'

But Socrates headed for the door, anxious to escape the oppressive aura of the cluttered room. The two-dimensional puppets staring back out of tear-shaped eyes suddenly struck him as grotesque and threatening, not as comic caricatures. The sea captain Karagiozi was particularly disturbing with his big hooked nose and long segmented arms, and the prominent hump on a back that symbolically carried the weight of the world. Socrates responded to the puppet master's *'Adieu, mon ami'* with a hurried wave, rushing out of the door and along the street.

3

Petri scanned the dirt road behind the wooden look-out post, waiting impatiently for his friend, desperate to get to the Pussy Cat nightclub and enjoy a couple of hedonistic hours as a civilian. From the narrow wooden hut high on a hill, Petri overlooked a busy dual carriageway leading to the island's main airport. He stared down at the cars rushing past, at the dizzying glare of headlights, at people journeying to and from foreign destinations, and felt resentful, trapped – on the road to nowhere. Army life was killing him, swallowing up his youth, stifling his individuality and denying him a sex life. Moreover, it had claimed the long hair he was so proud of and dressed him in his least favourite colour – dark green – starched and prickly. When he got his release papers, in a matter of weeks, Petri planned to grow his hair, pierce his ear, get drunk every night, and become a more prolific lover than Richard Gere in *American Gigolo*.

The landing lights of an approaching aircraft flashed before him. The plane circled the runway, its tailfin heralding the arrival of long-limbed Scandinavian girls. It was early in the season but the tourist influx had already started and every week a new batch of Nordic beauties descended on the island. The locals steered clear of the beach in April but these hardy, sun-starved northern Europeans needed little excuse to strip down to their thongs and stretch out on the sand. British girls arrived too but they were not as attractive as the Scandinavians and tended to burn and blister in the sun. With such an abundance of foreign beauties on offer, Greek girls, with their large thighs and coarse hair, rarely turned Petri's head. His mother had started dropping hints about their neighbour Maria, saying she would make the perfect wife, endlessly listing her good credentials. 'She's pretty . . . she's hardworking . . . she loves cooking . . .', the latter a sure sign that she'd be destined to grow fat. 'She has a good reputation.' This remark above all rang in his ears like an alarm bell, warning him to keep his distance. A night of passion with a girl like Maria could trap a man for ever, get him marched up the aisle with one arm pinned behind his back.

White light flickered in the distance, through the tight clusters of spiny burnet that lined the winding dirt track leading to the look-out post. The unhealthy rumble of a car engine grew louder, spluttering like a heavy smoker coughing up sputum. A cream Lada pulled up on the opposing verge and Oresti climbed out of the driver's seat, wearing tight jeans and a white T-shirt with 'No Problem' emblazoned across the chest in black letters. It was a fitting statement for an easy-going youth who walked with a lazy, cowboy swagger and a Royale cigarette perpetually hanging from one corner of his mouth. Nothing was a problem for Oresti, especially when he was on leave from the army and the Pussy Cat beckoned. He had pale skin, sandy hair and green eyes, and was generally considered to be the best-looking among his friends, but his handsome, boyish face did not secure him the greatest number of conquests. Petri, with his almond-shaped eyes, streetwise charm and glut of sexual magnetism, never left the Pussy Cat without a woman on his arm.

'What took you so long?' Petri asked. 'I only have three more hours of sentry duty left. I have to be back by two a.m.' His attention was caught by the sight of a pair of feet sticking out of the Lada's back window. 'Hey, Oresti! Who's in the back of your car?'

'A friend. Come to stand in for you.'

'Your friend looks as if he has rigor mortis.'

'My friend will make the perfect sentry.' He pulled open the back door. Inside the car lay a mannequin, dressed in a cream suit festooned with gold sequins. Oresti heaved the mannequin out of the car and carried her across the road under his arm, setting her down on pointed feet before Petri. 'Let me introduce you to Hilda.'

'*Re!* I know you want a woman tonight but isn't this a little extreme?'

'Hilda will be standing in for you. They say the general will be passing by on the main road tonight on his way to pick up a visiting military dignitary from the airport. This sentry box is visible from the road. If the general looks up and doesn't see you standing here, he'll go crazy and you won't be leaving the army in a hurry.'

'You think we can fool him with a blonde mannequin?'

Oresti pulled off the backcombed wig and threw it into the hut. 'There's one problem solved. Now, give me your cap and take off your uniform. Your clothes are in the car

34

– I picked up the suit bag hanging in your wardrobe at home like you said.' He slipped off the mannequin's suit. '*Aman!* What a woman.'

'She has nice breasts,' Petri said, taking off his shirt and handing it to his friend.

'And a nice arse too.' Oresti patted the mannequin's buttocks. 'I hope it's not the only arse I get a feel of tonight.'

Petri climbed into the back of the car to put on his latest sartorial acquisitions – white suit, pink shirt and dark, wide-rimmed sunglasses with large lenses shaped like the compound eyes of a fly. Getting out of the car, he rubbed at the creases in his trousers, fingered the collar of his shirt and straightened his glasses.

'*Re!* What the hell are you wearing?' Oresti asked, forcing the mannequin's arms into an army jacket.

'This, *my friend*, is what you call *high fashion*,' Petri said, peppering his sentence with English learned from late-night American movies.

'And why the hell do you need sunglasses in the dark? To shield your eyes from the glare of that suit?'

'To look stylish and mysterious. We're living in the eighties, my friend, not the time of our grandfathers. You should get yourself a sharp suit and a pair of these shades if you want to pull a decent woman. Now, tell me, where did you find Hilda?'

'My uncle's clothes shop. I have to take her back before he opens up tomorrow morning and notices she's gone.'

He stood the mannequin, naked below the waist, in the hut and put the army cap on her head, pulling down the peak to hide the cobalt blue eyes and gaudy green eye shadow.

'Do you really think the general will fall for this?' asked Petri.

'I hope so, otherwise you will be in serious trouble.' Oresti planted a hurried kiss on Hilda's lips. 'Thank you, my love. I'll pick you up later.' He turned to Petri. 'Put your rifle in the boot of the car and let's go.'

Food smells oozed from the hatch of Costa's mobile van. Ketchup, mayonnaise, gherkins, piccalilli and sweet peppers stood in bowls lining the detachable metal counter and a roast leg of pork hung from a hook inside the cramped vehicle. Above a small awning was the hand-painted sign 'Maradonna Sandwish' beside which a cartoon sandwich, with matchstick arms and legs, grinned and kicked a black-and-white football. Short and stocky with wire-wool hair, Costa bore a startling resemblance to Argentina's footballer ace and unashamedly used this asset as a marketing ploy. Costa looked down at heel in his baggy shorts and greasy number ten football shirt but he had made a small fortune from his unassuming little van and was the unlikely owner of several apartments, a holiday home in the mountains and a silver Mercedes, which he kept in the garage hidden from the prying eyes of the taxman.

Petri ordered a sandwich and watched Costa slice beef tomatoes on a grainy wooden board, cut sesame-sprinkled *franziola* down the middle and warm the soft bread on his gas-fired grill beside rashers of streaky bacon. Petri's mouth watered as Costa spread the warm bread with margarine and filled it with bacon, halloumi, roast pork, tomato, cucumber and gherkins, before wrapping it in greaseproof paper and handing it across the counter.

Petri tore off the paper and took a bite of the sandwich, savouring the sharp, tangy flavours, enjoying a taste far superior to the greasy baked lamb, overcooked pulses and stodgy pilaffs served up in the army canteen. He regularly defied army regulations by ordering kebab from the takeaway opposite the barracks, to be delivered through a hole in the camp's barbed-wire fence. And once a week his mother Eleni would turn up at the barracks with a Tupperware container filled with home-cooked *pastichio*, *koupepia* and *keftedes*.

A restless queue had formed outside the Pussy Cat. Petri and Oresti walked to the front and were greeted with a firm handshake at the door by a bouncer operating a strict system of 'face control'. Petri's muscle-bound cousin Aristos, nicknamed Goliath, controlled entry to the town's busiest nightclub and was an invaluable ally. Crowned Mr Cyprus three years in succession, Goliath was a minor celebrity who looked like the Incredible Hulk mid-transformation – Dr Banner with thick eyebrows and a swollen forehead, just before his skin turns green. Goliath's pectorals bulged beneath a black Lycra T-shirt and his muscular buttocks threatened to explode from the seat of his trousers. He unhooked a blue cordon across the doorway of the club and waved the friends inside, pushing back a group of Scandinavian men who tried to follow them in.

'*Is full*,' he grunted, reinstating the cordon.

'*But you've let those two in*,' a tall Scandinavian protested, running a hand through his thick, blond hair.

'*Tonight, reservations only*,' Goliath replied, narrowing his deep-set eyes.

'But my girlfriend's in there. I've come to meet her.'

Goliath shook his head. 'The club is full. No more room.'

The men drifted away, knowing it was useless to argue, muttering 'fucking Cypriots' under their breath.

Plaster stalactites hung from the low-slung ceiling. The dance floor was a multicoloured Perspex chessboard, lit from beneath. One square flickered on and off, out of synch with the music. A disco ball revolved overhead, projecting shards of dizzying light around the dim cavernous room filled with smoke and bodies. Petri stood at the bar, chatting to friends, drinking Keo beer, his eyes roving discreetly. The club's ingenious lighting altered skin tone and hair colour; illuminated eyes, teeth, flecks of dust and white clothing, turning women's underwear fluorescent. Petri felt at home and alive here, in the company of friends, a world away from the barked commands of his commander-in-chief and the stranglehold of military life.

He took off his jacket, rolled up his shirtsleeves and scanned the room for Oresti. His friend had already made his move and was sitting on a nearby sofa beside a dark-haired girl whose head hung limply to one side; she was either drunk or suffering from some neurological disorder. Petri glanced at his watch – time was running out – he would have to act quickly to steal a kiss before he left the club. He hated being rushed and acting without a strategy, preferring to make eye contact with several women simultaneously, to play the field that way before pursuing the one who gave him the least attention. Petri liked a challenge and the thrill of the chase, to psychoanalyse his prey and ensnare the most difficult quarry.

A friend standing beside him at the bar moved closer to shout in his ear, *'Aman!* Look at that one. She's a goddess. A doll. What a body! What legs! And Petri, my friend, it's our lucky day – she's coming this way.'

Petri was mesmerised by the approaching vision. Not by the goddess in her entirety but by the luminous white thong visible beneath her dress, the scant triangle of fluorescent cotton that seemed to drift through the air towards him. Soon she was up close, standing at the bar by his side and poised to order a drink, seemingly oblivious to the effect she was having on the men around her. Every head had turned to stare at the beautiful girl with the plump lips and the long, platinum-blonde hair that hung down to her waist, yet no one seemed willing to make the first move, to offer her a drink, to risk being rejected publicly. While the competition dithered Petri stepped in, figuring he had as good a chance of success as anyone. In his experience beautiful women were usually grateful to any man with the courage to attempt conversation.

'You wanna drink?' he asked casually, in the American accent he had cultivated to impress.

She looked down at him, through large, blue-tinged eyes, a science-fiction fantasy, a beguiling creature from another planet.

'Gin fizz,' she said, smiling, revealing a perfect set of luminous Martian teeth.

'Whass your name?' he asked, noticing she wasn't wearing a bra, aroused by the outline of raised nipples beneath her tight T-shirt.

'Carina.'

'I am Pete.' Petri motioned to the barman and ordered

drinks. '*You wanna dance?*' he asked, deciding to push his good luck as far as it would go.

He was surprised and flattered when she nodded. Feeling like a man who had just won the lottery he led her on to the dance floor as Opus launched into an uplifting chorus of 'Live is Life'. Keen to impress, he performed the routine he had recently perfected, counting one, kick – two, leg behind – three, kick – four, twist. Carina clapped while she danced and Petri noted that she was somewhat uncoordinated, her long legs moving arrhythmically beneath her like lengths of shapely rubber. A space cleared around them as others stood back to watch and he felt like king of the dance floor, the Pussy Cat's very own Tony Manero. Ignoring the mocking looks of men who thought him a ponce, who envied his gall and his success with women, Petri punched the air and danced until he was out of breath, before taking Carina by the hand and leading her off the chequered floor.

He collected the drinks and his jacket and led her to a black leather sofa beneath an air-conditioning unit that blasted out cold, dusty-smelling air. Carina shivered, hugging her sides, and Petri wished he could close his lips around those nipples like elongated Verigo grapes.

'*You are cold?*' he asked.

She nodded and he draped his jacket across her shoulders. '*Where you from?*'

'*Sweden.*'

'*How long you gonna be here?*'

'*Two weeks.*'

'*How you find your holiday until now?*'

'*I like the weather very much.*'

'*How you find the Cypriot people?*'

'*Very nice.*'

'*And the Cypriot boys?*' Petri grinned.

'*They're OK.*' Carina smiled.

He reached out for her hand and squeezed it. She squeezed back, drawing her face close, her eyes dreamy, opaque. Petri was about to lean forward and plant a kiss on her lips when Oresti suddenly appeared. 'Say goodbye, Petri, we have to go.'

'Just a few more minutes.'

'You're late already. We need to get back right away, before they find Hilda.'

'I'm not leaving without her,' Petri said, before turning to Carina. '*Cam with me. We talk outside.*'

He refused to leave this beautiful girl in a cavern teeming with wolves just waiting to steal her from him. Carina stood up, still holding Petri's hand. She followed him through the crowded club and out of the door. They walked past Goliath, alongside Costa's mobile food van, bypassing the group of drunk and irritable Scandinavian men denied entry to several clubs that evening. A tall, blond man grabbed Carina by the arm and pulled her roughly towards him.

'*What the fack are you doin'?*' Petri shouted, pulling her out of the man's grip and standing her behind him. '*You wanna fight, man?*' He raised his fists.

'What the hell are you doing, Petri?' Oresti cried. 'That man is twice your size. He's going to kill you.'

'*That bitch is my girlfriend,*' the Scandinavian hissed, stepping forward.

'*Not any more,*' Carina called out, covering her face and starting to cry.

'*Not any more*,' Petri repeated.

'*You little shit!*' The Scandinavian threw a drunken punch that missed its target.

'Run! We're outnumbered.' Oresti pulled his friend by the arm. 'They're closing in on us like a pack of dogs. They're going to slaughter us . . .'

Petri was as scared as Oresti of being battered, of having his jawbone turned to splinters, but he stood firm. From the corner of his eye he could see the cavalry arriving. Cousin Goliath and his bouncer friends were closing in, edging their way forward with clenched fists, and before the Scandinavian managed to throw a second punch Mr Cyprus had grabbed him round the waist and lifted him off his feet. The other doormen, hungry for Scandinavian scalp, pounced, needing little excuse to rough up these clean-shaven men with no body hair, who wore tennis shorts and white sweaters tied around their necks. As dust, blood and spittle filled the air, Costa quietly stored away his condiments, removed his metal counter, closed his serving hatch, grabbed a Coke and sat in the driver's seat, munching nuts and watching the fight through his windscreen.

'Cousin, leave this to us,' Goliath called out. 'Take your girl and get out of here.'

'I owe you,' Petri called back, bundling Carina into the back of the Lada and climbing in beside her, adrenalin and Keo beer coursing through his veins as the car sped away from the kerb, its wheels spinning. Carina fell against him, crying. Holding her in his arms, he felt powerfully aroused by the feel of her breasts against his chest, the fruity smell of her skin and the look of gratitude in her teary eyes. As the Lada sped down the wide street, the glare of street lights intermittently lighting up Carina's beautiful face, Petri felt like James Bond at the end of a mission, the unruffled hero claiming his woman. He swept back Carina's hair, pressed his lips against her gin-tasting mouth, and for a few brief, wonderful minutes reality was suspended and all that mattered in the world was the taste of her mouth, the smell of her hair and the feel of one perfect breast cupped in the palm of his hand. Ten minutes later he was back at the look-out post, getting changed and loading Hilda into the car, at the same time asking for the name of Carina's hotel and promising to ring her as soon as he could.

The next morning Petri was summoned to the office of his commander-in-chief, Baizanos, a fearsome disciplinarian from Athens who enjoyed meting out punishments. 'You'll be confined to base for a year,' his friends laughed as he set off on the long walk to the commander's office, past the latrine, through the canteen, and along a corridor smelling of disinfectant. The commander had his spies in camp and Petri was sure he knew about Hilda and the fight outside the Pussy Cat last night. He knocked on the office door and waited, ready to confess and accept his punishment, determined not to be belittled. The commander was always on his back, trying to break his spirit, accusing him of being surly and insubordinate, punishing him indiscriminately, misusing the power he wielded only within the confines of this camp. Outside the barracks Baizanos was a joke. With no social graces, he could not get a woman without the aid of his wallet.

'Come in.'

Petri walked into the small office lined with metal filing cabinets, and saluted. Baizanos was sitting behind his desk, twirling a pencil, his eyes narrowed suspiciously.

'Stand straighter,' he barked. 'Don't slouch, Sergiou.'

Petri straightened his back and stared ahead of him, resentful that he was answerable to this man he did not respect.

'That's better. At ease now, soldier.'

Petri put his hands behind his back, waiting to be told that his time here would be extended yet again for dereliction of duty, delaying his escape from the army.

'Sergiou, certain information has come to my attention.' Baizanos rose from his seat and walked round the desk to stand before Petri with a look of disdain on his face.

'I can explain . . .'

'You don't need to explain.'

'But, Commander, I do.'

'Close your mouth for once and listen.' The commander's garlic breath wafted into Petri's face, making him feel sick. 'The general drove past your sentry box last night, three times as it happens, and he told me something I can hardly believe. In fact, I told the general he was mistaken, that his eyes had deceived him, but he didn't take kindly to being contradicted.'

'The general wasn't mistaken.' Petri dry-swallowed and held his breath.

'You would say that, wouldn't you? But I tell you right now, I'm not at all convinced. I don't trust you, Sergiou – never have and never will. You're a slob, a layabout – always were and always will be. And it pains me to tell

44

you what the general said, it really does, because I am one hundred per cent sure he was mistaken.'

'But—'

'Shut up! Don't speak. The general said he saw you standing as straight as a presidential guard in your sentry box last night, looking in his own words like "a professional soldier", someone the army can be proud of. I thought perhaps he had driven past another sentry box, but no, it was definitely yours. He has asked me to pass on his compliments and to give you a week's leave.'

Petri stamped his foot and saluted and fought the urge to kiss his commander-in-chief on both cheeks.

4

Socrates could hear the taxi driver's booming voice before he turned into his friend's street. Marco's father was bellowing as usual and Socrates stopped outside the house to listen. His friend lived across the paved village square and down a narrow back street in the shabbier part of the village, on the densely populated housing estate built after the Turkish invasion to house refugees ousted from their properties in the north. Marco's father hailed from a village across the Green Line, the physical partition constructed in 1974 to confine the island's two ethnic groups to their respective sides, Greek Cypriots to the south and Turkish Cypriots to the north. The taxi driver often spoke resentfully of his lost inheritance and social standing, about how prosperous and carefree his life would have been if things had turned out differently.

'How many times a week must I eat chickpeas, woman?' he bellowed. 'Bring me some real food. Something that will fill me up, not blow me up.'

Socrates could not hear the wife's reply, though he guessed she was apologising. He imagined her hurrying to the store cupboard to find a suitable alternative to chickpeas, treading carefully around her husband's fragile temper. The taxi driver was tall and broad with jet-black hair, swept back and smoothed down with Brylcreem. He was the image of his late grandfather, Marcoulli Kabraras, whose faded black-and-white photograph hung on the living-room wall. The Kabraras clan were beefy, hairy, physically imposing men who were stubborn, aggressive and notoriously bad husbands.

'Hurry up! I haven't got all day,' the taxi driver complained. 'Fetch some bread and fry some halloumi. I have to leave for work in thirty minutes.'

Before the taxi driver had finished his sentence Irini had lit a gas ring and drizzled sunflower oil into a frying pan. Now, she fished an oblong of cheese from a jar of brine and cut it into slices, laying it quickly in the pan, turning it with a fork when it began to brown. Her face was hot and sweaty, warmed both by the heat rising from the pan and her exasperation. She could usually handle her husband's volatility by switching off, cauterising her own emotions, but today she was feeling sensitive, her head hurt, and the last thing she needed was the brute bellowing in her face. Once, early in their marriage, she had made the mistake of shouting back, of opening her mouth to express her anger and frustration. The taxi driver had punched her in the stomach, making her double over with pain and clutch the five-month-old baby enclosed within her abdomen. He showed no remorse after the event, no concern for the welfare of the child, warning her with a raised fist and hatred in his eyes never to antagonise him again. What was he telling her when he attacked her first-born in the womb? That he was in control, that no part of her was sacrosanct.

Making every effort to hide the fragility of her emotions, she set down a plate of fried halloumi and village bread on the kitchen table before her husband. He pulled the soft, pliable cheese apart and stuffed it into his mouth, mumbling curses as he ate. Recalling the pain and humiliation of that first punch triggered other painful memories. It always happened this way. She remembered one offence and then others came in rapid succession, as unstoppable and devastating as a mass of snow dislodged from the top of a precipice.

Fingering a strand of her dry hair, an image formed in her mind and intensified the headache, of soft curls falling on to a bare, concrete floor the day that Marco turned one . . . The taxi driver had come home from work that day in a filthy mood, to settle down on the sofa with a bottle of Chivas whisky and gripe about the cost of living. Irritated by the sound of his son banging on a plastic drum, he had confiscated the toy. On hearing that the instrument was a gift from the village grocer he had taken his wife by the arm and marched her into the kitchen. Why had the grocer bought his son a drum? He wasn't an uncle, a godfather, not even a friend. There was only one possible explanation in the mind of a man who trusted no one and considered his wife a possession. The grocer had bought a gift for the boy in order to impress his mother, and no man made moves on a married woman without some encouragement. 'I've seen the way you flick your hair when you walk down the street,' the taxi driver spat out, focusing his anger, not for the first time, on the chestnut hair that reached down to his wife's waist. Irini sensed what was coming and shook her head in denial, trying to appease him with the promise that she would keep her hair pinned up in future. 'Cut it off,' he had said, 'cut it all off to prove your innocence.' She agreed, hoping that by morning he would sober up and come to his senses. He left the kitchen briefly, returning with a large pair of scissors which he used to cut off the hair she had always loved, that so many had admired. From that day she had kept her hair cut short for fear of inflaming her husband and being subjected to the same humiliation.

Socrates bypassed the front door, walking through a narrow passageway that led to the back of the house where he picked up a small stone and threw it at his friend's bedroom window. Marco appeared at the window, beside him his six-year-old brother Mino and their sister Dora. Socrates had always admired his friend's good looks and athletic build. Walking beside Marco he felt proud and protected. What he himself lacked in stature, Socrates made up for in cunning, running speed, bravery and wit. Now Marco looked angry, his attention focused on the shouts filtering up from the kitchen. Mino was smiling as usual, seemingly oblivious to the commotion one floor below, and Dora wore her usual worried expression.

'I'm going to Andrico's house. Do you want to come?' Socrates asked.

Marco nodded.

'Can I come, too?' Mino asked.

'No. You're too young to be hanging about with Marco and his friends,' Dora said, draping an arm around her brother's shoulders. 'Let's go in my room and play together until things calm down.'

Dora was only nine but to Socrates she had always seemed older than her years. She flinched now at the sound of crockery shattering in the kitchen, drawing her young brother closer to her.

'I can't leave just yet,' Marco said. 'I'll meet you there. I won't be long. I have to go inside now.'

Socrates knew his friend would not leave the house until his father had left for work, until he was sure his mother and siblings were safe. Everyone in the village knew the taxi driver beat his wife. Neighbours heard her pleas and screams and the dull thud of her body being thrown against walls. They saw the bruises on her tired face, but felt they had no right to intervene. The men dropped hints when they played backgammon with the taxi driver in the coffee house, but never chided him directly. 'Wives can be a headache but they should be treated with respect,' they said, hoping he would get the message. Women gave the taxi driver a wide berth and called him a donkey but refused to interfere in his private affairs, telling themselves that every marriage had its ups and downs.

5

Andrico's house stood alone at the end of an unmade road on the outskirts of the village, nestled at the base of a chalky hill. From the left side of his simple, mud-brick cottage he looked out on to a village spreading like a fungal invasion, whitewashed villas colonising the ground year on year. On the other side lay unspoilt countryside, a view that had changed little in a hundred years, a harmonious landscape of overgrown fields and orchards, home to rabbits, birds, field mice, lizards and snakes. Behind the house loomed the hills, partially carpeted in spring greenery and dotted with gnarled olives, some as old as the nations that had ruled the island in succession: the Byzantines, Franks, Venetians, Turks and British. The oldest tree had a hollow trunk and for centuries had provided shelter for villagers escaping the persecution of whichever tyranny prevailed. These living monuments, workhorses of the tree world, still yielded an edible, crushable, curative yearly harvest; their dry leaves still burnt as incense in village homes.

Once a month Andrico walked to the village square to stock up on washing powder, flour, butter, pulses, cleaning fluids and other essentials. Sometimes children would follow him and mimic his lopsided walk, laughing and tossing stones at his back, calling him *'belo* Andrico' – crazy Andrico. The name-calling wounded Andrico who did not consider himself a fool, who was in fact proud of his accomplishments. He knew how to mix dough and bake bread, how to take a cutting and grow a fruit tree, how to milk a goat and make preserves, how to pickle octopus, cauliflower and capers. His mother had taught him many practical skills and he was largely self-sufficient, growing vegetables on a large plot at the side of the house, keeping chickens and a goat in the backyard.

His greatest joy was tending to the *chrysomila*, the apricot tree, that grew beside the house, on which flower buds were starting to unfurl. The fruit would swell in June and ripen ready for eating in July, before peaches, plums and cherries had reached their peak. Andrico often wondered why his mother had called her beloved apricot the 'tree of love'. Because the leaves were heart-shaped? Because the flowers could be threaded into garlands and worn by bridesmaids? Because she had planted it the year he was born as a symbol of her love for him? The real tree of love, she used to say, grew elsewhere on the island, west of the village in Paphos, over the hills and the Troodos mountain range, close to the spot where the Goddess Aphrodite rose from a foaming sea. In the garden of the goddess's temple, his mother told him, there grew a tree with yellow leaves and branches, bearing golden apples only Aphrodite was allowed to pick. And with these sacred apples she helped young people in love.

Andrico liked to hear his mother tell the story of

Atalanta and Melanion time and time again, never tiring of the tale about the virgin huntress as swift as a deer and the beautiful youth who fell in love with her. Dusting the living room now with a flannel cloth, he recalled the story and the soothing sound of his mother's sing-song voice: '. . . So Atalanta forced her suitors to compete against her, vowing to marry only the man who could outrun her. Droves of youths who tried and failed were put to death by her father, the black-bearded King Schoenus. But Melanion, determined to take Atalanta as his bride, beseeched the Goddess of Love for her help and she gave him three golden apples, picked from the tree in the garden of her temple in Cyprus. He scattered the apples on the ground as he ran, distracting Atalanta, crossing the finishing line before her and securing her hand in marriage. Oh, how the people of the kingdom rejoiced . . .' Andrico's mother always concluded her story on a happy note, putting a smile on her son's face, keeping from him the tragedy which later befell the lovers. Aphrodite, offended by the couple's lack of gratitude, conspired in their transformation from mortals into lions, condemning them to a savage life in the wilderness.

Baby Andrico left the comfort of his mother's womb reluctantly on a cold November morning, sensing perhaps in his neonate head that the world had little to offer him. The midwife thrust both hands inside his mother's dilated uterus and yanked him out before revealing his sex, slapping his buttocks and wrapping him tightly in a soft white sheet. 'It's a boy,' echoed round the maternity ward and brought tears to the eyes of a man pacing the hospital corridor, hoping for a son to take the name of his father. And so Andrico began life as Polycarpo, son of the local locksmith Patraclos, grandson of the late Polycarpo Senior, offspring of a woman desperately hoping this baby would cure her ailing marriage and entice a straying husband back to the marital home.

The baby on whom so many expectations were pinned was born with a conical head, squashed-up face and a shock of jet-black hair. The midwife was not unduly concerned by his appearance, saying he would soon fill out, and grow to be as handsome as his father. After several weeks of supping breast milk the newborn did fill out but his features remained flattened and friends and relatives began commenting, jokingly, that he was staggeringly ugly – a comment that wounded the proud mother and riled the disappointed father who had always been overly proud of his own looks. Several months later the baby failed a series of developmental tests and the doctor declared him brain-damaged, saying he would never walk or talk or lead a normal life. Andrico's mother cried for a week, clutching the baby to her chest, while the locksmith consumed a river of cognac in the local taverna. He felt ashamed of his son, blamed his wife's bad blood for the aberration, and refused to dishonour the name Polycarpo by assigning it to a sick child. The baby was hurriedly renamed Andreas, after the saint to whom his mother prayed for a miracle cure, and 'Andreas', a proud and distinguished name, slowly mutated to Andrico, a harsher, less endearing reworking, one more fitting for such a rough-hewn individual.

When Andrico was eighteen months old and beginning to walk (defying the doctor's pessimistic predictions) his father left, turning his back on his wife and the village, setting up home with another woman and marrying her polygamously. Henceforth Andrico's mother lavished every ounce of love in her body on the child she feared no one else would ever grow to love, making him her life's work. She taught him how to cook and keep house, how to tell the time and write his name, how to rear animals and grow plants, how to find contentment from within. Together mother and son enjoyed simple, quiet pleasures; they baked bread, picked wild flowers, planted vegetables and sang – created a modest and minimalistic world in which they were both profoundly happy. For twenty years Andrico led a contented life, until cancer claimed his mother and cut short his sheltered existence.

Two weeks after her funeral, devoid now of maternal protection, Andrico was gently coaxed into the back of a waiting ambulance and driven to a mental asylum in the neighbouring town, a rambling stone building surrounded by a tall fence topped with rolls of barbed wire. Andrico's uncle, refusing to take responsibility for his sister's problematic son, had convinced the authorities with fictitious anecdotes that his nephew was incapable of living independently, that he was a danger to himself and the community. After failing a series of psychological tests and suffering a panic attack in the presence of the island's chief psychiatrist, Andrico was formally committed and rehoused in the town's mental asylum. Whenever he protested or panicked or tried to escape, he was sedated with bitter-tasting pills or an injection of lithium. He spent his days staring through the wire fence at passing traffic, thinking about his mother, wondering if he had died and gone to hell, wishing he could go home. Five years later, when the asylum was forced to downsize, he was sent back home, to a property fallen into ruin. Memories of life in the asylum still haunted him and his worst fear was that one day, without warning, he would be taken back against his will to that place where people stared with vacant eyes and wandered the disinfectant-smelling hallways half-naked; where they screamed and rocked and resisted the chemicals forcibly injected into their veins.

The day after he arrived back home Andrico found a brown hand-delivered envelope in his letterbox filled with twenty pound notes, which he used to repair the house, re-stock the chicken coop and buy everything else he needed to restart his life. Every few months since his return from the asylum, he woke to find a brown envelope containing several hundred Cypriot pounds deposited inside the wooden box attached to his front gate. He had no idea who his benefactor was but liked to think that his mother had kept her dying promise to watch over him, that it was she who was sending him money from heaven.

Now Andrico dusted the makeshift shrine occupying a corner of his cluttered living room, polishing the walnut tabletop on which his mother's most prized belongings were displayed: her silver hair brush, a bottle half-filled with rose-scented perfume, a wooden jewellery box inlaid with mother-of-pearl, an icon of St Andrew clutching a scroll, a glass vase filled with plastic flowers, the tasselled shawl she used to sling around her shoulders on cool evenings. He polished the glass over the black-and-white photograph he cherished, taken before he was born, of his mother smiling, her eyes shining. This was how he remembered her. How she appeared to him in dreams. He kept a candle burning on the table that cast a flickering orange light across the shrine, bringing his mother's picture and belongings to life.

Hearing a shrill squawk from outside, Andrico knew that someone was approaching the house. He had learned to decipher the meaning of his pet magpie's calls in the same way a parent translates the cry of a child, interprets every utterance and intonation. Koko the magpie had blown on to his doorstep the year before, on a gusty day, a weak heartbeat faintly discernible inside his ribcage. Andrico had reared the chick on bread soaked in milk, on fruit, nuts and eggs, but failed in his attempts to return the magpie to the wild. Koko slept in a box on top of Andrico's wardrobe where he hoarded his finds and regularly flew into the village to visit his favourite places: the coffee house where he was offered candied fruit and sips of cold beer; the bins behind the café-arcade where he scavenged scraps of leftover meat; the churchyard on Sunday morning, scattered with breadcrumbs; Hector's backyard where a tethered donkey was a walking feast of bugs and corns. Villagers smiled and cursed and shook their fists when the gregarious bird swooped down to land on their heads, to steal keys, coins, valuables, lighted cigarettes. 'Watch out, here comes the thief,' they said, laughing, covering their heads and hiding their belongings.

Through the open window Andrico saw Koko side-skipping across the ground towards Socrates and Raphael. Excited by their arrival, he threw down his duster and hurried outside to greet the boys.

'Come inside and have some biscuits and a drink,'

he called out, intercepting them on their way to the shed.

'Thanks, but no,' Raphael replied. 'We want to ride our moped before it gets dark.'

Socrates' friend Raphael was as plump, soft and rounded as a plasticine Buddha. '*Zoumeros*' or 'juicy' the villagers called him to his annoyance, pinching his fleshy cheeks and grabbing the folds of his stomach. Raphael's mother resented these comments even more than her son did, and the unwelcome pinches and prods that accompanied them, since she remembered the mocking remarks she had had to suffer as a large child and plump teenager. Her weight had only ever been a hindrance to her in other people's minds, never in her own. At home Raphael was a pampered mother's boy who lounged about like an overfed cat, but out on the street, amongst his peers, he was feared and generally treated with respect.

'Why don't you come with us? We'll take you for a ride,' Socrates offered.

Andrico shook his head, terrified by the prospect of mounting the dusty old vehicle that looked as if it might fall apart at any moment.

Koko flew up into the air and landed on Socrates' shoulder. Reaching up gingerly, he gently stroked the bird's white chest, his face turned away from its long, powerful beak. Andrico drew closer, coaxed the bird on to his own shoulder and watched the boys head for the disused shed at the side of the house, filled with their belongings and turned into a den. He liked having them close by and had given Socrates, Marco and Raphael permission to use the shed as they wished, not knowing that behind its wooden slats they stored firecrackers, gun cartridges, matches and gunpowder, and unaware that these boys were in fact too young to ride the moped they were now hurriedly wheeling out of their den. The three friends had pooled two years of savings to buy the moped from an unscrupulous garage owner who'd asked only for a parental signature on the purchase contract and been happy to accept a forgery scribbled by Socrates.

The two boys climbed on to the torn leather saddle. Socrates turned the key in the ignition and the moped spluttered into life, the exhaust coughing out pungent black fumes. Unsettled by the noise, Koko screeched loudly and shook his head from side to side as if he were displeased.

Marco came riding up the path then on his bike, calling out to his friends, 'Hey! Wait for me.' He jumped off his bike, propped it against a tree and patted Andrico on the back before climbing on to the back of the overloaded vehicle, flattening the back tyre. Socrates budged forward and propped his legs up on the front fender, while Raphael complained about the squeeze, saying he could hardly breathe and felt like the filling in a sandwich. Socrates turned the throttle and the moped wobbled as it shot forward, the back wheel eating up the ground like a cheese grater, shredding the earth and throwing up dust and gravel.

Andrico waved and Koko flew up into the air to follow the boys on their precarious journey along the craggy, unmade road that led to the grassy foothills, following the furrowed tracks used only by farmers to access their vines, goats and olive trees. The whirring engine unsettled a venomous blunt-nosed viper on the road that thrashed about before vanishing into the gladioli-scattered scrubland.

6

'Don't forget we're fasting, Socrates.'

'OK, Mama.'

'Don't eat any meat, fish, butter, oil or milk. Do you hear me?'

'Yes.'

'And don't forget to come back home for lunch, I'm cooking beans.'

Eleni's instructions fell on deaf ears. Socrates nodded and walked out of the door, jangling the change in his pocket that he intended to spend on a cheeseburger, fries and strawberry milkshake. He was sick of beans and boiled vegetables, bread and olives. His soul was not being cleansed by abstention but becoming embittered by it. He felt hungry all the time and craved the foods he was not meant to have: chocolate bars and ice cream, lamb chops and sticky pastries. Carrying a shoebox under his arm, he ran along the road that led to Marco's house. He had inventive, dangerous, resourceful plans for this box and its contents, plans he was keen to share with his friends. It was the first day of the Easter holidays. Two weeks of freedom from the classroom and the droning, nasal voice of Mr Hadjimichael lay ahead. Socrates had been woken earlier than usual that morning by Koko who flew in through his bedroom window and pecked him on the head. This was a regular occurrence in the mornings but unwelcome at the start of the holidays when he had hoped to have a lie-in.

The taxi driver's freshly polished Mercedes looked out of keeping with the unkempt house it was parked outside. Socrates peered through the passenger side window at the plump leather seats and the polished dashboard, at the trinkets suspended from the rear-view mirror: a blue stone to ward off the evil eye and a large silver crucifix – superstition and religion juxtaposed. Socrates wished his father had the means to buy such a car and imagined himself sitting proudly in the passenger seat with the window wound down and Dalaras blaring from the stereo. He turned with a start at the sound of smashing crockery and the taxi driver's gruff shouts. The walls of the refugee house were paper-thin and afforded the occupants little privacy, thrusting passers-by into the maelstrom of their domestic disputes. Socrates stood at his friend's gate feeling like a voyeur, wondering if he should creep away and come back later, listening guiltily to the taxi driver complain that his wife Irini was lazy, that *he* had been short-changed at the altar.

'Why is my favourite shirt flapping like a flag on the washing line when it should be hanging in the wardrobe? I wanted to wear that shirt today but I can't, can I, because my wife is a slob. I work all day to put food on your table and clothes on your back and what do I get in return? Nothing. No appreciation. No thanks. Zero respect . . .'

Irini clawed at the eczema on her knuckles, scratching at the crusty patches until they leaked fluid. She knew she had to contain her frustration, to keep her mouth shut, to smother the flames not fan them. His favourite shirt had become the bane of her life, a symbol of her husband's irrationality. He had taken it off the previous day and dropped it at the foot of the bed, as he did with all his clothes. Irini had washed it early in the morning with the rest of her whites, kneading the cotton with cracked knuckles in the kitchen sink, wondering if she would ever have the good fortune to own a washing machine. For sure, her husband would never buy her one. He resented spending money on the house and grew angry whenever he was asked to put his hand in his pocket to improve it. After hanging the shirt out to dry, Irini had prayed for a blast of sunshine, fearing her husband would wake up in a bad mood and demand the one item of clothing he could not have.

'Why don't you wear another shirt?' she suggested.

'Why? Why? I've already told you why. Weren't you listening? I want to wear that one. Is it so difficult for you to understand?' He was naked to the waist and reeked of sweat and sweet aftershave.

The three children stood in the doorway watching their father rage against this minor injustice. Irini fought to stay calm for their sakes, though her stomach was in knots and she felt like crying. The children had seen too much in their lives already: their mother knocked off her feet, slapped across the face, pinned against the wall, swatted with all the respect afforded to a mosquito. Irini saw hatred in the eyes of her eldest and feared it was only a matter of time before he snapped and struck out at his father. What she feared most of all was that Marco might follow his father's example and become a violent husband in his turn.

'Papa, you have dozens of shirts hanging in your wardrobe.' It was Mino who spoke. The six year old had yet to learn that the taxi driver could not be swayed by reason when he was blinded by anger.

'Shut up! I don't remember asking for your opinion.'

Dora pulled her young brother towards her and held him in her arms, kissing the top of his head before whispering, 'Don't speak,' in his ear.

'Go upstairs, now.' Irini sent the children away with a hostile note in her voice, to protect them, before turning to her husband. 'Your shirt might be dry by now. Let me go outside and check.'

'Don't bother. I'm already late for my appointment. Go upstairs and fetch me another one.'

Irini climbed the stairs wearily and ran her hand along the row of shirts in his wardrobe; some he had only worn once, others not at all. The taxi driver collected shirts in the same way that some women collected shoes or handbags – he liked owning, stockpiling and admiring them. In the house he penny-pinched but on himself he lavished both money and close attention. He had his hair cut regularly, trimmed his moustache with the precision of a topiarist, and visited the barber several times a week for a shave. He kept his nails clean and expected his shoes to be polished for him every day. The gold chain around his neck was as thick as rope and the chunky gold signet ring he took off only when he showered was as lethal as a knuckle-duster when he lashed out at his wife. Irini pulled out a white silk shirt and carried it downstairs, feeling resentful that her own wardrobe contained nothing but a few loose-fitting skirts and bleach-stained tops.

The taxi driver dressed hurriedly, glancing at his watch, complaining he was late. Irini did not ask where he was going. Such probing only irritated him. Why ask when she already knew why he was lathered in aftershave and had insisted on wearing his favourite shirt? Why he blew into his hand and sniffed his breath. She knew he was late for a meeting with his mistress, a woman who lived in the neighbouring village, whose husband was conveniently away for most of the year, working on a digger in the Arab Emirates. The shirt she had suffered for, the one she had washed with painful knuckles, was for the benefit of another woman. And while that other woman was wined and dined in late-night tavernas, Irini struggled to feed and clothe her children; while the taxi driver grew fat on whisky and *mezedes*, his wife and family wasted away. Sexual jealousy did not enter into the equation. Irini was grateful to the mistress for satisfying her husband in bed, though she found it hard to understand how any woman could find him desirable.

Socrates waited for the shouting to die down before knocking on his friend's front door. The taxi driver answered it with a broad smile, inviting him in, patting him affectionately on the back, asking after his father. This pleasant man seemed to bear no relation to the bully Socrates had heard shouting only moments earlier. The taxi driver's good-natured smile fooled many people into believing he was a decent man. He seemed in good spirits, oblivious to the funereal atmosphere in the house. Marco, his mother and Dora greeted their visitor sullenly. Only Mino smiled and ran up to Socrates, his natural good cheer impervious to the misery around him.

'I'm on my way to the arcade. Are you coming?' Socrates asked his friend.

'Not now. I'll meet you there.'

'Go and have a good time,' his father said. 'And straighten that miserable face of yours.'

His mother nodded, wanting her son out of harm's way. 'Yes. Go, son.'

Dora reached out for Marco's hand, seemingly reluctant to see him leave.

'Let your brother go, Dora,' Irini said. 'And take Mino out into the yard to play.'

Outside, Marco took a sibling under each arm. 'Don't go back inside until Papa leaves,' he said. 'Make sure you don't get in his way. Do you hear me? I'll get back as soon as I can.'

A film of dirt covered the tiled floor of the café-arcade. The air was a grim cocktail of stale grease and tobacco. The stagnant pong of raw sewage wafted into the tired establishment. Errant cockroaches scuttled across the floor and over the feet of the clientele. The haggard-looking owner stood at the counter, a smouldering cigarette hanging from the corner of his mouth. Flaps of skin hung like flaccid breasts below his tired eyes, making him look older than his years. Kyriaco spent his days making Greek coffee and frappé, handing out change for the machines, flipping burgers, and plunging his hand down blocked toilet bowls when his customers ignored the handwritten requests (accompanied by a diagram for the illiterate) kindly asking them to throw their used tissue into the bin provided.

The arcade was open six days a week from eight in the morning until twelve midnight, and from two to ten on Sundays. While other shop owners enjoyed an afternoon siesta in summer, Kyriaco stayed open throughout the day. He slept for short periods on a chair in the kitchen or catnapped upright, leaning against the display fridge. On a number of occasions, warmed by the soporific heat rising from the hotplate, he had nodded off while cooking food, toppling forwards and burning the palms of his hands. Life had become an ordeal for him, hard and unrewarding; the daily grind had finally ground him down. Conceding defeat and on the verge of a breakdown, he had applied to the Department of Employment for permission to hire a worker from the Philippines and was expecting his first employee to arrive any day.

Sunday mornings were Kyriaco's only respite from drudgery. On Sundays he went to church and then on to the graveyard where he laid flowers on his mother's grave. Yes, he was a devoted son who missed his mother, but Kyriaco had other, more pressing reasons for visiting the cemetery. Graveside vigils were a crucial part of a plan he was hatching to change his life, secure his financial future and escape the arcade for ever. His plan was only weeks away from fruition, he was sure, but until then he had to knuckle down and get on with the business of running the arcade and keeping his customers happy.

'All right, boys?' he called out to the three friends sitting around the games console that doubled as a table.

Raphael raised his hand in salute while keeping his eyes on the Pacman that Socrates was skilfully manoeuvring along the interconnected paths. He had already won several lives and was rapidly totting up points. When finally his Pacman was ingested by a floating ghost he finished as top scorer, adding the name 'Cholera' to the top of the leader board, consigning 'Zaphiri' to second place.

'Fuck it! We're all out of money and I'm starving,' he said, leaning back in the leather-upholstered chair.

'Don't worry. We have plenty of money.' Marco pulled a ten-pound note from his pocket and laid it on the glass screen.

'Where the hell did you get that?'

'From Papa's trouser pocket.'

Raphael shook his head. '*Re!* He's going to murder you.'

'He won't notice. He carries a wad of cash in his back pocket, though he always complains about being broke when Mama asks him for money. He won't miss ten pounds, believe me. Now, who wants a Coke and a game of Flipper?'

'Look, Michali's hogging the Flipper. He'll be on it all day, as usual.'

A small, thin boy expertly worked the buttons on the Flipper machine, keeping the ball bearing in play, activating a tower of lights that flashed on the electronic front panel.

'He's never off that machine. Where the hell does he get the money? His father's ill and hasn't worked for years and his mother's only a cleaner at the school – she can't earn that much,' Raphael said.

Marco scanned the room before speaking. 'I've heard Hector gives him money.'

Socrates pulled a face. 'Why? Is Hector his granddad or something?'

'No. They're not related.' Marco leaned forward to whisper. 'I've heard he pays Michali for jerking him off at the back of the arcade.'

Raphael screwed up his face. '*Yax!*'

'I should have let that hornet sting the wanker.'

'So is Michali one of them? You know . . . homosexual?' whispered Raphael.

'I think he just likes playing Flipper,' Marco replied, casually.

Raphael motioned towards the shoebox lying at Socrates' feet. 'What's in there?'

'Things. I'll show you when we get to the shed.'

Zaphiri pushed open the door of the arcade and walked in, chewing gum. 'Hey, Cholera!' he shouted. 'Have you set fire to any more beds lately?'

'Not today. I've been too busy beating your score on Pacman. Have you learned to make firecrackers yet or do you want me to give you a few lessons?'

The taunt was a reference to the previous Easter when Zaphiri's homemade firecrackers failed to ignite. Every year on Holy Saturday boys gathered in the churchyard, their pockets stuffed with firecrackers, ready to mark the resurrection with a chorus of small explosions. At midnight when the priest shouted '*Christos Anesti*', Christ has risen, and the congregation banged on the wooden benches, the boys lit the fuses on their firecrackers and threw them on the ground. Socrates' firecrackers, generously stuffed with gunpowder and shot, exploded spectacularly, lighting the darkness with iridescent metal pellets.

'This year I will have the best firecrackers in the village,' Zaphiri boasted.

'You'll be buying them from Pyrgo then!' Socrates riled his enemy by implying he had to purchase the firecrackers from the local supplier who lived in the neighbouring village. Pyrgo sold watermelons for a living but at Easter he supplemented his income illegally, by making firecrackers and selling them to children. Every boy and girl in the village knew of Pyrgo's existence and where to find him, but surprisingly the police were ignorant of his criminal activities.

'This year I'm going to cause the biggest bang you've ever heard. Get ready to cover your ears, Zaphiri,' Socrates warned.

Marco and Raphael glanced at one another, raising their eyebrows, wondering what their friend had in mind, guessing the white shoebox contained their answer.

7

A welcome breeze blew through the shed door, cooling the boys. Makeshift seats were arranged around a low table fashioned from a pile of car tyres and a square sheet of melamine. Socrates sat on an upturned beer crate, covered with an old cushion. Raphael reclined in the wooden carcass of an armchair lined with a piece of foam stuffing, while Marco sat on a wooden chair with a damaged wicker seat and a short, unsteady leg. A dry tree trunk, with short branches coming off it, was propped against the wall and provided perches of different heights for Koko, who liked to observe the goings-on in the shed. The shelves of a storage unit, plucked from the rotting piles of discarded furniture at the village dump, were lined with objects found, borrowed and stolen. Tools and empty paint tins, old radios and lamps, jars filled with stones, beetles, cicadas, a sparrowhawk chick preserved in red wine vinegar. The boys owned a collection of syringes taken from the bins at the back of the doctor's surgery and washed beneath the tap in the village square. Some still contained dried blood, others the glutinous remains of yellowing liquids injected into patients' veins. In hot weather the boys filled these syringes with water and used them to squirt at each other from considerable distances. Firecrackers ran the length of one shelf, a stockpile manufactured in the days leading up to Easter – small triangular paper parcels fitted with homemade chewing-gum fuses.

Socrates lifted the shoebox on to the melamine table, pulled off the lid and took out a crumpled plastic bag and ten packets of Hollywood chewing gum.

'Is that it?' Raphael asked, looking unimpressed. 'I was expecting to see something a little more exciting.'

Koko hopped through the open door and jumped up on to the highest perch.

'Your problem is you have no imagination,' Socrates replied with a self-satisfied grin.

'You have more than enough for all three of us.'

Socrates held up the empty box. 'This is the most important component in my plans.'

'Come on.' Marco was losing patience. 'Tell us what you have in mind.'

Andrico stepped gingerly into the shed, not wanting to disturb them, carrying a tray laden with fizzy drinks and homemade biscuits, keen to please the boys and make them feel welcome. He liked their company and was happy they had filled his empty shed with their paraphernalia. When they were not around he liked to pore over their belongings, to pick them up and study them and guess their uses. He was fascinated and unsettled by the sparrowhawk in the pickling jar, and intrigued by the paper parcels he had been warned by Socrates not to touch. Sometimes he sat in Raphael's comfortable armchair and fell asleep for hours. His dreams were always pleasant in the shed where there were no ghosts, where he had only known happiness in the company of his three young friends.

They were good boys who treated him with respect, not like the other children who laughed when he passed them in the street, who threw stones at him and called him cruel names. Their taunts upset and angered him, made him feel like yelling and lashing out. He hurried away instead and locked himself inside the house, not wanting to disappoint the mother who was watching over him from heaven. Andrico felt the essence of his mother hovering close by, a protective loving force, and every time he found a brown envelope in his letterbox he knew she had not abandoned him.

He yearned for her physical presence still, for the feel of her soft hand against his cheek and the tender touch of her fingers smoothing down his hair, adjusting his collar. He missed their walks arm-in-arm into the village, where she would chat to neighbours, banter with the fishmonger, share a joke with the friendly grocer. Without his mother beside him Andrico lacked the confidence to approach people and initiate conversation, to exchange anything more than a cursory greeting. He preferred to walk into the village after dark when he was invisible, to retrace the steps he had taken with his mother and relive the happiness he had felt when she was alive.

Lately, he had stopped going out at night, convinced that someone was following him, lurking in the shadows ready to pounce. He had heard footsteps close behind and his name called out but, turning round, had seen only darkness, heard only the background hum of insects.

And home was no longer the sanctuary it had once been, not since he had seen a face at his darkened window, staring in at him. He had slept uneasily that night and in the morning had tried to convince himself that the face was nothing more than a dirty smear on the windowpane. Whether real or imagined, the incident had frightened him so much he had taken to drawing his curtains at night. When he felt particularly vulnerable he would lead the goat into the house and get down on his knees to lay his head against her warm flank and feel the solace of a living body, a beating heart beside him, and pretend he was not alone.

After handing round the drinks Andrico broke off a piece of biscuit and offered it to Koko in the palm of his hand. The bird pecked at the biscuit, breaking it up, flinging his head back and swallowing down the crumbs. Andrico took a five-pound note from his pocket and laid it on the table. 'Here. Take this and buy yourselves something nice,' he told the boys.

Socrates shook his head. 'It's too much, Andrico. Take it back. Keep it for yourself.'

'I have plenty of money, more than I know what to do with. I found another brown envelope in my letterbox this morning.'

'*Aman!* I wish someone would send me money,' Raphael said.

'Don't you want to know who it's from?' Socrates asked. 'I'd be desperate to find out. I bet it's your uncle.'

'It's not him. He hates me and never comes to visit.'

'Who else would send you money if not a relative? Do you want us to try and find out?'

'No, no. I don't want to know,' he said, hurrying out of the shed.

'So. What's your big idea?' Marco asked Socrates. 'And why do we need so much gum?'

'To make a really long fuse.'

The friends had already made dozens of fuses for their firecrackers with chewing gum, fashioning it into thin strips and rolling it in gunpowder extracted from shotgun cartridges.

'What for?' Raphael asked, fearing the reply.

'The loudest firecracker this village has ever heard. Instead of wrapping gunpowder in silver foil, like we normally do, why don't we put some in this nylon bag and set it in concrete in the shoebox? Can you imagine how loud a bang it would make if we managed to ignite it and explode the concrete?'

Raphael raised his eyebrows. 'Are you planning to blow up the church and the congregation, too? Socrates, face facts, we're not talking about a firecracker here. What you're planning to make is a bomb!'

The magpie screeched and hopped about on the upper-most perch.

Marco smiled. 'Even Koko thinks it's a bad idea.'

'We won't put it in the churchyard. I don't want to hurt anyone, I just want to turn a few heads, that's all, and get one over on Zaphiri. We'll put the thing round the back of the church, out of the way, behind the old toilet block. We'll make sure no one's around when we set it off. Did you know that on some Greek islands they throw sticks of dynamite at Easter? Now that's really dangerous.'

'My mother's going to kill me if she finds out. This is not

a good idea. And anyway, we don't have any gunpowder left.' Even as Raphael spoke he knew it was useless to protest.

'I'll steal some more cartridges from my father's drawer,' Marco offered. 'He's got loads of them. He won't notice if half a dozen go missing. He keeps the drawer locked but I know where he hides the key.'

The taxi driver was a dedicated member of the hunting fraternity. Every Sunday morning during the hunting season, he dressed in khaki and followed a convoy of action-hero lookalikes headed for fields and woods to shoot, if not each other, then hares, legal game and migrant birds: unwitting turtle doves, house martins and warblers, temporary visitors to the island. When he wasn't annihilating the wildlife population with a gun, the taxi driver used nets and limed sticks to harvest *ambeloboulia* – songbirds. He liked to eat them pickled, beak, bones and all, and wash them down with Chivas.

'Slow down, you two. Perhaps we should think some more about this. Discuss it.'

Marco pulled a face. 'What's there to discuss? You're like an old woman sometimes, Raphael. If you don't have the balls to do this then go home and do some embroidery with your mother.'

Raphael thought for a moment. 'There's a new house being built up the road from ours. I'll get the cement mix.'

'Good.' Socrates was pleased his plan was coming together. 'Now I think we should choose a name for ourselves, for our organisation.'

'The Good, the Bad and the Ugly?' Marco suggested.

Raphael shook his head. 'No way. You two will get the good names and I'll get stuck with "Ugly". How about the Secret Society of Fearless Bastards?'

'Yes, I like it.' Socrates looked around the wooden shed. 'And we can call the shed Ponderosa, like the ranch in *Bonanza*, and make it our duty to protect this place from those with unscrupulous intent.'

'And who's Andrico in this fantasy world of ours?' Marco asked.

'Well, he's always bringing us biscuits, so he can be the Chinese cook on *Bonanza*, Hop Sing.'

8

It was a bright evening, the sky a canvas of unbroken blue the colour of forget-me-nots. The faint trill of cicadas was drowned out by the clang of saucepans drifting into the street through open kitchen windows, mingling with the animated chatter of housewives gossiping over backyard walls. A dented Mazda 323 drove slowly along the pot-holed village road in third gear. The driver had his eyes on the road but his mind on the toned thigh he was gently caressing.

Petri was so hot with desire he felt he might spontan-eously combust before the pretty blue eyes of the girl beside him. He wanted to stop the car and ravage her but she was 'not ready' to be ravaged, she was 'not ready' for anything more than a kiss and the gentle touch of a roving hand. 'I need time,' she'd said. She wanted to be sure Petri was 'serious' before she let herself go, before she trusted another man. She was happy to lie topless beside him on the beach and let him rub oil on her back and buttocks, driving him wild, but she was 'not ready to have sex'. Petri had never felt so passionate about any woman, so sexually aroused, so close yet so far from his ultimate goal. He listened to her drone on about her feelings, nodding his head sympathetically, his balls on the brink of bursting.

Petri drove past his brother walking along the road with his two friends. He stopped the car and called out, 'Hey, Socrates, go home. Mama's worried about you. She said you promised to go back for lunch.'

Socrates approached the car, his gaze drawn to the girl sitting in the passenger seat. She had the bluest eyes and the whitest blonde hair he had ever seen in the flesh. Such girls usually only appeared on billboards wearing tight-fitting Levis or in magazines posing with perfume bottles or advertising shampoo. He glanced down at Petri's hand resting proprietorially on the girl's tanned leg and felt in awe of his brother.

'Eh, Raphael,' Petri said. 'Close your mouth. Haven't you ever seen a woman before!'

Petri turned to wink at Carina, feeling proud to have her sitting beside him, knowing he was the envy of every man he met. He often wondered what she saw in him and how he had managed to charm her with such ease. When he looked into the mirror he did not see Tom Cruise staring back at him, but a chancer with the luck of the devil. Being seen out with Carina had elevated his kudos about town. More women were giving him the eye and more men the cold shoulder. Carina's jilted lover had gone back to Sweden and she had extended her stay by a week, spending every day with Petri. The couple shared a lilo, the shower and a bed, kissing and touching one another while Petri waited impatiently for the signal to go further. But time was running out. She was due to leave in a matter of days. Petri's protestations of love were having no effect and so he had decided to take an unprecedented step, to speed things along and prove his good intentions – to introduce his girlfriend to his mother.

He turned back to his brother. 'What have you been up to? Nothing too dangerous, I hope. Don't forget what happened last year. How you went back to school after the Easter holidays with your hair and eyebrows singed.'

'I made a silly mistake. I should never have put my face so close to that firecracker. Don't worry, I've learned my lesson.'

'And you promised Mama that you wouldn't make any firecrackers this year. Do you remember? You haven't broken that promise, have you?'

'No. Of course not.'

'And what about you two?'

Marco and Raphael shook their heads and looked down at their feet.

'I know you three so well I could have given birth to you. I know you're all lying and I intend to keep a close eye on you. Now, get back home, Socrates, Mama's waiting for you.'

'Will you give us a lift?' Raphael asked.

'I don't have time. I'm on my way back to town.'

'Come on, Petri. I love your car and it won't take long.'

'I hope it's just the car you love, you rascal. Come on then. Get in.'

The three boys climbed into the back. Carina turned to smile and say, '*Hello*.'

'Hello. *How are you?*' Raphael asked.

'*Fine, thank you*,' Carina replied.

'*And what is your name?*'

'*Carina.*'

'*Re!* Can you speak English?' Socrates asked, surprised by the self-assured way his friend had addressed the girl.

'A few words of English. A bit of French.'

Marco smirked. 'Go on then. Speak some French, if you're so clever.'

'*Carina, voulez-vous coucher avec moi?*'

Carina blushed. Petri slammed his foot on the brakes and turned to give Raphael a withering look. '*Re!* What the hell are you saying? Get out of the car, now. You can walk home.'

'What's the matter? What did I say?'

'You just asked my girlfriend if she wants to go to bed with you.'

Socrates and Marco burst out laughing.

'Sorry, I didn't realise. I was just saying the words of that song. You know the one. I didn't know what I was saying, I swear it. I've always been useless at languages.'

Petri put a hand on Carina's shoulder. '*Raphael he say sorry. He dasen' anderstan' what he's said.*'

'*It's OK.*'

Just then, Maria walked past the car and waved at the boys. Raphael craned his neck out of the window.

'Where are you going?' he asked.

'To the bus stop. I'm on evening shift at the airport.'

'Why doesn't Petri give you a lift? He's going into town.'

'*Re!* I'm not a taxi service,' Petri whispered. 'And where do you suggest she sits? On my head!'

Maria caught sight of the disgruntled expression on Petri's face and quickly shook her head. 'No, thanks. I'm fine.'

'She's pretty, that Maria,' Raphael said. 'Shame she's my second cousin.'

'And if she weren't, do you think she'd look twice at you?' Marco asked.

'Pretty! Everyone thinks she's pretty,' Petri said, grimacing. 'Where exactly are they looking? I don't see it myself. She's too short and dark for my liking.'

As Petri pressed his foot on the accelerator and drove past Maria, though, he could not help but notice the curve of her swaying hips beneath the tight-fitting pencil skirt, her rounded calves and slim ankles, the shirt stretched taut across her large breasts. Maria was no longer the shy and awkward, brace-wearing girl he remembered but a shapely woman in a tight-fitting Cyprus Airways uniform. In his mind's eye he suddenly imagined her naked, wearing heels and her airline cap, and this unbidden image unexpectedly aroused him. He squeezed Carina's thigh to break the spell and chase away erotic thoughts that felt vaguely incestuous.

Petri pulled up outside Marco's house just as the taxi driver sped away, the wheels of his car spinning, the moody lament of Kokotas blasting from the stereo. When the Mercedes rounded a corner and disappeared another sound could be heard: that of Dora calling out for help and Marco's mother screaming.

'What the hell's going on?' Marco pushed open the car door, jumped out and headed for the back yard. Socrates and Raphael hurried after him.

Petri turned to Carina. *'Stay here. I cam back. OK?'*

He climbed out of the car and followed the boys along the narrow path that led into the rectangular yard where Marco's mother was wailing and his sister Dora was trying in vain to climb the thick trunk of a carob tree. Petri looked up to see Mino hanging upside down from the tree, his ankles tied to a rope attached to the uppermost branches. He was naked to the waist and red in the face, his cheeks wet with tears as he struggled like an escapologist to free himself. Stretching up, then falling back down, lacking the strength to reach his bound feet.

Marco took his mother by the shoulders and shook her. 'Mama! Mama . . . where's the ladder? Mama . . . where's the ladder?'

'Papa threw it over the back wall,' Dora called out. 'I tried to climb over but I couldn't manage.'

Marco clawed his way over the high concrete wall, scratching his shins and tearing his trousers, leaping into the overgrown field behind the house. He lifted the wooden ladder out of the undergrowth, nettles stinging his hands, and passed it over the wall to the others who propped it against the tree. Petri quickly climbed up and reached out for Mino, grabbing him by the leg and untying the rope tied around his ankles. The knot was loose and quickly came undone. The small boy had been seconds away from dropping head first ten feet on to the hard earth below. As he carried Mino down and eased him into his brother's waiting arms Petri felt a sticky substance on the child's skin. Mino's family gathered round him, crying, kissing him and smoothing down his hair. Dora's cheeks were red and streaked with tears.

Irini wrapped her son in a sheet and carried him into the house.

'What the hell happened?' Marco asked his sister.

'He did it. Papa did it. He hung Mino from the tree.'

'And why is he all sticky?' Petri asked.

Dora could not speak for crying, burying her face in her hands.

Petri pulled the girl close. 'Please, Dora, tell us exactly what happened.'

'Papa smeared Mino with honey so that he would get stung by bees. Mama tried to stop him but he just pushed her away. I was too scared to try and stop him. I watched him tie my little brother to that tree and I did nothing! I didn't even open my mouth to say a word. I could have stopped him but I didn't even try . . .' Dora began sobbing, her small hunched body shaking.

Petri lifted her up and held her in his arms. Moved by her tears, his own eyes watered. 'There's nothing you could have done. You're just a little girl. Your papa's a big strong man. You mustn't feel guilty.'

'But I do. And I'll never forgive myself.'

'What made him do it, Dora? What made him angry?' Marco asked.

'He said Mino stole some money from his pocket. Mino swore he didn't touch the money. Mama told him she took it but Papa wouldn't believe her. He said Mino was a thief and had to be punished.'

Marco cried out and slammed his fist into the tree. He flinched momentarily, before wiping his scratched and bleeding knuckles on his T-shirt. Socrates could feel the intensity of his friend's anger and pain but could not relate to it. He had stolen money from his father's pocket many times yet he had never known the threat of physical punishment, the menace of paternal brutality.

'I took that money to spend in the arcade,' Marco said, his thick eyebrows knitted together. 'He knows damn well I took it, but I'm too big to hang from a tree . . . so what does he do instead? He hangs my little brother up to punish me. If he does anything like that again, I'm going to kill him. I swear to God, I'm going to kill him.'

Unbeknown to Petri, Carina had climbed out of the car to watch the drama unfold. In a state of numb disbelief, she had watched Petri scramble up the ladder and untie the small boy. She could not help but notice the healthy bicep that swelled as he gripped the child by his leg. The tenderness he showed to the crying girl brought a tear to her own eyes. Those action-packed minutes confirmed what Carina already suspected – that Petri had a heart of gold and was a being far superior to any man she had ever dated before. As she made her way back to the car she made a firm decision to reward her boyfriend's heroism.

Petri thought he was climbing into the car with the same sexually reticent girl he had left some time earlier. So it came as somewhat of a surprise when on the drive back to town she began to nibble his ear and massage between his legs. She ordered him to stop the car, clambering into the back seat while the Mazda weaved along the quiet country lane and then swerved into a potato field, flattening several dozen plants and sinking into an irrigation ditch. Petri leaped over the back of the driver's seat as Carina pulled a condom from her handbag.

The lane was not as quiet as they might have hoped. A potato farmer's double-cabin truck rattled along it and came to a stop outside the gates of the field. A hardy-looking man with dusty boots climbed out. His brow was furrowed and his bony cheeks pitted with acne scars. Deep lines around his mouth made him look perpetually displeased and his whole face looked as if it had been carved from a weathered log and stained the colour of burnt sugar. Stick in hand, the farmer charged towards the Mazda, surveying his damaged crops, giving little thought to the goings-on inside the car with steamy windows – ruined potatoes uppermost in his mind. He lifted his stick in the air and brought it crashing down on the roof of the car.

Carina screamed. Petri pulled up his trousers and put his face to the window, the unused condom slithering out of his hand.

'You wanker!' the farmer shouted. 'What the hell are you doing in my field?'

Petri made sure Carina was covered up before climbing out of the car to talk to the farmer.

'You should be ashamed of yourself.' The farmer shook his head, his wide nostrils flaring. 'I worked myself to death planting these potatoes and look what you've gone and done.'

'OK. Calm down, I'm sorry. I can't have caused that much damage. The potatoes are underground.'

'You've killed the mother plants, you idiot. Several dozen by the looks of it.' The farmer glanced into the car and frowned. 'Couldn't you find a better place to do your business? There are plenty of cheap hotels in town. And where are you from? What's your father's name?'

'Leave my father out of this.'

'I've seen you before, haven't I? In the village . . . I know your face. Aren't you the son of Niko Sergiou who works in the village building society? Yes, you're Sergiou's son, I'm sure of it. You're the image of your father. I think I need to have a word with my old friend the clerk . . .'

'This is between you and me. I'll pay for any damage I've caused.'

'Do you have a job?'

'I'm a soldier. Just tell me how much I owe and give me a little time to find the money.'

A smile crossed the farmer's lips. He realised Sergiou's son had been sent by God, that his prayers had been answered. He had a crop of potatoes to harvest and no one to help him, until now.

'I'll tell you what, come back tomorrow morning at four and help me dig up some of these potatoes. I'll even give you some to take home to your mother. If you don't come, I will be forced to go and see your father.'

'I'll be here at four,' Petri said, feeling resentful that half a day of precious leave would be wasted labouring in a field.

Carina did not speak a word all the way back to the hotel and her knees were angled inauspiciously towards the passenger door. The silence between them was awkward. Petri tried to think of something amusing to say, to make her laugh, but the jokes and anecdotes that came to mind he could only tell in Greek. So he smiled inanely instead, hoping to infect her with good cheer. He wondered if the language of love really did transcend words, as he liked to think, whether a person could radiate their thoughts and speak with their eyes and be fully understood. He reached out for Carina's leg, hoping to rekindle her passion, but she nudged his hand away and sighed, as if he were responsible for the appearance of the potato farmer and her acute embarrassment. He was beginning to realise that his Scandinavian goddess was entirely mortal and, like every woman he had ever known, could blow hot or cold.

9

The police motorbike came out of nowhere. Its powerful engine growled threateningly, making a mockery of the moped's whiny drone. Sergeant Stelios Georgiou astride a Honda V7 sped towards the three wise monkeys perched on the saddle of a decrepit moped spewing black smoke from its exhaust. He refused to let any monkey outwit or escape him. No vehicle fit for the rubbish dump would outrun his superior 248cc-engine with its six-speed gearbox. True, these three renegades had escaped him in the past but now, on the open stretch of uphill road that led to the school, they did not have a chance. They thought they were clever, covering their faces with neckerchiefs, but they would never be as smart as a man who'd left the police academy with a commendation and was headed for a glittering career in the police force.

Socrates glanced over his shoulder at the policeman and urged Raphael to go faster. The burly officer, wearing dark shades and tight black trousers tucked into long leather boots, looked like the dark and menacing force in a television thriller.

'Lean forward,' Socrates shouted over the whir of the

engine, and all three boys craned their necks, hoping to make the moped more aerodynamic.

'We don't have a chance,' Raphael called, swerving to avoid a pothole, sweat beading on his forehead and under his arms.

'Listen to me and we'll get away,' Socrates replied. 'Quickly, take the next right.'

Raphael turned right. The moped struggled up a slight incline, losing power and speed. Marco turned to see the policeman baring his white teeth at them. 'He's right up our arse! Go faster, Raphael.'

'It's not up to me.' Raphael struggled to keep control of the moped, to avoid potholes and keep them from crashing. 'It's useless. He's going to catch us. This thing won't go any faster.'

'Turn in here . . . now!'

'What! Through those bollards? I can't. We'll crash.'

'Just do it. It's our only chance.'

Raphael swung the moped round and manoeuvred it through the tight space between two metal posts, picking up speed along the pedestrian walkway, bumping down a set of steps into the playground. He headed for the main road on the other side of the school that led out of the village to the seafront.

Stelios Georgiou pulled up sharply, cursing under his breath. The Honda was too wide to fit through the bollards erected to stop cars and motorbikes from using the walkway and school playground as a short cut. He circled the school three times, peeved that the boys had temporarily got away, intent on catching them. He was enjoying himself in a job that gave him licence to ride his bike at dangerously high speeds. In a village where serious crime was rarely committed, a policeman had to be grateful for such minor infringements.

Stelios Georgiou had hoped he would be stationed in the old colonial building in town, housing the district office, not some sleepy backwater. He had joined the force anticipating excitement, respect, high-speed car chases, and the opportunity to fire a machine gun. So far he had dealt with domestic squabbles, acts of minor vandalism, speeding motorists and underage boys riding mopeds. He had shot dead a number of stray dogs suspected of carrying rabies and confiscated several dozen firecrackers. The three wise monkeys had so far eluded him but he had their cards marked and he was closing in on them. He had been unable to trace the owner of the moped because the number plate was missing but he was determined to catch the boys, lock them in a cell and let them stew there for a couple of hours before telephoning their parents. They were a danger to themselves and to other road users. They had to be caught for their own good, before they wrapped themselves around a lamp post.

Raphael slowed the moped along the seafront road. A westerly wind swept across the friends, infusing their hair with sand and saltwater droplets, making it curl. The wide expanse of pebble beach they rode alongside was deserted. Ridges of water raced across the surface of the sea and swelled into waves that lashed the shore. Socrates lowered the neckerchief that felt hot and moist against his face. Raphael veered right and pulled on to a tarmacked area, a favourite spot for picnickers who gathered here every evening with their barbecues and skewered meat, with strings of light powered by a generator and beer bottles cooled in drums of ice. He parked the moped beside a tree, alongside a battered blue Fiat, and climbed off, desperate to relieve himself.

'I need to pee,' he said, walking away.

Socrates caught him by the arm. 'Shhh! Listen.' The unmistakable sound of a Honda engine could be heard in the distance then growing louder. 'First, my friend, you need to take a swim.'

Socrates hurriedly laid the moped on the ground close to the Fiat before running across sand and pebbles, throwing off his T-shirt, slipping out of his shoes and diving head first into the sea. His friends followed, stifling shrieks when the cold seawater chilled their warm skins. They surged forward through the water, falling to their knees and ducking their heads below the surface when the police motorbike came into view. Raphael came up first, coughing and spluttering, saltwater stinging his eyes and pouring from his nostrils. Then Marco raised his head above the waterline, shivering and cursing the policeman. Socrates stayed underwater for another minute and could have stayed longer had Marco not yanked him up by the arm. Socrates liked to hold his breath under water until he grew dizzy.

The friends were wading back to shore when they heard a voice call out to them, a fisherman shouting from a rocky outcrop nearby.

'Get down, get down! He's coming back.'

They heard the motorbike through waterlogged ears and dropped back into the sea. When they stood up again, all three of them gulping air, the fisherman shouted, 'He's gone, you're safe,' and beckoned them over. They dripped water across the variegated grey pebbles, Raphael's training shoes squelching and oozing water. Socrates picked up his T-shirt before climbing the mound of jagged rock that projected into the sea. The fisherman sat on a flat ledge, a metal rod held in his right hand and pressed against his body. He had a friendly, boyish face and unkempt hair, stiffened by sea spray. He wore jean shorts, flip-flops and a checked shirt with the sleeves rolled up. His skin was golden-brown and his cheeks flushed from sitting too long in the sun. Water gently lapped the algae-covered rock below his feet. Three large sea bream glistened in a blue plastic bucket beside him. He reached into his khaki rucksack, pulled out a tea towel and offered it to Socrates.

'Here. Use this to dry yourselves off.'

Socrates rubbed his hair before handing the towel on. The sun had already begun drying a crust of salt on his skin.

'So, why was the policeman chasing you?' the fisherman asked.

'Because he's a donkey,' Marco replied.

'Then you're old enough to be riding that moped?'

'Not exactly, but nearly.'

'And how old are you, exactly?'

'Thirteen,' Socrates lied.

'What . . . even him? He looks older.' The fisherman motioned towards Marco.

'He's younger than me.'

'Thirteen and riding a moped – do your parents know?'

'No, of course not. They'd kill us.'

The fisherman smiled. 'Don't look so worried. It's no big deal. I did the same thing at your age. You'd think the police had better things to do than waste their time chasing boys on mopeds.'

He laid the fishing rod down beside him and pulled a bottle of beer from his rucksack, biting off the top with his teeth.

'I wish I could do that,' Raphael said, impressed by the strength of the fisherman's jaw.

'It takes lots of practice. I wouldn't try it if I were you unless you want to lose a couple of teeth.' He put the bottle to his lips and took a long drink.

'Can I have some?' Raphael asked. 'I'm really thirsty.'

'If you're too young to ride a moped, then you're too young to drink alcohol.'

'My father lets me drink.'

'I'm not your father.'

Socrates peered into the bucket. 'I've always wanted to know how to fish. My father keeps promising to teach me but he hasn't got round to it yet.'

'Then sit down and I'll show you how it's done.'

The boys perched on the rock to watch the fisherman take a lump of dough from a plastic bag and break off a small piece. After dousing it with a reddish-brown liquid squeezed from a small plastic bottle, he rolled it into a ball and attached it to the hook at the end of his fishing line.

'How long did it take you to catch those bream?' Marco asked.

'Only an hour. I've been very lucky today.'

'Where do you live?' Raphael asked as the fisherman

93

flicked his line into the water. 'We're from the Plakariso village.'

'I have a close relative in your village but I live in town. My name's Poli.'

'What do you do?' Marco asked.

'Whatever pays. Mostly bar work. I fish during the day, and when I'm not working I fish at night too.'

'What a life,' Raphael remarked.

'I love fishing. Looking out to sea relaxes me. This is a good place to sit and think or just switch off and forget everything and everyone. Here, hold this and keep it steady.' Poli handed Socrates the rod and rolled down one of his shirtsleeves in which he kept a packet of Senior Service. Flipping open the lid, he pulled out a cigarette and put it in his mouth before striking a match, protecting the flame within his cupped hand.

'Can I have one?' Raphael asked.

'You're too young to be ruining your health.'

Raphael pulled a face. 'I'm not a child. I've smoked before. Plenty of times. I bet you were smoking by the time you were my age.'

'I'm not a good example to follow. I started smoking when I was eleven. I was on twenty a day by the time I was your age.'

'Eh! What's the big deal, then?'

'OK. Take one.' The fisherman threw the cigarette packet and matches into Raphael's lap. Socrates watched his friend light up and inexpertly suck on the cigarette, his cheeks plumping up as he drew smoke into his mouth before exhaling in exaggerated fashion. He was about to reach out for the packet too when he felt the rod dip and saw the cork float disappear beneath the surface of the water.

'Something's happening,' he said, feeling his heart start to race.

'You've caught a fish, I'd say.' Using his free hand, Poli helped Socrates pull a small, silvery fish out of the water and toss it into the bucket. The fish battled for life, flicking its tail fin, choking on air, perishing finally after one last defiant twitch.

'I'm going to eat well tonight,' Poli said, patting his stomach. 'Fish cooked on the barbecue, basted with oil and lemon and washed down with St Panteliemon. What could be better!'

'I want to learn how to fish,' Socrates said, wanting to relive the thrill he had just experienced.

'Then come back tomorrow at around six in the afternoon and I will teach you. Fetch three bamboo sticks and I will bring the bait and tackle.'

10

Raphael's strong hands were made for arm-wrestling, removing tight lids from jars, for cracking walnut shells and fighting his enemies. They were not designed for threading fine fishing line on to a small wire hook and securing it in place with a tricky knot. So after his friends had finished their bamboo rods and cast off, following Poli's instructions, Raphael was still struggling with his own, complaining about his ineptitude and resisting the urge to throw the whole annoying contraption into the sea and walk away.

'I need help, Poli. I can't do it.'

'You won't learn if you don't do it yourself. And anyway, your line is far too long. Cut it down. Don't you remember me telling you that the line has to be the same length as the rod, and that before you tie on a hook you need to attach a float? I'll pass you one.'

'I've got a head like a marrow. I never remember anything. Ooofou! I'm never going to get the hang of this, I'm useless. To tell the truth, I'm more interested in eating fish than catching them.'

Poli reached into a plastic bag full of wine corks and handed one to Raphael.

'How come you've got so many corks?' Socrates asked.

'Don't you remember me telling you yesterday – I work in a bar. I collect up the corks at the end of the night and pierce them with a hot skewer. Why spend money on something when you can make it yourself? When I was younger I used to get my weights for nothing too, by climbing up electricity poles and stealing their metal registration numbers.'

Raphael threaded the cord on to the line and moved it up and down. 'How do you keep the float in place?'

'Here, take this matchstick and push it into the hole. When you get the hang of tying on one hook, I'll show you how to make a double hook so you can catch two fish in one go.'

Socrates was holding his fishing rod with both hands and watching the float intently. The surface of the water was smooth and so clear he could see several feet down. Concentric rings gently rippled from around his float as he waited impatiently for a fish to swallow the bait. He wanted to be the first to catch one. He wanted his fish to be the biggest and most impressive.

'You've nearly finished, Raphael. Good. You see, you *can* do it,' Poli said. 'Now, just take a pinch of the dough, roll it into a ball and thread it on to the hook. And don't forget to add a few drops of the liquid in the plastic bottle to your bait.'

'What is it?'

Poli touched his nose. 'My secret! A magic potion that draws the fish close. When you're an expert fisherman I will tell you what it is.'

'Nothing's biting, Poli,' Marco said. 'I don't think we'll catch anything today.'

'Just wait. Something will, eventually. It always does. To be honest, it's not the best day for fishing. The sea's too calm, it's too hot and there's no wind. I always catch more fish when the sea's rough and the fish are a little more active and hungry.'

Suddenly, Socrates' float began to tremble and he felt the same rush of excitement he had experienced the previous day. 'Poli, the float's moving! What do I do?'

'OK. Stay calm. You need to pull the fish out of the water, slowly and carefully.'

Socrates could see a large, dark shape looming beneath the surface of the water. 'It's a big one.'

'Yes, it is. Probably a mullet.'

'How can you tell?' Marco asked.

'Because most fish shoot upwards, grab the bait and head straight back down again. The mullet is clever. It plays with the hook, circles it, rests it in its mouth and pushes it along. The float doesn't go straight down as it does with other fish but disappears into the water diagonally. Don't do anything until the float keels over.'

All Socrates' senses were honed on the dark shape. His friends drew closer, craning their necks over the ledge of rock to get a better view.

The float began to keel over. 'Now . . . slowly shepherd the fish towards you. Tire it out, and make sure you don't stand up because it's strong enough to pull you into the water.'

Socrates tugged at the line and felt it grow taut.

'No! Not like that, more gently. It's a big fish. If you pull it up too quickly you might split its mouth and lose it, or else your fishing line could snap. Drag it towards you slowly, Socrates. That's it . . . you're doing it . . . well done! Just a little further and the fish is yours . . . it's getting closer . . . now take the net with your other hand and reach down . . . scoop up the fish . . . it's too heavy to pull out of the water . . . good, you've got it!'

Socrates pulled the net out of the water feeling triumphant. A grey mullet that weighed at least 3 kilos, thrashed about in the net, splashing him with seawater.

Raphael patted his friend on the back. 'You're very lucky, catching a fish like that.'

'It's not just a matter of luck,' Poli said. 'Fishing is about skill, patience and how well you prepare your rod. It seems our friend here is a natural fisherman.'

Raphael's stomach gurgled. 'I'm starving. I wish we could throw that fish on the barbecue right now.'

'Why don't we?' Poli said. 'Since you're not so keen on fishing, Raphael, you go and collect up some stones and dry wood so we can build a fire. Gather twice as much wood as you think we'll need because it always burns down quicker than you expect. I'll show you how to cook your catch on the beach, fresh from the sea. You will never have tasted better fish in your lives, I promise you.'

As Raphael walked away Marco's cork float began to vibrate, a fish snapping its jaws around the bait and impaling itself on the hook. He pulled a small, grey-marbled fish with silvery fins from the water and reached over to unhook it.

'Don't touch it,' Poli warned. 'Let me do that. That

unassuming-looking fish is a *kourkouna*. It can give you a nasty sting, the back fin is poisoned.'

'Can it kill you?' Socrates asked.

'No, but the sting is very painful, ten times worse than the sting from a nettle, and the pain can last as long as a week.' Poli carefully unhooked the fish and tossed it into the bucket. 'Whereas mullets are clever, *kourkounes* are stupid fish and can be caught easily. I once attached six hooks to my line and caught half a dozen in one go.'

Raphael climbed on to the rock to see what his friend had caught. 'What's that? A sardine! What kind of fisherman are you, Marco? How do you expect us to fill up on that?'

'There's plenty of meat on it. Pick it up and take a closer look.'

Marco and Socrates shared a conspiratorial smile. Before Poli had a chance to warn him off, Raphael had picked up the fish and felt the prick of a spiny dorsal fin piercing the skin of his right palm. He cried out, dropped the fish back into the bucket and rubbed his hand frantically while his friends fell about laughing.

'You wankers! It feels like I've just closed my hand around a globe thistle or a prickly pear. The pain is terrible.' His palm began to burn and throb.

'Don't worry, it won't kill you,' Marco said. 'But you won't be able to wipe your arse for a week.'

'Watch it! I can still throw a good punch with my left fist and smash that good-looking face of yours.'

'Sure! If you can catch me.'

'How do you expect me to build a fire now, without the use of this hand?'

Marco put down his rod and stood up. 'Come on, I'll help you. I'm bored of fishing.'

'Wait!' Poli pulled a net out of the water. It contained several sea bream, with silver-grey stripes running their length. 'I think we have enough fish for our meal. Let me show you all how to prepare the fish for cooking and how to build a fire.'

The boys crowded round Poli as he crouched at the water's edge to scrape the scales off the fish using his penknife. He slit each one open and pulled out the guts with his finger, the water lapping at the shore carrying away the pink entrails. After washing his hands in the sea, he fashioned skewers from long, thin twigs, scraping off the bark and sharpening the ends. He found a sheltered spot behind the rocks, dug a shallow pit and built a stone circle around it while the boys collected up more wood. They filled the makeshift barbecue with driftwood, twigs and dry grasses that smoked when lit before glowing orange. Each boy held a fish threaded on to skewers over the embers that hissed and spat as juices dripped on to the burning wood. Using their fingers they pulled at the cooked flesh and hungrily packed it into their mouths, agreeing that the fish, flavoured by the salt on their hands, was the best they had ever tasted.

Afterwards Socrates leaned back on his elbows feeling full and content, not caring that his face, his hands, his clothes reeked of fish, proud to have caught his own meal. He had always loved hunting and foraging, filling his stomach with nature's offerings: nuts and berries, roots, stolen fruit and edible hillside mushrooms. He had once killed a sparrow using his sling, plucked its feathers, removed the intestines, splayed it out on the metal rack his mother used to toast bread and cooked it over a naked gas flame. He ate the tough meat with pride, feeling a great sense of achievement, though the flesh was burnt and unpalatable.

'Who taught you how to do all this stuff? To fish and cook on the beach?' he asked Poli.

'I taught myself. A man quickly learns the art of survival when he's hungry. I lived on the beach for a while when I was a kid. I ate what I caught and slept on the sand, beneath the stars.'

'And your parents let you?' Raphael asked.

'My mother died when I was very young and my father, well, he disappeared. My sisters and I were brought up in an orphanage. I hated the place and ran away when I was sixteen. I lived on the beach for a few weeks before finding a job and a place of my own. I've been looking after myself ever since.'

Socrates was more impressed than saddened by Poli's description of his unsettled life and wanted to hear more. 'Where is your father?'

'Who knows? They say he went to England.'

'Don't you miss him?'

'You can't miss what you don't know. I was very young when he left. In fact, I hardly remember him at all. What I know for sure is that he was a wanker who turned his back on his own family.'

'My father's a wanker too. He hits my mother,' Marco said, this confession surprising his friends who were unused to hearing him being so open about his feelings or criticising his father to strangers. But then Poli did not feel like a stranger but more like an old friend, an older and wiser brother. It was easy to relax in his company.

'We all have our cross to bear, Marco,' Poli said, getting up to douse the dying embers with sand.

11

Irini listened to the distant sound of goats bleating as she made her way to the church on foot carrying a basket of flowers. The farmer was up early as usual, milking his herd in an enclosure close to the refugee quarter, beyond a cluster of giant cactuses that masked the sight of the smallholding but not its malodorous scent. Irini held her breath as a gust of wind infused with animal smells wafted over and enveloped her. A feral cat with matted fur hurried across her path, a rodent's tail hanging from its mouth. The grating crow of a cockerel pierced the air. A canine howl chilled Irini's blood, sparking deep-seated superstitious fears, reminding her of her late grandmother who was quick to cross herself whenever she heard a dog's sad lament warning of a death in the family.

She was more than tired, beyond exhaustion, functioning on autopilot, a headache stabbing her temples. She had not slept properly since her youngest son had been strung up from the tree. Hatred, anger and guilt kept her awake at night and pummelled her insides, making her feel perpetually nauseous. How could a man do such a thing to his own child? How could a mother stand by and watch? Why hadn't she taken a knife to her husband? Recurrent visions of Mino swinging from that rope like a man on the gallows haunted her. The image seemed etched to the inside of her eyelids, denying her rest, torturing her whenever she tried to sleep.

Her mouth felt dry and acrid from the spoonful of vinegar she had swallowed for breakfast and the vegan diet she had lived on for almost forty days. It was Good Friday, a day when only the sour condiment would cross her lips in recognition of the vinegar that Christ supped as he suffered on the cross. Irini had never fasted for so long or so stringently. This year she felt a greater need than ever to cleanse her body and soul. This year the words of St Basil struck her with a powerful resonance: 'To receive the Spirit we must withdraw ourselves from evil passions. When we do this, the Spirit can uplift our hearts and through Him be brought to perfection.'

Victora was approaching from the opposite end of the deserted street. Irini considered crossing the road to avoid him but did not want to appear unfriendly. She liked the quirky old man and often stopped to chat to him but today she was in no mood for his searching questions and sympathetic looks. 'He can read the future . . . he talks to the dead . . . he can curse you with his eyes . . . he visits the graveyard at midnight,' villagers said of the puppet master, making Irini feel a little afraid and uneasy in his company. She believed the world to be full of supernatural forces, some benevolent, others evil and destructive. A superstitious woman, she avoided any activities that might heap more bad luck on her shoulders. After a funeral she never returned home straight away for fear of bringing death back with her. Whenever a coffin passed along the street outside her home she hosed down her front step in an effort to wash death away. She kept stored scissors shut to seal the mouths of neighbours who might gossip about her, and closed cupboard doors behind which evil eyes lurked, wanting to do harm.

The puppet master greeted her with a warm smile and reached out for her hands. His touch was both unsettling and strangely disarming.

'How are you, Irini?' he asked.

'Very well, thank you, Kyrie Victora.'

He looked at her quizzically as if he did not believe her, as if he could see through her lying eyes a black morass of pain.

'You look tired. You have been working too hard.'

'Easter is a busy time.'

'Easter is a time to be enjoyed, a time to rejoice. Christ suffered on the cross so that we could all have a better life.'

'I wish it were so. I think we were put on this earth to suffer.'

'You mustn't think like that.' His eyes were suddenly too probing and intense and she wanted to snatch her hands back and hurry away. 'Your life may seem unbearable at the moment, Irini, but you have the children and your health and things will get better, I assure you . . .'

His voice was so kindly and compassionate, his gaze so loving, that her throat tightened and it took some effort not to cry. Though she feared Victora's powers she knew in her heart that he was a good man who wished her no harm. As he talked about hope and a better future he

106

gently stroked her hands and she felt herself succumbing to a warm and heady sensation. His touch felt reassuring and paternal. It was as if the spirit of her late father had entered the old man's body to console and comfort her.

'These are not empty promises, Irini. Your future will be peaceful, fulfilling and prosperous. You will lose before you gain. Suffer before you profit. Grieve before you heal. What you mustn't do is try to force the pace of change. A person's fate cannot be rushed. Never forget the values your parents instilled in you. Cherish your goodness. And in God's name, my child, forget the terrible deed you are contemplating.'

Irini pulled her hands free, shocked that the puppet master might actually have picked up on the vengeful plan taking shape in her mind.

'I have to get to the church, I'm already late.'

'I won't keep you any longer. But don't forget what I said.'

Irini hurried away, not daring to glance back over her shoulder.

The church was empty. Irini headed for the altar where she unpacked her basket of Easter lilies and hyacinths beside the carved wooden sepulchre in which an effigy of Christ lay on an embroidered cross. The other women would be arriving soon with armfuls of spring flowers donated by the parish and inside the hallowed stone walls the murmur of female voices would reverberate. Spring buds would be threaded together and floral wreaths fashioned to decorate Christ's tomb, the flowers symbolising the fragrant myrrh with which His body was anointed. In the evening the bier would be carried outside the church and villagers would pass beneath it while the priest sprinkled them with cologne.

The silence was oppressive and the thick smell of incense, candle wax and lilies was making her upset stomach churn more than ever. Irini had come early in the hope of finding peace, a place of comfort for her tormented soul, but the gaunt and harrowed faces of the saints staring down at her from the iconostasis only intensified her own feelings of misery. And as she stood over the sepulchre, staring down at Christ's effigy, she realised that forty days of fasting had been a waste of time. While her thoughts should have been chaste and virtuous on the day of Christ's funeral, they had never been more sinful. She snapped the stalks off her lilies and laid the large white heads in a neat row ready for threading, her mind focused on the different ways in which she might murder her husband. Was this the terrible deed the old man had picked up on? If so, she would have to avoid the puppet master in future, lest he try to weaken her resolve.

The thought of killing the taxi driver made her feel warm and jittery. The dark life inside her head was the only one *he* did not control. Was it so wrong to take one life when she could save three others – those of her children? She wanted nothing for herself, she felt dead inside, immune to real joy, but the children were still full of life and had every chance of being happy if *he* were not around. Time was running out for them too. Their father was blackening their souls with every passing day. Dora was a frightened mouse who jumped at the sight of her own shadow. Mino had begun wetting the bed, and Marco's eyes spoke of hatred and revenge. He was nearly as tall as his father and it was only a matter of time before he gave in to his anger. How much longer would he stand by, fists clenched, watching his mother being abused?

'Just leave your husband, divorce him,' a well-meaning friend had once said, as if the solution were really that simple. Pack a suitcase, take the children and *arrivederci*. Irini had taken this advice and moved in with her parents, breathing a premature sigh of relief when beds were made up for the children and they had all put on their pyjamas. That evening the taxi driver barged his way into the house, wild with rage. He tore the net curtains from the window, kicked over the armoire and smashed up the television, threatening to kill his wife if she did not return home by morning. Irini's sick father, bent over with arthritis, could only stand and watch, tears pouring down his cheeks. That evening Irini repacked her bags and returned home, to spare her parents further pain. A week later, when her father died of a heart attack, Irini blamed the brute for his death and wished that he would burn in hell. 'Why didn't you call the police when he smashed up the house?' her friend had asked naively. How easy it was to comment from the sidelines! The taxi driver had friends in high places. His cousin *was* the chief of police. He came from a large, well-connected family who were quick to back him up whenever he got into trouble. Irini only had her fragile mother to turn to.

And there was worse to come. Without his wife's knowledge the taxi driver began visiting his widowed mother-in-law on his way home from work. He bought her a new television set and expressed his desire to make his marriage work, apologising for his violent outburst, saying he was ready to turn over a new leaf, to become a good husband and father. The key to domestic bliss, he told his mother-in-law, was financial security and a bigger house for her grandchildren. If she sold her own house, and bought something smaller and more practical, she could give her daughter a lump sum and watch her live like a queen. He persuaded his mother-in-law to sign the house over to him, and as soon as she did so he sold it and pocketed the proceeds. He moved the gullible widow into cheap rented accommodation on the fifth floor of an apartment block. His gold signet ring, bought a week after the house was sold, was a painful reminder to Irini of her husband's treachery.

If God Himself were to stand before her and plead her husband's case, if He asked her to forgive, she would shake her head and dig in her heels. She would look God straight in the eye and say, 'no way, not a chance.' Her mother's mental health had deteriorated rapidly after the loss of her husband and her home. She was beginning to forget, to repeat herself, blaming the onset of senility for her memory lapses. Irini believed she was blanking out the recent past because it was too painful to remember.

Irini had been forced into a corner. She would only be free when her husband ceased to exist. As he munched his breakfast in the morning, hunched over the kitchen table, she imagined plunging a sharp knife into his hairy back and turning it, watching the life spurt out of him, hearing his pain. This gory vision was quickly followed by a sickening fear of being separated from her children. Who would raise them if she spent the rest of her life locked up? Not her sick mother. The brute's family would take them in and probably do them more psychological harm than their father had. No, stabbing him was not the answer. She could not risk getting caught. In films, murderers cut brake cables to send their victims careering over cliff edges into deep ravines, but Irini knew nothing about cars and tampering with his brakes might put other road users at risk. In films, the perpetrators of such crimes hired assassins to do their dirty work or killed their victims with a range of poisons: arsenic, cyanide, hemlock. Irini's plan needed thought and preparation and more courage than she feared she had.

The sound of footsteps startled her. When she looked up she saw Eleni approaching, felt her own cheeks flush and hoped her wicked thoughts could not be read on her face. Eleni carried a large bunch of carnations and greeted her with a kiss on each cheek. Niko's wife was a handsome woman who radiated marital contentment, a woman who had clearly never known physical or psychological abuse. Irini envied her innocence and mourned the loss of her own. She was not as old as she looked and still remembered the carefree girl she used to be. The lively, trusting girl with the ready smile and the lovely hair, who turned heads when she walked down the street. A fragile lily crushed in the hands of a brute. Little if anything of that girl remained. Now, Irini wore the hardened mask of a troubled woman. She believed prolonged pain could be read in a person's face, in the dark shadows beneath the eyes, in frown lines and premature wrinkles. She hoped it was her face and not her intimate thoughts that the puppet master had read.

'I thought I'd get here early,' Eleni said, unwrapping the flowers. 'There is so much to do today. I still need to bake my *flaounes* and make some *daktyla*.'

'I have to clean the house when I get back.'

'You mustn't do any housework today. They say it's bad luck.'

Irini arched her eyebrows. 'I think I've had my fair share of bad luck lately.'

Eleni smiled sympathetically, knowing her neighbour was referring to the assault on Mino. Everyone in the village had heard how the boy had been dangled dangerously from a tree. Hearing a first-hand account of the rescue from her son, Eleni had felt sick inside yet she had stopped her husband from confronting the taxi driver, saying it was best to stay out of other people's business. The taxi driver was large and intimidating and she worried about her husband's physical safety. Standing now before Irini and sensing her pain, Eleni felt guilty for having turned a blind eye and putting her own family first. Someone had to help this poor woman before a tragedy occurred that could not be reversed. But no one wanted to break up a marriage or deny three children a father.

'How is Mino?'

'He hasn't smiled since it happened.' Irini was grateful to be asked and glad that people knew what her husband was capable of. When the taxi driver was found dead one day, only his kin would shed a tear.

'Children are stronger than we give them credit for. He will get over this.'

'Maybe. But I won't.'

'We women all have our fair share of misery,' Eleni

sighed, and began breaking up the carnations that the flower girls would throw like confetti on to the sepulchre at the evening service.

'You're lucky, Eleni. I don't think there's a better man than your husband in the entire village.'

'That may be so but God has given me two incorrigibly disobedient sons. Socrates is out of control, he's like a wild animal, and Petri is determined to break my heart and shatter my dreams.'

'In what way?'

'Tomorrow, on the holiest day of the year, he is bringing his Swedish girlfriend home to meet us. I have a thousand jobs to do – I haven't got time to play hostess to my son's girlfriends. I've told him so, but he won't listen. I just pray to God he doesn't want to marry her.' Eleni quickly crossed herself.

'What does Niko say about this?'

'What does my husband always say? Nothing, of course. He's not happy about it but he won't put his foot down either. That's my husband all over. Too easy-going. Isn't that why the boys think they can do whatever they want, why they're as wild as savages? And what am I supposed to say to this girl tomorrow? I don't speak English. She doesn't speak Greek. How are we meant to communicate? Using sign language? Speaking double Dutch? I'm very disappointed in my son, Irini.'

'Your son is happy and healthy, that's all that matters. The rest is unimportant, believe me. Let him enjoy his life while he can.'

'I couldn't stop him if I tried.'

12

A hot sun beat down on Socrates' back as he cycled up the steep hill on his way to the neighbouring village. He pedalled hard through a landscape dotted with carobs, oleander, juniper bushes and pines, an area of lowland once thickly forested. The trees hacked down over the preceding centuries by a succession of invading forces from the East and used to build ships; the finest pines razed to the ground by locals, dragged to the nearest market and sold to producers of resin and pitch. The sparse and scrubby woodland was now awash with spring flowers, enlivened by the bright yellow heads of thistles and sky-blue petal clocks on stems of dwarf chicory; by lilac flower bundles crowning wild leeks and purple florets emerging from the hearts of globe artichokes. Within weeks this evanescent spectacle would bleach and wither and give way to an arid landscape of dry grasses, cheered only by evergreen trees and stalwart, flowering shrubs.

Socrates glanced over his shoulder and was pleased to see that Marco and Raphael were some distance behind. He liked to lead, to arrive first, to cycle so hard his muscles ached and his heart pounded in his chest. Marco's long legs worked the heavy pedals of his late grandfather's tall bike. It was still fitted with the cooling box in which his grandfather had once kept homemade rose-cordial sorbet and mastic-flavoured ice cream, sold to tourists on the beach and shoppers in town. Now, the box contained Marco's penknife and the few coins he needed to make his yearly purchase from Pyrgo. Some way down the hill, Raphael sat astride a red Raleigh chopper, panting and sweating, worn out by the effort of climbing the slope, his energy sapped by the intense heat, his right palm still throbbing from the sting inflicted by the spiny fish. He stopped to rest beneath the shade of a pine, to wipe his brow, blow on his hand and take a sip from his water bottle.

Socrates flew over the brow of the hill and landed with a judder, the bike threatening to come apart. He took his feet off the pedals and freewheeled down the incline hunched over the handlebars, the wind cooling his face and blowing back his bushy hair. The bike felt like an extension of his body, a detachable appendage on which he could twist and turn and fly. He had mastered its quirks and idiosyncrasies and rode fearlessly. Inherited from his brother, the bike pulled to the left, the back wheel had a slow puncture, the brakes were dangerously worn and the frame was dented and warped. Sections of it fell off intermittently and new parts were screwed, glued or welded on.

Socrates pulled on the brakes and the worn pads screeched as they rubbed against the back tyre. He put his feet on the ground, wearing a small hole in the sole of his training shoes, and came to a stop outside Pyrgo's house, built on a large unkempt plot surrounded by a tall, metal fence. A mangy dog with a matted black coat was tethered to a post in a back yard littered with bone fragments and rubbish. The dog barked ferociously when it saw Socrates, baring yellow teeth, running as far as its rope leash would allow, not quite reaching the fence. While he waited for his friends Socrates stooped down to talk to the dog, noticing its rheumy eyes and the bloated purple ticks sucking blood from its ears. He felt sorry for the neglected mongrel and wondered if he should return one night when Pyrgo was asleep to liberate the dog and take it to the animal sanctuary nearby, set up by a retired English couple. Saliva dripped from the dog's jaws as it growled and barked and tried in vain to leap at the fence. Marco and Raphael approached cautiously.

Pyrgo stuck his head out of the kitchen window. 'What are you three doing? What do you want?' He turned to the dog. 'Shut up, Linda.'

He raised his hand in the air and the dog fell silent, its shoulders drooping as it wearily dragged its rope leash back across the dusty yard.

'We want three walnut ones,' Socrates replied.

'Give me fifty cents each and you can have them. Come through the gate, Linda won't hurt you. That stupid dog only knows how to bark.'

The boys walked through the gate and deposited their change into Pyrgo's palm. Linda pricked up her tick-infested ears but did not move. Pyrgo disappeared into the kitchen. He reappeared several minutes later at the open window with a paper bag, handing each boy a firecracker the size and shape of a walnut, containing gunpowder wrapped inside a ball of brown twine. These firecrackers ignited with a loud bang and were a valuable addition to the friends' growing arsenal. Pyrgo retracted his head through the window and closed it without saying goodbye.

'Where shall we put them? I don't want to get caught again,' Raphael said, remembering the previous Easter when a policeman had forced him to empty his pockets of firecrackers before grabbing his ear and marching him home. After a long lecture from his mother, Raphael had promised he would never touch another firecracker as long as he lived.

Marco lifted off his saddle to reveal a secret compartment. 'I can fit two under my seat. This is where my grandfather used to keep his cigarettes and his takings.'

Socrates unclipped his bicycle lamp. The aluminium carapace, heated by the sun, was blisteringly hot, scalding his fingers. 'I'll put the other one in here.' He flicked open the Perspex front, moved the bulb to one side, inserted the firecracker and clicked the cover shut.

On the journey back to the village Socrates felt pleased with himself, confident that no policeman would ever think of searching his bicycle lamp. A number of boys in the village had already been searched by Sergeant Stelios Georgiou and had had their firecrackers confiscated.

The midday sun was baking hot. A mist of condensation rising from the road turned the stretch of grey tarmac into an iridescent lake. Socrates manoeuvred the bike with only the lower half of his body, arms by his sides, a T-shirt tied around his hot head, the sun burning his bare chest. He picked up speed, swerved to avoid a pothole, squinting into the white light obscuring his vision. Not only was the sun scorching his chest, it was simultaneously heating up the aluminium carapace connected to the mangled frame of his bike. Behind the Perspex cover the heat intensified, baking and searing the walnut firecracker. As Socrates pulled at the handlebars, raising the front wheel off the ground, the temperature soared, setting alight the fuse on the homemade device. A tiny flame quickly travelled to its core, igniting the gunpowder, and with a thunderous bang the bicycle lamp exploded. Startled by the noise, Socrates veered off the road and crashed at high speed into a tree. He lay on the ground motionless, stunned and in pain, his vision blurred and his head aching. Several minutes later his friends were standing over him looking worried, calling out his name as if from a distance, trying to disentangle his limbs from the wreckage of his bicycle.

'Are you all right?' Marco asked. 'Speak to us, Socrates. Are you all right?'

Socrates wished that he had worn trousers, not shorts. His legs were scratched and bleeding. His face hurt when he tried to smile and one side of his body looked as if it had been rubbed with a cheese grater.

'Socrates, are you all right?'

'I'm fine.' His voice was hoarse. It hurt his throat to speak. He looked at the blackened bicycle lamp, feeling irritated that a firecracker costing fifty cents had gone to waste. Glancing across at Marco's bike, lying on the ground by the side of the road, he was tickled by a thought that made him laugh out loud.

Raphael raised his hand in the air and made a gesture

with his fingers, as if twisting the lid off an imaginary jar. 'You've lost it, Socrates.'

'What the hell's so funny?' Marco asked, pulling his friend up by the arm.

'It's a good thing this happened to me and not to you,' Socrates replied, through his laughter.

'You're a mess. Your clothes are torn, you're scratched to bits . . . and you're thinking about me?'

'Just thank God your firecrackers didn't explode.'

'Why?'

Socrates motioned towards the saddle with an irrepressible smile. 'They might have blown your balls off.'

13

Holy Saturday was the busiest day of the year and one that Socrates had been eagerly anticipating. He woke up earlier than usual and made his way to Loulla's house, excitement churning his stomach, his mind focused on the day ahead and the many things that needed to be done. The exploding walnuts bought from Pyrgo the day before and dozens of homemade firecrackers had to be stored in the deep crevices that punctured the mud-brick wall surrounding the churchyard, ready for collection and ignition at midnight when the church bells tolled Christ's resurrection. The gunpowder-filled concrete brick was ready and had to be positioned beside the disused toilet block behind the church. A new block had been built the previous year, with separate facilities for men and women. Now, no one ever used the crumbling mud-brick structure that housed a primitive hole in the ground leading to a cesspit. Socrates planned to light the chewing-gum fuse at midnight and keenly anticipated the resulting bang which promised to be phenomenally loud.

He found Raphael and Marco peering over Loulla's back wall, eyeing up a pile of wooden beams.

'The wood's still here,' Raphael said, looking pleased. 'The widow won't notice if some of it goes missing.'

Every year the children of the village collected wood for the churchyard bonfire on top of which sat an effigy of Judas Iscariot. The widow's store of thick, dry wood looked perfect for burning and was a lucky find. Tino and Zaphiri rounded the corner on their bikes, dismounted, approached the wall and staked their claim to the beams.

'No, that's our wood,' Socrates said. 'We saw it first.'

'I don't see your name on it, Cholera,' Zaphiri replied.

Raphael stepped forward and loomed over him. 'My friend's name is Socrates. Show him a bit more respect, otherwise I'll crush you.'

'I'm not scared of you. It's her I'm worried about.' Zaphiri pointed towards the house. 'What if she's in?'

'What's there to be scared of?' Socrates turned the latch on the old woman's back gate and walked into the yard. 'She's never in at this time of day. She gets up early and goes to the cemetery to visit her husband's grave, and then she spends the rest of the day at her daughter's house.'

'Those beams look heavy. It's going to take all five of us to carry them to the bonfire. Let's share the wood,' Marco said, following Socrates through the gate.

'Zaphiri! My Zaphiri.' The voice was Stephania's. The girl approached, addressing her cousin, grabbing the hem of his T-shirt. 'Will you play hide and seek with me?'

He scowled and pushed her away. 'Get away from here. I have things to do.'

'Please. I have no one to play with.'

'I told you to get lost. I'm not playing with you.'

Stephania turned to leave, her eyes watering.

'Wait.' Socrates recalled the girl's treachery on the day he'd set fire to his bed and sensed an opportunity to take revenge. 'I'll play with you, but only in there.' He pointed to the old woman's rundown house.

Stephania shook her head. 'No way. I'm not stepping foot inside that house. Loulla's a witch and might put a curse on us.'

'Then go home to your mother and leave us alone.'

The crumbling house looked like a fitting home for a witch. The wooden doors and window frames were warped and flaking, and the once vibrant blue shutters had weathered to a sickly pallor and hung from their hinges. Sheets of exterior plaster had come away, revealing crumbling courses of mud bricks, each painstakingly made from straw and local clay by Loulla's grandfather. The exterior walls were riddled with deep holes, housing snakes, lizards, birds and mice. Children in the village believed Loulla could curse a person by waving her hand in the air, and the old woman, who liked being feared, made every effort to live up to her reputation. When she crossed a child in the street she widened her eyes, flared her nostrils and waggled her fingers, mumbling the Lord's Prayer under her breath. She chuckled quietly to herself when the victims of her convincing performances ran away shrieking.

The manner by which her husband Sotiraki had met his death only intensified the fear she engendered. Sotiraki had been the local gravedigger and caretaker of the village cemetery, an imposing man with an enormous moustache that curled upwards at the ends. He dug each new grave single-handed, using a pick to break the earth and a spade to shovel it out. One day he was found dead lying beside a freshly dug grave, a corner of his black pantaloons pinned to the ground with the pick. According to local folklore, Sotiraki had finished digging the grave and thrown down his pick, not realising he had pinned his baggy trousers to the ground. When he had tried to walk away and found himself unable to move he'd panicked, thinking the dead were trying to pull him down into the grave. The man was frightened, quite literally, to death, villagers said to one another in the days following, crossing themselves in rapid succession. The coroner confirmed that Sotiraki had died of a heart attack, a verdict which the villagers took as confirmation of their theory. In actual fact, a daily packed lunch of bread and lard, lovingly prepared by Loulla, had seen to it that the blood vessels around the gravedigger's heart were thickly lined with arterial plaque. Sotiraki had been living on borrowed time, every fatty sandwich taking him a step closer to his death.

'If you're sure she's not in then I'll play too,' Tino said, covering his eyes. 'You all go inside and hide and I'll count to a hundred.'

'Come with me.' Socrates grabbed Stephania by the arm and pulled her towards the house.

The back door was open which came as no surprise to the intruders, as villagers of Loulla's generation rarely locked their doors. The children walked into a rudimentary kitchen, a remnant of the early 1900s, a time before electricity and running water, fitted gas cookers and off-the-shelf units. Loulla shunned such modern conveniences that cost a fortune and made a woman lazy. Her only concession to modernity was the thick black cable that climbed the bare concrete wall and travelled along the ceiling, supplying power to a naked bulb. She still washed her clothes in a deep stone sink and hung them outside to dry. She still heated her water by means of a wood-burning stove, and scrubbed the floor on all fours. There were no cupboard doors in the kitchen; a dirty floral curtain was drawn across her plates and saucepans; and there was a blue metal bottle supplying gas to a simple, two-ringed hob.

The children hurried out of the kitchen and along the hallway, looking for somewhere to hide. They followed one another into a dark bedroom, cold and dank, where heavy curtains, not quite shut, hung at the window. A shard of sunlight shone across the embroidered cover of a lumpy, four-poster bed. Socrates shuddered when he saw a photograph of the gravedigger hanging on the wall, lit from below by a candle. Stephania saw the picture too and shrieked, grabbing hold of Socrates' T-shirt, saying she was scared and wanted to leave. She stared in fear at the old woman's walls that were hung with crosses and icons and framed photos of long-dead, severe-looking ancestors.

Raphael quickly hid behind the curtain. Marco and Zaphiri dived under the bed. Socrates pushed Stephania into a tall wardrobe, resembling a coffin turned on its head, and locked her in, scratching at the door to frighten her, smiling to himself as she rattled the lock, trying to get out. When he heard Tino call out, 'Ninety-five . . . a hundred . . . whoever I find I will spit on!' he leaped into the bed, covering his head with the thick bedspread that smelt of dust, sweat and mothballs. As Tino entered the room an elongated shape in the bed beside Socrates rose up, lifting the bedspread and discharging a shrill wail. Tino yelped and ran out and Stephania hammered on the door of the wardrobe, screaming and calling out for help. The phantom uncovered its head. It had white hair and no teeth. It was ugly and wrinkled with sunken eyes, flared nostrils and puckered lips. It took several seconds for Socrates to realise he had jumped into bed with Loulla, who proceeded to lift her arms in the air and recite the Lord's Prayer.

'Run!' he shouted, leaping out of the bed and racing out of the door, followed by the two boys from under the bed.

Loulla reached for the dentures on her bedside table, fishing them out of a glass of cloudy water. She filled her mouth with the ill-fitting teeth, water dripping down her chin, as Raphael struggled out of the window, scraping his belly on the rotten frame. Stephania remained locked in the wardrobe, banging and crying, believing her life was at its end. The boys ran a short distance from the old house and took cover behind a water tank from where they could hear the stomp of Loulla's heavy, flat feet on the concrete floor. They watched her chase a tearful Stephania out of the front door with a broom and heard her virulent curses. The boys fell about laughing before creeping back to the house and stooping below Loulla's bedroom window. They heard the creak of bedsprings as she climbed back on to her mattress, waited until she started snoring, then sneaked back into the yard to collect the beams and carry them to the bonfire.

*　　　*　　　*

The smell of cheese pastries baking in a clay oven drifted over the high stone wall, making Socrates' mouth water. Lent did not come to an end until midnight but Socrates was determined to sample his mother's Easter pastries now. He spied on Eleni through a hole in the back gate, watching her empty the clay oven of breads and pastries using a *fournofkio* and lay her delicacies on the outside table to cool: *boxamadia*, firm, aromatic breads sprinkled with black cumin and anis seeds; and *flaounes*, golden pastries filled with halloumi, Easter cheese, fresh mint and sultanas. Like most of the women in the village Eleni made enough *flaounes* to share with her friends and neighbours while taking in their offerings gratefully, comparing the taste of other women's pastries with her own, wanting hers to taste the best. Socrates heard the sound of voices from inside the house and watched his mother disappear indoors. He ran into the back yard, stole three *flaounes* and joined Marco and Raphael at the front of the house.

'*Re!*' Marco said. 'Your brother's just arrived with his girlfriend. They've both gone into the house.'

'Both?' Socrates was surprised. He knew his brother had an active love life but he had never known him to bring a girlfriend home.

'Perhaps he's going to marry her?' Raphael said, biting into a warm *flaouna*.

'I hope so. Then he'll move out and I can have his bedroom.'

Petri's bedroom was on the ground floor in an adjoining annexe and had a separate outside entry, private bathroom and toilet.

'I'm going inside to see what's going on. Wait here. Hold this and don't eat it,' Socrates said, handing his pastry to Raphael.

He found the family gathered in the parlour and greeted Carina with an embarrassed nod, unsettled once more by her good looks. He stood in the doorway staring down at her long legs, listening to his father try to make polite conversation in English, wanting to laugh at his strange pronunciation. The parlour, a stuffy old-fashioned room smelling of jasmine disinfectant, was reserved for the most important guests. In this room his mother kept her most precious figurines, china vases and glassware sitting on embroidered doilies. A hard, uncomfortable three-piece suite, arranged around a marble coffee table, was covered in a prickly brown material with an embossed pattern that left indentations on bare legs.

Petri sat beside Carina on the sofa. Eleni chose to stand, wiping her flour-dusted hands on the skirt of her apron, hoping her unwelcome guest would not stay too long. The house was a mess; there were courgettes, peppers and tomatoes to stuff, a million jobs to be done. She tried not to look at the girl's bare legs that were crossed and shamelessly on display up to the thigh. Any fool could see why her son was besotted. What man could resist the charms of blonde-haired, blue-eyed temptress wearing a tea towel for a skirt? She could only hope that the Scandinavian was a passing fancy, a dalliance, one of many girls her son would date before settling down. This girl did not have the makings of a good wife. This girl would always draw other men's glances and make her husband jealous. If only Petri would open his eyes a little wider and look around him, he would see that his rightful match lived closer to home.

Eleni was grateful to her husband for trying to make conversation. Anger had tied her tongue and banished from her mind the few words of English she knew. *Hello – goodbye – thank you very much – my name is Eleni.* A stifled conversation she did not fully understand ensued, punctuated by smiles and head nodding, with Niko bowing subserviently like a waiter. Why was he doing that? Grinning like a crazy man and cocking his head to one side when *she* spoke? Why else! Because a man did not stop being a man when he had a ring on his finger; because the old dog had been charmed by the minx too. Eleni could read her husband's face like a book and today she wished she could rewrite the narrative.

Niko ignored the dirty look on his wife's face. 'Sit down, Eleni,' he said in Greek.

'I have jobs to do.'

'And we have a guest.'

Petri glared at his mother. 'You're being rude, Mama. Sit down.'

'If you won't sit down then why don't you make Carina a cup of tea or a Greek coffee?' Niko's generous smile angered his wife as did the easy way he uttered the girl's name.

'If you smile any wider, Niko, you'll split your lips.'

'I'm sure she'd love to try one of your *flaounes*.'

'Don't the Scandinavians fast over Easter?'

'I'll have one too, Mama,' Petri said.

'No way! Lent isn't over for you until midnight,' Eleni said, shaking her head. 'Next you'll be changing religion.'

She turned to leave and saw Socrates skulking in the

128

doorway, learning from his brother's bad example, staring quite blatantly at the girl's legs.

'I'll go and make tea,' she said, grabbing her youngest son by the arm and pulling him out of the room, wanting to limit the damage caused by Carina's visit. She had lost one son to a foreigner and was determined not to lose a second. 'Come with me, Socrates. I have a job for you.' She led him into the kitchen and handed him a plastic bag filled with pastries.

'I want you to take these to Andrico. He likes my pastries. It's a shame that poor man doesn't have any relatives to spend Easter with.'

'What about his uncle?'

'His uncle is a mule, a relative in name only. He treats his own nephew like a leper. His poor sister would turn in her grave if she knew what her son had been through since her death.'

'Did you know her well?'

'Everybody knew her. She was a lovely woman, kind to everyone and a perfect mother. She grew the best apricots in the village and made the finest preserve I have ever tasted. The poor woman took a wrong step in her life and paid dearly for her mistake. Not that she was to blame.'

'What happened?'

'She married the wrong man. She's not the first and won't be the last woman who has suffered at the hands of a bad husband. I cross myself every day and thank God for sending me your father. Now, take those pastries carefully, don't shake the bag around, and don't eat any yourself. OK? And I suppose you had better say goodbye to her before you go.'

'Carina?'

'Yes, *her*.'

Petri walked into the kitchen then, holding Carina's hand. 'Mama, we're going to my room for a while.'

Eleni flushed with anger. 'Do you have to? It's Holy Saturday.'

'And?'

'And we must all live virtuously for at least one day!' Did she have to spell it out? Did she have to say that sex before marriage, beneath a mother's roof, on the most sacred day of the year, was a sin?

'Don't worry. We're only going to listen to some music.'

Eleni turned to Socrates with a glare. 'Why are you still here? You have a job to do. Go on.'

Socrates hurried out of the house with the bag and found his friends sitting on the front step. 'Quick! Petri's taking his girlfriend to his bedroom. Let's go and have a look through the window.'

Raphael sprang to his feet. 'Holy Virgin!'

The boys crept round the side of the house and took it in turns to peer through the narrow gap between the drawn curtains, each voyeur delivering a whispered commentary. Marco watched the couple sit on the bed and draw close to one another. He saw Petri stroke Carina's hair and slide his hand up and down her back. Socrates watched the couple's lips touch, tenderly at first, then with greater passion, and was aroused by the sight of them hungrily exploring each other's mouths with their tongues. He did not want to look away when his time was up but Raphael yanked him away from the window, demanding his turn.

'But the real action is just starting,' he complained.

'Then let me take a look and you can have another turn.'

Raphael stared through the window in disbelief, his legs weakening as he watched Petri ease Carina down on to the bed and begin pulling up her skirt.

'*Re!* What's happening?' Socrates asked.

'What *isn't* happening! My friend, everything's happening. People pay to watch this kind of thing. He's on top of her . . . he's pulled up her skirt . . . I can see her knickers. They're white, the tanga-type . . .'

'Get down! It's my turn again.' Marco pulled at his friend's arm.

'I'm not moving. No way. He's pulling her top off now . . . My God, she's not wearing a bra!'

'Can you see her breasts?' Socrates asked, feeling the bulge in his underpants swell.

'Yes. Both of them. They're amazing, fantastic, just like you see in the magazines.'

Raphael's face was pressed against the windowpane, his breath steaming up the glass. Marco tried to shove him out of the way but he would not budge, his eyes glued to the couple writhing against one another. Suddenly, a stone flew over Raphael's head, hitting the window and cracking it, the erotic display inside coming to an abrupt end. Petri shot up and Carina hurriedly dressed. Socrates turned to see Stephania hurling a second stone that hit him squarely on the forehead.

'That's for locking me in the wardrobe,' she screamed, before running off.

Socrates had barely recovered from the shock and pain

when the curtains parted, the window flew open and his brother caught him by the arm.

'*Re!* What the hell are you doing?'

'Nothing.'

'Have you been spying on us? Did you see anything?'

'No. We were just passing.'

'Then why is my window covered in your breath? And why is the glass broken? Get away from here. What does a man have to do to get some privacy in this country? All three of you, get lost. Now.'

Carina was fully dressed by the time Petri turned back to the bed.

'*Let us go and drink some tea with your mother,*' she said.

'*Why we no lie down?*' Petri wanted desperately to start where they had left off, to pull off her clothes and feel her skin against his.

Carina opened the door and walked out, leaving Petri hot and unsatisfied and furious with his brother.

The bag of pastries swung from the handlebars of Socrates' bike as he rode vigorously, banging against the metal frame. His mother's warning to him to ferry the pastries carefully had fallen on deaf ears. He stopped at the gates of the village cemetery to wait for his friends who were some distance behind, Marco struggling on his unwieldy bike and Raphael stopping, as usual, to rest. Through the cemetery gates lay an ordered landscape of stone crosses, plaster angels and marble tombstones fitted with compartments in which lighted candles flickered. Fresh flowers and potted plants decorated the well-tended graves where widows and grieving relatives knelt, pruning and polishing; paying homage to the dead whose faces were embossed on ceramic ovals affixed to their headstones. The gravedigger's mausoleum, a gift from the village to a long-standing public servant, was an elaborate structure of Italian marble surrounded by a wrought-iron fence.

Socrates spied Victora wandering among the graves holding a bunch of carnations. He looked at peace among the dead beneath the gently swaying branches of a eucalyptus tree. He knelt before a simple gravestone, unwrapped the flowers and slotted them singly into a vase already half-filled with wild flowers. Sitting down, he pulled a knife and an apple from his pocket and began slicing and eating the fruit. When he'd finished eating he started talking to himself, gesticulating, nodding and smiling as if the headstone were a living person.

Socrates wondered what, if anything, Victora could hear. A voice in his ears, a verbal exchange in his head, a spiritual sensation he alone could decipher? If Victora could commune with the dead then perhaps the graveyard was as noisy to him as the vegetable market on a Saturday where customers murmured and stallholders competed with one another to be heard. Socrates had often wished he could communicate with his late grandfather, his namesake, a man with whom he felt a strong spiritual connection. Standing over his grandfather's headstone he often found himself talking to the polished marble slab as if below it lay a sentient being. 'Hello, *papou*, how are you?' he would say. 'I miss you – what's it like in heaven?'

One day, sifting through junk in the roof space of his home, Socrates had come across a box with his late grandfather's name written on it. Inside, he found a suit that smelled of camphor, a worn leather wallet, a green beret, a knife, a pistol, several bullets, and a stack of letters addressed to his grandmother, sent from a British military prison. In the letters his grandfather wrote about the harsh treatment he was suffering at the hands of the British who had held him captive for a year after he was found guilty of being a member of EOKA, the underground organisation fighting for the island's independence from British rule. It was among these letters that Socrates had found a document he'd slipped into his pocket and now kept hidden beneath a loose floorboard in his bedroom. On that yellowing sheet of paper, torn and stained, his grandfather had jotted down the ingredients required to make a bomb. Much of the writing was illegible, where the paper had thinned and the blue ink had been worn away, and the methodology was written in a code he could not decifer, yet it was this recipe sheet that had inspired Socrates to try his own hand at bomb-making. Lying in bed at night he often imagined his grandfather as a young man, crouched in a cave, assembling devices that were later used to ambush military vehicles, blow up Government buildings, and fight a well-armed colonial power.

Victora stood up and reached into the pocket of his jacket, taking out a large white handkerchief which he used to dab his eyes. Socrates had spent some time in the cemetery reading the inscriptions, familiarising himself with the ages and identities of the dead, but he was unfamiliar with the name etched on the simple tombstone facing Victora. Socrates remembered the puppet master mentioning that his parents were buried in a cemetery fifty kilometres away and he wondered if the grave before which Victora now shed tears was that of his lost love, the woman he had been prevented from marrying.

He turned to see Kyriaco dragging on a cigarette, ambling towards him. The arcade owner had closed his shop for the afternoon and was determined to put his free time to good use. He was freshly shaven and wore his father's musty blue suit made by the best tailor in town, a double-breasted classic which he saved for his visits to the graveyard. The trousers were a little short but the tailoring was fine, and what did it matter that a second man could fit inside the jacket when it was made of the finest quality, pinstripe cashmere?

Kyriaco threw down his stub and mashed it with his foot. 'What are you doing here?' he asked Socrates.

'I'm waiting for my friends. They lagged behind a little on their bikes.'

'How's your papa? I haven't seen him for a while.'

'He's fine.'

'Your brother drove past me a little while ago. Is he out on leave again?'

'Yes. He's at home with his girlfriend.'

'The blonde girl who was sitting in his passenger seat?'

'Yes. She's Swedish.'

'I don't know why that boy wastes his time on foreign girls when there are so many nice women in this village, women crying out for love and romance. Why else do you think I've come here?' He motioned towards the grave-yard.

'To visit your mother's grave?'

'No. Today my mission is a happier one. This, my young

135

friend, is the best place to pick up a woman, to find a girlfriend. Don't look so incredulous. Most of the women who come here are single, widowed, desperate to be loved . . . and they're not short of money, either, if you know what I mean.' Kyriaco rubbed his thumb and forefinger together.

While other men dressed up to go to bars and clubs, Kyriaco groomed himself for a visit to the village cemetery where he was a master of the art of picking up widows. He had never had much success in conventional settings. If he looked at a woman across a crowded dance floor she would invariably turn away unless her sexual favours were for sale. In the cemetery, though, women vied for his attention, they enjoyed his company, they cried on his shoulder and let his hands wander up and down their backs. Most of his conquests, not unlike his suit, were past their prime, but they were women none the less and hungry for company. In the cemetery Kyriaco knew what to say, how to charm and seduce, and how to use the pain of bereavement to his own advantage. He had a devoted band of black-clad women eating out of his hand, and half a dozen or so who regularly invited him into their beds for hurried sessions of guilty sex.

Kyriaco's ultimate target was Sophia, an asthmatic sixty-two year old who visited her late husband's grave three times a week. She was lonely, childless, and the owner of several beachside building plots worth a small fortune. Kyriaco imagined apartment blocks on these prime sites with his name painted in black letters across the top – Kyriaco's Court or Kyri's Hotel Apartments. When he married Sophia and took charge of her assets he would sell the arcade, buy a wardrobe full of made-to-measure suits, and drive around the village in a gold Mercedes with a foot-long cigar sticking out of his mouth, a metaphorical middle finger to all those who had dismissed him over the years. The move would be mutually beneficial. Sophia had much to gain: a companion, a chauffeur, and a man about the house who would sit dutifully at her bedside when her time came to leave the world.

14

Andrico reached up into the apricot tree and began to saw through a branch. Every April he pruned the tree as his mother had shown him, thinning out short branches loaded with weak spurs and cutting back long branches by a third, to keep the tree producing healthy replacement wood and encourage a good yield of fruit. At the beginning of June he would thin out the pea-sized fruitlets to one per cluster, to ensure the tree grew large, healthy apricots. Later, after the stones formed, he would thin the fruit again, knocking off the fledgling apricots from the highest branches using a bamboo stick. What he liked most of all, what he loved doing, was picking the ripe fruit, gently plucking the reddish-gold apricots and loading them carefully into boxes lined with cloth, his mind drifting back to his mother and her stories about fabled beings and golden apples.

She had liked to relate mythical tales while she plucked apricots, transporting her son to a world inhabited by cruel and powerful gods who controlled the destiny of mortals. No story had excited her more than that of the fierce competition that ensued between Hera, Athena and Aphrodite at the wedding celebration of Peleus and Thetis. The Goddess of Discord, Eris, angered that she had not been invited to the banquet, threw a golden apple into the gathering, inscribed with the words 'For the fairest'. Hera, Athena and Aphrodite, three goddesses who prized their looks, gave Paris, Prince of Troy, the task of deciding which of them was the most beautiful, and when he gave the apple to Aphrodite she rewarded him with the love of Helen of Troy and thus set in motion the Trojan Wars. Andrico remembered this story with some sadness, recalling his mother's animated face and the intonation of her voice, the way she always repeated her tales at his insistence with undiminished vigour and enthusiasm.

Koko's call, announcing visitors, pierced the air, arresting Andrico's attention. The bird hopped about agitatedly on the windowsill before flying away. Andrico put down his saw, shook the dust from his hair and hurried to the front gate, feeling tired suddenly from his early start that day and the many jobs he had completed. He had spent the morning peeling onions and boiling up the skins to produce a coppery dye to colour eggs collected over several days from the chicken coop, afterwards polishing them with olive oil and cotton wool. Easter had been his mother's favourite time of year and to honour her memory he tried to uphold her traditions by festooning the house with flowers, baking fresh bread, and colouring dozens of eggs. The smells and colours of Easter cheered him and went some way towards distracting him from the permanent hollowness he felt, living without her.

He was glad to see the three boys standing at his gate and gratefully took the pastries Socrates handed him. He opened the bag, caught a whiff and was conveyed back in his memory to a busy kitchen at Easter time, filled with nuts and spices and bags of sugar, dusted with flour, smelling of cloves, cinnamon and blossom water. Koko settled on Socrates' shoulder, surveying the world through glassy, pinhead eyes. Andrico envied the bird's friendliness, but feared that his love of people and frequent raids on the village would one day get him into trouble.

He pulled an untidy wad of cash from his back pocket and peeled off three five-pound notes, handing one to each boy. 'A present for Easter,' he said.

'You've had another envelope already? So soon after the last one?' Socrates asked.

'I always get a little extra at Easter.'

Raphael thanked Andrico and walked across to the shed. Marco slipped the note into his pocket, deciding to give it to his mother.

'I'm curious to know who sends you that money and why,' Socrates said.

'I think I might have seen him.'

'So it's a him? When did you see him?'

'I saw a man's face at my window again last night and found the envelope this morning. I thought he had come to do me harm but it seems I was wrong.'

'Do you have any idea who it was?' Socrates asked.

'I didn't get a close look. I was so scared I closed the curtains and locked myself in the bathroom. It was a youngish man, that's all I know.'

'One day I'm going to find out who that man is, I promise you.'

Raphael wheeled the moped out of the shed and

climbed aboard the saddle, saying he was going for a ride. Turning the ignition key and twisting the throttle, he shot off along the road that led to the hills behind Andrico's house.

'Keep Koko locked up in the house tonight,' Socrates warned. 'The firecrackers may scare him.'

'I always do.'

'And don't get scared yourself if you hear a really loud bang. It's nothing to worry about.'

'I normally stuff my ears with cotton wool at midnight. Don't worry about me.' Andrico looked across at the red chopper leaning against the fence, admiring the bright colour and the comfortable-looking leather seat. 'If I could ride a bicycle I would buy one just like that,' he said.

'You can't ride?'

'No. Mama tried to teach me once but I couldn't get the hang of it.'

Socrates coaxed Koko on to his hand and placed him carefully on the fence. 'It's easy. There's nothing to it. Why don't you have a go now? Come on. We'll help you.'

'Yes, give it a try,' Marco said, taking Andrico by the arm and leading him towards the chopper.

Infected by the boys' enthusiasm, Andrico mounted the saddle and nervously took hold of the handlebars. He pushed down on the pedals, the boys supporting him on either side, and cautiously eased his way along the road like a child graduating from four wheels to two. He meandered along the gritty lane trying to balance, testing the brakes, putting his feet down whenever he felt he might fall, feeling exhilarated when for short stretches he travelled along the road unaided, with the boys running

141

along behind him. It wasn't long before he was riding alone, feeling inexplicably happy, the wind tousling his hair, shouting: 'Look, my friends. I'm flying!'

Raphael heard Andrico's shouts and headed back to ride alongside him.

'Do you want to go faster?' he asked, wanting to give Andrico a thrill he would not forget.

'I can't go any faster.'

'First of all let's stop. Good. Now, reach out and grab my arm. Put your feet straight out in front so they're not touching the pedals and I'll pull you along. We three do this all the time, it's great fun.'

Andrico clutched Raphael's arm nervously and the moped slowly pulled away, towing him back to the house. Excited by this new experience he asked to be towed along the lane again, ignoring Marco's protestations that the stunt was too dangerous for a novice cyclist. Raphael rode the moped as slowly as he could, only picking up speed when Andrico called out 'Faster, faster'. He rode up and down the lane, egged on by Andrico's whoops and laughter, until the chopper's front wheel hit a stone and wobbled momentarily. Panicking, the inexperienced rider lost his balance and crashed into the moped. Raphael veered off the road, hitting a fence, while Andrico hurtled in the opposite direction and was thrown head first into a shallow ditch. The two boys watching ran to help, lifting the moped off Raphael and pulling him upright, before rushing across the lane to Andrico who lay face down in the dry trench.

'You've killed him, Raphael. He's not moving,' Marco screamed. 'Why did you go so fast?'

'Because he told me to.'

'And if he'd told you to drive off a cliff, would you have done that too?'

Koko hopped along the road towards them, screeching. He jumped down into the ditch and on to Andrico's back, frenziedly pecking his head in an effort to wake him, marching up and down the lifeless body, seemingly in a state of hysteria. He kept pecking at Andrico until several minutes later he slowly regained consciousness and rolled, groaning, on to his back. The three boys helped him to his feet and led him back to the house where they cleaned his cuts and bandaged his ankle and used an ice pack to settle a swelling on his forehead while all the while Koko wove frenetically in and out of their feet, shaking his head and chattering angrily, as if he were giving the boys a telling-off.

15

Villagers packed the church holding unlit candles. A bustling crowd crammed the stone courtyard listening to the priest's sung liturgy of the Easter Vigils and the cantor's melodic hymns. They waited expectantly for the moment of Christ's Resurrection, his passage from death to life, the point at which mourning gave way to joy and forty days of fasting came to a welcome end. Judas Iscariot burst into flames, crackling and twisting as if in agony, on top of a roaring pyre. The atmosphere was electric and highly charged. Children fed the inferno with sticks, their faces taking on a ruddy glow, the dancing flames reflected in their wide eyes. Floodlights fitted for the occasion lit up the thirteenth-century Gothic church, giving it a foreboding but uplifting ambience.

Eleni stood beside her husband staring up at the church, wanting to feel intensely spiritual but unable to focus on the liturgy, to detach herself from niggling worries. The priest's operatic boom absorbed her momentarily before other, more mundane, concerns infiltrated her consciousness, multiplying like a virus, blinding her to the beauty and significance of the service. A surge of manic energy had carried her through the day, allowing her to complete all the tasks she had set herself: preparing a banquet for Sunday's eating fest; baking dozens of pastries, skinning and gutting a spring lamb to be spit-roast over charcoal embers; cooking the egg and lemon soup to be eaten after midnight mass. She was mistress of her kitchen, boss of the house, an accomplished housewife, she ruled the roost . . . but she had lost control of her sons. Her lips moved in time to the Lord's Prayer but her mind was on Petri and his penchant for foreigners. Was she destined to have a Swedish daughter-in-law? What would the neighbours say? What did people in Sweden eat? What in God's name was she supposed to cook for her in-laws? Petri had promised to come to the service without *her* but like his brother was nowhere to be seen. How many firecrackers were stuffed in her youngest son's trouser pockets? Might he blow off a finger this year or damage his eyes? Would she be visiting Accident and Emergency after taking Holy Communion as she had done the previous year when Socrates had set fire to his eyebrows and singed his hair? Eleni glanced enviously at Michali standing passively beside his mother, his hair neatly combed and centre-parted, his church suit freshly laundered. Now, there was a son to be proud of – a quiet, compliant, soft-spoken boy who stayed out of trouble.

Socrates knelt behind the disused toilet block attaching a length of toilet paper to his chewing-gum fuse, extending the combustible cord to give himself more time to get away when the shoebox device was finally ignited later that evening. Several metres away Marco was retrieving the firecrackers hidden in the churchyard's mud-brick wall, gingerly sliding his hand inside the holes, wary of being bitten by a snake. In the courtyard Raphael wove through the crowd, on the look-out for plain-clothes policemen. He brushed past Sergeant Stelios Georgiou, dressed in tight white trousers and a silk shirt, who had been instructed by his chief officer to confiscate any firecrackers and note down the name and address of offenders. Stelios Georgiou carried out this duty grudgingly, sick of handling petty misdemeanours, peeved that three years of police training had led him to this dead-end place.

While Eleni made the sign of the cross and kissed the gold crucifix hanging round her neck, Petri's lips kissed Carina's pink cheek, then her small earlobe, followed by her smooth shoulder. She lay beside him on the bed in his private annexe, moaning contentedly. Having consumed several glasses of St Panteliemon, she was gigglier than usual, less inhibited, more receptive to the touch of his wandering hands. She was leaving for Stockholm the following day and Petri knew it was now or never – and what better time to consummate their relationship? Most of the village had gone to church and would not return home until the early hours of the morning. They had the house and the street to themselves. Petri hoped that two weeks of heavy petting would imminently and magnificently reach a natural conclusion.

Meanwhile the liturgy was reaching its theatrical climax. The village *muhktar* flicked a row of switches, throwing the church and congregation into darkness. Burning embers smouldered in a corner of the paved yard. Judas sizzled and dissolved into ash. A portly priest dressed in a long embroidered robe and tall black hat stood at the arched wooden door, holding a lighted candle, calling for all evil spirits to leave the stone building. Villagers held their breath, exhaling communally when the door flew open and the priest invited his congregation to 'come and take the Holy light'. They surged forward and lit their candles, the light fanning out, transforming the church and yard into a mystical sea of flickering wicks, thick with the resinous smell of candle wax. The sombre mood of the past week was shattered by the peal of church bells and exploding firecrackers and the stirring chant of the Resurrection hymn sung by the priest and his congregation.

In the field behind the church Socrates and his friends twirled burning strips of wire wool in the air over their heads, red-hot sparks of metal shooting off, lighting up the darkness. Afterwards, they lit their homemade firecrackers and threw them on the ground. The fuses hissed before the paper cartridges exploded into brief, effervescent balls of light. The walnut firecrackers packed with shot were more impressive, igniting with a loud bang; a shower of white sparks bursting from their core. When all that remained of the firecrackers was charred paper and string, the friends turned their attention to the brick. They made sure the disused latrine was empty before lighting the end of the toilet-paper fuse and running to take cover behind the trunk of a carob tree a short distance away, Socrates estimating the device would explode in twenty seconds.

From his hiding place he could see the concrete brick but not the taped-off entrance to the latrine nor Hector padding slowly along the darkened path that led to the crumbling structure. Tired of queuing for the toilet, and with his intestines groaning, he'd decided to use the abandoned block. He was pleased Lent had come to an end – he was sick of eating vegetables and pulses – too much fibre in his diet was playing havoc with his digestive system. He pulled at the tape stretched across the entrance, felt his way along the familiar mud-brick walls, pulled down his pantaloons, squatted over the hole and began relieving himself.

The boys grew concerned. Twenty, thirty, forty seconds had passed without the anticipated bang.

'Perhaps the toilet paper went out and didn't carry the flame to the fuse,' Marco said.

Socrates felt disappointed. 'Perhaps my plan was flawed.'

'I think the fuse was faulty,' Raphael said. 'It was too thick and we didn't have enough gunpowder left to roll it in.'

Socrates stood up. 'Let's go and check.'

'What if it goes off, Socrates?' Raphael was more concerned about dirtying his new trousers than injuring himself. He had promised his mother he would keep them clean.

'Don't worry. If it hasn't gone off yet then it won't go off at all.'

Hector pulled up his pantaloons, tightened the drawstring and reached for the wall, his eyes still unaccustomed to the darkness. As the boys walked across the field, debating remedies and hypothesising, the brick exploded with a deafening blast, knocking them off their feet and crumbling the latrine's mud-brick wall, dislodging a rotten beam that dropped on to Hector's ill-fated head. A rousing chorus of *'Christos Anesti'* was brought to an abrupt end by the resonating boom, as were Petri's efforts to seduce Carina. He had worked long and hard using every weapon in his erotic arsenal – ice cubes, honey, his mother's homemade pistachio ice cream. She was as pliable as wet clay in his hands, poised to submit, and a second before the brick detonated had called out *'Fuck me'*. The deafening boom collapsed both the toilet block and Petri's erection. He leaped out of bed, pulled on his trousers, his shoes, the shirt his girlfriend had torn off, and rushed out of the house, panicking when he heard in the distance the sound of women screaming. He knew from his military training that he had just heard the sound of a bomb and wondered if the island were being invaded yet again.

Villagers crowded round the toilet block, trying to work out what had happened. The boys crouched behind the tree, the circle of people surrounding the latrine obscuring their view. Socrates realised from the muffled cries that spread through the crowd as quickly as the holy flame that someone was trapped beneath the rubble. He thought he heard the name 'Loulla'. He watched Sergeant Stelios Georgiou waving his arms around and issuing orders that were ignored. A woman screamed, saying her son had been buried alive, before falling into the arms of the man standing behind her. Petri squeezed through the crowd where he found a group of men lifting Hector out of the wreckage by his arms and legs. The old man's head hung lifelessly, swinging from side to side, reminding Petri of the spring lamb suspended from a hook in his father's shed. Hector's shirt had ridden up revealing a thin stomach and bony ribcage, his pantaloons were ripped and he was covered in white dust and cobwebs.

'Put him down on the ground,' Petri called out. 'He may have broken a bone.'

'That's the least of his worries,' someone called back. 'The old man is done for.'

The priest looked on in dismay, wondering whether he would soon be administering the last rites, so soon after rejoicing Christ's rebirth. Hector was set down on the ground and Petri knelt down beside him, struggling to remember the first aid he had been taught at the military academy.

'I need something to lay his head on and a blanket to keep him warm.'

'Your father's gone to call for an ambulance,' the *muhktar* said, rolling up his jacket and handing it to Petri.

'And, everyone, stand back. Give us some space. I might need to resuscitate him.' The prospect of planting his mouth on the old man's dusty lips, while he could still taste Carina, was repellent. He took hold of Hector's frail wrist and felt for a pulse. He could feel his own heart thumping in his chest but could not tell if blood was still pumping through the old man's veins. He leaned forward to speak to Hector while a woman covered the widower's body with a blanket.

'Can you hear me? Can you hear me? Hector, can you hear me?'

Onlookers murmured and crossed themselves, asking the Holy Virgin to intervene, to grant the old man a few more years of life. Fearing Hector was dead, Petri began to lose the confidence which had possessed him when he first came upon the scene. Soldiering had taught him how to use a machine gun, how to throw a grenade, how to launch a missile; the army had equipped him with the skills required to kill a man but had left its work unfinished, offering no guidance on how to handle death. Petri was sickened by the vision before him. He wanted to pump the old man's chest to restart his heart; he wanted to leave the army and never touch another weapon as long as he lived; he wanted to hold Carina in his arms and feel her life force flow through him.

He refused to give up. 'Speak to me, Hector. Speak to me.' He felt the widower's hand twitch and wondered if this was a sign of life or an involuntary muscle spasm before rigor mortis set in.

'Holy Virgin! His foot just moved. It seems the old man hasn't eaten all his bread yet,' the *muhktar* called out.

A gasp rose up from the crowd.

'CAN YOU HEAR ME?' Petri shouted.

Hector stirred, opening his eyes wearily. 'They can probably hear you in the next village,' he croaked, spitting dirt from his mouth.

Shouts of 'He's alive!' rang out.

'Tonight,' the priest announced loudly, clutching his gold crucifix, 'we celebrate a second resurrection.'

The sun had begun to rise but Socrates had yet to return home. Eleni was having trouble swallowing her *avgolemoni* soup. She glanced despondently at the pastries, the red eggs, the boiled chicken and the soup laid out on the starched white tablecloth, and felt all her efforts had gone to waste. She had expected all the family to be gathered round the table, breaking their fast together, her boys cracking eggs after the meal as they had done when they were younger. Now, sitting opposite her husband in the otherwise empty house, Eleni felt like crying. Petri had driven into town to take Carina to her apartment, saying he wouldn't be back until next lunchtime, and Socrates had disappeared into the incense-scented ether. A tear trickled down Eleni's cheek. A spoonful of rice caught in her throat. There was a dull ache at the pit of her stomach. She had more than a niggling suspicion that Socrates was involved in the commotion at the church.

'Where is that boy?' she said. 'Where can he be hiding?'

'He's probably gone home with one of his friends. I'm sure he'll be back before long.'

'I hope he's . . .' Not involved in the explosion, she wanted to say, but held back, not wanting to mar the holiest day of the year still further by slandering her own son.

'He's fine. Don't worry.'

'It's not him I'm worried about. It's that poor old man lying in a hospital bed.'

'He'll be fine too. He was sitting up before the ambulance came. Hector will live for ever. That man has more lives than a cat.'

'What if our son . . .' She couldn't help herself.

'Let's wait and see what he has to say.'

'And you think he'll tell us the truth?'

'Eat your soup, Eleni, and stop fretting.'

Socrates skulked in his back yard, readying himself for confrontation, cooking up a story to justify his late return, hoping his eyes would not betray him when his father looked into them. Where should he say he had been all

152

this time? How much should he admit to knowing? How would he explain the rip in the seat of his new trousers caused by the blast knocking him off his feet? He wanted to kick himself for not rushing home as soon as the crowd began to disperse, to change his trousers and sit dutifully at the table waiting for soup. He could handle his mother's angry outburst. She would shout for a while, whether he was guilty or not, and threaten to beat him with the sweeping brush, before offering him a bowl of soup and ordering him to eat. His father was a different matter. He said more with his eyes than his wife could say with a thousand hollered words. One wounded look from his father and Socrates feared the truth would come flooding out. He braced himself, pushed open the back door and walked into the kitchen, trying to look nonchalant.

'Here he is. I told you he wouldn't be long, Eleni,' his father said with surprising cheeriness. '*Christos Anesti*, son.'

'*Alithos Anesti*, Papa.'

Eleni pursed her lips, struggling to keep a lid on her anger. 'Where have you been?'

'I went home with Raphael.'

'I see. So, you had soup at Raphael's house? I must call his mother and thank her.' Eleni knew her son was lying and was determined to catch him out.

'I didn't go inside the house. We were playing outside.'

'Come on. Sit down and tell us everything you've been up to tonight. We didn't see you at church,' his father said. 'But wash your hands first. They look filthy.'

Absentmindedly, Socrates turned to the sink.

'My God!' his mother cried. 'Your new trousers are

153

ripped and as black as coal. How did that happen? What have you been doing? Trailing across the ground on your buttocks? Didn't I tell you to keep those trousers clean?'

'I'll go and change.'

'Stay where you are,' Eleni bellowed, her anger erupting. 'Stay right there and tell us what you were doing tonight and why you are so late. You did it, didn't you! You made that bomb that blew up the toilet block and almost killed poor Hector. What the hell were you thinking! What has that kind old man ever done to you? First, you nearly see him off with a stone, and then you blow up a building that collapses on his head. You should be ashamed of yourself. People go to prison for doing things like that – and, believe me, if the police turned up on my doorstep right now to take you away, I wouldn't try to stop them. I'd give you up with pleasure. Perhaps that's the only way you'll learn your lesson.'

Socrates shook his head, his eyes watering, a lump forming in his throat.

'Eleni, give him a chance to speak.'

'Why? So he can lie to me like he always does? If I find out you were responsible, Socrates, I am going to kill you.'

'This is a very serious matter, son. The police have already started making enquiries. Sergeant Georgiou even questioned me about your whereabouts tonight. Luckily, Hector wasn't badly hurt.'

Eleni made the sign of the cross. 'It wasn't his time to go.'

'But I . . .' The truth was lodged as uncomfortably as a fish bone in Socrates' throat.

'Don't say anything now,' his father said. 'I want you to have a good long think about what you want to say. In three days' time I want you to come and tell me the truth, OK? If you played a part in this affair we must find a way to put things right. For now, let's set all this aside and get on with enjoying Easter. Your mother has been cooking all day and deserves a little appreciation. Go upstairs and change your clothes and then come and join us at the table.'

Socrates left the kitchen, head bowed, knowing that eventually he would have to tell the truth and face the consequences.

Eleni shook her head. 'Why give him three days' grace, Niko? To give him time to think up a plausible story?'

'No. Because I want him to stew for a while and then come to me with the truth, not a knee-jerk lie.'

'Where did we go wrong, Niko? Why is our son so keen on starting fires and making bombs, on causing havoc? It's not normal.'

'How did you feel about my father, Eleni?'

'Why have you changed the subject? What does your father have to do with any of this?'

'Just answer the question.'

'Your father was a lovely, saintly man.'

'And what did Socrates think of his late grandfather?'

'He looked up to him, respected him, idolised him.'

'And have you forgotten that my lovely, saintly father was a member of a military organisation in the fifties? That he made bombs used to fight the British?'

'That's different. He was fighting for a just cause. He was fighting for our Independence. He wasn't making bombs for the fun of it.'

'True, but we talk about those days with great nostalgia and pride and tell stories about my father's heroism. For sure, those stories have influenced an impressionable boy like Socrates.'

'So we are to blame, then?'

'Yes, inadvertently. But the post-war climate, our island's history, years of occupation, Socrates' genes, have also played their part. That boy has inherited his grandfather's courageous, anarchic spirit. Just pray to God there isn't another war any time in the future because then our daring and foolhardy son would be first in line to fight for the freedom of this country.'

16

His plan would soon come to fruition. His life was about to change for ever. Within months he envisaged swapping the counter for a desk, his overalls for a suit, slavery for the good life. Kyriaco stood facing the fridge door, polishing his teeth with a serviette, smoothing down the collar of his white shirt, running a comb through his Brylcreemed hair. He stared at his distorted reflection in the fridge door, feeling unusually handsome. Any woman would be crazy to refuse him, especially an old one with missing teeth and few other options in life. He sniffed one armpit and then the other before blowing into his hand to check that his breath was fresh. Every inch of him reeked of cheap aftershave, applied liberally to his skin and clothes to mask the smell of fried food. Overzealous in his application, he had even sprayed between his buttocks and was now suffering acute irritation and fighting the urge to scratch.

He glanced at his watch impatiently. His father was due to arrive at any moment with the Filipino hired to help him run the arcade. The immigration office had finally issued his employee with a work permit and Kyriaco was cheered by the thought that his floor-scrubbing, toilet-cleaning, burger-flipping days would soon be over. He would come and go as he pleased, issuing orders and collecting the takings. He would act according to his status as employer with an air of detachment and cold professionalism. 'Don't make the mistake of being too hospitable. These people take advantage,' a friend had said. 'They steal from your till and pocket the takings. They use the phone whenever your back is turned to call their relatives. Start as you mean to go on.' Kyriaco planned to welcome the new arrival hurriedly before making his way to the cemetery to propose to Sophia.

A car horn sounded and a silver Honda pulled up outside the arcade. Kyriaco pulled on his jacket, straightened his back and assumed a lofty, superior expression. Through the greasy shop window he watched his father unload a heavy suitcase and hand it to a tiny woman who seconds later struggled through the door with her belongings. With 'start as you mean to go on' ringing in his ears, he decided to let her carry her own case, though he could see the feat required a great effort. She shuffled on small feet across the tiled floor, waist-length hair covering her face, and reached Kyriaco with a heavy sigh. Pushing back her dark hair and securing it behind her ears, she looked up at him with eyes as dark and shiny as black olives set in an adorable, feline face. Kyriaco's skin prickled. His stomach tightened. He was stunned into silence by this woman's perfect complexion and the lovely smile that plumped up her round cheeks.

'Hello. I am Bimbingan but you can call me Barbara,' she said, extending a hand.

He shook it, surprised by its smallness and the softness of her skin.

'*And what do I call you, sir?*' she continued.

'*I . . . be call . . . Kyriaco,*' he stuttered, hoping she would not think he had a speech impediment.

'*Mr Kyriaco, pleased to meet you.*'

'*Not Mr. – Jass call me Kyriaco.*' He felt himself grinning and bowing, wishing he could slip Barbara into his pocket and carry her around with him for the rest of the day. How could he play the big white chief when this woman made him feel like a gangly, bumbling, inarticulate fool? How could he pull rank when what he really wanted to do was scoop her up like a tiny pet and sniff her hair? He was desperate to know what she thought of him. Had he made a good first impression? Did she like what she was looking at? Did the brown stains on his teeth, the bags beneath his eyes and the terrible suit repulse her? He felt like a man on a first date. And what did she think of the arcade? Had she noticed the greasy fingerprints on the front window, the burn marks on the plastic tables, the slimy gunk that had accumulated in every corner?

'*It is a nice place. Very nice,*' she said, looking around, assuaging his fears.

'*Thanks you.*' Sweat began beading on his forehead. It was a hot day. Too hot for a cashmere suit and such unexpected excitement.

'*Where can I put my case?*' she asked.

'*Cam with me. I show you bedroom.*'

He picked up the suitcase and led the way, forgetting his earlier resolution, thinking only that Barbara was far too small and delicate to carry such heavy luggage. He led her through the galley kitchen, where unwashed plates were piled high, and opened the door to her makeshift living quarters. He had thought himself clever, converting his old storeroom into a bedroom at minimal cost, but now as a cockroach scuttled across the dirty, tiled floor of the cramped space he felt ashamed. This dark room with bars at the small window, furnished with a camp bed and a wooden chair, was unfit for a cat. The state treated its criminals with more respect. He hated the idea of Barbara sleeping in that squalid place beneath the sickly light of a low-wattage bulb. And he had given no thought to where she would wash or shower and felt horribly embarrassed.

'This room is jass for now. For one, two weeks. After, I promise, I find you somewhere better. OK?'

She shook her head and looked up at him gratefully, making him feel criminally negligent. She had travelled thousands of miles on trust only to reach this dark and dingy cell. A room airily described as 'palatial' by his friend and 'more than adequate'. 'Over there they live in squalor,' he had said. Well, his friend was a donkey! This room was a stinking pit. And this woman was at his mercy, vulnerable, reliant, he had a duty to treat her with respect. How many girls like her had come to Cyprus to work as waitresses and ended up as strippers or prostitutes, abused by unscrupulous employers who preyed on their powerlessness? He wanted to protect Barbara, to find her cosy lodgings; he wanted to reassure her that she had fallen into safe hands.

'Today arcade closed. You rest,' Kyriaco said. *'Tomorrow you start work. I go now, you eat. Take whatever food you want. Plenty of food in the kitchen.'*

She nodded. '*Thank you. You are a good man. Tomorrow, I work hard for you. Tomorrow, you see what Barbara can do.*'

He left the arcade feeling heavy-hearted. He wanted to stay longer in her company but his future beckoned, albeit somewhat less urgently than it had before Barbara's arrival. He headed for the cemetery in his Datsun Cherry, rehearsing the glib lines that he hoped would secure him an affluent wife with a parcel of beachside land. The closer he came to the cemetery, the more he felt a sinking sense of doom as if his life were coming to an end, not beginning anew. He found Sophia on her knees, vigorously polishing her husband's marble tombstone. Hearing his footsteps, she turned and smiled. Not a captivating smile like Barbara's but a stingy, tortured half-smile that could easily be mistaken for a grimace. The smile of a troubled soul, a grieving widow, a woman who wanted the world to know she could never be truly happy again.

'Sophia, how are you today?' Kyriaco helped her to her feet.

'Eh! As well as can be expected. As well as a woman alone in the world can be.'

Sophia never admitted to feeling more than tolerably well. When asked about her health she usually reeled off a litany of aches and pains, prefixed by the phrase 'God put me on this earth to suffer'. Kyriaco was suddenly aware of the self-conscious way in which she smoothed down her skirt and the unusually bright lipstick applied to her over-fleshy lips. He had spent the best part of a year flattering her, showering her with compliments, being manipulative and disingenuous, but now that his prize stood before him, primed and ready for the taking, he was having second thoughts.

Casting aside his doubts, he took her by the hand. 'It's not easy being alone, especially on a day like Easter Sunday when everyone is at home celebrating Christ's resurrection with spouses and children. We are both lonely souls, Sophia. I don't even have a dog to call my own.'

She nodded empathetically. 'My poor Kyriaco, you should find someone. Get married. You're not like me, you're young. You don't have to be alone.'

'I have found someone, Sophia. Someone very special.'

The glazed eyes that gazed back at Kyriaco were hopeful, besotted, expectant; the skin around them tired, dark and lined.

'And who is this lucky woman?' she asked, and he knew from the look on her face that she was poised to hear her name and fall into his arms.

The name 'Barbara' hovered on the tip of Kyriaco's tongue, the pretty face in his mind's eye interposing itself between a grotty arcade and a swathe of first-rate building plots by the sea.

'You are the lucky woman, Sophia.'

'What exactly are you saying, Kyriaco?' She moved a step closer to him.

'I want you to . . .' He hesitated, fighting the urge to scratch the itch between his buttocks, feeling as if he were inching towards the edge of a precipice. From the corner of his eye he saw a magpie swooping towards him and recognised it as the tame bird that came to the arcade for scraps of food. He forced out the words 'marry me' just as the bird flew down on to his head and sank its claws into his scalp, trying to steady itself. Startled by the bird's rapid descent and clumsy landing, Kyriaco cried out. Sophia, reminded of a scene in Hitchcock's *The Birds*, thought Kyriaco was being attacked and started screaming and waving her hands in the air. Frightened by the noise, Koko took off and circled overhead three times before landing on the headstone Sophia had just been polishing.

'My God.' She crossed herself. 'That bird attacked you.'

'No, he was just being friendly. That's Andrico's bird, Koko. He comes into the arcade sometimes.'

'Is it a magpie?'

'Yes.'

'You know they're a bad omen.'

'I don't believe that.'

'Why else do you think the bird is sitting on my husband's grave?'

'To rest, probably. Now, tell me, Sophia, will you marry me or not?'

Before she could answer, Koko began screeching and gobbling and doing a sideways jig on the headstone.

'Will I marry you?'

Her words were obliterated by the bird's angry-sounding squawk.

'Yes. What's your answer? Don't keep me waiting.'

Koko shook his head vigorously from side to side, as if he were saying no, and made a commotion that turned heads in the graveyard.

Sophia crossed herself and kissed the gold crucifix hanging from her neck. 'You have to leave right now and never speak to me again,' she whispered, wiping off her lipstick with the back of her hand.

'Why? What's happened? What have I done?'

'Don't you understand? That bird is a sign, a signal from my husband. He doesn't want me to get remarried. He's angry. Jealous. That's why the bird attacked you. I should have known better than to betray him in front of his very eyes.'

'What eyes? He's dead!'

'Please, Kyriaco, leave before the bird attacks you again. We have no future together. I am destined to be alone for the rest of my life. I'm sorry. Please go.'

Kyriaco walked away, head lowered, Koko skipping along behind him, chattering, demanding a treat from the man who always gave him scraps of meat and bread.

'He's following you out to make sure you leave,' Sophia called out, falling to her knees and polishing the marble with renewed vigour.

At the cemetery gates Kyriaco couldn't help but smile. He was not in fact disheartened by the outcome but unexpectedly and wonderfully relieved.

He turned to the bird. 'Thank you, Koko. Thank you, my friend, for rescuing me from my own stupidity.'

Kyriaco climbed into the Datsun and headed back to the arcade to look in on Barbara and make sure she had everything she needed. The first thing he noticed when he arrived were the front windows, freshly polished and glinting in the sun. The smell of garlic, onions and spices hit him when he walked through the door, whetting his appetite. In the kitchen two pans spouting steam bubbled on the cooker. He glanced into the bedroom and was surprised by its transformation. Swathes of coloured silk in fuchsia, ochre and emerald hung at the window, covered the bed, hung from the wall. The suitcase lay open at the door. Inside were exotic foodstuffs in brightly coloured packaging. A bunch of wild flowers arranged in a tall frappé glass stood in a corner of the room. The grim cell had been brought to life with a profusion of colour and unfamiliar scents.

Barbara walked into the kitchen through the back door, her hair tied back, her cheeks flushed. Kyriaco wanted to say he liked what she had done but her sudden appearance made him feel self-conscious and tongue-tied.

'Is smell nice,' he said, sniffing the air.

'You like we eat together?'

He nodded and she busied herself setting the small table in the kitchen.

'You want I help?' he felt compelled to ask though the voice inside him still muttered 'start as you mean to go on'.

'No. Please sit.'

He sat and watched her, feeling like a guest, marvelling at her speed and agility in the kitchen, knowing he had struck gold. How different she was to Sophia who walked with the air of a woman tired of living, who shuffled along as if she were carrying the weight of the world on her shoulders. Barbara spooned steaming, sticky rice into a serving plate and set it on the table followed by a rich, sweet-smelling stew.

'Is look very nice,' Kyriaco said, feeling ravenous.

'It is Adabong Baboy. Pork cooked with vinegar, peppercorns and soya sauce.'

'You find this soya sauce in my kitchen?'

'No, I bring it with me, and the rice and the spices.'

165

They ate in comfortable silence exchanging friendly, appreciative looks. The peppery stew stung Kyriaco's mouth, made his eyes water and warmed his insides. It made a welcome change from the grilled meat and hot sandwiches he was used to eating alone. Kyriaco felt inexplicably happy. No high-class restaurant or expensive taverna could have given him more contentment than he felt sitting in his cramped kitchen opposite Barbara, eating the spicy pork dish that cleared his sinuses and sharpened his senses.

17

The day of reckoning had arrived. Three days had passed since the toilet-block incident. Socrates listened at the door of his bedroom, waiting for his father to go to work, intending to creep out of the house and delay the inevitable confrontation with his parents until the evening. The explosion was not the only crime he had to answer for. Everyone in the village had heard of the theft of Loulla's roof beams, and several witnesses had reported seeing Socrates carrying the wood to the churchyard. How was he to know the widow had spent all her savings buying new beams for her crumbling roof, that her house was on the verge of collapse and she lived in fear of her roof caving in? No one had thought to complain about that on Saturday night, he thought indignantly, watching the roof beams crackle on the biggest bonfire they had ever seen, but now the village was up in arms about the theft. Loulla had provided the police with a list of suspects, saying that a gang of children had broken into her house on Easter Saturday and assaulted her.

Socrates wondered what was going on downstairs. His father should have left for work several hours ago but instead was playing host to a series of early-morning visitors. Angry male shouts filtered into his bedroom from the kitchen and Socrates feared a terrible confrontation awaited him there. Perhaps Hector's condition had worsened? As far as Socrates knew, the widower had been sent home from hospital the day after the explosion with minor cuts and bruises. Perhaps the men downstairs were discussing the most recent development. News of the bomb had caught the attention of the island's archbishop who was planning a visit to the village to address the local congregation and urge the guilty parties to give themselves up.

The front door slammed shut. The house fell silent. Assuming his father had left for work, Socrates took off his shoes and stole quietly downstairs, anxious to make his escape. As he turned the latch on the door, holding his breath, his father called out to him.

'Socrates, please come into the kitchen.'

His voice was uncharacteristically sombre. Socrates walked on heavy feet along the narrow corridor that led to the kitchen, his stomach clenching. The mood he encountered there was far worse than he could ever have imagined. His mother was standing at the sink crying, her face buried in her hands, and the whites of his father's eyes were bloodshot. Socrates felt sick. A bitter taste filled his mouth. He was sure now that the old man was dead, that the shock of being buried alive had proved too much for his heart. Starting to tremble, he took a seat at the kitchen table.

'We've had some very bad news this morning,' his father said.

'Terrible news.' His mother looked at him with anguished eyes.

'I don't know how to tell you this. It's not easy . . .'

'Just tell him, Niko. He needs to know.'

'I will. But how, Eleni? Tell me how? What words do I use?'

The wait was tortuous. 'He's dead, isn't he, and you think I killed him, don't you?' Socrates blurted out.

His father looked puzzled. 'Who? What are you talking about?'

'Hector.'

'This has nothing to do with Hector. The old man's fine and will probably outlive us all.'

'Then, what do you have to tell me?'

'A boy in the village was attacked, son.'

'Who?'

'We can't tell you who.'

'Why?'

The colour drained from his father's face. 'The boy was attacked in the field behind the arcade. A man did very bad things to him. Unspeakable things. Do you understand what I'm saying, Socrates? He was molested.'

Socrates nodded, though he wasn't exactly sure in physiological terms what his father meant.

'I don't want you going anywhere near that field, not until the man's caught. Do you hear me?' His mother's anguish turned to anger. 'In fact, I don't want you going anywhere alone at night. Stay with your friends at all times. Listen to me, Socrates, and take heed of my words for once in your life. Don't go anywhere alone after dark. The same thing might happen to you.'

'You must listen to Mama. This is a very serious matter, son.'

'What is the village coming to when children are no longer safe to roam?'

Eleni felt so angry she wanted to scream, to tug at her hair, to strike out with her fists. Nothing of this nature had ever happened before in the village. The abomination made her want to lock up her sons and never let them out of her sight. Gone for ever was the carefree era when doors were left unlocked and neighbours drifted in and out without invitation. Now it appeared there were maniacs on the loose, walking the streets, preying on young children. Society had changed beyond recognition. Mass tourism was a scourge. Those scandalous American late-night movies, that were practically pornographic, turned men into monsters.

'The police will probably want to ask you some questions. To find out if you know anything.'

'Questions?'

'Yes. They'll want to know if you've seen anyone suspicious hanging about near the arcade. Do you know anything at all that might help the police, son?'

Socrates shook his head, struggling to make sense of the news, Hector's alleged crimes behind the arcade coming to mind.

Sergeant Stelios Georgiou felt a flutter of excitement in his chest. At last a real crime had been committed, one he could cut his teeth on. He had spent the morning conducting interviews, speaking to the arcade owner, a number of boys who used his establishment, and the

170

Filipino waitress who'd found the victim. After giving a brief statement in hospital the night before, the traumatised boy had turned his face to the wall, refusing to speak further. So far the policeman had gleaned that the child had left the arcade through the back door at ten last night and was walking home when a man pounced on him from behind, putting a hand over his mouth to stop him screaming. He had no description of the attacker, no eye witnesses. The only detail the boy recalled vividly was the smell of blood on the perpetrator's hand.

Villagers milled about outside the arcade voicing their outrage, their disgust, threatening to hunt the molester down and decapitate him. Unbeknown to Sergeant Georgiou, a group of villagers armed with shotguns had squeezed into the cabin of a truck soon after the news broke, to search the surrounding countryside and administer their own justice. They had already accosted three farmers at gunpoint, taken pot shots at a fruit picker, and chased a hapless tourist hitching a lift. All the vigilantes had sons of their own and felt a violent sense of revulsion.

The area behind the arcade had been cordoned off and forensic officers were due to arrive at lunchtime. Villagers crowded round the cordon, staring at an area of unimpressive scrubland with patches of trampled grass and bare soil, littered with ice-cream and sweet wrappers. The onlookers shook their heads. They pointed to a child's upturned sandal lying on the ground, a poignant symbol of the crime that had taken place. The poor boy had obviously fought back, they said to one another, but the devil had overpowered him.

171

Earlier that morning there had been another visitor to the crime scene, one that breached the cordon unseen and had stolen a vital piece of evidence. A black bird with a white chest and a fondness for all things shiny had swooped down from a nearby rooftop to pick up a metallic object glinting in the grass, flying back home to store his precious find in a box on his master's wardrobe.

Inside the arcade all attention was on Barbara who was still recovering from the shock of finding the crying boy outside the back door of the arcade. Kyriaco sat with an arm around her shoulders, consoling her, feeling guilty for using the raw emotions stirred by the crime to his own advantage. He was offering his new employee comfort, he told himself, stroking the soft skin of her forearm, squeezing her lovely fingers and smoothing down her fine hair. With Kyriaco acting as translator, Barbara told and retold her tale to villagers hungry to hear every gruesome detail, whose questions were more searching than Sergeant Georgiou's.

Socrates walked into the arcade and joined a group of villagers listening to Barbara's account. He wanted to find out as much as he could, to piece together the clues and discover the identity of the victim. Zaphiri turned to acknowledge him with a friendly nod. Today there were no animosities and rivalries. Today all boys were one homogeneous group united against a common enemy, an enemy who could so easily have targeted any one of them. Socrates listened eagerly to Barbara's account of the events of the previous evening. About how she had mopped the arcade floor, gone outside to throw away the dirty water and found the boy slouched on the ground, crying, his face grazed and dirty. Only after speaking to him softly for some time did she manage to coax him inside and treat his grazes with iodine. After asking his name, she had wrapped him in a blanket and telephoned her employer at his house who in turn alerted the police and called the victim's parents. The boy's father limped into the arcade with a walking stick, Barbara said, and collapsed when he caught sight of his injured son.

Marco came up behind Socrates. '*Re!* I've just been questioned by the police. So has Raphael. Come on, let's sit over there and talk where no one can hear us.'

Socrates followed his friend to a table at the far end of the arcade.

'What did you tell them?'

'Nothing. What could I tell them! I don't know anything.'

'About Michali getting money from Hector for doing things to him behind the arcade.'

'That might just be idle gossip, and anyway, I don't want to get Michali into trouble if it is true.'

'But he's the one who's been attacked.'

'How do you know?'

'I just do. Look around you, Marco. That kid practically lives here but he's the only boy who hasn't turned up. And the Filipino woman said the boy's father walked with a limp and used a walking stick.'

'You're right! It's got to be him. The wanker who did this picked an easy target . . . but it can't be Hector. He's too old and weak.'

'You'd be surprised. He's much stronger than he looks. He bruised my wrist when he grabbed hold of me for firing a stone at his head. Maybe we should speak to the police about him?'

'No way. That story might not be true. And after what we did to Hector, I doubt he could do anything to anyone. Perhaps it was our teacher, Kyrios Hadjimichael. He's a pervert. Katerina says he's always pressing up against her desk when he talks to her. But no, on second thoughts, it can't be him. He likes young girls, not boys.'

'He's going to get what's coming to him. I'm going to teach him a lesson he won't forget after the holidays.'

'What about Victora? He's strange. Always hanging around kids with those puppets of his.'

'That's his job!'

'Nobody knows much about his past. He's got no wife. No family.'

'There's no way it was him. Victora's a good man. He invited me into his house last week. It was great in there, and he gave me something really amazing.' Socrates took the marble out of his pocket and passed it to his friend.

Marco surveyed the glass sphere cynically before handing it back. 'Did he do anything strange to you while you were in the house?'

Socrates shook his head, remembering the wet kiss planted on his hand and the old man's ominous predictions.

'They say he can do magic tricks, that he can see into the future,' Marco said. 'But I don't believe anyone truly knows what's going to happen to us. People who believe in that kind of stuff are pretty stupid, if you ask me.'

18

It was Sunday lunchtime. The soldiers were at rest. The heat had seeped into their bones, making them feel languid. They snoozed, leafed through newspapers, played cards and backgammon. Petri lay on his bed, reading Carina's first letter, struggling to decipher three pages of loopy handwriting, skipping over words he did not understand. He sniffed the perfumed paper and traced the small hearts framing her flowery prose. He closed his eyes, conjured up her face, and pressed his mouth against the pink lipstick smudge at the bottom of page three below a blurred section of text where Petri assumed her tears had dripped and smeared the ink. He was gratified by the thought that she was miserable without him.

He kissed the photograph sent with the letter in which he sat beside her on a bar stool. She looked incredible and he wondered, not for the first time, what she found so appealing in him. The man who stared back at him from the photograph, holding up a bottle of Keo, was a dark, mischievous-looking demon with a skewed smile. Surely Carina was far better suited to the tall, fair Scandinavian wearing the white tennis jumper who had been roughed up outside the Pussy Cat. Petri wondered jealously if her ex-boyfriend was already making moves to win her back.

He had not expected the tidal wave of emotion that hit him in the airport departure lounge as he said goodbye to Carina. Upset she was leaving, and suffering from a terrible hangover, he had struggled to hold back tears, not wanting to cry in public. Confronted by the calamitous prospect of never seeing or touching her again, never consummating their relationship, he knew that in the annals of his life Carina would be remembered as his first true love. He had wiped away her tears, stroked her soft hair, kissed her salty lips long and hard, and given her half a silver heart, hanging the other half from his own neck.

'*Our hearts can only be whole when we are together. I will come back in the summer and find a job,*' she had said. '*And we can live together.*'

'*I wait for you,*' he had replied, promising to be faithful, believing wholeheartedly that he would stick to that promise.

When the speaker announced her flight was boarding, Carina had drifted away tearfully, glancing back at him intermittently until she disappeared from view. Afterwards Petri drove to their favourite stretch of beach near the airport and parked the car beneath a palm tree, turned his stereo on full blast and drank a bottle of cheap whisky, his eyes welling up every time a plane flew overhead. Then he fell asleep and woke at midnight with leaden limbs, his mouth dry and bitter-tasting.

A soldier friend came to whisper in his ear, '*Re!* Get up. Oresti's parked outside the barracks, he's waiting for you. He's got two Norwegian girls with him.'

'Good luck to him.'

'One of them has come for you. A girl called Alva.'

'I'm not interested in that girl. I don't even fancy her. She has the face of a ghoul.'

After Carina's departure Petri had thrown himself into army life with uncharacteristic vigour, obeying the rules and showing no interest in the outside world. For ten miserable days he had mourned his loss, feeling no inclination to look at another woman, sparking Oresti's concern. This was not the Petri he knew and admired, the man who loved and left without compunction. Oresti had finally persuaded him that an evening out at the Pussy Cat would do him good. Petri had gone along, intending only to eat a Maradonna sandwich and drink a crate of Keo. As he sat at the bar looking moody and detached he caught the eye of a Norwegian holidaymaker called Alva, a buxom girl who liked a challenge and enjoyed casual sex. Alva had seen Petri out with the blonde stick insect some days before and thought he might appreciate a change, a woman with a little more meat on her bones. She pulled him on to the dance floor and cavorted before him. Though flattered, Petri was unmoved by the erotic way she swayed her hips, immune to such overt seduction so soon after the departure of his beloved.

The soldier standing over his bed pulled a disgruntled face. 'I wish to God I could take your place. I haven't been laid in six months. What's your secret, my friend? How do you get all these women chasing you?'

'Go and tell Oresti I'm not coming.' He slipped Carina's letter back into the envelope and stashed it inside his pillowcase.

'He said if you don't go out, he'll never speak to you again. The girls are leaving. He's taking them to the airport.'

Petri got up reluctantly and walked across the quadrangle towards a group of soldiers urging a new recruit called Stavraki to bite the head off the live chameleon thrashing about in his hand. Stavraki entertained his fellow soldiers by eating anything that moved, including lizards, beetles and cockroaches. Petri stopped to watch, joining in the countdown from ten to one, cringing when Stavraki put the chameleon's head in his mouth and lopped it off, blood and green guts running down his chin, triumphantly throwing down the decapitated body. A soldier standing beside Petri leaned forward and vomited. Another ran into the barracks and returned with a box of Cif washing powder and a bottle of water for the finale of the Stavraki show. The recruit spat out the gory contents of his mouth, leaned his head back, poured in washing powder and water and gargled, soapsuds pouring down his face, the men around him laughing and holding their stomachs.

Petri walked on and climbed through a hole in the barracks' barbed-wire fence. He found Oresti parked a little way off with the two girls in his car.

'Climb in. Let's take them to the airport,' he said. 'You'll be back in an hour. No one will even notice you've gone.'

'OK. If it's just to the airport, I'll come.'

In the back of the car Alva and several cans of beer awaited him. The big-eyed girl with long black hair and a jowly face looked even more like a ghoul than he remembered. Petri greeted her coldly by raising his eyebrows before reaching for a beer and settling back in the seat. Oresti pulled away from the kerb and turned up the stereo until music blared deafeningly from the back speakers, making the whole car vibrate. A pale girl in the front passenger seat moved her head in time to the beat, dragging on a cigarette, her dark eyes underscored with shadows.

Half a dozen empty beer cans already littered the floor. From the corner of his eye Petri noticed Alva's large breasts jiggling every time the Lada hit a bump in the road. He turned to glance at the short white skirt riding up her generous thighs, and catching a glimpse of her black knickers began to feel aroused. He swallowed down the lager and tried to focus on Carina and her pretty face, but his eyes kept drifting back to that skirt and the large quivering breasts squashed beneath a tight-fitting T-shirt, to the outline of prominent nipples.

Oresti was fondling the pale girl's leg with his left hand and pressing down hard on the accelerator. He took the detour Petri knew well, to a secluded stretch of unmade road behind the airport, a well-known lovers' lane. Petri pulled the ring on a second can, his senses dizzied by the drink, the smoke, the loud music and Alva's breasts. Oresti swerved into a gravel lay-by and slammed his foot on the brake before leaning across the gear stick to kiss the girl beside him. Alva fell against Petri, refusing to budge, looking up at him with lovelorn eyes, her hand moving up his thigh, her fingers unbuttoning his fly and rummaging inside his trousers. Petri's body caught fire and the flames consumed all thoughts of Carina.

'*Come on,*' he said, grabbing Alva by the hand and climbing out of the car, leading her through a field of tall weeds and trampled grass towards a solitary carob tree where he kissed her passionately beneath a canopy of leathery leaves. In a state of sexual delirium he pulled Alva down and climbed on top of her, easing off her knickers while she loosened his belt. With no talk of condoms, of the future, of anything at all, he entered her while she moaned and wriggled and clawed his buttocks. The excitement was too great, the heat too intense. Thirty seconds later Petri drew back and ejaculated on a bed of nettles. He had no intention of sending Alva away with a parting gift, to have her return to the island nine months later brandishing a paternity suit and a baby with a ghoulish face.

'*You gonna miss the flight,*' he said, pulling up his trousers, knowing he had cheated her, left her hanging.

Alva adjusted her clothes and sat up looking flushed and disappointed, wincing from the nettle stings on her back. Her white T-shirt was grass-stained and her skirt crumpled and creased, but when they got back to the car she was remarkably forgiving, sidling up beside him on the seat and rubbing her hand up and down his leg.

At the airport Oresti smooched with the pale girl behind a magazine stand while Petri was left holding Alva's hand. The airport departure lounge was heaving and he hoped he would not see anyone he knew. Alva pulled a clean top from her holdall and changed out of her soiled T-shirt, exposing her bare breasts in the departure area as easily as if she were standing on a beach, attracting amused and affronted gazes. Petri's cheeks burned. In the cold light of day, beneath bright artificial light, she struck him as staggeringly unattractive. Why had he cheated on Carina with such an unworthy rival? How could he have touched this girl at all? As soon as he got back to the barracks he would take a shower and wash the unsavoury smell of her away. Alva took a camera out of her knapsack and asked a passer-by to take a picture of her and Petri embracing. He wondered why she was behaving as if this were the end of some passionate holiday romance, not welcome closure on a sleazy afternoon, a seedy romp in a field of nettles. Why were there tears in her eyes? Perhaps this was how she had scripted the end of her holiday, bidding a tearful farewell to some Mediterranean Lothario. Everything had fallen into place at the very last minute. She had got her man and would have stories to tell, notes to exchange, and photographic evidence.

On his way out of the departure lounge Petri spotted a pretty girl sitting behind a check-in desk, quite obviously staring at him. He flashed her a smile, looking quickly away and feeling embarrassed when he realised the girl was Maria. Her curly hair had been blow-dried straight and she looked chic, lovely, and nothing like the unremarkable girl in his mind's eye. Petri hoped she had not seen him with Alva and jumped to any wrong conclusions. Not that he cared what Maria thought since she meant nothing to him. But then, why had he blushed? True, she had changed beyond recognition, but he reminded himself that not so long ago Maria was a scrawny girl with unsightly metal wires lashed across her teeth. Now she waved to him with a wry smile before leaning over to speak to the girl beside her. Both of them laughed out loud and Petri hurried out of the exit doors, knowing he had been seen with Alva and become the butt of Maria's joke.

19

It was a warm, windless night. The tall aromatic trees towering over the tombstones gave off a medicinal smell. The inky blackness of the graveyard was pierced by iridescent flickers of candlelight glowing in the headstones behind glass and perspex covers. Perched on the saddle of his bike, Socrates waited impatiently for his friends. They had agreed to meet him outside the cemetery gates at 1 a.m., so they could cycle to the beach together and go night fishing with Poli. But Raphael had fallen asleep on his bed, forgetting to set his alarm clock, and Marco was sitting with an ear to his bedroom wall, listening to his father shouting, unwilling to leave lest his mother needed him. Socrates had managed to escape the house without waking his parents, ignoring his mother's warning not to go out alone at night.

He stared through the cemetery gates at the eerie landscape contained within the high stone wall. The nearest house was half a kilometre away. No one wanted to build near the cemetery, to open their curtains on to a necropolis, to be reminded each day of their own mortality. Socrates wondered how many coffins had passed through the wrought-iron gates, how many blood relatives were stacked one on top of the other in family graves. As his eyes grew accustomed to the darkness, he noticed a dark figure moving along the path between the headstones. His first impulse was to cycle away, to escape this apparition, but the need to know more about this oddity was stronger than his fear. He backed his bike up behind the gatepost, peeking round the stone pillar at the slow-moving figure with the hunched shoulders and the masculine gait. When the phantasm stopped to strike a match and light a cigarette, his identity became clear. He had a trimmed white beard, a domed beret worn at a rakish angle, and was dressed in a dinner jacket with tails. The puppet master strolled casually through the dark graveyard, seemingly at ease with the surroundings. Socrates wondered why he spent so much time with the dead. Why he spoke to spirits, and what he said. This man could breathe life into inanimate objects, his paper puppets, yet he shunned the living, kept himself to himself, lived an eccentric, itinerant lifestyle. The fishing rod slipped from Socrates' shoulder and clattered to the ground, shattering the silence, alerting Victora to prying eyes.

'Who's there?' he called out, walking briskly towards the gate.

Socrates reached for the bamboo stick and pressed down on the pedals of his bike, racing away from the old man who spooked him more than any ghost. Perhaps Marco was right, after all. Perhaps the puppet master was Michali's attacker. Perhaps he wandered through the village at night searching for lone children to accost. Socrates' heart thumped in his ears as he pedalled, heading for the coastal road and the safety of the fisherman's company.

The moon was a bright white globe on the horizon ringed by a golden hue. It cast a beam of yellow light across the blue-black sea, highlighting the gentle ripples that raced across the surface of the water. Socrates listened to the sloshing sound of the ocean as it washed over the sand. He scanned the dusky beach for his friend and noticed the end of his cigarette first, burning a hole in the darkness.

'You've come alone?' Poli asked.

'Yes, the others didn't turn up. I don't know why.'

Poli flicked away his cigarette. 'That's probably for the best. They don't take fishing as seriously as you do. They lark about too much. Tonight, my young friend, you need the patience of a fisherman and the stealth and strength of a hunter.' He looked at the rod held in Socrates' hand. 'Why have you brought that?'

'I thought we were going fishing.'

'We are, but not with rods . . . with a spear . . . with this.'

Poli bent forward to pick up a metal rod lying at his feet and handed it to Socrates. It was heavier than it looked, made of solid metal with a cord running through an eyelet at the end of the handle. Socrates fingered the sharp point and felt powerful to be holding such a lethal-looking weapon.

'Now, hand it back and roll up your trouser legs. Tonight we'll be getting wet.'

Poli lit a paraffin lamp while Socrates rolled up his trousers. They walked to the water's edge and began wading out to sea, Socrates contemplating the seeming impossibility of spearing a moving fish.

'You hold the lamp and move slowly,' Poli explained. 'Shine the light on the surface so we can see what's underneath . . . and hope to God you don't step on a jellyfish. And another thing – don't let the lantern touch the water because the glass might break.'

Poli fumbled in the tight pocket of his trousers with his free hand and pulled out the plastic bottle he always carried with him when he fished. Unscrewing the lid with his mouth, he sprinkled a dark liquid into the water, emptying the bottle.

'What did you pour into the sea?' Socrates asked.

Poli pushed the lid and bottle back inside his trouser pocket. 'My magic ingredient. Something to attract the fish.'

'What was it?'

'Every fisherman has his secrets and this one is mine.'

The water was cold against Socrates' skin. Wet sand squelched through his toes. He saw the outline of a small fish and shone the light in its direction. It darted away. Poli held the spear poised above the surface of the water, the end of the cord tied around his wrist.

'How will you ever catch one? They move so fast.'

'Don't you know that fish sleep at night? Some of them stay absolutely motionless, others lean against the rocks to rest.'

'And do they close their eyes?'

Poli laughed and patted Socrates on the shoulder. 'No, my friend. They don't have eyelids.'

The water reached past Socrates' knees. He wondered

when Poli intended to stop walking. Soon the water would be waist-high. He felt a quick tap on his shoulder and heard a whispered 'Stop'. A dark shape hung in the water. Poli angled his spear, the muscles in his face tightening. With a loud cry he thrust the spear into the sea, agitating the sand, the water clouding. He pivoted the spear upwards with a triumphant smile, an impaled fish flapping its tail, its mouth gaping. Awed by the fisherman's skill, Socrates felt a surge of pride in his new friend. He desperately wanted to get his hands on the spear now and have a go himself. Poli carried the fish back to the shore and laid it on the sand before returning to hand Socrates the weapon.

'Come on. Give me the lamp and have a try.'

'Really?'

'Of course. But it's not as easy as it looks.'

Socrates mimicked the fisherman's stance, honing his concentration. Too eager to catch a fish and impress Poli, he stabbed impatiently at the water several dozen times, at blurred shadows in the water, soaking his clothes but catching nothing. When the spear grew too heavy to hold, he handed it back to Poli, feeling disappointed.

'I can't do it,' he said.

'Don't worry. I didn't catch a fish the first time I tried. I had to practise for months before I mastered the technique. We'll come again with a lighter spear and you can have another go. Come on, let's go and rest. You must be tired.'

They waded back to shore. Socrates sat down on the sand feeling exhausted, his clothes uncomfortably wet against his skin.

'I need to get home before my parents wake up,' he said, starting to feel cold.

'Forget your parents. I think they have too much control over you. You're not a kid anymore – you're old enough to make your own decisions. Stay and keep me company a while.' Poli sat down and lit a cigarette. 'Take one, if you want,' he said, tossing Socrates the packet and a lighter.

'Thanks.'

Socrates pulled a cigarette from the packet and lit up. Resting on one elbow, he stared up at the feverish moon overhead and a sky dotted with stars, filling his mouth with smoke and letting it seep out, feeling more manly than he had ever felt before.

'Did I ever tell you I have a close relative in your village?' Poli said.

'You did, but you didn't say who.'

'I'd rather not if you don't mind. It's a problematic relationship. Doomed, in fact. I wish we were close but that's never going to happen. Not in this lifetime.'

'Why not?'

'My life has always been complicated, Socrates. My relative and I are fated to live apart. That's how we began life and that is how we will end it.' Poli lay down, propping his head on his folded hands.

'I might know your relative.'

'You probably do. Everyone knows everyone in the village, don't they, and nobody's affairs are private. That's why I'm glad I live in town. Nobody gives a damn what you do there.' He yawned. 'I'm tired. Maybe I'll get some shuteye on the beach. Have you ever slept on the beach, Socrates?'

'No. But I've always wanted to.'

'Perhaps it's a good time to start. Close your eyes. Relax. You'll never have a better night's sleep.'

'But I'm wet and cold. I need to change.'

'I have some shorts in the car. You can wear them, if you like.'

A car passed by on the beach road. The darkness was starting to thin. Socrates glanced at his watch and realised it was time to go home. His mother woke up early and he had to get back before she discovered that the body-shaped mound in his bed was actually a rolled-up blanket.

'I have to go. Mama gets up very early.' He sprang up and hurried towards his bike.

'Are you coming fishing tomorrow afternoon? I'll be here, waiting.'

'I'll try. See you then.'

20

Irini found comfort in kneading the bed sheets in soapy water, working quickly, establishing a rhythm. She unleashed her anger on the heavy sodden sheets, pounding them with her fists, the friction hurting her cracked knuckles. She muttered to herself, 'The demon, the devil, the bastard.' Her husband's offences were lodged immovably at the forefront of her mind and needed little excuse to flood her consciousness and drive her to the brink of madness. He seemed to forget his crimes the day after they were committed. Each morning he was reborn a new man, all sins expunged, all transgressions forgotten. Irini could not put the past behind her so easily. She did not want to forget or forgive the man who'd duped her mother, sent her father to an early grave, and strung her son up from a tree. Mino seemed to have recovered his old spirit now but he kept a safe distance from his father and was still wetting the bed. For five consecutive mornings Irini had changed her son's sheets, turned his mattress and aired his room. Now, as she drained the suds and lifted the wet sheet out of the sink, she imagined with great satisfaction that the wad of cotton she wrung tightly between her hands was her husband's thick neck.

She was startled by a knock at the door. Her friends rarely came to visit, fearing they might find the taxi driver at home, preferring to keep their distance from the unhappy household, as if marital disharmony were a contagious disease. The children were at school. Her husband had gone to work. Irini felt too agitated to answer the door and hoped her caller would drift away if ignored, but the knocking continued, growing louder and more urgent. She wiped her hands dry on a tea towel, brushed the perspiration from her forehead and smoothed down her messy hair. As a young woman she had taken care of her appearance and never gone out without applying lipstick, without glancing in a mirror. Now, she avoided mirrors and any other reflective surface in which she might catch a glimpse of the dowdy woman she had become.

Irini answered the door to a tall man with wavy black hair swept back from his dark, sharply defined face. He was dressed in a blue pinstripe suit and a white shirt worn open at the neck to reveal a gold cross nestled among tufts of curly chest hair. On his long fingers he wore an assortment of gold rings, and he clutched a fat cigar that leaked pungent white smoke from its smouldering tip. A metallic silver Mercedes was parked outside the house, as perfectly polished as the man's patent-leather shoes.

'Is your husband in?' he asked, his smile revealing a gold incisor.

'No. He's at work.' Irini felt painfully aware of her drab appearance and was cowed by this man's powerful, yet somewhat sleazy, persona.

'Does he come home for lunch?'

'Sometimes.'

'Then I'll come in and wait. I'm a friend of his. I need to talk to him, urgently.'

He walked past her into the house without waiting for an invitation and sat down on the sofa, looking around the tired living room with a look of disapproval.

'Would you like a coffee?' Irini asked, wanting to escape the man's unnerving aura.

'Yes. Thank you. No sugar.'

Irini went into the kitchen where she filled her *imbriki* with water and added a spoonful of coffee, her hands trembling. She was unused to having strangers in the house or to meeting her husband's friends and felt ill at ease. She put the pan on the heat and began to stir, the heat warming her already flushed cheeks. When the coffee bubbled and rose to the rim of the saucepan she poured it into a demitasse and returned to the living room, handing the small cup to the man.

The fat cigar lay in a glass ashtray on the coffee table now, its tip crumbling slowly away. Sitting opposite him on a wooden dining chair, Irini felt too nervous to speak. She feared the taxi driver might come through the front door at any moment and fly into a rage, that he might accuse her of flirting with his friend. He had a jealous streak and was quick to accuse his wife of behaving inappropriately. The grocer, in particular, continued to rile him, and he had warned his wife with raised fists not to fraternize with the shopkeeper. Widowed in his early-thirties, the store owner was a kind, self-effacing man who regularly entertained his customers with comic anecdotes

191

to make them laugh. Visits to the grocery had once been the highlight of Irini's week but now she shopped there quickly, avoiding eye contact with the puzzled shopkeeper whose conversational efforts she rebuffed.

The taxi driver was unpredictable, a bubbling cauldron of irrationality. The most absurd of accusations could fly without warning from his lips. He never looked at his wife as if she were desirable or worthy of attention yet he would kill any man who dared to tamper with his property.

'How do you know my husband?' she asked.

'He comes to my establishment at the weekends. I've helped him out on a number of occasions.'

The man's deliberate vagueness sparked Irini's curiosity. What kind of establishment did this shady character own? Not one he wished to name, not a restaurant or a bar. Irini guessed he was the owner of a gambling den or some dingy cabaret where men went to pick up prostitutes. Plucking his cigar from the ashtray the man got up, walked over to the window and pulled back the net curtain.

'Perhaps you'd like to leave him a message,' Irini said. 'As I told you before, my husband doesn't always come back for lunch.'

'I really need to speak to him face to face. I've been trying to pin him down for weeks.'

'I don't see him myself much. He's always working.'

'Is that what he tells you?'

The man smiled wryly, as if he knew more about her husband than she did, but his smile was quickly displaced by a look of annoyance.

'Your husband drives a black Mercedes these days, doesn't he?'

'Yes.'

'Well, he's just driven past without stopping. Why did he do that, do you think?'

Irini shrugged.

The man let the curtain drop, turned from the window and tutted. 'It seems your husband doesn't want to see his old friend. It seems he wants to play games with the maestro. I suppose I'm left with no choice but to leave him a message. Tell him Pantelas the Scorpion came to visit and is not a patient man. Tell him it's time to pay up or face the consequences. Tell him I'll come back in two days' time at ten in the morning to collect my money.'

Pantelas' eyes darkened, his brows knitted together, and his hulking physical presence filled the small room. Irini sensed instinctively that this man had a violent nature yet she did not feel personally threatened because he did not have that all-too-familiar look of the woman-hater in his eyes. And it was gratifying to know that someone made her husband tremble, as he made her tremble, and that one day soon he might even get a taste of his own medicine.

She considered the pseudonym Pantelas had brandished like a gun and realised she was standing before one of the island's most notorious criminals. A recent news report came to mind about the arrest of the nightclub owner Pantelas Charalambous, alias The Scorpion, for running an illegal gambling den. Irini wondered then why this high-profile felon was standing in her home, doing his own dirty work. Surely he employed hoodlums for such menial tasks as debt collection? She could only assume that her husband owed a lot of money and that previous attempts to make him pay up had failed.

'. . . and tell him that his house is a disgrace, that he's all show and no substance. Tell him he should be ashamed of letting his family live in squalor while he acts the big man, driving around in his flashy car.'

With that The Scorpion turned to leave, reiterating his threat to come back in two days and thanking Irini for the coffee he had not touched.

She was sweeping the living-room floor when the taxi driver stormed into the house and charged towards her, his face clenched into a fearsome scowl, his right arm outstretched. Her whole body tightened in anticipation of his attack. He grabbed her by the neck without slowing his stride and pinned her against the back wall, her head slamming against the bare plaster. She dropped the broom and tried to loosen his grip, struggling to breathe, her eyes watering. His fingers were too strong and unyielding and she felt herself growing dizzy, losing consciousness, convinced he had come to kill her.

'Why the hell did you let that goon into my house, you stupid woman?' he screamed, bringing his face close to hers, foaming at the mouth like a rabid dog, smelling of stale sweat and whisky. 'What did he want? What the hell did he tell you?'

He loosened his hold just enough to let her speak. 'He said you owe him money,' Irini managed to whisper hoarsely, before he clamped his fingers tight around her neck again.

'What else did he say?'

'He wants it repaid.'

'Does he now! What a surprise. And what did you say?'

The front door opened then and the children, back

194

from school, piled into the house. Dora screamed and Mino ran straight out. Marco marched across the room, grabbed his father by the shoulders and yanked him backwards. The taxi driver stumbled, tripped over the broom and fell heavily on to his side, becoming wedged between the sofa and the coffee table. Marco picked up the broom and began beating his father, his jaw clenched tight, his eyes wild with rage. The taxi driver covered his head, his body jerking with every blow. Irini pleaded with her son to stop but she knew he had lost control, that he was venting twelve years of accumulated anger and frustration. Irini held Dora in her arms, turning her away from the horrible spectacle she was unlikely to forget. The beating continued for some time until Mino ran back into the house followed by Socrates' father who tackled Marco, pushing him on to the armchair, grabbing the broom from his hands and flinging it across the room. Then he sat on the boy, trying to absorb his anger and calm the madness that possessed him. The taxi driver lifted himself off the ground and staggered towards the front door, his nose bleeding, his eyes crazed and bloodshot.

'I'm going to kill you and your mother,' he said, pointing first at one and then the other.

He walked out of the house, climbed into his car and drove away, leaving Niko to console and comfort the traumatised family.

21

Hilda, the statuesque mannequin with the bouffant hair, took centre stage in the window display of Miki's boutique. A sign in fluorescent yellow lettering hung above her head proclaiming the arrival of new stock. She stood legs astride, hands on hips, wearing a short jeans skirt and a tight Lycra top, her feet stuffed into black, patent-leather shoes with six-inch heels. The summer stock had become a talking point in the village with young local women flocking to the boutique to try on clothes that scandalised their parents. Socrates had overheard his mother calling Miki's boutique a 'den of iniquity resembling an Amsterdam bordello'. Curious to see what she meant, he had walked to the clothes shop with his friends to stare through the window.

'What a doll,' Raphael said, eyeing up Hilda.

'She *is* a doll!' Marco said, less impressed by the plastic vision of perfection.

'Do you think she's wearing knickers?'

'Why don't you go in and find out?' Socrates suggested.

'How?'

'Just lift up her skirt. There's not much of it.'

'Not a chance. I'm not doing that. Why don't you go?'

Socrates could not resist a challenge. He walked brazenly into the shop and approached the mannequin, avoiding the gaze of the sullen assistant standing at the cash desk. Climbing into the window display, he slipped his hand up Hilda's skirt and ran his fingers over bare plastic buttocks.

'*Re!* What are you doing?' the assistant called out, standing up and charging towards him.

Socrates jumped off the raised platform and dashed out of the shop and across the road, calling out, 'She's not wearing knickers,' over his shoulder to the friends who chased after him, laughing.

'You should be ashamed of yourself,' the irate assistant shouted from the door of the shop, waving her hand in the air. 'I know who you are, and don't think I won't tell your mother.'

At that moment, across the square, down a narrow street, outside a shabby house, Koko was busy filling a cylindrical nook with small stones and pieces of gravel. Stephania sat on a nearby wall watching, absorbed by the magpie's antics, keeping her distance, not wanting to scare him away. She longed to call the bird over and stroke his shiny plumage but feared a nip from his strong beak. Amused by the magpie's eccentric side-skip across the road and back again, she smiled to herself.

When Koko had finally finished his laborious task he flew up on to the opposite roof gutter, scouting for insects. Stephania was still smiling when the door of a shabby house flew open and the taxi driver walked out, climbed into his Mercedes and turned the key in the ignition. She nearly fell backwards off the wall when the exhaust pipe exploded and the finely tuned engine, fitted with a silencer, growled like a tractor. The taxi driver got out of the car and stared in astonishment at the small stones blocking the end of his exhaust pipe before scanning the road for the culprit and settling his angry gaze on Stephania. Fearing she would be blamed and conscious of this man's evil temper, she pointed upwards, saying: 'The bird did it.'

The taxi driver stormed back into the house while Stephania sat helplessly on the wall, willing Koko to fly away. She screamed and ran for her life when the taxi driver returned, brandishing a hunting rifle. Koko took flight, jauntily alighting on the neighbouring roof and running along the gutter, thinking the man below was playing some sort of game. The practised hunter, who hated wasting bullets, chased the bird along the street, fingers resting on the trigger.

Socrates and his friends were still laughing and running along the road in the direction of Marco's house. Raphael was first to see the gun pointing upwards and the magpie preening its feathers.

'*Re*, Marco!' he shouted. 'Your dad's going to shoot Koko.'

'Koko! Koko!' the boys screamed, jumping up and down and waving their arms in the air, imploring the bird to fly away.

He stopped preening to look at them and a second later a blast rang out and Koko tumbled from the eaves into the front garden below. The taxi driver hurried to the spot where the bird had fallen and, irritated that its wings were still flapping, decided to finish the job he had started. He fired again at close range before walking away, revelling in the sweetness of revenge, wondering how much it would cost to get his exhaust fixed, angry to have wasted two bullets on a mangy bird.

The boys rushed over to Koko, their hearts pounding, wanting to believe he was still alive and could be saved. But what they saw when they reached the bloody spot was a mangled, bloody creature with its lifeless head thrown back. Socrates began to cry and soon all three boys were wiping their eyes, and cursing the taxi driver, and wondering how to tell Andrico that his best friend was dead.

'Why did he do it?' Socrates asked. 'Why did he kill Koko?'

'Because he's a wanker,' Marco replied, hating his father more than he had ever hated him before, more even than when he hit his mother or strung up his brother.

Raphael pulled a handkerchief from his pocket and blew his nose. 'We can't leave him here. We can't let the cats eat him.'

Socrates nodded. 'We have to take him back to Andrico so he can bury him.'

'We can't take him back like that, all covered in blood.'

'You two stay here. I'll run home and get some bandages.'

Socrates ran along the street feeling wretched, his feet banging hard against the tarmac, the wind slapping his face, rapid motion offering some relief from his misery. He found his father in the hallway and ran into his arms, tearfully relating his story about the taxi driver's brutality. Niko tried to calm his son with comforting words but all the while anger and resentment bubbled inside him.

Enough was enough. This time the man had killed a bird; next time he might take a pot shot at his wife or his son. Something had to be done before it was too late. Niko collected several rolls of bandage from the kitchen cupboard and a bag of safety pins and handed them to Socrates.

'Wrap up the magpie, take him back to Andrico and leave Marco's father to me,' he said, intending to rally the support of other men; to confront the taxi driver and put a stop to his sadism.

'What are you going to do, Papa?'

'That's my business. You get off now and do what I told you.'

Socrates ran back to the street where Koko lay dead and began unwrapping several rolls of bandage. The bird's once-shiny plumage was spotted with glutinous patches of dark, coagulating blood. Together the friends swathed the bird, shrouding all evidence of injury, securing the bandage in place with a dozen safety pins. Finally they wiped their hands clean on Raphael's handkerchief, disposing of the bloody rag in a nearby bin.

'Come on. Let's go to Andrico's house,' Socrates said, cradling the dead bird in his arms.

Marco bowed his head. 'I can't go. I'm too ashamed. How can I tell him Papa killed Koko?'

'He doesn't need to know.'

'I just can't face him right now. I'm too angry. I need to go home and make sure Mama's all right.'

'I'll go back with Marco,' Raphael said, fearing his friend might attack his father a second time.

Socrates understood and walked away, clutching the bird

to his chest, wondering how to break the news to Andrico. The sudden realisation hit him that he was carrying death in his arms as Victora had predicted. Perhaps he had taken the puppet master's prophecies too lightly and should not have dismissed his fanciful riddles as nonsense. If the old man really could see into the future then more tears and betrayal lay on the horizon. Socrates' eyes welled up as he walked across the square in a daze, stroking the bird's soft head to comfort himself.

As he walked through the square he caught the attention of Tino and Zaphiri who were sitting on the ground playing with marbles.

'Hey, look!' Zaphiri called out. 'Cholera's crying like a girl.'

They laughed and followed Socrates along the street.

'What are you holding in your arms? Why are you crying? Did your mother batter you for blowing up the toilet block?'

'Koko's dead. He's been shot,' Socrates said, in a deadpan voice that stopped them in their tracks. 'I'm taking him back to Andrico so he can bury him.'

'Who shot him?' Tino asked.

Socrates shrugged, not wanting to link Marco to this crime.

'Poor Koko. Poor bird,' Zaphiri said, grabbing his friend by the arm and heading back to the square, allowing Socrates to continue his unhappy journey alone.

Andrico was sweeping his front step and humming the tune to 'Samiotisa', a song his mother used to sing. He stopped humming and raised the broom in salute when he saw Socrates approaching, paying little attention to the white bundle he held in his arms. It was not until the boy had stopped at his front gate, seemingly reluctant to step beyond it, that Andrico registered the black tail feathers protruding from the white sheath.

'What happened to Koko? Where did you find him?' he asked, throwing down the broom, his mind refusing to register what he was seeing.

'He's been shot.'

Andrico took the bird from the boy's arms. 'Give him to me. I'll soon make him better.'

'He's been shot,' Socrates repeated, unable to spell out the truth.

'He's been injured before. He's always getting himself into trouble, my Koko. Always flying off into the village and annoying people.'

'You can't make him better. Not this time.'

'I have a way with animals, Socrates. Magic healing fingers, Mama used to say.'

'No amount of magic can heal Koko.'

'You don't believe me? Then just wait and see.'

'But he's dead.'

Andrico looked down at the bird and felt nauseous, noticing now the spots of blood that had seeped through the bandage. He tried to stay calm, to control his breathing as his mother had taught him, shaking the bird vigorously in his hands in the hope of waking him up. But the magpie's lifeless head flopped from side to side and his eyes no longer shone. Panic hit Andrico like a tidal wave, head on, submerging and suffocating him. He squeezed the bird to his chest and let out a piercing, animalistic cry that rose up from the depths of his being and reverberated across the hills. The world around him suddenly liquefied. The boy, the gate, the trees beyond were all underwater too, their outlines warped and hazy. As he struggled to breathe Andrico thought that at any moment he might drown in his own pain. He felt the boy take him by the arm, lead him into the house and ease him into the rocking chair. Small fingers smoothed down his hair. A friendly voice spoke soothingly in his ear. He wanted to climb into bed and never get up; he wanted death to take him, too, like it had taken every being he had ever loved.

'Don't worry, Andrico. Everything will be all right. We'll bury Koko in the garden and make him a special cross. Everything will be all right, Andrico. I'll find you another magpie chick. Yes, I'll fetch you another one. In fact, I'll go right away and search the woods.' Socrates headed for the door, promising to come back as soon as he could.

He ran along the unmade road and into the scrubland beyond, heading for a wooded area outside the village where magpies were said to nest. Fired up and determined to find Andrico another magpie chick, he leaped across several dry ditches, waded through waist-high grass, walked half a kilometre and came across a grove thick with carob, olive and citrus trees where he began his search for a nest. The sun had begun to set and migrant birds filled the treetops, chattering and warbling, singing to attract a mate or to claim their territory. A flock of bee-eaters with turquoise breasts and yellow throats flew by before landing in a wobbly row on an overhead telephone wire. A blue-breasted swallow swooped down to pluck an insect from a bush before rising up and disappearing inside the thick foliage of a carob tree. Walking through the darkening grove, Socrates began to feel anxious. The chatter grew harsher, more hostile, as if the birds were warning him to leave their enclave and keep his hands off their young. The trees and bushes seemed thick with wary, disapproving eyes, charting his course.

Socrates spotted a magpie's nest nestled in the branches of an olive tree. He climbed the squat trunk easily and examined the elaborate, domed structure. Of all the nests that Socrates had ever seen this was the most robust, a ball of sticks lined with mud and dry grasses. Through an indistinct opening, he could hear the call of hungry chicks. Grabbing on to a branch for support, he forced his hand through the hole, defiling the nest, snapping twigs, making the frightened fledglings squeal. He closed his hand around a soft, warm, throbbing body and gently began pulling it out through the opening.

Suddenly, an adult magpie appeared beside him on the tree and began squawking indignantly. Ignoring the ranting bird and hoping he would not be attacked, Socrates began his descent. The bird followed him down, hopping from branch to branch, showering him with high-pitched curses. It continued its tirade on the ground, tearing up the earth with its beak in angry protest. Socrates knew in his heart that it was wrong to steal the chick but he hurried away nonetheless, the mother's harsh cackle ringing in his ears. He quickly escaped the grove and walked through an open field. A swallow flew by before doubling back. Then four swallows flew by in formation, swooping low as if to frighten him before heading off. Socrates convinced himself that they were reconnoitring, gathering information about his position to take back to the chick's mother. Feeling exposed, he quickened his stride.

He was half expecting the attack but was surprised by its ferocity. The magpie came out of nowhere, diving down to claw his head before flying off into the distance. Beside itself with rage, it swooped down again and again, intent on taking back its offspring, making a noise so harsh and grating that Socrates finally surrendered the chick so he could cover his ears. He put it on the ground and ran as fast as he could back to the village, too frightened to glance over his shoulder in case the bird attacked him again.

As he neared the first houses, his heart still pounding, he stopped to catch his breath and heard a muted grunt coming from behind a roadside tree. The sound came again, louder this time, accompanied by the snapping of twigs underfoot.

'Hey! Who's there?' Socrates called out, afraid he was being followed, hearing a faint yet familiar voice whisper his name. 'Socrates . . . Socrates . . .'

He ran all the way home without stopping, bent over with cramp, telling himself over and over again that the wind was playing tricks with his mind.

22

The arcade and its tired owner had undergone a facelift. The walls had been freshly painted. The lino-covered floor shone. Small glass vases filled with spring flowers sat on polished tabletops. Kyriaco flipped burgers on a shiny grill pan, wearing a starched white overall and chef's hat. Barbara's magic touch had transformed the jaded establishment and breathed new life into its proprietor. Order and cleanliness reigned. The takings had gone up, bolstering Kyriaco's confidence. He had plans to expand and diversify, to turn the shopfront into an American-style diner, to buy a jukebox. Now Kyriaco viewed his little world through new eyes, through the freshly polished, rose-tinted spectacles of a man besotted. The thought of wealthy widows and his past life made him cringe. Some benevolent force must have sent the magpie, he thought, to save him from his own foolishness. What a shame the bird was dead now, gunned down by the idiot taxi driver. Kyriaco was no animal lover, but he would always be grateful to the magpie for putting his life back on track and giving him the chance to experience true happiness.

Barbara handed him a plate of sliced cucumber. *'You OK, boss?'* she asked, her small hand brushing against his, making his heart flutter.

'Very OK.'

He wondered if she had any idea how he felt about her. He guessed she did and hoped she felt something, anything, for him too. Kyriaco had never believed in love at first sight or the notion of two souls becoming one; the stuff of romantic fiction, of asinine books that made silly women cry and expect too much from life. But now as Barbara hovered nearby, as he yearned to reach out and touch her, the word 'love' took on a mystical significance for him. Money could not buy it, that much he knew. It came of its own accord and took possession like a spirit. It cast a spell, played cruel games and plunged daggers into the heart. The fear that she might never grow to love him made Kyriaco want to curl up and perish.

On the night of the attack on the boy he had moved her into the spare room of his own small house. It was meant to be a temporary measure until he found her somewhere else to live, but he had grown comfortable with the set-up and consigned flat-hunting to that far-off tomorrow he hoped would never come. Barbara was good-natured, jolly, laughed easily, and seeing her smiling face first thing in the morning lifted his spirits. He had always hated mornings, facing each new day with a sigh of resignation, a mug of strong Greek coffee and half a dozen Senior Service. Now he woke to the sound of the radio or her singing and walked into a kitchen flooded with sunlight, the table laid with breakfast plates and tea brewing in a pot. She had opened his eyes to a new style of living and given him a reason to get out of bed in the morning. He loved her company and shunned the solitude he'd once treasured as freedom from disturbance, following her from room to room like a devoted Labrador. He would happily be her lapdog, her slave, her minion, anything she wanted him to be. He realised, with a sick feeling in his stomach, how desperately lonely he had been before Barbara had come into his life and that if she were ever to leave him he would spend the rest of his sorry life grieving over her departure.

Hector walked through the door of the arcade, batting away a cockroach that flew across his sightline, casting a disapproving glance at the three boys huddled in a corner drinking 7Up. 'The devils,' he muttered under his breath, though he had no real evidence that Socrates and his friends had been responsible for his brush with death. His bones still ached from his premature burial beneath a pile of masonry and he had been advised by his doctor to take things easy. But he was not one for lying in bed, especially when the village was teeming with gossip, when there were one hundred and one permutations of the same sad story to be heard. Hector was keen to find out what Kyriaco knew about the attack on the boy, what his Filipino waitress had witnessed first hand. It was common knowledge that the victim was Michali and that the boy had not shown his face in the village since the night he was molested.

'Ach! What a terrible affair,' Hector began, unaware that the boys in the corner were honing in on his conversation. 'I haven't been able to sleep properly since I heard about the boy. Who would have thought a thing like that would ever happen in the village?'

Kyriaco nodded, half-listening, his attention focused on the speedy way Barbara refilled the new plastic ketchup bottles shaped like tomatoes. He didn't have the stomach for bad news, for banter that might dampen his good mood.

'Michali is such a good boy. Not like some of these ruffians in the village.' Hector glared at the group huddled round the corner table, not noticing the cockroach that scuttled lightly across his bandaged foot and ran across the tiled floor.

'I haven't seen the youngster since it happened. He used to come in here every day to play Flipper and eat a burger.'

'I used to give him money whenever I saw him so he could play on your machines. His family are so poor they hardly have enough to buy food.'

Kyriaco sighed and turned back to his grill pan, having had his fill of doom and gloom, wanting to be left alone with his warm and satisfying romantic thoughts, failing to see the armoured brown bug that ran in an arc across the white-tiled wall right in front of his eyes.

'Do you want a couple of fried eggs, Hector?'

The old man rubbed his stomach. 'I won't say no. Eggs are the only thing I can eat these days with my crumbling teeth.'

Marco leaned forward to whisper, 'You see. I told you Hector gave him money.'

'Yes. Because he felt sorry for him,' Socrates said.

'So he says. Perhaps he's just trying to deflect suspicion with that story.'

'OK, Marco. So we can't strike him off our list of suspects yet, but who else could have done it?'

Marco glanced at the arcade owner. 'Maybe it was Kyriaco. That man's a weirdo, always hanging around the cemetery.'

Socrates shook his head. 'He goes to the cemetery because he's trying to hook a rich old widow, he told me so himself.'

'I think he's in love with the Filipina. Have you seen the way he looks at her?' Raphael fluttered his eyelashes. 'We need to find a person who walks around with the smell of blood on their hands.'

'Blood?' Socrates queried.

'Yes. I overheard someone in the bakery say Michali smelt blood on his attacker's hands. Maybe it was the butcher?'

'Too obvious,' Socrates replied. 'And anyway, he's my mother's cousin. He's a really good man and very religious.'

'So what!' Marco said. 'You think everyone who goes to church is virtuous? The so-called pious women in this village are also the worst gossips, back-stabbers and busy-bodies – believe me. They have nothing better to do than criticise other people. They get down on their knees every Sunday because they feel guilty, not because they love God. Anyway, I don't think it's the butcher either – I still think it's Victora. I don't trust that man. He's strange and scary.'

Socrates felt it was time to confess. 'To tell the truth, I couldn't get out of his house quick enough. I didn't want to tell you this because I felt embarrassed but . . . Victora kissed my hand.'

'*Yax!* And you let him?' Raphael said.

'I didn't know he was going to do it. And he said some strange stuff too about loving children. It made me feel sick. And I know he carries a knife in his pocket because I saw it with my own eyes. And another thing, he wanders the cemetery at night—'

'So *now* do you believe me? I've been telling you all along that Victora did this. All we have to do is prove it. We'll have to break into his house and search for evidence.'

Raphael sighed. '*Aman!* First we make a bomb that nearly kills an old man, and then we break into someone's house on the basis of a hunch? We're all going to prison, and they won't let us out until we're old and grey. There's no point trying to convince you that this is a bad idea – so I won't even try. When do you intend to carry out this break-in, Marco?'

'When do you think, dummy? On the day of the shadow theatre. You've seen the posters. Victora's performing in the village square in a couple of days' time.'

'But I wanted to watch that.'

'And you will. You can be our look-out. Let us know if anything unexpected happens. Like Victora coming home early.'

The door of the arcade swung open then and a hunched boy walked in nervously, crushing a cockroach under-foot. He stopped and looked around him, scanning the eyes that stared back for signs of condemnation or ridicule. Hector's opaque gaze watered. Kyriaco smiled weakly, his eggs starting to smoke on the grill. Barbara covered her open mouth with her hand and hurried into the kitchen.

211

Socrates broke the silence. '*Re*, Michali,' he shouted, trying to sound casual. 'Do you want to play Flipper?'

Michali nodded and followed Socrates and the other boys to the machine at the far end of the arcade.

'You go first,' Socrates said. 'But prepare to be beaten.'

Michali smiled weakly. 'But I don't have any money.'

Raphael reached into his pocket, pulled out a coin and pushed it into the slot. 'This one's on me.'

The machine flashed on, a column of coloured blocks lighting up Michali's pale face. The game absorbed him completely, his eyes following the ball bearing's erratic course.

'He'll be playing forever at his rate,' Marco said.

Hector approached and stood watching. He pulled a five-pound note from his pocket and put it down on the glass surface of the machine.

'Here you are boys. Buy yourselves some drinks.'

Michali looked at the money and froze, taking his eye off the game, losing the metal ball. Socrates noticed Marco eyeing the old man suspiciously and wondered if the rumours about the widower and his activities behind the arcade were true after all.

'*Re!* What's wrong?' he asked, putting a hand on Michali's shoulder.

The boy shook his head. 'Nothing.'

Socrates grabbed the note. 'Good. I'll get some change and four Cokes.' Just as he reached the counter a woman's high-pitched scream rang out.

Kyriaco froze momentarily before throwing down the metal scraper he was using to clean the grill and hurrying into the kitchen, adrenalin pumping, his blood pressure soaring. That piercing scream had been Barbara's and as he ran his stomach clenched at the thought that he might find his beloved girl dead, electrocuted by the cord of the dodgy kettle he had bought on the cheap, felled by the loose tile he had been meaning to fix. What he found when he reached the kitchen was Barbara cowering in a corner, her face twisted with fear and revulsion and an army of cockroaches marching in through the back door. He looked around him, wondering what to do first. Take Barbara in his arms and comfort her – or fight the invaders with the aerosol he kept under the sink? Socrates ran into the kitchen behind him and Kyriaco turned to see the boy grimace, then harden his features as if readying himself for battle.

Sidestepping cockroaches, Kyriaco walked out of the back door and Socrates followed. Outside he found that the manhole cover leading to the drains had been removed and out of the sewage pipe surged thousands of cockroaches, unsettled by daylight. They caked the floor and encrusted the toilet wall, scrambling over one another, their antennae twitching, making Kyriaco's skin crawl, unsettling his stomach.

'Quickly, let's put the cover back on to stop any more escaping,' Socrates said, spurring a stunned Kyriaco into action. He stooped beside the boy to replace the heavy cover, his face twisting in disgust as a succession of vile insects scurried across his hand and up his bare arms. Kyriaco could stomach most living creatures, even the most despised. He had no problem co-existing with rats, snakes, spiders or scorpions and had once befriended a mouse that lived in the roof space of his house, feeding it crisps, nuts and food from his plate. But cockroaches were a different matter together. They lived in sewers, feasted on dead things and human excrement. They were demonic and if decapitated could live headless for up to a week. In the event of humanity destroying itself with nuclear weapons, these loathsome bugs would colonise the earth.

'What next?' Socrates asked.

Barbara tiptoed towards Kyriaco, holding three bright yellow aerosol cans, her shoulders and arms drawn in as if she wanted to disappear inside herself to escape the insects.

'All-out attack,' Kyriaco said, grabbing two cans from Barbara and handing one to Socrates. 'You climb up the ladder at the side of the toilet block and attack them from above. I'll strike from below.'

Barbara pulled the lid off the remaining can and began spraying the area around her feet, gingerly at first and then with vengeful enthusiasm. Socrates quickly climbed the ladder and peered over the edge of the toilet block at the shiny, brown legion scuttling erratically towards him.

'Right, get ready, Socrates. Finger on the trigger. One, two, three . . . and fire!'

Socrates sprayed from above while Kyriaco steadied his shaky legs, angled the nozzle upwards and pressed down on the plunger cap, stunning the insects with pyrenthroid nerve poison. Dozens plummeted like stones with a ping-ping-ping to the ground below, falling on to their backs and pedalling their legs frantically, unable to right themselves. Kyriaco sprayed the black cloud that hovered over him, dizzying the cockroaches that dropped in handfuls on to his head, his shoulders, his back, and then struggled to find a footing on his skin and clothes. He wanted to scream and run away, to tear off his clothes and jump into the nearest shower, to scrub himself all over with a scourer, but Barbara was watching and he kept telling himself to be a man, to show her he had nerves of steel. So he sprayed with one hand and flicked away cockroaches with the other, his stomach twisting itself into knots.

'You all right, boss? You all right?' Barbara screeched, spraying him with insecticide, a kind act he realised but one that was choking him; that might, if she persisted, even kill him.

He opened his mouth to say yes, and to cough, and felt antennae brush against his lips and the head of a cockroach entering his mouth. He spat the insect away and nodded furiously in reply, trying to look unflustered, summoning all his reserves of courage and nerve to spray the aerosol, bat away insects, endure the toxic smell of insecticide, fight his own violent revulsion and the impulse to flee – and all for the sake of love.

All three of them sprayed until the aerosol cans ran out and the thick wall had been defeated; until piles of insects lay on their backs fighting for their lives, and others had scurried away or flown to safety. Kyriaco thanked Socrates for his help while plucking a dead cockroach from his chest hair. He waited for Barbara to go back inside before walking into the toilet block, entering a cubicle, locking the door and sticking a finger down his throat.

23

Irini busied herself in the kitchen frying a large, fatty chop for her husband, sprinkling it liberally with salt and wishing it were ground glass instead. She had heard a person could be killed with glass, murdered slowly but surely. How simple it would be to take a tumbler from her shelf, crush it in a pestle and mix the powder in with her husband's food. How satisfying to watch him eat and know that every mouthful brought him closer to death. Especially since food was so important to him, a mark of his status as male provider and superior being. The taxi driver was top of the eating hierarchy in his household, expecting the best cuts of meat and the largest portions. On Sundays when the family ate lunch together the children waited for their father to serve himself first before reaching out for the serving plates. Irini rarely sat down for long, flitting from table to kitchen at her husband's bidding, to fetch more bread, to cut more salad, to top up his whisky glass. She picked like a bird on whatever was left on the table after everyone else had finished eating.

He arrived at twelve. The first thing he said as he stepped through the door was, 'I'm hungry. Where's my food?'

Irini speared the pork chop, dropped it on a plate, poured over the fat he liked to mop up with bread and carried his meal into the living room. He was sitting on the sofa watching television and reached out for the tray without acknowledging her presence, a snub that always niggled her. The rules of engagement in her parents' home had been so different, so decorous and respectful. Her father never ate without praising the cook, never came home without planting a kiss on his wife's lips. As a child she had taken her parents' loving relationship for granted, never imagining that the unassuming couple would come to epitomise married bliss, the unattainable, a yardstick against which she measured her own failed union. Now, as she watched her husband hacking at the meat and chewing it noisily, Irini felt sick and resentful and angry with herself for marrying a barbarian. As a newlywed she had sought reassurance and praise. 'Are you enjoying the food?' she had asked him every mealtime, wanting desperately to please. 'I'm eating it, aren't I?' came the ungracious reply. He'd saved his verbal skills for the criticism and stinging insults that made his wife shrivel up inside and want to die.

When he'd finished eating, he lifted the tray off his legs and laid it on the sofa beside him. Irini knew the drill. She carried the tray back into the kitchen and prepared his coffee just as he liked it, with two sugars and a layer of froth floating on top.

'Sit down,' he said, almost kindly, when she handed him the coffee. 'I want to talk to you.'

She perched on the edge of the sofa, waiting to hear what he had to say, watching him pull a brown envelope from the inside pocket of his jacket.

'That Mafioso is coming back here tomorrow morning for his money. I want you to give him this envelope – OK? The cash is all in there, everything, including the interest.'

'Wouldn't it be better for you to give it to him?'

'I don't want to see him. Just give him the envelope and make sure you don't open it. In the meantime, put it somewhere safe, somewhere those thieving children won't find it.'

'I'll put it under our mattress.'

'Good idea. Do it now, before they get home from school.'

Irini climbed the stairs, clutching the thick envelope to her chest, wondering how much money it contained. A braver woman might have waited for her husband to go to work before steaming open the envelope, but Irini knew there would be hell to pay if he ever found out. Where had he suddenly found the money to pay off his debt? From some back-street lender, a loan shark? Or did the envelope contain the proceeds from the sale of her mother's house? Maybe his girlfriend had baled him out, paying for services rendered? Irini resented having to do her husband's dirty work, aggrieved that he had no qualms about letting her face the notorious gangster alone. She slipped the envelope under the mattress and was on her way back downstairs when the doorbell rang. Her husband pulled a resentful face. He had been hoping to stretch out on the sofa for his afternoon nap. Irini opened the door and was surprised to see Socrates' father Niko, the village priest and the local *muhktar* all standing on her doorstep. She feared momentarily that they had come bearing bad news about the children.

Niko smiled and touched her shoulder reassuringly. 'Can we come in and talk to your husband?' He looked apologetic.

'Yes, of course. Come in.'

She offered to make coffee and disappeared into the kitchen, straining to hear from the doorway the conversation that ensued. The men greeted her husband formally and sat down, wasting no time in making clear the purpose of their visit. The neighbours were concerned about the shouts and screams heard emanating from the taxi driver's house. Rumours had circulated that he had strung his son up from a tree. People had complained that he had charged through the village brandishing a gun, and had killed a tame magpie for no apparent reason. Irini listened keenly, glad that her husband was finally being held to account. When she carried the coffees back into the living room on a tray, she was surprised by the innocent expression on his face. He turned to her with the hissed command 'Leave the room' before a false smile curved the corners of his deceitful lips. Irini hated that smile for it had been her undoing, fooled her into believing that the taxi driver was a good man and had the makings of a good father. She wondered if it would now fool the three men who had come to rescue her. Setting down the tray, she hurried back into the kitchen.

'Yes, I shot the bird. But I had no idea it was tame.'

From the kitchen Irini listened to the first of her husband's lies.

'It was Andrico's bird. Surely you've seen it before in the village?' Niko said.

'One magpie looks like any other, and that bird nearly

219

blew the engine of my new car. It stuffed my exhaust pipe with stones and cost me thousands of pounds in repairs. Did anyone in the village tell you that?'

'No,' the *muhktar* said, glancing at Niko.

'You should be thanking me, not criticising me. I saved the village a lot of trouble and expense. That bird was a nuisance, always stealing things and attacking people.'

'It never attacked anyone,' Niko said.

'I don't understand what all the fuss is about.' The taxi driver turned to the *muhktar*. 'You go hunting, don't you?'

The *muhktar* nodded.

'You're happy to kill birds all day long then you come here bleating because I killed crazy Andrico's pesky crow!' He laughed, his confidence snowballing as he scored his first point over his inquisitors.

The *muhktar* took a deep sigh. 'OK, let's forget the bird. Let's say you did us all a favour there. What about our other concerns?'

'What concerns? That I strung my son up from a tree? What can I do if you choose to believe idle gossip?'

'Idle gossip! My son Petri untied Mino from that tree. He saw the evidence with his own eyes!' Nico exclaimed.

'What evidence? Did he see me string my son up?'

'No. But your wife said . . .' Niko knew as soon as he had uttered these words that he had made a grave mistake.

'My wife is not well, she's sick in the head, did you know that? She has her own version of the truth. Mino was playing with a rope swing and he got tangled up in it. I didn't touch him. I must thank your son next time I see him for releasing Mino.'

Niko shook his head in frustration. He knew there was

no point arguing with a man prepared to tell a blatant lie, who was willing to declare his own wife insane in order to save his own skin. Worst of all Niko could see that the *muhktar*, who had only come under duress, was being swayed by the taxi driver's lies.

The priest leaned forward in his chair. 'But, son, I've heard from reputable sources that you frequently beat your wife – and as a man of God I cannot condone such an action.'

'With all due respect, Father, you don't have a wife or children, you don't live in the real world, you don't know what goes on in people's homes, you don't know the difficulties that families face these days just trying to make ends meet. Most of all, you don't have any idea what horrors I have to put up with. Niko was here the other night when my own son tried to kill me. Isn't that right, Niko?'

Both the priest and the *muhktar* looked at him reproachfully, clearly irked that he had persuaded them with half-truths to intervene in another man's domestic arrangements. It seemed the waters here were muddy, the taxi driver's guilt unproven. They had come against their better judgement and would leave red-faced.

'Is this true, Niko?' the priest asked.

'The boy was protecting his mother.'

The taxi driver shook his head in denial. 'From what?'

'From you.'

'Did you see me touch his mother, Niko?'

'No. But I saw the marks on her neck.'

'And assumed I had made them?'

'Well, who else would have done?'

'I told you already, she's sick up here.' The taxi driver tapped his right temple with his forefinger. 'She made those marks herself to turn the children and the village against me. She does it all the time. And look here.' He took off his jacket and unbuttoned his shirt, revealing a mark near his collarbone, the scar left by the jagged edge of a beer bottle thrown at him outside a nightclub. 'This is where she tried to stab me, to kill me. You have no idea what I have to put up with! She lashes out all the time and I push her away, trying to protect myself. You can't condemn me for doing that, can you, Father?'

The priest hung his head. The *muhktar* rose from his seat. The coffees sat on the tray untouched. Niko felt sick inside, knowing this was the worst of all possible outcomes.

'And she steals from her own husband, did you know that? I used to have a signet ring, which I wore all the time. I took it off one day to shower and it disappeared from the bedroom. My wife was the only person in the house yet she put her hand on the Bible and swore she did not take it. If she can lie to her own husband, in the face of God, then she can lie to our friends and neighbours.' The taxi driver's prized ring *had* gone missing, that much was true, but it was not his wife who had taken it.

'Courage, son, and patience,' the priest said, taking the taxi driver's hand. 'Everything will work out for the best.'

'Thank you, Father. For being so understanding.'

'Sorry,' the *muhktar* said, throwing Niko a hostile glare. 'Next time I am persuaded to stick my nose into other people's business, I will make sure I get my facts straight.'

The taxi driver waved goodbye from the doorway with an amicable, forgiving smile. Irini stood shaking in the kitchen doorway, distressed and humiliated. She had hoped her husband would lose his temper and show his true colours, that her rescue party might at least coerce him into treading more carefully in future. She should have known that he would never lose his temper in public, that he could turn his rage on and off at will, that he was capable of the most treacherous lies. The lies he had told would now pass from husband to wife, from friend to neighbour, and soon the entire village would think her insane and her husband the victim. Who could blame him for cracking occasionally when he lived with the constant strain of a lunatic wife? they would say. Irini leaned back against the kitchen wall and waited for her punishment, for the inevitable confrontation with this man who was ready to blame others for all his own wrongdoing. Better to face his anger now, while it was still manageable, rather than let it fester and intensify and explode in her face later in the day when the children were present. The taxi driver made sure the men had rounded the corner before marching into the kitchen and putting his face up close to his wife's.

'What the hell have you been saying?'

'Nothing. Not a word.'

He pressed his palms against the wall, trapping her in the U-shape of his body. 'It's probably for the best anyway. Now at least they all know that you're as crazy as your mother.'

'I'm not mad and neither is my mother.' Cowed by his overpowering aura, the best she could do was whisper her defiance, though she felt like sinking her nails into his cheeks.

He laughed sadistically. 'Who the hell does Niko think he is anyway? Coming into my house and telling me how I should live my life. The wanker! And to think I was a best man at his wedding, he called me *koumbare* . . . He should pay closer attention to the goings-on in his own house before criticising others. He should keep a closer eye on his womanising son and his whore of a wife.'

He stressed the word 'whore' and pressed his groin against Irini's stomach. She felt him grow hard and began to panic. She tried to duck beneath his arm, try to escape, but he pushed her back against the wall.

'That hussy is always dressing in tight skirts, always shaking that big arse of hers when she walks down the street. If you had a big arse like that I would keep you locked up at home. I would keep your big arse locked up.'

Closing his eyes, he pulled up Irini's skirt and started stroking her thigh, making her feel nauseous, her abdominal muscles tightening. For a year he had not touched her and she had hoped he would never touch her again. He unzipped his fly with one hand and pulled down his wife's underwear with the other while she tried to separate her mind from her body, to focus on a section of peeling plaster above the sink. But the overpowering stench of his breath and underarm sweat kept hauling her mind back to the rough hand clawing between her legs. Gagging, she turned her face away from his and felt the coldness of the wall against her hot cheek.

'That hussy, that big-breasted whore, that bitch with the big arse . . .'

He pressed against her so hard she thought he might squeeze her to death, cause her to rupture, crush her ribs.

The back of her head bashed against the wall and pain shot through her abdomen as he began stabbing and ripping, leaving bruises no one would ever see, lifting her off her small feet, conjuring up behind his closed eyelids salacious images of his buxom neighbour. Irini prayed he would finish quickly, before the children got home from school, reminding herself that she was an empty vessel, a dead thing, a walking corpse. He spat out the word 'Bitch!' before ejaculating and falling away, leaving traces of his slime between her legs. Breathing heavily, he zipped up his trousers and left the kitchen. Irini pulled up her underwear, smoothed down her dress, and tried to take a step forward but her legs crumpled beneath her.

24

Socrates' concentration was focused on the football. He had already scored three goals and secured victory for his team. Tino was marking him, taunting him, had tripped him over several times and stamped on his hand. Now, he tugged at Socrates' shirt tail to tackle the ball off him and race away. Socrates was a faster runner and sprinted ahead to hover in the goalmouth. 'Save this!' Tino shouted, booting the heavy leather ball with all the force he could muster, hitting Socrates squarely in the face.

Shock and pain dizzied him. Blood spurted from his nostrils and dripped from his chin on to his white school shirt. Through the haze of stars before his eyes he saw Tino laughing and a surge of blinding anger engulfed him, blocking out the sound of the end-of-break bell. He ran with the ball after Tino, chasing him off the tarmac pitch and crossing the line beyond which ball games were not allowed, booting the ball as hard as he could, aiming for the back of Tino's head. His shoe flew off and followed the same trajectory as the ball, missing the target, smashing through a classroom window and hitting Stephania on the head as she sat embroidering a copy of the Last Supper.

The screaming began instantaneously as splinters of glass showered the breaktime sewing class. Socrates doubled back, looking for an escape route, but was blocked by the flow of children gathering round the window. When Mr Hadjimichael, recently promoted to deputy head, charged out of the school entrance holding a brown loafer aloft, Socrates knew there was no escape.

'Sergiou,' he screamed. 'Come here. Now!'

Head bowed, Socrates walked across the bustling playground towards the teacher who grabbed him by the ear and stooped to bellow in his face.

'*Re!* What have you done? What got into you? You're in big trouble now, you stupid boy!'

The teacher's pungent garlic breath was unbearable and greater torture than the fingers pinching his ear. The screams from across the way had died down but Socrates could still hear raised voices, girls crying and the grating sound of glass being swept across a tiled floor. He could feel blood drying inside his own nose and wanted to pick at it. Had the teacher not noticed the injuries inflicted by Tino, his bloodstained school shirt?

'You're undisciplined, out of control, a disruptive influence. Wait until the head hears about this. He'll have you expelled' – the head, a keen advocate of corporal punishment, was attending a conference in Greece; Socrates knew he would not be feeling the thwack of wood against his palms for at least three days – 'and I wonder what your father will have to say too. And your mother. You won't get away with this, Sergiou, I can promise you that. Let's go straight to my office, you useless piece of firewood . . .'

Socrates could not give a damn about the threatened wooden ruler but he cared deeply about his father's opinion. The toilet-block incident had not been mentioned since Michali's attack but it was only a matter of time before the subject reared its ugly head. The teacher dragged Socrates along the hallway by the ear, past students milling about outside their classrooms, too scared of Mr Hadjimichael to laugh or call out. Like most of his classmates, Socrates hated the deputy head who constantly belittled his students with caustic insults, calling them 'firewood', 'deadheads', 'brainless'. The children had names of their own for Mr Hadjimichael. They called him 'Hansel' because he was fair-haired with chiselled facial features and reminded them of a German. The girls who sat at the front of the class called him 'Porno' because he pressed his groin against their desks when he spoke to them and they were convinced that he wore baggy trousers to hide his erection.

Socrates unchained his bike and pushed it out of the school gates. His friends were waiting for him outside. Raphael sat astride the chopper and Marco was perched high on the seat of his late grandfather's bike.

'What did Hansel do to you?' Raphael asked.

'Sat me on a chair in the library. I've been staring at a whitewashed wall for three hours.'

'You escaped lightly. The whole school's talking about the window. Stephania was taken to hospital and had to have stitches in her forehead.'

'I'm really in for it then! Hansel said he's going to punish me tomorrow and telephone my parents. I don't

228

want them to find out. Mama has threatened to keep me locked up in the house if I get into any more trouble.'

'Well then, you'd better enjoy your last day of freedom,' Marco said. 'Let's go and get the moped and have a ride.'

In the distance, police sirens could be heard wailing.

'Wait,' Socrates said. 'Something must have happened in the village . . . the sirens are getting louder . . . I think they're coming in this direction . . . Christ, they're heading down this road. You don't think the police are after me, do you?'

Marco shook his head as two police cars and a white van hurtled past. 'What – for kicking a ball through a window?'

Socrates jumped on his bike. 'Quick, let's follow them.'

The boys cycled after the police vehicles, excited by the prospect of coming upon a crime scene. Alarmed by the sound of sirens, villagers hurried to their doors to see what was going on. Many followed the convoy on foot. One man shook his head and tutted, complaining to his neighbour that the village was becoming as noisy and dangerous as New York. When the convoy rounded the next corner Socrates grew concerned, knowing it was headed for Andrico's house. He wondered if their friend had hurt himself? Had his home been broken into? Had he been attacked by the man at his window? What in Christ's name had happened requiring the deployment of two police cars and a van?

Socrates watched events unfold with a sense of disbelief. Andrico was in his front garden, dragging a rake across the soil. The convoy pulled up, tyres screeching, and two policemen burst out of the front car and charged him, forcing his arms behind his back and locking them in place with handcuffs. He looked bewildered as he was led along the front path and out of his gate. Clearly panicking, he broke free and ran blindly along the unmade road, stopping before the ditch in which he had lain unconscious, beyond which was a flimsy metal fence and scrubland. With nowhere to run he stared with wild eyes at the policemen closing in on him, settling a terrified gaze on Socrates that begged him for help. Seconds later the officers had pounced on Andrico, dragged him by the shoulders to the waiting car and had bundled him, kicking and wailing, into the back. Face down on the back seat he did not see Socrates staring in through the back window with tears in his eyes, nor Sergeant Stelios Georgiou pull the boy roughly away.

'Where are you taking him? What has he done?' Socrates shouted as the police car drove away.

'We're taking him to the station for questioning.'

'Why?'

'I can't tell you. It's a police matter. Go home.'

'But he hasn't done anything.'

'How do you know that?'

'I just do. I know Andrico.'

Marco and Raphael came up behind him.

'What's going on?' Raphael asked.

'They're taking Andrico to the police station for questioning. I keep telling this idiot that he hasn't done anything but he won't listen.'

'Hey! Mind your language.' The sergeant pinched Socrates' ear before walking away.

'But he's a good man,' Socrates called after him. 'He

hardly ever leaves his house and he wouldn't hurt a fly. He's our friend.'

The sergeant stopped and turned, suddenly more interested in what the boy had to say. 'Really? A friend, you say? How friendly was he?' He pulled a notebook and pen from the inside pocket of his jacket and began scribbling. 'What's your name?'

'Socrates Sergiou.'

'And who's your father?'

'Niko Sergiou. He works in the village building society.'

'Well, tell your father to bring you to the police station tomorrow afternoon. I have some questions to ask you.'

The officer walked away, turning his attention to the crowd clustering around Andrico's gate.

'What the hell are they doing now?' Socrates watched in dismay as two plain-clothes officers wearing gloves began emptying the wooden shed. 'We're done for. They'll find the moped and our fingerprints all over it and come for us next.'

'Holy Mary! What about the shotgun cartridges?' Raphael said as his armchair was loaded into the van. 'And what do the wankers want with my chair?'

Socrates felt ill watching Pondorosa being looted, the homestead he had vowed to protect. The pact he had made with his friends seemed ridiculous and childish now.

'Let's split up,' he said, 'and find out what the hell's going on. I'll stick with Sergeant Georgiou. Marco, you hang around by the shed. And, Raphael, go round the back and have a look through the windows of the house.'

His friends left as the *muhktar* strode determinedly towards the young sergeant. News of the police swoop had reached his ears and as head of the village he intended to find out what was going on.

'What's happening? Why have you taken Andrico?' he asked.

'I wish I could tell you.'

In fact, Sergeant Georgiou was desperate to tell all, to announce through a loudspeaker that he had solved the crime of the century. He fully expected a commendation for his efforts, his dogged and careful pursuit of the clues, the unearthing of irrefutable evidence. Like the unassuming sleuth Columbus, his favourite TV cop, he had used his wits and ingenuity to nail a dangerous criminal.

'What have you found in the shed?' the *muhktar* asked.

'What haven't we found! Syringes, fuses, shotgun cartridges, explosive devices . . .'

'So what are you telling me, in a roundabout way? That Andrico blew up the toilet block?'

Socrates' stomach lurched.

'I wish that were his only crime.'

'Don't tell me he attacked the boy?'

Sergeant Georgiou raised his eyebrows. 'I didn't say anything. Not a thing.'

'My God! Who would have thought it? The man was so quiet. He kept himself to himself.'

Several people standing in the crowd heard the shocking news and hurried away to spread it. The bare facts took on a life of their own, giving birth to mutant offspring. By evening the gossip mills were spinning at full speed and Andrico was declared guilty by public consensus. Wild stories circulated apace. He had injected his victims with a sedative to dull their senses. He had lured boys into his

232

shed by offering them chewing gum. He had stockpiled enough gunpowder to blow up the entire village. A man of his age living alone had to be a sexual deviant, some said. Alas, there was truth in the sordid rumours that Andrico used his goat for sexual gratification, that he drilled holes in watermelons and filled them with his semen. In heated debates, that went on until the early hours of the morning, the villagers raged against a system that had allowed such a dangerous man to leave the asylum and live in their midst.

25

Irini relived the trauma of the previous day again and again, kneading and squeezing Mino's soiled bed sheets in the sink. The showers she had taken that morning and the night before had failed to wash the smell of her husband away. His odour lodged tenaciously in her nostrils and every time she inhaled she was reminded of the violation. Her head hurt. With wet fingers she fingered a tender swelling behind her ear. How much more could she take before losing her mind? Before the taxi driver's lies became a self-fulfilling prophecy, before she swallowed a handful of pills and ended it all? Tantalised by death, she had contemplated suicide many times, held pills in her hand even, imagined falling asleep in a warm bed and never waking up to see his smug face, breathe in his bad smell or hear his gruff voice. But how would she ever rest in peace, knowing the barbarian and his family were raising her children?

A knock at the kitchen door startled her. The Scorpion had arrived earlier than expected and his dark shape loomed ominously behind a pane of frosted glass in the metal-framed door. Irini dried her hands and took a deep breath. She pulled open the door and Pantelas walked into the kitchen, greeting her hurriedly before requesting his money. Irini was about to turn and climb the stairs, to collect the envelope from beneath the mattress and hand it over, when something stopped her. An ad hoc plan crossed her mind and she spoke it aloud before considering its flaws and consequences, before it had fully taken shape.

'He hasn't left it,' she said, surprised by the sincerity of her tone.

'Is he planning to bring it to me himself?'

'Not as far as I know.'

Pantelas' expression darkened. 'Are you sure you gave him my message? You told him exactly what I said?'

Irini nodded. She felt no fear at all, though the huge man began to pace the kitchen, clenching his jaw. What could he do to her? Beat her up? Pull out a handful of her hair? Slap her across the face? Her own husband had done far worse.

'Then your husband is a very stupid man. I know he has money because my associates tell me he's out every night, drinking with his friends and playing cards.' The Scorpion swept his hand across the kitchen worktop. Picking up a crystal decanter that contained her husband's whisky, he pulled out the stopper, sniffed the contents and smiled wryly. He held the neck of the decanter between thumb and forefinger and swung it gently back and forth as if poised to drop it. 'Your husband drinks Chivas! *Aman!* He does have expensive tastes.'

'Yes, my husband can afford to drink Chivas and smoke cigars but the children and I live on a pittance.'

The Scorpion seemed taken aback by Irini's snide comment, her breaking of ranks. He stoppered the decanter and put it back down on the worktop.

'I have two friends waiting in the car outside, ready to come in and empty this house, to take my first instalment in goods.'

'They're very welcome to do so, but look around you. Do you see anything worth taking? If you do, it's yours, take it with pleasure. Everything in here is so old and broken, I doubt you could give it away. The television works when it wants to, the sofa belonged to my grandmother, and every piece of crockery in my cupboard is chipped from overuse or being flung across the kitchen. Anyway, if you take our things my husband won't suffer, not one bit. He hardly comes home as it is.'

Irini noticed The Scorpion glance at a photograph of the children, hanging on the wall behind her.

'Do you have children, Mr Pantelas?' she asked.

He nodded.

Irini held The Scorpion's gaze. 'I have three and they have all suffered enough at the hands of their father. Please don't make them suffer any more.'

'In this household it seems the wife has the balls,' Pantelas said, shaking his head and looking thoughtful. 'I tell you what. As a favour to you, I will give your husband one last chance to make amends. Tell him to come to my club tomorrow with the money and I'll forget all about today. I will even pour him a glass of Chivas. I won't have anyone saying The Scorpion doesn't have a heart.'

Pantelas thrust his hand into his back pocket and pulled out a thick wad of notes. He peeled off five twenties, laid them on the kitchen table and turned to leave.

'Mr Pantelas, I don't want your money. I can never pay you back and my husband . . .'

The Scorpion silenced her by putting a finger to his lips. 'This is not a loan. It's a gift.'

Before she could protest he had walked out and closed the door behind him. Irini stared at the money numbly, suddenly shocked by what she had done. She fought the urge to chase after Pantelas and admit her deceit, to thrust the envelope into his hands and nip her treachery in the bud. She heard a car start and the purr of a finely tuned engine. As The Scorpion drove away Irini realised that she had set in motion an inexorable chain of events, at the end of which someone was destined to be stung. She wondered where her courage and poise had come from and realised with a rush of exhilaration that she could be strong and assertive and fearless, that she was finally exercising control over her own life.

The brute arrived home an hour later. She heard the familiar sound of his car pull up outside. Acting on impulse, she stuffed the twenty-pound notes into her apron pocket and darted up the stairs to retrieve the envelope, hiding it somewhere he would never think to look: in the back of a cupboard beneath the lid of a casserole pot. By the time her husband had climbed out of the car and walked through the front door, Irini felt breathless and clammy with sweat.

'He came then?'

'Yes.'

'And did you give him the money?'

She nodded.

'Thank God. And did he say anything?'

She took a deep breath. 'He said he doesn't want you going anywhere near his club ever again.'

The taxi driver laughed. 'Does he think I'm mad! I never want to see that venomous shit as long as I live.'

The reference he made to his own longevity made Irini shudder. She realised with a sinking sense of dread that she had hoodwinked a violent criminal and put her husband's life in grave danger.

26

The air in the maths class was thick with expectation. Mr Hadjimichael was scribbling sums on the blackboard. Socrates slouched in his chair at the back of the class, waiting. In the front row Katerina struggled to restrain the hilarity tickling her insides. She giggled uncontrollably. The teacher silenced her with a hissed 'Shhhh', his back to the class. Blushing, Katerina turned to smile at Socrates who noted with satisfaction the look of gratitude and admiration in her eyes. His punishment for breaking the window had not yet been meted out and he expected to be called into Hansel's office at the end of the lesson, by which time yet another offence would have been added to his record sheet. If he faced expulsion anyway he had nothing to lose. He would walk out of the school gates with his head held high, in a blaze of glory, having impressed the prettiest girl in class and taught Hansel a lesson he was unlikely to forget.

Outside, the village glazier was busy replacing the broken window. Socrates listened to the distant sound of sawing and hammering, wondering how his parents would take the news of his expulsion. He feared his father's reaction, yes, but he did not feel guilty for breaking the window. Why should he when he had not intended to shatter the glass, to scare the sewing class and wound Stephania? He had avoided her in the playground all morning, not wanting to see the row of black stitches on her forehead, though he considered her injury to be, in part, divine retribution for her role in Koko's death. A remorseful and tearful Stephania had confessed to her friends the part she had played in the magpie's demise and her guilty secret had spread like wildfire, reaching Socrates' ears and making him furious. The doctor should have sewn Stephania's lips together, he thought resentfully. Her big mouth was more lethal than a million shards of flying glass.

Mr Hadjimichael turned from the board and pointed his ruler at a boy sitting in the third row. 'Pyroyiannis! Look at the first equation on the board and tell me the answer.'

The teacher took a step forward and Pyroyiannis breathed in sharply.

'What! What's wrong? Has someone cut out your tongue?'

The teacher knew something was up. His pupils were subdued one minute and snickering the next. He felt vulnerable, exposed, and expected a projectile to hit him on the head at any moment.

Pyroyiannis scanned the board and mouthed the answer.

'Good, that's correct, but I want the answer quicker in future.'

Next, the teacher pointed his ruler at Katerina and walked some way towards her desk. She flinched and leaned back in

240

her chair. The teacher tried to read the girl's expression; her body language and the terrified look in her eyes. Why had she flinched? What was she up to? He scanned the scheming faces and averted gazes of his pupils for clues. What nature of torment lay in store for him? Perhaps some joker had brought in a stink bomb. How droll . . . and unoriginal! Maybe he would return to his office and find a cockroach in his sandwiches or a bug squashed between the pages of the class register.

'Come on. Think, my girl. If you can! If there's a brain in your head. What's the answer? Quickly.'

Katerina's mind was not on equations but on the plot she had conspired in, that was likely to get her into serious trouble. Socrates' idea had seemed exciting and heroic first thing in the morning, Porno's just deserts. She had always hated the way her maths teacher pushed his groin against her desk, the suggestive way he fumbled in the pockets of his baggy trousers. So, she had given Socrates the go-ahead to attach a dozen drawing pins to the front of her desk, the points sticking out, secured in place by other drawing pins pressed into the wood. Now as the teacher approached, with an ugly scowl on his face, Katerina lost her nerve and her hands began shaking in her lap.

'Perhaps you left your brain at home?'

She glanced over her shoulder at Socrates, fearing that at any moment she might burst into tears.

'No one can help you. And especially not him! He can't even help himself. Look at the board, not at your class-mates.'

Mr Hadjimichael strode forward and glowered down at the girl, disdain twisting his lips. She shrank away from him, a tear trickling down her cheek, and he stepped forward, to deal a final crushing blow to her ego, to make an example of her, to show the class that he would not be toyed with, disrespected. He drew his face close to the girl and a terrible pain shot through his groin as a drawing pin pierced his left testicle. He screeched like an animal caught in a spiked trap, jumped back and fought the urge to clasp a hand over his genitals. The class burst out laughing, their hilarity intensified by the teacher's expression of agony and the blasphemous litany that shot from his lips. He staggered backwards, thinking he was about to faint, but managed to hold himself upright by leaning against a pillar. When he saw the line of drawing pins running the length of the girl's desk, he felt a surge of violent, irrepressible anger.

'Kabraras, Tyras, Sergiou,' he shouted, addressing the usual suspects, 'go to my office. Now!'

Mr Hadjimichael hurried out of the classroom and headed for the staff toilet to examine his testis. The teacher's greying underpants were spotted with blood. Bile rose into his mouth when he saw it and his head swam. He gently lifted up the warm sac between his legs and inspected it. The only damage he could see was a tiny red pinprick but Mr Hadjimichael, a dedicated hypochondriac, became unduly concerned about the risk of infection and the possibility of long-term damage to his reproductive gland. Despite his aversion to children, the bachelor had hoped that one day he would father a family of his own. This hope was fading fast now. Eligible, educated, attractive women were hard to come by in a village full of peasant stock. Mr Hadjimichael knew his own worth and absolutely refused to lower his standards or take second best. Good things come to those who wait, he told himself, and wait he did, though the fair hair he was so proud of was thinning and faint lines criss-crossed his once-handsome face. His features were hardening in line with his manner which was becoming more obdurate and severe by the day.

He pulled up his trousers, straightened his back, and marched out of the toilet cubicle muttering curses under his breath. The unruly trio he had selected for punishment slouched outside his office in disorderly fashion. When he had children of his own he would raise them correctly, strictly, produce perfect specimens of humanity. He would spawn doctors, lawyers and accountants, suit-wearing prodigies who would make him proud and support him financially in his old age. The undisciplined boys outside his office were hopeless losers who would grow up to be farm labourers, builders or shopkeepers, if they were lucky. He marched them quickly into his office and ordered them to stand in line in front of his desk.

'Stand up straight,' he barked, making them jump, heartened by the look of fear in their eyes. He had the troublemakers where he wanted them and intended to have all three expelled. 'So. Who was responsible for the attack on my person?'

The boys shuffled their feet.

'If no one owns up, then you will all be punished.' He put his face close to Raphael's. 'Do you understand, Tyras?'

Raphael nodded.

The teacher moved on to Marco, looking him up

and down contemptuously. The boy was too tall to be intimidated at eye level, too broad to be cowed by the teacher's physical presence. Only words could cut him down to size.

'And you, Kabraras. Must I call your poor mother into the school, yet again? She cried the last time, do you remember? And you promised to knuckle down, to work hard and stay out of trouble. You haven't kept that promise, have you? You lied to your mother. Lied, lied, lied! Go on the way you are and you will come to nothing, you will end up driving taxis like your father. Is that what you want?'

The teacher purposely left Socrates and his most stinging comments until last. 'Sergiou, I am certain you played a hand in this. You are the lynchpin, the instigator, the rotten apple in this group. You are deadwood, my boy, only fit for the fire, and I will not be waiting for the headmaster to come back before I expel you. You will leave right now.'

Socrates cleared his throat.

'Do you have something to say, Sergiou? No? Then I must assume from your silence that all three of you are jointly responsible for the attack on my person and you will all face the consequences.'

'Sir,' Socrates said.

'Yes?'

'I did it. My friends had nothing to do with this.'

'*Re!*' Raphael said. 'Tell him the truth. We were all involved.'

'No. I did it, sir. It was my idea.'

'But . . .'

'Shut up! Enough!' the teacher silenced Raphael. 'Kabraras, Tyras, go back to the classroom. Collect up your friend's belongings and put them outside my room. I will be sending him home in disgrace.'

When the two boys had left the room Mr Hadjimichael began pacing the office, his arms behind his back. 'I can hardly believe your gall, your stupidity, your downright wickedness. You are a disgrace to this school and to your parents. You are a fiend, a devil, nothing but trouble. And this time you've really done it. This time there is no escape for you, my boy. There is no good reason for what you did. No explanation. The attack on my person was unprovoked and malicious.'

'But there was a reason, sir.'

'Don't be ridiculous. What reason?'

'Katerina's scared of you.'

'Me? Why? What are you talking about?'

'She said you rub your . . . erm . . . trousers against her desk every time you speak to her.'

'My trousers? What are you talking about?'

Socrates glanced at the teacher's fly. 'She thought you were . . . you know . . . doing dirty things . . . and she was well . . . erm . . . scared . . . and I decided to do something about it.'

The teacher felt faint for the second time that day, falling from his lofty moral high ground with a thunderous crash. He sat down heavily on the chair behind the desk, his stomach knotting, his face burning red hot.

'How could she think such a thing? How terrible. And do all the girls in the class think the same way?'

When Socrates nodded the schoolmaster wanted the

tiled floor beneath his chair to open into a chasm and swallow him up, the gaseous furnace in the bowels of the earth to burn him to a crisp. He had never courted popularity at the school, wanting only to be feared and respected. To be thought of as depraved was horrifying, soul-destroying, a terrible, monstrous, unthinkable slight.

'You have to tell them they're wrong, Socrates.' He found himself addressing the boy by his first name, requesting his help, desperately needing him as an ally, an intermediary. 'I would never dream of doing such a terrible thing. It pains me even to talk about the matter. Why didn't you come and tell me sooner?'

'I felt too embarrassed and I thought you wouldn't believe me. I hoped the drawing pins would make you realise.'

Mr Hadjimichael fell silent, wondering if he would ever be able face the girls in his classroom again. True, some of them were exceptionally pretty, and yes, he had had improper dreams featuring schoolgirls in gym skirts, but surely he could not be held responsible for the workings of his subconscious mind. In the classroom he was a con-summate professional, his thoughts as chaste as those of the monks at the revered monastery at Stavrovouni.

'Sir, you said you were going to send me home. Shall I leave right now?'

'No,' the teacher said, panicking suddenly.

If the boy were expelled, questions would be asked by the headmaster on his return from Greece and the answers supplied could prove very embarrassing. The teacher would not have his reputation sullied, not when he had his sights set on promotion, on eventual headship.

And there was another delicate matter to consider. A boy had been molested outside the village arcade, had he not? Accusing fingers had pointed in all directions, with single men firmly placed in the villagers' sights. What would happen if Katerina's unfounded accusations reached the ears of the police? Might he be considered a danger to children? A freak? A possible suspect?

'On further consideration I don't think there is any need for expulsion. You appear to have had a valid reason for your actions,' he said slowly.

'What about the window I broke yesterday?' Socrates was disappointed. He had come to terms with the prospect of expulsion and had actually been looking forward to going home to watch a repeat episode of *Bonanza*.

'I'm sure that was an accident. You didn't set out to injure poor Stephania, did you?'

'I was aiming for Tino but he ducked.'

'Exactly. Perhaps in future you should aim for the goal.'

'But I shouldn't have crossed the line.'

'No. And I'm sure you won't do it again.'

'There's a good chance I will, if you don't punish me . . .'

'I think you should go back to the classroom now. I'll ask one of my colleagues to take over the lesson.'

'Won't you be coming back?'

The schoolmaster could not summon the strength to stand up, let alone address a class. 'I don't feel too well. I think I shall go home and lie down.'

27

Kyriaco stepped gingerly on to the flat roof of the arcade holding a plastic bucket and headed for the water tank, a sweltering sun beating down on his head. Barbara was standing at the foot of a wooden ladder down below, waiting for an answer to the drinking water mystery. Several customers that morning had complained that the water served with their Greek coffee had a strange, unpleasant, slightly rancid taste.

The large tank on the roof had been fitted the previous year to provide the arcade with a constant supply of running water, even during the summer months when the precious resource was rationed. Strictly speaking, the tank water should only have been used for washing and toilet flushing but Kyriaco saw no harm in filling both his kettle and the plastic Agros Mountain Water bottles which he sold to his customers. He considered it lunacy to pay good money for nature's free gift to man when tank water looked and tasted identical to its costly counterpart. People were easily fooled and few could tell the difference between tank water and the supposedly superior stuff allegedly drained from natural springs in the Troodos mountains.

Lifting the heavy, galvanised, baking hot lid he peered over the edge of the tank. He expected to see a dead pigeon floating on the surface of the water but instead, to his surprise and shock, he saw several pieces of disintegrating turd. The pong of excrement wafted into his face, turning his stomach. Kyriaco knew at once who had tainted his water supply and decided to turn them in to the police. Earlier that week he had barred Tino and Zaphiri from the arcade for teasing Michali about a tear in his trousers, and the two boys had left swearing vengeance. He suspected the same two jokers of having removed his manhole cover, triggering the cockroach invasion.

'*Everything OK, boss?*' Barbara called up.

'*No, everything not OK.*'

Kyriaco used the bucket to fish out the turds before climbing down the ladder to share the details of his gruesome find with Barbara. She baulked and ran indoors as instructed to turn on all the taps in the arcade and empty the tank. Kyriaco disconnected the water supply, closed up the shop and telephoned the village police station, saying he had a serious crime to report. Sergeant Stelios Georgiou arrived ten minutes later, ready to put his Columboesque powers of detection to the test. The arcade owner had reported an emergency, claiming his water supply had been poisoned, his livelihood threatened and the mortal health of his customers put at risk. The evidence that faced the sergeant on his arrival at the arcade was rather less dramatic and obviously the work of pranksters.

'So, someone took a dump in your water tank?' he said, thinking the matter trifling.

'And probably pissed in it too.'

'But you only use that water for washing, right? So it's unlikely that anyone would have been poisoned.'

'I use it to make tea and Greek coffee too.'

'But that water is boiled, which would probably kill off any bacteria. That's all you use tank water for, isn't it?'

Kyriaco nodded, sweat beading on his palms. 'Yes, of course, just for making tea and coffee.' He was glad that Barbara could not understand the lies he was telling in Greek.

'Have any of your customers fallen ill as far as you know?'

Kyriaco shook his head.

'I'll let the village doctor know about this but I doubt very much that anyone's been poisoned.'

'Let's get to the nub of this, Sergeant. I know who did it.'

The officer opened his notebook wearily and scribbled down the names, promising to make his own enquiries and report back. He left the arcade owner sitting thoughtfully at a table, trying to summon the energy to climb back on to the roof and disinfect the tank.

'*Do not look so sad, boss. Everything is gonna be OK*,' Barbara said, sitting beside him and touching his hand gently, making his whole body tingle. Kyriaco tried to interpret the meaning of her touch. Was it a tender stroke, a manifestation of her natural tactility, or just a there-there pat such as one might employ to calm an unsettled dog? The sun shone through the freshly polished window, lighting up Barbara's hair, making it look too shiny to be real, like doll's hair. How often he had wanted to sniff that hair, to wind it round his hand, to bury his face in it,

250

to drape it over his own head. He knew in his heart that Barbara was too good for him, too pretty, too clever and able and wise. The woman sitting beside him was an angel who deserved far more than a life of turd-filled water tanks and roach-infested drains.

He patted her hand in a friendly, proper manner. *'Don' call me boss. Call me Kyriaco. Please.'*

'OK. I will call you Kyriaco, boss.'

Her smile made him smile back though his tortured heart cried.

'Not Kyriaco, boss. Jass Kyriaco.'

She turned to look into his eyes. *'You know something? You are a good, good man. A very kind man.'*

Kyriaco was taken aback by the comment. His eyes watered. He had never considered himself a good man but rather a schemer and phoney who turned on the charm to get what he wanted. Only now, sitting beside Barbara, did he feel that he had the potential to be genuinely good, a man who cried and empathised and knew how to love. In the deep recesses of his Machiavellian soul Barbara had struck gold, a stratum of untapped goodness.

'Hey! Why are you crying?' she asked. *'Do not worry about nothing. I will help you clean the tank. We will do it together. Life is not so bad, Kyriaco.'*

He looked at her longingly, hoping his face spoke for him, articulating his hopes and dreams, his fear of rejection. She drew close, reached for his hand and stared into his eyes with such intensity he thought his pounding, overwrought heart might explode in his chest, that his life might end in that blissful moment. But he lived on and there were more electrifying feelings to come when she

251

craned her lovely neck upwards and pressed her mouth against his. Her lips were plump and soft, her kisses spiced and heady. Kyriaco closed his eyes, wishing he could stay glued to her mouth for ever, a harmless leech, a love-lorn symbiotic parasite. Surely this kiss was unequivocal. A declaration of deeper feelings. But how deep? He wanted clarification, to hear her say she loved him with all her heart.

28

Socrates heard the sound of his brother's car horn and rushed out of the house before his mother could ask where he was going. He could not face her interrogating look, not when he was feeling so edgy, guilt-ridden and tense. She had a knack of reading his face, deciphering his mood and knowing when he was up to no good. He had avoided her all afternoon, staying in his bedroom behind a locked door, waiting on tenterhooks for his brother to arrive and drive him to the police station where he planned to confess his crimes in the hope of saving Andrico. He climbed into Petri's car and slumped down in the black, leather-covered seat.

'So what was so urgent that you had to call me at the barracks?' Petri asked.

'I have to go to the police station.'

'Couldn't you go with Papa?'

'I don't want Papa to hear what I have to say.'

'What the hell have you been up to?'

Socrates told his brother about the Easter bomb and the secret den and the illegal moped, about the mountain of evidence that had wrongly incriminated Andrico and strengthened the case against him.

'You're a devil,' his brother said nonchalantly, starting the engine and pulling away from the kerb. 'But then again, so was I at your age. I'm no angel now. Promise me you'll stop this stupid bomb-making business? It's not a joke. You might end up killing someone one day or blowing yourself to pieces. You don't want to do that. Life becomes interesting when you get to my age.'

'With women, you mean?'

'Yes. And cruising in your car, and partying all night on the beach with your friends. I'm being discharged in a couple of days and then we can spend more time together, hanging out, doing things. But we can't do anything, can we, if you go injuring yourself and end up in hospital? Now, let's go to the police station and see what we can do to help Andrico.'

Sergeant Georgiou was standing behind a wooden counter, filling out a form. He looked up, acknowledging Petri with a nod before turning to Socrates.

'I've been expecting you. Who's this? Your brother?'

'Yes.'

'Why didn't you come with your father?'

'It's better he came with me,' Petri said. 'There are things he's too scared to admit in front of Papa.'

'Follow me.' The policeman grabbed a notepad and pen from the counter and led the brothers into a sparsely furnished room with white-gloss walls, tinged yellow. A naked, unlit bulb hung from a length of grey cord. The rhythmic hum of cicadas drifted in through the open window. The officer sat on a plastic seat behind a wooden desk and took a packet of B & H from his shirt pocket. He offered Petri a cigarette before lighting up himself, settling back in his chair and telling the brothers to sit down. A metal ashtray on the tabletop overflowed with crushed butts, filling the room with a stale, alkaloid stench.

'Now, Socrates. Tell me how well you knew Andrico?' the sergeant began.

'Very well.'

'How often did you visit him?'

'We went to his house four or five times a week.'

'Who's we?'

'Me, Raphael Tyras and Marco Kabraras.'

'Did Andrico invite you into his house?'

'Not really. We went into the shed.'

'He took you into the shed?'

'No. We used his shed as our den.'

'So you know what kind of things Andrico kept in there?'

'He didn't keep anything in there. Everything in that shed was ours, most of it taken from the rubbish dump. The syringes we took from the bins behind the doctor's surgery. So, you see, Andrico hasn't been injecting children with chemicals like everyone's been saying. We used those syringes to have water fights.'

'I see. That's very interesting.' The officer eyed Socrates disapprovingly. 'So you're one of the wise monkeys I've been chasing through the village on that old moped?'

Socrates nodded and lowered his gaze.

'Andrico shouldn't have let you use his moped. You're too young to ride it.'

'It wasn't his, it was ours. Mine, I mean. I bought it from a garage and hid it in the shed.'

'Andrico gave you permission to hide it?'

255

'We didn't ask his permission. He didn't seem to mind. He didn't know we were doing anything illegal. He's not that . . .'

'Clever? You'd be surprised. Andrico is much brighter than he looks.'

'He trusted us, that's all.'

Petri turned to his brother. 'How the hell did you manage to buy a moped? Are you sure it wasn't Andrico's?'

'Yes, I'm sure. He can't even ride a bike, let alone a moped, so what use would it be to him?' Socrates hesitated. 'Look . . . I forged Mama's signature . . . that's how I bought it. But don't tell her, please. She'll kill me.'

The policeman was scribbling furiously in the notepad and shaking his head. 'Don't tell me the cartridges were yours too?'

'They were. We had a lot more but we cut them open and used the gunpowder inside to make firecrackers at Easter.'

'Those things are lethal,' the police officer said, clicking his tongue several times against the roof of his mouth.

Socrates fell silent, fearing Sergeant Georgiou's reaction when he told him about the bomb.

'Come on,' Petri urged. 'Don't clam up now. Tell him the rest. Tell him everything.'

Socrates shook his head. 'I can't.'

'Yes, you can, and you will. You can't let poor Andrico take the blame for your actions on Holy Saturday.'

The police officer rose to his feet and stared down at Socrates. 'Don't tell me you and your friends blew up the toilet block?'

'I did it. My friends weren't involved.' Socrates stared at

the cigarette smouldering in the ashtray, slowly crumbling away. His body stiffened as he waited for the officer to bellow at him, to tell him he was under arrest and lead him away in handcuffs.

'That was a very dangerous and stupid thing to do. Don't ever try a stunt like that again. You could end up killing someone. As it is you saved the church the effort of demolishing that old block – it was falling to pieces anyway.'

Socrates was surprised by the officer's big brotherly tone, by his apparent reluctance to take the matter any further.

'So now you won't be charging Andrico for the explosion?' Petri asked.

'That's not why we arrested him. That's not why we have him in custody. I'm afraid the charge against him is a great deal more serious, and the reason I asked your brother here today was to find out if Andrico hurt him in any way.'

'No, he never hurt me. Never. Don't you understand! Andrico hasn't done anything. He hasn't hurt anyone. He's a good man who loves his animals. He hardly ever leaves his house.'

'Did you know he was seen wandering the village the night the boy was attacked? Did he have friends in the village? Did you see him that night?'

Socrates stood up and began gesticulating. 'Look, Andrico preferred to go into the village at night, when it was dark and no one could see him or make fun of him or throw stones at him.'

'Who threw stones at him?'

'Some of the kids in the village.'

'Then I don't suppose he liked children very much?'

'He liked us because we were kind to him. He even made biscuits for us.'

'Biscuits.' The officer sat down and began scribbling again. 'And did they taste nice?'

'Not really. But we ate them because we didn't want to hurt his feelings.'

'And did you feel sleepy afterwards?'

'No. *No*.'

But it seemed the officer refused to abandon the theory that Andrico drugged his victims. Socrates was growing increasingly frustrated, realising that he could not help his friend, that a wrong word might actually make matters worse.

'And did he give you money?'

'Sometimes. He was generous.' Socrates wondered if he should mention the mysterious brown envelopes.

Petri turned to him. '*Re!* Why did you take money from such a poor man?'

'He's not poor. Someone sent him . . .' Socrates decided to keep his mouth shut about the money deposited in Andrico's letterbox. Nothing he had said so far seemed to have helped at all.

'And did he ask for favours in return for the money?' the officer prompted.

Socrates shook his head and sat down, biting back tears.

'Look, I shouldn't be telling you this but it might help you to understand why the case is so strong against Andrico. The man was covered in scratches and bruises

258

when we arrested him. He had obviously been involved in some sort of struggle.'

'No. I can explain that, too.' Socrates' frustration was intensified by yet another wrong conclusion. 'He fell off a bike and injured himself.'

'I thought you said he couldn't ride a bike?'

'He couldn't. That's why he lost his balance and fell off.'

'He must have been going at some speed.'

'Forget it.' Socrates hung his head. 'I have nothing more to say.'

The officer looked thoughtful, then smiled. 'Perhaps there is a way you can help Andrico. If you help me, then perhaps I can help you.'

Sergeant Georgiou had no intention of doing a deal with this boy, of scuppering a case he had solved single-handedly. He simply wanted information and was prepared to lie in order to get it.

'I'm sure you've heard about the arcade owner's water tank.'

Socrates nodded. The whole village had heard about the turds in the water tank.

'Do you have any idea who contaminated the water?'

Tino and Zaphiri had boasted about the stunt, warning their friends to stay away from the arcade. Socrates shook his head.

'*Re!* If you know anything at all then speak up,' Petri said. 'You want to help Andrico, don't you?'

'And the culprits will get no more than a telling-off, I promise you. After all, it was just a silly prank.' The officer's tone sounded genuinely forgiving and generous.

Socrates knew he had been forced into a corner and had to choose between helping his friend and betraying his enemies. 'Tino and Zaphiri did it,' he said, cringing as he spoke.

'I thought so. Right. Good.' The officer stood up. 'I think you've told me all I need to know.'

'So, what's going to happen to Andrico? Are you going to let him go?'

'I'll see what I can do. I'll pass on all the information you've given me to my superiors.'

'You'll tell them he didn't do anything? That he didn't attack anyone?'

'Could you wait outside for a minute while I have a private word with your brother?'

'Wait for me in the car,' Petri said.

Socrates walked to the car feeling confused, his confidence in the efficacy of the law shaken. What chance did a helpless, illiterate man like Andrico have against the might of the police force? Against the Public Prosecutor? Socrates climbed into the front passenger seat trying to focus on the dim, yet definite ray of hope – the police officer's promise to help. Minutes later Petri opened the driver's side door and climbed in beside him.

'What did he say?' Socrates asked.

'You don't want to know.'

'Tell me. Please.'

'But I promised I wouldn't say anything.'

'Why? What is it?'

'You really don't want to know.'

'Please, Petri, tell me. Now.'

'OK. But you're not going to like what I'm about to say.

I'm sorry to tell you this, Socrates, but Andrico hasn't got a hope in hell of being freed.'

'But the police officer said . . .'

'Police officers say anything when they're trying to get information.'

'So he tricked me! I should have kept my mouth shut. Why have they got it in for Andrico? Why won't they listen?'

'They haven't got it in for him. This may be hard for you to accept, but the police have concrete evidence. This information is strictly between the two of us, OK? Don't tell your friends.'

Socrates nodded.

'The police found Michali's christening cross hidden in Andrico's house. That cross was torn from the boy's neck the night he was attacked.'

Socrates felt numb and confused, tears filling his eyes. 'I don't believe it.'

'*Re!* Why are you crying? Why are you so upset? Why do you care so much about that man? Did he do anything to you – anything at all?'

'No, no, no!' Socrates cried, shaking his head, burying it in his hands.

'It might help you to know that Andrico has a good lawyer. Someone very generous is paying for his defence. No one knows who's footing the bill, not even the police. It seems there is more to Andrico than meets the eye.'

29

The small kitchen window at the back of Victora's house had conveniently been left open. Using Marco's linked hands as a foothold, Socrates climbed through it on to a laminated worktop resembling white marble, and jumped down to unlock the back door. Marco walked in, quickly closed the door and scanned the room. Wasting no time he began pulling open drawers and searching cupboards while Socrates rifled through the small, vinegar-smelling larder, picking up and replacing bags of pistachio nuts, bulgur wheat, pudding rice, flour and pulses. He pushed aside jars of fruit and vegetables preserved in thick syrup: sweet cherries, baby aubergines, grapefruit, apricots and walnuts. After his depressing visit to the police station, Socrates was more determined than ever to prove Andrico's innocence and he hoped the puppet master's house would yield incriminating evidence.

The three friends had spent the morning in the square, watching Victora build his stage set and position his props. A large crowd had slowly gathered to watch a show that appealed to children, parents and grandparents alike, everyone laughing at the Chaplinesque antics of Karagiozi.

Hector and his friends listened to the show from their coffee-house seats, remembering their youth, lamenting the march of time and the advent of television, nodding their heads knowingly when the harangued puppet argued with his wife or fell out with his employee, when he complained about having no money. Victora operated several characters at once, flipping them over, turning them back to front, making them dance, babble, box each other's ears and sing. And while the children laughed at Karagiozi's high-pitched voice and silly clothes, the old men shook their heads, empathising with the character, a man of the people who struggled in vain to change his fate, who challenged authority and social norms, who would, like them, spend his life struggling to make ends meet.

'There's nothing of interest in here,' Marco said, hurrying out of the kitchen and along the hallway. 'You go upstairs. I'll search the living room.'

Socrates quickly climbed the stairs and entered the bathroom that smelled of must and mould and cheap cologne. The suite was enamel, basic, decades old and lacklustre. The bath was cracked, a thick layer of limescale had formed around the base of the gold taps and the toilet bowl was ringed with grime. Socrates searched the plastic cabinet above the sink. It contained a razor, a comb, a small pair of scissors, shampoo, nail cutters and a clear bottle of pale yellow aftershave. There were no pills, creams or potions inside the cupboard, nothing unusual, nothing suspicious, nothing to link Victora to a crime.

The first two bedrooms Socrates entered were sparsely furnished. Bare mattresses lay on simple, wooden bed frames, the cupboards contained nothing but sheets and towels, no curtains hung at the windows. These tidy, unused rooms seemed to Socrates a reflection of Victora's lonely life. The third bedroom was as opulently decked out as the living room. Red velvet curtains were drawn across the window, blocking out the sun. Socrates switched on the light. A weak bulb shone through a tasselled, satin shade giving the room a melancholic air. Beside a double bed covered with a blue silk spread stood an oddly shaped chair with a red cushioned seat and high back, suitable only for a tall, skinny sitter. The terracotta-coloured walls were lined with colourful canvases: fantastical landscapes hung beside childlike portraits. A forest scene over the bed depicted exotic birds with hooked beaks, staring through lush green foliage. There were portraits of men and women with angular faces and large, two-dimensional eyes, painted in blocks of thick, vibrant colour. Socrates felt the eyes were staring at him, following him round the room, witnessing his crime.

He opened the puppet master's large wardrobe and, using the red chair, climbed up to search the top shelf. There he found dusty cravats, broken ornaments, scrunched-up newspaper and discarded puppet limbs. His search of the armoire base yielded only fluff and old shoes. Remembering his grandfather's habit of hiding money, private documents and even bullets in his footwear, Socrates poked his hand inside each of the shoes before rummaging through the pockets of the clothes, starting with a striped waistcoat hanging on the left and working his way through every item of clothing, searching shirts, coats and trousers. He found loose change, several lighters, a packet of chewing gum, cigarette paper, tobacco, matches and a small penknife with a rusty blade. He slipped this into his pocket, wondering if Victora might have used it in the attack.

In the deep, silk-lined pocket of a long cashmere coat, more suited to the Russian climate than the Mediterranean one, Socrates felt something round and heavy. Pulling it out, he saw it was a metallic golden fruit, not much bigger than a walnut. At first he thought it was a pomegranate, the kind given as a gift at weddings to bestow fertility on the newlyweds, but on closer inspection he realised the glistening globe he held in his hand was a golden apple. He thought the object so beautiful and unique, so wasted in the wardrobe, hidden from the world, that he slipped it into his own pocket, doubting the puppeteer would notice its absence. If the object had been precious to him, if he had thought it worthy of attention, surely he would have displayed it on the mantel in his living room. In all probability the puppet master had forgotten the apple's very existence and was unlikely to mourn its loss. Reaching into the other pocket of the cashmere coat, Socrates found the black-and-white photograph of a young woman. She was sitting on a wooden bench and wearing a simple white dress. He knew instinctively that this was the woman Victora had talked about, the woman he'd fallen in love with. The photograph was worn thin, edges torn and the print cracked and grainy. Only the eyes were sharp and well defined. They seemed to be full of joy. There was something strangely familiar about those eyes. Socrates knew he had seen them somewhere before but, try as he might, could not put a name to the face.

Marco came bounding into the room. '*Re!* We have to go, right now. Raphael's outside. He says Victora's packing up.'

'Already?'

'Are you deaf? Can't you hear the rain?'

Socrates pushed the curtain aside and was surprised to see heavy raindrops pelting the window and the ground outside, and a torrent of water coursing down the street. Engrossed in the search and focused on identifying the woman in the picture, he had not heard the deluge outside the puppet master's window.

'Come on! Close the armoire and let's get out of here. Before we're caught.'

Socrates pushed the door shut, switched off the light and ran out of the room still clutching the photograph. He stuffed it hurriedly into his pocket alongside the golden apple and the penknife.

30

The taxi driver reverently opened the oak case and lifted out the double barrel of his 12-bore shotgun. He held it to his nose and breathed in the satisfying scent of gun oil. The door to his study was locked. His family were asleep upstairs. The sun was several hours away from rising. Beneath the weak light of a low-wattage bulb the taxi driver, kitted out in military garb, cleaned the 28-inch barrels with a metal rod and lint before assembling the gun and buffing it lovingly until it shone. He paid special attention to the engraved side plates and the elegant double trigger which allowed him to fire two cartridges seconds apart and gave him a greater chance of hitting his target, of spattering his prey with lead shot.

No woman had ever moved him like his Purdey, the Rolls-Royce of shotguns, manufactured in London, England. He viewed the elegant weapon with pride and proprietorial satisfaction. Handling the Purdey, pulling the triggers, watching birds drop like stones from the sky, made him feel inexplicably happy. Happier than when he was playing blackjack; than when he was spending the night with his girlfriend; even than when he was cruising down the palm-lined seafront in his Mercedes. His life beyond this was a mess. He knew his wife and children hated him. His girlfriend was constantly on his back, nagging like a spouse, saying she loved him, demanding his attention and presents he could not afford. What's more, her husband had discovered she was cheating on him and had threatened, on his return from the Arab Emirates, to hunt down her lover and shoot him in the head. The taxi driver had made a firm decision to end the affair as soon as he could and stick to prostitutes in future. They might make demands on his wallet but not on his time. At least The Scorpion had been paid now and was off his back.

The Purdey's unerring reliability was the only certainty in his life and it came at considerable cost. A man who worked hard, who supported a wife and a girlfriend, deserved a few luxuries in life, the taxi driver had told himself frequently to justify his actions. And it was this philosophy that drove him to sell his mother-in-law's house and use some of the money to buy a gold ring and a pair of shotguns. Had he not supported his wife during their marriage and shouldered the financial burden of a family? Had he not taken on a woman with a microscopic dowry? If war had not broken out in 1974, if the island had not been invaded, if the Turks had not taken his home and his inheritance, he would have aimed higher than a spouse with an ice-cream man for a father. He would have expected a sizeable dowry from his bride. Yes, he had promised to buy a new house for his wife and children on selling his mother-in-law's home but on reflection had decided there was nothing fundamentally wrong with the existing family abode. Why waste good money on breeze blocks and mortar when he was a refugee and the Government had a legal obligation to house him? The Government and its institutions did not need not know that this particular refugee could in fact afford several properties of his own, that he declared only a fraction of his income and kept the rest hidden. He liked to keep things simple, pay for everything in cash, and keep no more than a few pounds in his bank account.

Each month he spent a small portion of his earnings and stockpiled the rest (along with his substantial winnings from the blackjack table) beneath a section of floorboard in the spare room of his mother's house. No one, not even his beloved mother, knew about the stash. He had no real plans for the money, it was simply his security blanket, a guarantee that he would never be penniless again. Like the magpie he had killed without compunction, the taxi driver had a compulsive, pathological need to hoard. He had more than enough money to buy the pair of Purdeys for himself but once his money was put away it pained him to touch it, to plunder his mountain of cash. The balance due to The Scorpion, lost in one evening on the blackjack table, had been a terrible blow. He had hoped to pay back his IOU slowly, when his luck turned in the gambling den, but The Scorpion had proved an impatient and threatening creditor. How he had hated lifting that floorboard, scooping out wads of cash and giving it away! He felt like strangling his wife for inviting the Mafioso into his home.

A car horn sounded outside followed by raucous male laughter and the bark of a gun dog. The shooting party had arrived earlier than expected, anxious to drive to the hills and claim their stamping ground. The taxi driver strapped on his cartridge belt, picked up his shotgun and holdall and left the house. Three friends and a caged dog sat in the back of the double-cabin truck. Vangeli was at the wheel. All four men wore khaki battle dress, camouflage jackets and chunky lace-up boots. Vangeli had a black neckerchief tied around his forehead and a greasy black stripe painted down each of his cheeks. The bony grey dog barked hungrily and whirled around the metal cage trying to find an escape route.

'Hurry up, my friend,' Vangeli said. 'The pheasants await us.'

The taxi driver climbed into the front passenger seat, standing the Purdey beside him, barrels pointing downward to prevent oil from seeping into the stock and causing it to crack prematurely. Vangeli pressed his foot down on the accelerator and pulled away from the kerb. He drove out of the village and headed for the neighbouring town.

'We're going the wrong way,' the taxi driver said.

'We have to make a slight detour.' Vangeli raised his eyebrows. 'Our good friend Costa in the back is in the mood for fishing, not hunting.'

The two men laughed conspiratorially, 'fishing' being their euphemism for picking up women.

'More fool him. I would choose hunting over fishing any day of the week. Women are nothing but trouble.'

Vangeli drove into the town suburbs and headed for the bright lights of the cabaret district, lined with seedy clubs and dingy basement bars. When the fluorescent lights of

Chicitettas's Paradise and Fantasy Island came into view the taxi driver felt energised. He stuck his head out of the window of the truck and whistled at two peroxide blondes, tottering to work on dangerously high heels. In this gaudy corner of town reality could be forgotten and fantasies lived out. Dumpy, balding men could bed gorgeous redheads wearing sequinned hot pants, and shy teenage boys could lose their virginity for a pocketful of loose change. At double the price a punter could buy himself a multicultural threesome, twin sisters, a virgin. Here, a dissolute taxi driver could cheat on his wife and his girlfriend at the click of his fingers and think himself urbane, a real man. There were women to suit every taste. Statuesque East Europeans who towered over their clients like dominatrixes. Short, smiley Filipinas, warm-hearted vixens who would reputedly do anything to please a man in bed. And there were shows of every description to titillate and draw in the clientele: pole dancing, topless burlesque-style can-cans, naked women with snakes draped round their necks.

Vangeli pulled up outside a pub decked floor to ceiling in glossy pine and staffed by sullen-looking barmaids. Costa jumped down from the truck and stood at Vangeli's open window. He pulled off his camouflage jacket and handed it to his friend, revealing a black, sleeveless T-shirt that hugged his flabby stomach.

'We'll pick you up from here tomorrow night at eight,' Vangeli said. 'Have a good time, my friend.'

The others planned to spend the night in a guesthouse and enjoy two uninterrupted days of hunting.

'I'll give you a couple of my hares to take home to your

wife,' the taxi driver called out, smiling. 'You can't go back empty-handed.'

Twenty minutes later the truck was travelling in convoy along a country road leading to the hills, through early-morning mist. A line of vehicles stretched out in front and to the rear, packed with men in combats brandishing shotguns. An unwitting British tourist, travelling in the opposite direction and unaware of this Sunday morning ritual, thought he was witnessing a show of military might, a procession of the Home Guard on its way to the front line.

Good shooting ground was scarce and highly sought after, always claimed on a first come, first served basis. Hunters eagerly colonised the island's hills and plains, shooting skyward or across open fields. Such overcrowding inevitably led to many injuries and the occasional death. The most fanatical were prepared to take greater risks for their sport, foolishly venturing into the UN buffer zone to find wild partridges and turtle doves, firing shots at anything that moved, including the occasional patrolling UN soldier.

Vangeli drove through a small village square invaded by hunters, who sat at roadside cafés drinking Greek coffee and frappé. A feeling of camaraderie and friendly competition infused the air. Thousands of men had been let loose with their favourite toys to do what men do best: to exercise their masculinity, to strut through the wilderness like cockerels, to hunt down and kill their dinner. The uplifting peal of Sunday morning church bells in hilltop belfries would soon have to compete with the head-splitting sound of gunfire.

Two miles out of the village Vangeli pulled up beside a field where thyme, prickly broom and spiny burnet grew in clumps. Metre-high thistles with mauve heads and forked spines towered above the long grass. Vangeli climbed out of the car, licked his forefinger and raised it in the air.

'Perfect,' he called out. 'The wind is blowing in this direction so the hares won't smell us coming. Let's go.'

The taxi driver climbed out of the car and began to prepare his gun: snapping it open, loading the cartridges, draping the Purdey over his arm like a waiter with a napkin. The dog was released from its cage and ran around in circles, sniffing the air, before heading off into the field, nose to the ground, tail wagging. The hunters followed, fingering their triggers, scanning the bushes for movement, poised to gun down the first hapless animal that strayed across their path.

31

Petri stared at the underside of his green army cap feeling elated. On the peak he had drawn a series of boxes representing each month spent in the army, and inside these boxes he had marked off the days. With great satisfaction and a sense of disbelief, he marked off the thirtieth day of the twenty-seventh month with black biro before packing his bag and walking to the gate. By rights he should have served only twenty-six months in the army but his tour of duty had been extended on account of the times he had absconded from the barracks without permission. In reality Petri had served only twenty-two months behind the barbed-wire fence because he had enjoyed sixty days of official leave and had managed to wangle an additional three months' sick leave. A doctor friend at the hospital, who owed him a favour, had wrapped his healthy right leg in plaster, written him a sick note and sent him off with the X-rays of a man with a compound fracture. The medics in camp suspected trickery but were reluctant to question the integrity of a fellow doctor.

It was late afternoon. In the branches of a lemon tree beyond the camp's periphery a robin sang. 'I will soon be as free as that bird,' Petri muttered to himself, the joyful singing whetting his appetite for civilian life. He handed his discharge papers to the sergeant on duty and his heart began to race. He felt like a hibernating creature waking up from a long, wearisome period of dormancy. No more early starts, he thought happily. No more idiots bellowing in his face and telling him what to do. No more cleaning latrines, polishing shoes or watching Stavraki bite the heads off lizards for entertainment.

Thoughts of freedom had been uppermost in his mind in the weeks leading up to his discharge. Freedom from sentry duty and parades, from rules and regulations. Freedom from the suffocating yoke of coupledom. Petri's passion for Carina had cooled considerably yet she had made firm plans to come back to Cyprus and work over the summer. Carried along by her enthusiasm and not wanting to disappoint, he had foolishly offered to find and pay for an apartment where they could live together. But as yet he had no job lined up, no income, no real plans for the future. Petri blamed himself for encouraging Carina's extended visit and wished to God he had never asked Barbara at the arcade to write a love letter for him in English. He had given her free rein to woo his girlfriend while he sat drinking frappé with Kyriaco. '*Write whatever you want*,' he had said, nonchalantly lighting a cigarette. Barbara, an avid reader of romantic novels, had written three pages of whimsical prose, comparing Carina's lips to ripe strawberries and her hair to liquid gold. The letter, which Petri sent without bothering to read it, convinced Carina that her Mediterranean sweetheart had the soul of a poet, that he was a higher being, of the uncommon breed of man who could fathom the workings of a woman's heart.

The duty sergeant was taking his time examining the discharge papers. He looked Petri up and down disparagingly.

'I should lock you up just for wearing those clothes,' he said.

'I'm a civilian now,' Petri replied, adjusting the collar of his pink shirt defiantly, slipping his hands into the pockets of his white trousers.

'You're not a civilian until I sign these papers.'

'Then sign them.'

A group of soldiers walking past the exit gate began wolf-whistling.

'Travolta's being discharged,' one of them shouted.

With a mocking smile the sergeant signed the papers and handed them over. Petri put on his dark glasses, bade farewell to the laughing soldiers with his middle finger, and sauntered out of the gate without looking back. Oresti was waiting for him outside, revving the engine of the Lada impatiently. Petri threw his bag into the boot of the car beside a lorry battery and climbed into the passenger seat, ready to try out the new device his friend had rigged up. The lorry battery was connected via an adaptor to a transmitter the size of a shoebox, and the transmitter was attached by a long wire to an antenna fixed to the roof of the car. Oresti was an electronics wizard who operated his own pirate radio station from his bedroom. Keen to test this new gadget he had fashioned, he headed into town looking for a traffic jam.

There was a hold-up at the traffic lights on the main thoroughfare. Oresti sidled the Lada up beside a green

Honda in which two young women sat, singing along to a Dalaras song, their windows wound down.

'Let's try it now,' he said.

'What do I have to do?'

'Turn the dial on the car stereo until we're tuned into the same station as the girls.'

Petri slowly changed the channel as instructed until the Dalaras track blared from the speakers.

'Now, turn the dial on the transmitter until the song cuts out. If we interrupt our frequency, then we interrupt theirs at the same time.'

'Just theirs?'

'No, everyone within a thousand metres or so, but the girls are the only ones we're interested in – unless you've got your eye on the fat guy in the Nissan?'

'No, I prefer the girls, especially the one in the passenger seat.' Petri turned the transmitter dial, interrupting Dalaras on a high note.

'Good.'

'And now?'

'Pick up the microphone attached to the transmitter and talk. It's as simple as that, if it works, which it should.'

'Hello,' Petri said, putting the microphone close to his mouth, surprised to hear his own voice coming through the speakers. He glanced across at the girls in the Honda who looked bewildered. They could hear his voice too, transmitted through their radio.

'Hello, ladies,' he said, while Oresti sniggered beside him. 'How are you today?'

The traffic began to slither forward. The girl in the passenger seat put her ear to the radio.

'Yes, I'm talking to you in the polka-dot top and the hooped earrings. What's your name? Tell me your name?'

The girl fingered her earrings and squealed, her shrill cry an expression of delight and fear. 'Hey,' she said, and turned to her friend, 'the radio's talking to me.'

'Don't be stupid,' her friend replied.

Petri could clearly hear their conversation through the open window.

'She's not being stupid,' he said, slumping down in the seat to avoid being seen, struggling to suppress his laughter. 'What's your name?'

'Tell him your name,' the girl at the wheel said, spooked by the surreal experience, convinced that some supernatural force had infiltrated the radio and was trying to make contact.

'Anna,' the girl said timidly, glancing out of her open window into Oresti's car.

Petri leaned forward so that his face and the microphone were in full view. 'Anna. Pleased to meet you,' he said, smiling.

The two girls shrieked with laughter.

'You devils,' Anna said. 'How did you do that?'

'That's our secret. See you later.'

The friends drove away and spent the rest of the afternoon scaring young women out of their wits, laughing so much their sides hurt.

'Let's do one more and then go and have a drink,' Petri said. 'If I laugh any more I'll be sick. You're a genius, my friend.'

Oresti drove alongside a car in which three girls were chatting over the strains of a synthesised beat.

'Look at that one in the back, she's gorgeous. Talk to that one,' Oresti said.

Petri turned the dial on the transmitter and began talking to the girl with the tight-fitting top and long black hair, telling her she was beautiful, a goddess. The girl's reaction was muted, as if knowing that the outlandish phenomenon she was experiencing had a simple explanation. She did not scream out like her friends in the front of the car but simply turned her head to the left and stared up at the antenna on the Lada and then down, straight into Petri's eyes.

'Baby, do you know what I'd like to do to you tonight?' Oresti shouted into the microphone.

'*Re!* Stop it,' Petri said, switching off the microphone, his cheeks burning. 'That's Maria from the village. She's practically family.' He switched the microphone back on. 'Maria, tell your friend to pull over. We need to talk.'

The two cars pulled up, one behind the other. Petri and Maria climbed out and walked towards each other.

'So, is this how you like to spend your time?' Maria said, hands on hips. 'Bothering women! Your mother would be very proud of you.'

'We only did it for a laugh. Sorry if I offended you.'

'No, I'm not offended. Why should I be? Anyway, I didn't quite catch what your friend said. What was it again?'

'Forget my friend, he's a fool.'

Petri glanced down at the cleavage bursting from Maria's V-neck top, as appetising as a slice of cool watermelon in summer. He felt angry with himself and hardened his expression. Maria was forbidden fruit, a temptation he had to resist.

279

'Aren't you dressed a little provocatively?' he said, staring into a face that struck him as peculiarly beautiful, not perfect like Carina's but quirky and beguiling. He noticed the sensuous curve of her generous bottom lip and the green flecks, like shards of emerald, that brightened her hazel eyes.

'Do you think so?' she said proudly, though she knew he had meant to be critical.

'Does your mother know you dress like that?' He kept his tone brotherly. It did not match the sexual thoughts swimming around in his head. He wanted to dive into that cleavage, to thrash about in the deep, flower-scented valley between her breasts.

'What my mother doesn't know won't hurt her. At least I'm covered up. Not like that girlfriend of yours who stripped off at the airport.'

'She wasn't my girlfriend.'

'You were kissing her.'

'I was just saying goodbye.'

'With your tongue.'

Petri flushed.

'Anyway, I'm going. The girls are waiting.' Maria walked away, shaking her head.

'Hey! Why are you shaking your head like that?' he called after her.

She stopped, then turned to face him with a scornful look. 'Because Cypriot men are impossible to please. We cover ourselves up and you don't give us a second glance, preferring to spend your time with foreign women. We show a bit of flesh and you think we're sluts.'

Petri watched Maria climb into the car and be driven

away. He wanted to call her back, to carry on talking, to tell her she was wrong, though he knew she was right. He found himself contemplating the possibility of going out with Maria, of dating a woman he could fully communicate with, of squeezing that curvaceous girl in his arms and kissing her lips. A strange, unpleasant feeling of urgency, guilt and nausea overwhelmed him. He walked back to the car, realising he had to act quickly before it was too late, to end a relationship that would tie him down, limit his experience and keep him from Maria. He climbed back into the car and asked Oresti to drive him to the village arcade.

Half an hour later he was sitting in a plastic booth, opposite Barbara and Kyriaco, begging the Filipina scribe to write an apologetic letter that would let Carina down gently. Barbara shook her head.

'Bat the gel, she's caming in a week. Please, you gotta help me.'

'You gonna break the poor girl's heart if you tell her you do not love her,' Barbara said.

'Then, you write and tell her, Petri he's dead.'

'I cannot do such a thing. I cannot lie to the poor girl.'

'Bat you lie before.'

'No. You told me that you love her, so I tell her that you love her. Where's the lie?'

'And it take you three pages to say tha? Wha else you tell her?'

'In my letter is said you miss her, you want her to come back, that you keep her picture in your pocket, that maybe one day you will marry her.'

'Wha! I never say tha.'

281

Kyriaco looked across at Barbara wishing he could whisper a marriage proposal into her sweet, tiny ear, wondering if it was too soon to broach the issue of their future together. They were sharing a bed and living as a couple; he was married to her in spirit if not on paper. They had installed a television and a video recorder in the arcade and when business was slow in the evenings would sit together, watching films and munching popcorn.

'Why don't you telephone her?' Kyriaco suggested in Greek. 'Be straight.'

'Because I don't have the balls, my friend.'

'There's no other way.'

'I suppose you're right. I'd better go and call her right away. I can't put this off any longer.' Petri stood up and walked out of the arcade, searching his brain for suitable lies.

'*Yong people these days!*' Barbara said, tutting. '*They fall in love one day and out of love the next.*'

Barbara was only twenty-six yet she did not consider herself young. She had grown up quickly, starting work at the age of ten in a cigarette factory to support her mother and younger siblings, and she was still supporting them, sending half of her salary to Manila each month.

'*Me, I only fall in love one time,*' Kyriaco said, hesitantly.

'*Who with?*' Barbara teased, knowing she was wanted and adored, enjoying the power she wielded over this soft-hearted man.

'*With you,*' he replied, hoping she would say she loved him too. '*And you . . . do you lav me, Barbara?*'

'*You are a very kind and loveable man.*'

Telling him he was worthy of love was enough to bolster his confidence.

'*Barbara, I want to ask you samthin'.*'

'*Yes, Kyriaco. What is it?*'

He wanted to reach out for her hand but his palms were too sweaty. He wiped them dry on his trousers and took a deep breath to steady his nerves. Should he go down on one knee? Clasp a flower between his teeth? Hand her a ribbon-tied package containing a ring? He knew the arcade was the wrong setting for a marriage proposal but he could wait no longer.

'*Barbara.*' He wanted to tell her that she meant every-thing to him, that without her he was nothing, but his poor command of English meant he could only use the simplest of phrases to express his feelings.

'*Yes, Kyriaco?*'

'*Marry you me?*' The words came out jumbled, garbled, not as he had intended.

'*How could I say no?*'

She did not say yes and for a moment Kyriaco wondered if she had actually consented. '*You say no?*'

'*No. I say yes.*'

'*Thanks God.*' He took her in his arms and kissed her on the lips, overcome and tearful, hardly able to believe his good fortune.

Barbara did not love Kyriaco passionately, nor did she consider him handsome. Her love for him was the gentler kind, born of respect and admiration. She knew the arcade owner was a good man who worshipped her, and that was reason enough to accept his proposal. Kyriaco had no idea as he held Barbara in his arms that in the space of eighteen months she would give birth to twin boys, that her mother and sister from the Philippines would join her, that he would buy a bigger house to accommodate them all. That he would forget his get-rich-quick schemes, banish his father's suit to the back of the wardrobe, concentrate on nurturing his growing family, and die a happy, fulfilled and beloved old man.

32

Socrates stood his bike on the tarmacked area, kicked off his sandals and walked barefoot across the warm sand. He climbed the rocky outcrop, carrying a backpack and a bamboo rod, and sat down beside the fisherman, greeting him with a handshake. The wind lashed his face, blowing away the fusty cobwebs clouding his brain and tangling up his thoughts. He unpacked his bag, feeling glad to have escaped the village and its wagging tongues, fed up of hearing about Andrico's arrest. Theory, speculation, exaggeration and tall tales formed the basis of local opinion. 'The man was sick in the head,' villagers said, or, varying the theme: 'Only a sick man could do such a thing.' The village idiot was the perfect suspect in many ways, a convenient scapegoat, an outcast who could be erased from village life without upsetting the status quo. A number of Andrico's relatives lived locally but none was prepared to fly in the face of the consensus and support him. In fact, his uncle was his most outspoken critic, saying he had warned the authorities that his nephew was unstable and quite possibly dangerous. This same uncle had called Social Services the day after his sister died asking for Andrico to be institutionalised, refusing to take emotional or financial responsibility for his half-witted nephew. For him the arrest was a blessing, a chance to wash his hands of the shameful relative, a genetic stain on the family reputation. The arrest would finally silence villagers who had criticised him over the years for turning his back on his own flesh and blood.

The gist of Socrates' statement to the police had somehow become common knowledge. Everyone knew about the contents of the den and tended to believe Sergeant Georgiou's interpretation: that Andrico had lured boys to his property by filling the shed with enticements. Question marks now hung over Socrates' head. Why did Andrico give him money? Had he been molested too? Drugged perhaps? Was he too scared to own up? His mother had questioned him at length about his relationship with Andrico, saying she would forgive him every sin he had ever committed in exchange for the unadulterated truth. Only here, sitting on the rocky outcrop preparing his rod before an undulating sea, did Socrates feel at peace. The village and its machinations were a million miles away. In the company of the fisherman, Socrates felt no pressure to talk but only a quiet determination to catch the biggest fish.

'It's a great day for fishing,' Poli said. 'Just the right amount of wind stoking up the water.'

'Good. I've promised to take Mama a big fish home to cook for our lunch tomorrow.'

'Do you know when the best time of all to fish is?'

'When?'

'Just after the local shepherd has been here with his animals. He drives them on to the rocks and they fall into the water one by one and swim to the shore, getting cleaned up in the process. After five hundred sheep have jumped into the sea, the water literally changes colour, becomes a kind of muddy red, and thick with matter that fish love to eat. This area around the rocks teems with fish for several hours.'

'When does the shepherd come?'

'There's no set day or time. I come here so often that I've stumbled upon him several times. It really is a sight worth seeing. The sheep swim around, their heads bobbing up and down, and when they reach the shore they shake off the water, just like dogs drying their coats.'

Socrates fashioned a cork float using his penknife and secured it in place with a match.

'You're doing a great job there,' Poli said. 'I've never seen a finer rod. You're a quick learner, my friend.'

Socrates had learned that the more attention he paid to his rod the greater chance he had of catching a fish, and the more fish he caught the more Poli paid him compliments. The fisherman had begun to feel like a brother to him, a fixture in his life. Socrates knew he had a knack for fishing and that he was a better fisherman than his friends. Marco lacked the necessary patience and Raphael's plump fingers were not made for the delicate job of preparing a line. Socrates was determined to become as good a fisherman as Poli, to buy a boat of his own one day and spend all his free time by the sea.

He broke off a piece of the dough his mother had mixed for him and began rolling it into a ball. She approved of his new hobby, believing it would keep him out of the village, out of harm's way and out of trouble.

Poli pulled the small plastic bottle from his rucksack and unscrewed the lid. 'Put some of this on your dough and you'll catch a monster.'

'That stuff again. Your magic ingredient. Please, tell me what it is?'

'First, open your hand.' Socrates stretched out his hand and Poli drizzled a dark red liquid into it.

'OK, I'll tell you, but only you. It's pig's blood. The fish can smell it a mile off and radiate towards it. Sometimes I put a few drops in the water before I start fishing, like I did the day we fished with the spear. Mix it in with your dough, quickly, before it dries.'

'Does it really make a difference?'

'Just wait and see.'

'Where do you get it from?'

'The local butcher gives me a jar from time to time.'

Socrates cast off with a flick of his hand and sat waiting for a fish to bite, his eyes fixed on the float. He did not have long to wait. Five minutes later it began to judder.

'It's a mullet,' Poli said.

'How do you know?'

'Because they never swallow the hook straight away. Don't you remember me telling you? They play with it, rest it in their mouths, swim around it. And this one's a big one, at least a kilo. I can see its outline. Prepare yourself for battle, my friend.'

Socrates' muscles tightened. The float juddered for a while and then stopped moving.

'I've lost it, Poli. It's gone.'

'It will come back. Trust me and have patience. That dough is far too tasty to resist.'

Suddenly the cork moved forward and then sideways along the surface of the water.

'You see. What did I tell you! It's pushing the hook along. Any moment now it will bite.'

The float keeled over and moved diagonally underwater.

'Pull it back. NOW!' Poli said.

Socrates stood up and began wrestling with the strong fish, trying to keep his line taut. He tugged until his arms hurt, dragging the fish closer to the rocky shore, leaning back to keep from losing his balance.

'Slowly does it . . . that's it. You've got it, it's tiring. Just a little longer and that fish will be yours. Here, take this with your other hand. Do the whole thing yourself.'

Poli handed Socrates the net and he quickly scooped the fish into it before sitting back down with his catch feeling exhausted, exhilarated and proud of himself, imagining his mother's look of delight when he presented her with their supper.

Poli slapped him playfully on the leg. '*Aman!* What luck. That's the biggest fish you've caught yet.'

Keen to cast off again and capitalise on his luck, Socrates lifted the fish out of the net and dropped it into the blue bucket. Poli put down his own rod and reclined, resting his back against his holdall and closing his eyes. 'I had a late night last night. I think I need to get some sleep.'

'But you won't be able to help me if I catch something.'

'You don't need my help any more. You're an expert.'

Socrates cast off, hopeful he would catch a large sea bream, his mother's favourite fish. She liked to sprinkle the fish with white wine and olive oil and cook it on a bed of sliced onions and potatoes. Socrates was so lost in thought, staring out to sea, that he hardly noticed Poli stretch out one arm and place a hand on his leg. He turned to look at the fisherman whose eyes were shut and whose rhythmic breathing suggested he was asleep. Socrates wanted to move the hand that felt hot and clammy against his skin but he did not want to wake his companion or, worse still, offend him by suggesting the gesture was inappropriate. He tried to focus once again on his float but Poli's fingers began to move, to stroke his leg lightly and drift closer to his shorts. Perhaps he was dreaming about a woman, Socrates thought. He froze when Poli slid his index finger under the leg of his shorts and continued upwards, touching the sensitive skin beneath the boy's underpants, his finger wriggling, tickling, arousing.

Socrates wanted to run but felt fused to the rock, his body flushing so hot no wind could cool him down. He wanted to flee but he was also curious to know what would happen next, to live this new experience through to its conclusion. Poli used two fingers, then three, and then his whole hand to rub between Socrates' legs, to massage the area that had only ever been explored by the boy's own fingers before. He felt himself grow hard and could think of nothing but the intense and novel sensation, the expert fingers that made him tingle all over and moved like the legs of a spider. The muscles in his groin tightened and a pleasurable explosion took his breath away. He had come before, in wet dreams, but never with such intensity. He turned to Poli, whose face was flushed and wet with perspiration, whose eyes were now open and staring at him, whose other hand fumbled inside his own shorts.

Overcome with revulsion, Socrates sprang to his feet, climbed quickly off the jagged rock and sprinted across the sand.

'Socrates, where are you going? Come back,' Poli shouted after him. 'Let's talk. We need to talk.'

The boy jumped on to the saddle of his bike, leaving his sandals where they lay, and headed for the safety of the village. He cried as he cycled, feeling confused and guilty, the uncomfortable wetness in his underpants a constant reminder of the sin he had allowed to happen. Why had he let the fisherman touch him? Why hadn't he fought him off or run away? How could he have taken pleasure from such a wicked act? Why hadn't he realised the moment blood was poured into his hand that he was in danger? He sniffed his palm, pulled on the brakes of his bike and threw up by the side of the road, realising now that his newfound brother was Michali's attacker. His friend had betrayed him, just as Victora had predicted, and Socrates felt a fool for trusting this man he knew so little about. He contemplated cycling to the police station and reporting the fisherman in the hope of saving Andrico but knew he could not face the mocking sergeant again, or describe what had taken place without feeling dirty and ashamed. The whole village would find out and then he would be branded with the same indelible stain as Michali.

33

Irini heard a truck pull up outside the house and hurried into the kitchen to open the oven. The potatoes were pale and the pork joint raw. She turned up the heat and hoped her husband would not demand his meal as soon as he walked through the door. If she cooked a roast too far in advance he complained the meat was tough. If the roast was not ready on time he accused her of being idle. Irini wondered why he had arrived home so early from his hunting expedition. Normally, it was well past midnight before he walked through the door, reeking of drink, his bloodstained catch draped proudly over his shoulder. She dreaded the thought of spending her evening plucking pheasants, skinning rabbits and picking lead shot from animal flesh.

The house had been wonderfully calm for two days without the brute. Irini had used The Scorpion's gift to take the children to the cinema, to buy them popcorn and a Margharita pizza, enjoying an evening of simple, peaceful pleasures. Tonight, the children had gone to bed early, guessing their father would arrive home drunk and in an argumentative mood. Irini braced herself for the taxi driver's entrance, expecting the sound of a key turning in the lock but hearing instead a knock at the door. She froze. Maybe The Scorpion had come back with a truck in which to take her belongings as he had threatened. Maybe he knew she had been lying and had returned to demand his money. Irini opened the door to find Vangeli, eyes as red as pomegranate seeds, clutching the Purdey to his chest.

'Irini *mou*.' My Irini, he called her, stepping forward into the house. 'I'm afraid I have some very bad news. Very bad.'

'What is it?'

He closed the door behind him, lips trembling and downturned, his face looking slightly clownish. 'There's been a terrible accident. Really terrible.'

The children were upstairs in bed. She had just spoken to her mother on the telephone. All the people she loved most were safe and sound. His expression failed to move her.

'What's happened?'

'Are the children asleep?'

'Yes.'

'Thank God. I couldn't face them as well. I hardly have the strength to face you.'

'Please, tell me what's happened.'

His red eyes watered. 'My dear Irini, your husband has been shot.'

'Is he in hospital?'

She knew what was coming but wanted the truth spelled out. Vangeli wiped the sheen from his forehead using the back of his sleeve and took a deep breath.

'Perhaps you should sit down.'

He took her by the arm and led her across the room, laying the gun on the coffee table and sitting on the sofa beside her.

'Irini *mou*.' He took a dirty white handkerchief from his trouser pocket and noisily blew his nose. 'Your husband is dead. Another hunter shot him accidentally. We tried to save him but we couldn't. He lost too much blood. He died in my arms, Irini. The poor man died in my arms.'

Vangeli broke down then, crying with gusto as he relived the tragedy and described the scene of the dying hunter lying in a pool of his own blood. He squeezed Irini in his arms, wailing in her ear, wetting her neck with his tears, while she stared apathetically at the back wall, hoping the children would not wake up. She felt numb, incapable of reacting. A woman who loved her husband might have succumbed to the drama of the moment and cried her eyes out, but Irini had wished the taxi driver dead more times than she cared to remember and could not genuinely mourn his loss.

Vangeli looked into her vacant eyes.

'You're in shock,' he said. 'It hasn't sunk in yet, has it?'

She shook her head.

'You shouldn't stay on your own tonight. Shall I go and fetch your mother?'

'No, I'll be fine. Go home to your wife.'

Vangeli stood up. 'I expect the police will be along soon. I wanted to come before them, to break the terrible news to you myself. Your husband was my best friend and I loved him dearly.'

Irini could not help the subtle twist of her lips that

suggested disapproval of this friendship. Oh, yes, they had been close. Partners in crime, in fact. Egging one another on like naughty schoolboys, gambling and womanising together, laughing like hyenas at each other's dastardly stunts and reprehensible behaviour. She walked Vangeli to the door, knowing he was shocked by her coldness, her dry eyes, her composure. She had never been one for theatrics and could not feign sorrow.

She spent the following day in a stupor, dressed in black, carried along by the etiquette of bereavement. First thing in the morning there was the body to identify in the hospital morgue, after which she broke the news to her children and consoled them as they cried, surprised by their outpouring of grief. Marco seemed both angry with himself and upset at having lost a parent. Irini guessed he felt guilty for threatening to kill his father, a threat that had seemingly reworked itself into a curse. A steady stream of friends and relatives wandered through the open door to comfort the newly widowed woman and her children. The taxi driver's mother fainted and had to be revived with smelling salts. His sister wailed and hugged her sides, loudly eulogising her brother. 'He was a good man, a good husband and a good father,' she repeated over and over again, and all those gathered nodded in agreement, reinforcing the lie.

Irini made coffee and stood on the sidelines while the taxi driver's kin stole the show. Her composed air was noted by his mother and would never be forgiven or forgotten. In the years that followed, Irini's mother-in-law would slander her mercilessly at family gatherings. 'That

295

woman has a heart of stone,' she would say repeatedly, not bothering to ask herself why. She talked about her daughter-in-law's aloof manner, her ineptitude as a wife, her slovenly appearance; insulting her without compunction or understanding. She buried the sordid truth about her philandering son and his violent nature deep in her subconscious, not wanting to speak ill of the dead or face the fact that she had nurtured a monster. And buried beneath her feet, under the floorboards of her home, was her son's stash of treasure which she never discovered, thousands of pounds' worth of ill-gotten gains that over the ensuing years were chewed up and shredded by nesting mice, which simply went to waste.

At the end of the day, when everyone had finally departed and the children had gone to bed, Irini sat down on the sofa trying to fathom why she felt so utterly lost and empty. Her prayers had been answered without her needing to bloody her own hands yet she felt incapable of rejoicing, of looking forward to the future. When her gaze fell upon the gun propped against the wall, a notion took shape in her mind that had lurked in the shadows of her consciousness all day.

'I killed him,' she muttered. 'I killed him,' she repeated, her heart racing, her pulse resounding in her ears. The shooting was no accident. The Scorpion had carried out his veiled threat. Why hadn't she given him the money? Why had she lied to such a dangerous man? How could she rob her own children of a father? She would take the envelope and burn it, get rid of any evidence linking her to the crime. For the first time, since hearing of her husband's death, Irini visualised him writhing in a river of blood like some fallen Adonis and realised the true horror of the murder she had conspired in.

Pacing the room, consumed by guilt and self-loathing, she did not hear a car pull up outside her house, the click of heels along the front path and a man clearing his throat on the front step. A loud knock at the door made her jump and intensified her anxiety. Her nerves were shredded and she doubted she could face anyone without breaking down, maybe even confessing her crime. She willed her visitor to go away but the knocking continued, until finally a man poked his head through the partially open window, making her scream out.

'I didn't mean to scare you,' The Scorpion said gently. 'I've come to see how you are.'

Irini wanted him to leave, to recede into the darkness. What did this man want? Surely he had settled his score with her husband. What more could he take? Perhaps he had come with his goons to finish her off too.

'Aren't you going to let me in or would you rather I climb through the window?'

Was this a joke or a threat? Was his smile kindly or menacing? Irini could not tell. She opened the door to the man she believed to be her husband's murderer and stood shaking with fear and anger before him. Gone was the bravery and invincibility she had felt at their last meeting.

'Can I come in?'

Irini moved aside.

'I'm sorry to hear about your husband.'

As he walked into the room Irini waited for the 'but' . . . but I'm not satisfied . . . but I still want my money. If he asked for his money again she would give it to him and say her husband had had a change of heart.

'You're trembling. Sit down.'

'No, I'm fine. What do you want?'

'I don't want anything. I've just come to offer my condolences. I knew your husband well. Believe it or not, I liked him.'

Irini felt tears well up in her eyes for the first time that day.

'He was quite a character and I'm sorry for your loss.'

'Are you?' she asked accusingly.

'Yes, of course.'

'Then why did you take his life? Why did you kill him?' Even as the accusation left her lips, Irini feared the repercussions.

The Scorpion held up his hands and took a step back. 'What! I didn't touch him, I swear to you. If I had, do you think I would be standing here right now?'

'Then you've come for your money?'

'And who's going to give it to me? You? Now you have three children to raise alone? I've checked out your husband's account through a friend at the bank. It seems he was telling the truth about one thing at least. He doesn't have a penny to his name.'

Irini knew in her heart that this man who had told a thousand lies, who had cheated his way through life, who had the blood of several men on his hands, was telling the truth. She wanted to cry out, to scream, to express the pure joy that flooded the gaping hole inside her, but instead she wept unashamedly, covering her face with her hands to hide the irrepressible smile on her lips. The brute was gone, his monstrous presence erased. She would never have to see him, smell him or feel his hands upon her skin again; her son would never be strung up from her tree; her daughter would never again stand quivering in a corner, pale with fright. Family life could begin anew. The puppet master's prediction had come true.

Pantelas shuffled his feet, looking awkward, and patted Irini on the shoulder. 'I should leave. I didn't come here to make you cry, I'm sorry. But you do believe I didn't kill your husband, don't you?'

She nodded and wiped her tear-stained cheeks with her hands, noticing in the corner of her eye the Purdey propped up against the wall, the loathsome gun she had imagined aiming at her husband.

'Won't you take his gun?' she said quietly.

'His gun?'

'Yes, that one over there.'

The Scorpion moved across the room and picked up the Purdey, rubbing his hand over the silver side plate. '*Aman!*' he said, looking impressed. 'What a beauty.'

'He has two. The other one's in his study.'

'Do you know how valuable this is? How sought after?'

'I don't know and I don't care. I have no use for guns. If you like it, then take it. Take the other one as well. You'd be doing me a big favour. Perhaps the guns will go some way towards paying my husband's debt to you?'

'Quite a long way.'

'Then I insist. Come with me.'

Irini hurried into her husband's study and located his second gun in a cupboard. She gathered up all his hunting paraphernalia, cartridges and cleaning equipment, and handed the lot to Pantelas.

'Are you sure you want me to take all this stuff? You could sell it and make some money. God knows you need it. At least let me give you something.'

'No,' she said, shaking her head, desperate to be rid of her husband's belongings and their bad associations.

After The Scorpion had loaded up his car and driven away, Irini hurried into the kitchen to retrieve the brown envelope hidden beneath the lid of her casserole pot at the back of a cupboard. She tore it open, spilled the contents on to the kitchen table, and counted out £35,000 crisp Cyprus pounds, the sale price of her mother's home, the money her husband would have frittered away on more guns and jewellery for himself. Irini had never seen so much money in her life, yet it neither fazed nor impressed her and she felt no urge to rush out and spoil herself. She knew exactly how to spend this money. First, she would build an extension at the back of the house for her mother to live in and then, somewhere down the line, after all the children's needs had been catered for, she would buy herself a washing machine.

In a village ten miles away another woman was dressed in mourning while her husband was in a jubilant mood after a successful hunting trip. Earlier that day he had eaten the woodcock dish his wife had prepared, washed it down with ice-cold Keo and licked his greasy fingers clean. He had stood over his wife as she plucked the birds and singed them over a naked gas flame, taking great pleasure in her obvious discomfort. Unused to getting her manicured fingers dirty and sickened by the sight of blood, she had pulled out the intestines grimacing, the smell of innards making her feel nauseous. Following her husband's instructions, she had browned the woodcocks and their livers in butter and stewed them in dry white wine. When he had finished eating, the husband settled down on the sofa to watch the evening news, asking his wife to sit beside him. They listened to a report about a father of three from the neighbouring village who had been killed accidentally while on a two-day hunting expedition. News cameras zoomed in on a bloodstained combat jacket lying on the ground and interviewed the victim's friend who complained that there were too many hunters in the same area, that a tragedy of this nature was unavoidable. When the victim was named the husband smiled while the wife turned ashen, realising with horror that this death was no freak accident, that her husband had gunned down three woodcocks, two pheasants, a wild rabbit and her lover.

34

The village began to stir, roused by a cool breeze from its lunchtime sluggishness. Themi the butcher sat on the front step of his shop, picking roast pork from between his teeth with a match, while flies buzzed around the carcass of a hare hanging from a hook above his head. Giorgios brewed coffee on the single gas hob in the kitchen of his coffee house as men gathered beneath the vine-covered trellis outside to play backgammon and kill time. Hector sat in his favourite chair sipping coffee, surreptitiously ogling young women from behind the dark lenses of his shades, wishing he were several decades younger. He contemplated the social changes he had witnessed in his long life and thanked the Lord above for sexual liberation. He remembered a time when women wore long skirts, scarves, fussy underwear and shirts that buttoned to the collarbone. Nowadays, there was plenty of flesh on show to keep a man's eye busy, feed his imagination and set his loins on fire. Hector yearned to spend one last night with a young woman before he met his maker but he feared the excitement might prove too much for his heart. How he suffered, having a young man's mind lodged inside an old man's ineffectual body.

He saw Maria approaching from the far end of the street and thought how marvellous it would be to cup the girl's heavy breasts in his hands, to feel their weight and girth. He waved her over, knowing he would have to make do with breathing in her smell and touching her hand.

'Hello, *papou*,' she called out, addressing him respectfully as 'grandfather'.

'My girl, sit down. Let me buy you an Orangina.' Age conferred some advantages, giving Hector's trembling hands licence to roam and fumble. 'How are you? I haven't seen you for a while.'

'I'm fine. Working hard.'

'And growing.' Hector looked the girl up and down, admiring her curves. The spindly child had grown into quite a woman. 'We'll be marrying you off soon, no doubt.'

'I'm in no hurry, *papou*.'

Maria knelt down beside him and stroked his hand, fooled by the grey hair and the wrinkled skin into thinking him harmless, chaste of thought, saintly. Hector deserved neither trust nor reverence for beneath the innocuous exterior bubbled hot blood and ungrandfatherly thoughts. He leaned forward in his seat so that his knee was pressed lightly against Maria's breast and the withered snake inside his baggy, black pantaloons began to rear its aged head.

A car stopped beside the coffee shop wall. Maria stood up and waved. 'I have to get to work. Take care of yourself.'

'Who's that?' Hector motioned towards the car.

'It's Petri, Eleni's son. He's going into town and has offered to give me a lift to the airport.'

'Be careful of him. He's a womaniser,' Hector said, defaming the boy whose reputation he envied.

Maria hurried away. Hector sipped the last dregs of his coffee and scanned the road ahead for his next ocular victim.

An open truck trundled past, piled high with potatoes, caked in crumbly, red earth. Themi shouted huskily across the busy road, '*Re*, Giorgio. Make me a sweet coffee. Business is slow today.' A thumping bass blared from the open windows of a souped-up Suzuki saloon, its roof cut open like a sardine tin and customised with a sunroof. The driver's sun-baked arm dangled from the window, his fingers tapping impatiently on the door. More so when the traffic slowed and an old woman riding a donkey laden with grapes overtook him and carried on through red lights defying the rules of the highway. Three scrawny feral cats took advantage of the hold-up to dart across the road.

The shrill, repetitive drone of cicadas rang out from the branches of a pavement carob beneath which Socrates walked, swinging his blue plastic bucket. The hum of transparent wings rubbing together reminded him of the sound made by his simple harmonica fashioned from greaseproof paper and his father's fine toothcomb. He walked absentmindedly across the road, weaving his way through the traffic, passing the coffee shop, failing to notice the old man who recoiled in his chair at the sight of the boy who had tried to kill him several times. Socrates' mind was elsewhere, flitting from one troubling thought to the next, tortured by flashbacks to the episode on the rocks. Shame gnawed at his insides. Whenever he remembered the look on the fisherman's flushed face or the feel of his fingers, Socrates cringed inside. He couldn't bring himself to tell his parents or his brother what had happened and had avoided Marco and Raphael for several days, fearing they might read his face or question his refusal to go to the beach. Should he tell the police and ruin himself in the process? he had asked himself countless times. The answer always came back . . . no, no, no way. The violation would have to remain a secret he would carry with him for the rest of his life.

Glad to leave the village centre behind him, he quickened his pace. The gently undulating hills in the distance were a sprawling mosaic of parched earth, yellowing grasses and chalk-coloured limestone outcrops. He planned to take a walk in the hills later that day, to escape human contact for as long as possible and try to find peace. Veering off the asphalt road to walk through an orchard of citrus trees, studded with ripening fruit, he whistled to himself in an effort to lighten his heavy mood. But no amount of whistling could rid him of the lethargy and shame that riddled his system, that made him want to lie down beneath a tree, to fall asleep and forget. He tried to focus on the job he had to do; one he hoped would assuage his guilt. Andrico's animals needed feeding and Socrates carried with him a bucket full of vegetable peelings.

A police cordon no longer surrounded the house. Socrates approached it, half expecting Andrico to meet him at the gate with Koko perched on his shoulder, but nothing was as it had been. Life had lost its sweetness. Socrates felt as if he had eaten an accursed apple and was, like Adam, suddenly prone to emotions he had never before experienced: fear, loneliness and shame. Had he been walking around in a dream all his life, immune to reality, living in a fool's paradise? If so, it was no longer the case. Now, he could see the world for what it really was: unjust, corrupt, strewn with invisible obstacles a person could stumble over at any moment. For the first time in his life Socrates felt small and powerless, a pawn at the mercy of higher powers – his parents, the state, destiny and God.

Straggly weeds had already begun sprouting on Andrico's vegetable patch, between withering marrow, aubergine and cucumber plants, adjacent to tender green shoots that Socrates could not identify. The house itself looked neglected, though Andrico had only been gone for a matter of weeks, and the branches of the apricot appeared to have wilted, resembling a collection of downturned mouths, making the tree look forlorn. Socrates remembered the apricots he had picked and eaten the previous summer, the succulent yellow-orange flesh, tart and wonderfully sweet. Andrico had given him a bag of fruit to take home to his mother who had preserved the apricots in thick syrup and served them to her guests with Greek coffee.

Beyond the tree stood the shed, a lopsided wooden rectangle with a dirty grey window and a warped door hanging off its hinges. Socrates walked towards it and forced himself to step inside. He was dismayed by its bareness, his mind's eye reconstructing the cluttered interior he and his friends had painstakingly created. The Ponderosa they had childishly vowed to protect had been looted, destroyed, its magic extinguished. A chewing-gum packet lay at his feet, each strip a potential fuse for a firecracker. Marco's beer crate stood in a corner of the shed alongside Koko's tree-trunk perch. Bits of wood, torn paper and matchboxes littered the earth floor. Socrates picked up a matchbox and shook it to confirm there were matches inside before slipping it into his pocket.

The goat's plastic carton had recently been filled with fresh water and apples were piled high in a corner of the pen. The well-fed animal showed little interest in Socrates' vegetable peelings. The floor of the chicken coop had been scattered with seed. Some of the hens sat on the straw-covered ledge inside their enclosure while others wandered around the yard pecking at the ground. Socrates was curious to know who had tended the animals, who had scraped away the muck and droppings soiling their enclosures, who had brought the apples. All the villagers he knew had washed their hands of Andrico and kept their distance from a property that had assumed mythic significance as a house of horrors, the home of a beast.

A patina of grime covered the kitchen window. Socrates wiped the glass with his hand, blackening his palm, before peering into the kitchen. Inside he saw a mouse sniffing at the decaying contents of a plate on the table and he banged on the window to scare it away. A line of ants marched under the back door, parallel to another line travelling in the opposite direction carrying crumbs into a small crater with a hole at its centre. Socrates imagined the vast system of chambers and galleries beneath his feet where billions of ants fed and reproduced, recycled dead insects and pampered their queen. He knelt down and brushed the ants with his hand, watching them scatter before returning to their ordered columns. Then he rose to his feet, tried the back door handle, and was surprised when it gave and the door fell open.

He stepped into a kitchen slowly being colonised by wildlife. Ants looted the small pantry, mouse droppings littered the worktops, moth cocoons clung stickily to the bare plaster walls. Unidentifiable foodstuffs were green with fungal spores. The house had been left in a hurry and it felt to Socrates as if the owner had been chased away by a natural disaster or an advancing military force. He looked down at the dusty floor and saw footprints, bigger than his own, crisscrossing the lino. Someone else had evidently entered the house and even ventured beyond the kitchen. The herbs, cuttings and seedlings reared in margarine tubs on the windowsill had all perished. Withered stems and brown shoots trailed down over the sides of plastic containers. Walking into the living room, Socrates was dismayed to see that Andrico's cherished money plants, yuccas and geraniums had all met with the same fate. He set about watering the plants, filling a saucepan from the kitchen sink and drenching the parched soil in each pot.

The living room was hot, airless and smelled of decay. Socrates opened the window and a cool breeze blew in, airing the room and buffeting the grimy net curtains. He sat down on the carved wooden blanket box below the window, the wind cooling his face, and pulled the matchbox from his pocket. He opened it, took out a match and distractedly rolled it between his fingers before striking the tip, breathing in the sulphurous smell, watching the wood blacken and shrivel as it carbonised. When the orange flame had reached halfway, he licked his fingers and gently took hold of the tip, letting the wood burn right down to its base. Flicking the spent match out of the window, he struck another.

How would the net curtains burn? he wondered as the flame danced before his eyes then died. Would the light material ignite instantly like his bedspread? What sound would it make as it burned? Would it fizzle like wire wool or hair? He lit a third match, cupping his hand around the flame and impulsively putting it to the edge of the curtain. He did not anticipate the speed with which it would burn. The material smouldered momentarily before bursting into flames. Socrates leaped back and watched, believing the fire would stop once the curtain had disintegrated. Instead, a section of the burning material fell on to the hundred-year-old blanket box, setting it alight, and in an instant the dry window frame had caught fire too. Socrates ran for the saucepan, filling it up and flinging water at the oxygenated flames that spread uncontrollably, devouring the window, scaling the wall, splintering the glass. He grabbed the chequered blanket draped over the sofa and began beating at the window, the wall, the box, burning embers flying up into the room and singeing his hair. Remembering the hosepipe in the front garden he ran outside, turned it on from the outside tap and doused the window, drenched the living room, finally managing after what seemed like hours to extinguish the fire.

The frame had burnt away completely. Shattered glass lay on the ground. Socrates kicked at a section of loose plaster below the window that came away, revealing dry, fire-damaged mud bricks beneath. Angrily, he struck the wall again with his foot and watched it crumble. He looked down at the devastation, raked it with his foot and saw something shiny flickering among the debris. He bent down, picked up a gold ring inset with a small square of black onyx, and wondered if a builder had dropped it by accident into the render when the house was being built. Wiping off the dust, he read the name engraved inside the ring – Laki Kabraras – the name of Marco's late father, born at least fifty years after the house had been constructed. Perplexed, Socrates inspected the wall again and saw the end of a gold chain trickling out of a hole in the bricks and trailing down the side of the house. He pulled it out before using a stick to scratch at the mouth of the hole, gradually dislodging a store of screws, nails, buttons, bolts, hairpins, gold and silver jewellery. The hole was too narrow for a human hand to access but wide enough for a long, thin beak and Socrates realised he had found Koko's secret stash; that the compulsive thief had probably also taken Michali's christening cross from the field behind the arcade and implicated Andrico in a crime he did not commit. If he'd hidden it here, out of the way, the police might not have been so quick to arrest Andrico. Socrates felt a rush of excitement, stuffing his pocket with the bird's plunder, realising that with this new evidence he could save his friend without revealing his own secret. He stared through the gaping rectangular hole into the sodden house, strangely glad to have set fire to the curtains, knowing this fire was the work of fate. A movement through the back window caught his eye, a human shape moving across his sightline.

'Hey! Who's there?' he called out.

Socrates wondered if he had stumbled upon Andrico's

guardian angel, the person who deposited money in his letterbox, who cared enough to feed his animals, who was paying for his defence.

'Hello, who's there? Who are you?'

A face appeared at the dirty kitchen window and a familiar voice replied, 'It's me, Socrates. Your friend.'

Socrates froze. The fisherman was the last person he'd expected to see, the one person on earth he never wanted to lay eyes on again. Before he could run away or pick up the rake to defend himself Poli had appeared at his side, looking cheerful, extending a hand.

'It's good to see you.'

Socrates flushed with anger. 'Stay away from me – don't touch me.'

Poli took a step back, looking hurt, his eyes widening. 'Socrates, please, calm down. What's got into you? I thought we were friends.'

'I'm not your friend. Just leave me alone. Get lost. Why are you following me?'

'I'm not following you.'

'So you just happened to be here at the same time as me?'

'Yes, as it happens. Why are you treating me like this? I've been nothing but good to you. I taught you how to fish. I gave up my time for you. What the hell is wrong with you?' Poli showed no sign of regret, no hint of a guilty conscience.

'Go to hell. I hate you.' Socrates wanted more than anything to wound this man who had betrayed him.

'No, you don't. You hate yourself for what happened between us. But you don't have to feel bad – what

311

happened was simply an extension of our friendship, something natural and honest and good. And don't pretend you didn't enjoy it because I know you did. Ask yourself this question. How can something so enjoyable be bad?' Poli's self-assured tone was disarming, confusing. Socrates tried to gather his thoughts, to think of a reply, but his mind swam.

'Sexual pleasure is not a dangerous thing, my young friend – it's a part of life. Perhaps you weren't quite ready to face those wonderful feelings you had – I'm sorry if I scared you, but I'm not sorry for what happened between us. I care about you, Socrates, a lot. I love spending time with you, talking to you. I love everything about you. I would never do anything to hurt you, surely you believe that. I had a relationship with a man when I was your age – shared the happiest three years of my life with him. I could make you happy too, Socrates, if only you would let me. And there isn't that big an age difference between us . . .'

The thought of reliving the revulsion he'd experienced on the rocks, of having the fisherman's hands anywhere near him, appalled Socrates. 'I don't want to have a relationship with you. I can't stand you! I know what you did to Michali and I'm going to tell the police.'

'Tell them what?'

'Tell them the truth. That you're the attacker, not Andrico.'

'Do you want me to tell you the truth about your friend Michali? Do you? He was a very silly, greedy boy. A boy who thought he could have something for nothing. A boy who hassled me constantly for money, who paid me with sexual favours behind the arcade. One day I refused to pay him and that's when he made up that silly story about being attacked.'

'Why didn't he tell the police it was you?'

'Because he just wanted to scare me, extort more money from me. He doesn't want the police to catch me because then he'll have some explaining to do, as will you if you report me. You're not as innocent as you look, Socrates. You egged me on, admit it. You came to find me alone that night, without telling your parents. No one forced you to lie down on the sand beside me smoking cigarettes, and I don't remember you telling me to stop that day on the rocks. I would have stopped, right away, if I thought you didn't like it.'

'What about Michali's bruises?'

'The silly boy tried to fight me, to hurt me. I pushed him on the ground to protect myself. I never forced myself on him, ever. Not once. He was always a very willing participant in our relationship. He enjoyed himself very much, the same way you enjoyed yourself that day when we were fishing.'

Socrates knew he was being toyed with, manipulated, and felt a rush of cold hatred. This man had his arguments well honed, would swear black was white to suit his own purposes.

Poli looked pensive. 'The last thing I want to do is fall out with you, Socrates. Why don't we go into the house and talk this thing through? Find a solution.'

Socrates looked around him. The road was deserted. If he screamed for help no one would even hear him. Panicking, he turned and ran, his heart drumming inside

313

his chest, his throat stinging. Doubled over with cramp, he ran without stopping all the way to the police station where he emptied his pockets on the front counter before Duty Sergeant Stelios Georgiou.

'Andrico . . . didn't . . . do . . . it,' he said, breathlessly, his sides throbbing with pain. 'Look. Here's the evidence.'

'Calm down. Catch your breath, my boy. What are you talking about?'

'I have new evidence. Right here, in front of you.'

The policeman raised his eyebrows. 'You think a few nuts and bolts and a handful of jewellery are pertinent to the case?'

'This is all stolen. Look, this is Marco's father's ring.' Socrates thrust it into the policeman's hand. 'I found all this stuff in a hole in the wall of Andrico's house.'

Sergeant Georgiou shook his head, suddenly looking more interested. 'Ah, yes! I remember the taxi driver reporting the theft of his ring. I must pass it on to his poor widow.'

'Andrico didn't steal any of this. Koko did.'

'And who's Koko?'

'Andrico's pet magpie. He was always stealing things and stashing them away in cubbyholes.'

'And this means?'

'This means that Andrico didn't steal Michali's cross. Koko must have picked it up and taken it back to the house.'

The officer smiled. 'Thank you, Inspector Clouseau, but I'm afraid I don't agree with your interpretation of the evidence.'

Socrates knew he was being teased and angry tears

314

welled up in his eyes. The officer wasn't listening, wasn't taking him seriously, didn't want to understand. 'I'm telling you, Andrico didn't take the cross, Koko did.'

'And I'm telling you that if I go to my inspector with some ridiculous story about a bird, I am going to be the laughing stock not only of this station but of the whole town, maybe even the island. What you're telling me, as far as I can see, is that our suspect not only assaulted a boy but was also a kleptomaniac. I know you're having difficulty accepting Andrico's guilt but there's nothing I can do about that, I'm sorry. Now, go home and forget about him. He's not your problem. He'll be appearing in court in a couple of days and nothing and no one on earth can save him, not even his fancy lawyer.'

The policeman disappeared into a back office, leaving Socrates standing at the counter. A ceiling fan whirred above his head, circulating stale air. A fat beetle with antler-like mandibles ambled across the marble floor, past his feet. Cigarette smoke drifted out of the half-open door of the office and curled in the air like the tendrils of a fast-growing vine. The heat in the police station was oppressive and Socrates feared he might faint at any moment if he did not fill his lungs with fresh air. Exhausted and emotionally spent, he walked out of the station and slumped down on the front steps, burying his head in his hands and starting to cry.

35

Life as a civilian was rosy, a perpetual holiday. Petri slept during the day and spent his nights in the Pussy Cat. His favourite nightclub was a safe place to get drunk, to topple over, to fall asleep on a barstool. He was surrounded by friends and protected by his cousin Goliath, the doorman with striated biceps of Grecian granite. It was midday. Petri was up earlier than usual, sitting in his car parked close to the village bus stop, smoking a cigarette and drinking frappé made with three teaspoons of coffee, four sugars and half a litre of milk. His head clanged like a church bell and his sleep-deprived eyes ached inside burning sockets. A boiling sun shone through the windscreen, turning the car into a hothouse, making Petri feel listless and sleepy.

His eyelids drooped momentarily before he shook himself awake and focused on the bus stop, deciding to give Maria twenty more minutes of his time before driving away. If she failed to show up he would go back home, climb into bed and sleep the whole day. Perhaps he should not have come at all to intercept his neighbour and offer her a lift into work? What was he thinking of, obsessing about a girl from the village? A date with Maria would only complicate his life, make him the focus of local gossip and speculation. If his mother found out she might pressure him into marriage to 'save the girl's reputation' and . . . *finito*. No more nights out, no more romantic adventures, his life would be over before it had started. He would grow a belly, don the shackles of marriage and work like a dog for the rest of his life, trying to pay off a mortgage.

Perhaps he had acted too hastily in ending his relationship with Carina. He recalled their telephone conversation with some regret and considerable embarrassment.

'*I like you, Carina, but I mast forget you,*' he had said enigmatically, hoping this would suffice.

'*You only like me now? You don't love me any more?*' she had replied, sounding hurt, refusing to let him off the hook so easily, demanding a fuller explanation.

'*I want you to be happy, Carina.*'

'*I am happy.*'

'*One day, maybe, I make you sad.*'

'*No, I don't believe that.*'

'*Is better we split now.*'

'*Why?*'

'*Because one day you gonna leave me and break my heart.*'

'*I won't.*'

'*You will.*'

'*I won't.*'

'*I am no good man, Carina. No good.*'

'*Have you met someone else?*'

'*No. No, I promise. I don' even look at other girl.*'

'*Fucking lying Cypriot! Go to hell,*' was her final, withering utterance before she slammed down the receiver.

The caffeine was finally doing its job, perking him up, overstimulating his brain. Unbidden thoughts agitated him. He was at a crossroads in his life and had big decisions to make about the future. Should he get a job or go abroad to study? Should he stay in the village or look for work in town? Should he pursue Maria or keep his distance? Should he stake out the bus stop or drive away and escape the possible repercussions? Maria appeared in his rear-view mirror before he had made up his mind, walking determinedly, hips swinging beneath a tight pencil skirt, long dark hair trailing down her back. She strode past his car without noticing him and stopped at the bus stop to talk to the widow Loulla. Starting the engine, Petri drove slowly along the road and stopped just beyond the crooked metal post delineating the stop, pressing down on the car horn to get Maria's attention. She waved but continued talking to the widow and so he stuck his head out of the window and called out her name. Breaking off her conversation she approached the Mazda, leaning forward to speak to Petri through the passenger side window.

'I'm going into town. Do you want a lift into work?' he asked.

'Again? Two lifts to work in the same week!'

'I have jobs to do in town, that's all.'

'You look like death,' she replied. 'Your eyes are black. You should go home and get some sleep.'

The comment knocked his confidence. 'I had a late night last night.'

'And too much to drink?'

'No,' he lied, glancing at her bronzed cleavage that gave

318

off a sweet, flowery smell. 'I think I've got a cold coming on.'

'Then I'd better not get in the car with you. I don't want to catch anything.'

'You won't catch anything just sitting next to me.' He raised his eyebrows and she smiled coquettishly.

'No, it's fine. Really. The bus will be along at any minute.'

'But the bus is hot and I have air conditioning in my car.'

'Well, if you put it like that, how can I refuse?'

She took hold of the door handle and Petri's pulse began to race. She might be playing hard to get but he was master of this game. Soon she would be sitting beside him, her skirt hitched up just above the knee, her tanned legs visible from the corner of his eye.

'Kyria Loulla,' Maria called out to the widow, 'Petri's going into town. He's offered us a lift. He can take you to your sister's door – and he has air conditioning.' She turned back to Petri, raising her eyebrows. 'You don't mind, do you?'

Petri shook his head, realising she was playing games too.

'Praise God,' the widow said, lurching on arthritic hips towards the car.

Maria pulled open the door and helped Loulla into the passenger seat. Petri forced a smile, though his stomach clenched when the smell of must and camphor filled his nostrils, and the widow pulled up her skirt to air plump, misshapen knees, revealing short black stockings clinging to her fat calves. She turned the air-conditioning knob to full and wound up her window before settling back in her seat.

'Thank you, Petri,' she said, touching his hand with her clammy palm. 'It's so hot I thought I was going to die standing at that bus stop.'

Maria climbed into the back. Petri glanced at her through the rear-view mirror, thinking how pretty she looked, how unlucky it was to have Loulla in the car. The widow was the eyes and ears of the village, a notorious gossip who slithered from house to house like a terrestrial mollusc, leaving her residue wherever she travelled. She was undeniably entertaining, a great storyteller. A person could listen to her lewd and fanciful stories for hours without tiring. Even Petri, who considered himself above idle gossip, could not help but listen avidly to the conversation which ensued in the car.

'I don't believe he did it,' Loulla said. 'I watched Andrico grow up and never knew him to be violent, only soft in the head, poor soul. I don't believe he could hurt anyone, let alone a child.'

Maria leaned forward from the back seat. 'But they found the child's cross at his house.'

'Yes, so they say, but still I don't believe he committed the crime. And now that unfortunate man, who has had more than enough bad luck in his life, is locked up and awaiting trial. His poor mother must be turning in her grave. She was a good woman. A church-going woman. She raised that boy alone when the father left.'

'Why did he leave?'

'Because he couldn't bear to look at his son, because the man was filth.'

'Why do you say that?'

'He was a polygamist. He took a second wife without bothering to divorce the first and had three children by her. When his second wife died in a car accident he was left with three young children, which can't have been easy, I admit, but what did he do? He left them with his sister and went to England to find work. To make his fortune, he said. Well, he never came back, and never sent those children a single penny either. And the sister, well, she had five children of her own to raise and so she put her nephew and two nieces into an orphanage. God only knows what happened to them after that.'

'Didn't they have family in the village to look after them?'

'Not blood relatives, and certainly no one willing to take them in.'

'What a terrible story.'

'That man abandoned his own children and left a trail of devastation behind him.'

'So Andrico has siblings that he doesn't know about?'

'And never will, in all likelihood. That poor man is alone in this world. Only a miracle can save him from being locked up in an asylum for the rest of his life.'

Petri gazed at Maria in his rear-view mirror for a second too long, taking his eyes off the road, failing to notice that the car in front had stopped at red lights.

'Petri!' Maria called out.

He slammed his foot on the brakes and came to a screeching halt an inch from the car in front. The widow screamed, grabbed Petri by the shoulder, and thinking she would soon be joining her husband, called out, 'Sotiraki *mou*, I'm coming.'

'Kyria Loulla, you're not going anywhere for the moment,' Maria said. 'You're fine – we're all still in one piece. But perhaps Petri should keep his eyes on the road!'

The widow crossed herself and kissed the large gold crucifix hanging from her neck.

Petri shrugged and turned to smile at Maria. 'Sorry. I got distracted.'

The airport was his first stop. Petri climbed out of the car, determined to speak to Maria before she disappeared through the sliding doors leading into the departure lounge.

'What time do you finish work?' he asked.

'Not till late.'

'Can I take you out for a drink?'

'Not tonight. I have plans.'

'OK. See you,' he said, feeling disappointed, meaning goodbye for ever, refusing to beg this or any other woman.

'Why don't we meet at the bus stop at the same time tomorrow and talk about it then?'

'And will the widow be there?'

'No. She only goes into town once a week.'

Loulla wound down the window. 'Come on, Petri. My sister's waiting for me. You two love birds can talk later.'

'We're only friends, Kyria Loulla,' Maria replied.

The old woman raised an eyebrow. 'That's what they all say.'

Petri squeezed Maria's hand. She squeezed back and drew closer to whisper in his ear, making the hairs on his arms stand on end, 'They'll be marrying us off soon.'

'I'm not such a terrible prospect, am I?'

'No. But I'm enjoying my life at the moment and have no plans to settle down. No way. Not a chance.'

'Then we're perfectly matched.'

'You'd better go now and take Kyria Loulla to her sister's.'

'Yes. Thank you for lumbering me with the old woman!'

'And try to keep your eyes on the road this time.'

'There'll be nowhere else to look, will there? See you tomorrow.'

On his drive back to the village Petri relived the skin-tingling memory of Maria's breath tickling his ear and felt aroused. A warm wind blew through the open car window, brushing his ear, mimicking her warm whisper. Though he had known Maria all his life, he understood so little about her. He was keen to find out what made her tick, what made her smile and laugh, what turned her on in bed. Petri was intrigued and unsettled by Maria. She was both familiar and an unknown entity. When he looked into her eyes he felt she was a kindred spirit, the kind of girl he could, quite possibly, love and might even have a future with. Thoughts of Maria and the future intertwined in his head, linked inextricably, simultaneously scaring and exciting him. These thoughts occupied him all the way to the village, flooding his body with a warm feeling of optimism. As he drove past the police station he caught sight of his brother slumped on the steps and pulled the Mazda up sharply by the side of the road.

'*Re!* What's the matter? Why are you sitting like that?' he called out.

Socrates looked up. He wiped his eyes and shrugged.

'Come here and tell me what's wrong.'

Socrates stood up and walked across the street.

'Have you been crying?'

'No. I have dust in my eyes.'

'Don't lie to me. Tell me what's going on! Is this about Andrico again?'

Socrates blinked away fresh tears.

'Get in. Let's go for a drive.'

'Where?'

'Just round the block. So we can talk.'

Socrates climbed reluctantly into the passenger seat, feeling numb and uncooperative.

'You know you can tell me anything, don't you?' Petri said.

Socrates sighed and turned his head away to stare vacantly out of the passenger window.

'What are you afraid of? Speak to me. I can keep a secret, you know. Come on, Socrates, I know there are things on your mind.'

He nodded, suddenly wanting to tell his brother everything but not knowing where to begin.

'Please tell me what you were doing at the police station?'

'Presenting that stupid sergeant with new evidence. But he wouldn't listen to me, wouldn't take me seriously.'

'I don't understand why you're so obsessed with Andrico and his troubles. Why can't you let this matter rest and wait to see what happens in court?'

'Because he'll be convicted for sure if I don't try to help him.'

'OK. So tell me about this new evidence.'

Socrates told his brother about the fire he had started, about the crumbling mud bricks and the magpie's secret hoard including Laki Kabraras' ring. He still could not bring himself to talk about the incident on the rocks or the fear he had felt upon facing the fisherman again.

'How can you be so sure Andrico's innocent when everyone else believes he did it? Why do I feel there's something you're not telling me?'

Socrates took a deep breath before he spoke. 'I know who did it.'

'Who? Who did it, Socrates? Speak up. Is it someone I know?'

'No, you don't know him. I met him on the beach. His name's Poli. I thought he was nice at first. He made me a fishing rod and taught me how to fish. We cooked our catch on the beach and went night fishing together with a spear. I thought he was nice. I didn't know he would . . .' Socrates hesitated unable to find the words he needed to go on.

Petri pulled into a side street and stopped the car, turning to face his brother. 'Did this man do anything to you?' His voice was calm but his narrowed eyes were fiery and intense.

'I don't want to tell you. Don't force me to tell you! I feel too ashamed.'

'Did he touch you, Socrates? You have to tell me. I'm your brother and I love you and nothing you tell me can change the way I feel about you. Did this man touch you?'

Socrates nodded, confirming his brother's suspicions

and sparking a bellicose cry. Petri punched the leather steering wheel again and again with his clenched fist, cursing, his face turning red.

'I didn't know it would happen. I'm sorry,' Socrates said, his eyes streaming, fearing his brother's anger was directed at him.

'Why are you sorry? You have nothing to be sorry about.'

'But I let it happen. It's my fault. I let him touch me. I should have stopped him. I should have run away.'

'That's enough! You're not to blame. Not one bit. Don't ever say that again.'

'But . . .'

'But nothing. There are some very bad people in the world, Socrates. People without a conscience, without morals. I've never told anyone this, I was hoping I wouldn't have to, but a man tried to touch me once when I was your age. He sat beside me in the cinema and put his hand on my leg. I didn't know what was happening so I just sat there, frozen. I was scared, confused, and at the same time strangely curious.'

'And what happened?'

'The film reel stuck and the lights went on and the man got up and walked out. I had a lucky escape, Socrates, but I've never been able to forget that experience and I've always felt guilty for just sitting there, for not grabbing that man by the throat and squeezing the life out of him. That fisherman, Poli or whatever the hell his name is, took advantage of you, of your age and your innocence, your inexperience. Never forget that. Never. He was kind to you all right because he wanted to win your trust and get what he wanted, the damned son-of-a-bitch!'

'But I feel guilty.'

'Well, you shouldn't. Not a bit. You're not the first boy this has happened to and you won't be the last. Now, we need to go back to the police station so you can tell the officer everything you know about this man.'

Socrates shook his head. 'No, I can't. Mama and Papa will find out. My friends will hear about it. The whole village will know what happened.'

'An innocent man's reputation is at stake. You can't let Andrico go to prison, and you can't let the wanker who did this to you get his filthy hands on any other children. If I ever get my hands on him, I'll rip his head off.'

Socrates wondered if he should tell his brother where he had last seen Poli but decided against it, fearing Petri might start a fight.

'OK. Take me back to the police station, right now. Before I lose my nerve.'

Sergeant Georgiou stood at the front desk, yawning. 'Welcome back, Inspector Clouseau,' he said. 'What evidence have you brought me this time? Was Andrico's goat an accomplice in this crime? Should I go and arrest his chickens?'

Petri's eyebrows knitted together. 'My brother would like to make a statement, and I would ask you to take him seriously.'

'I've already heard what he has to say, and to be honest I've had enough of his ridiculous stories.' The sergeant had grown tired of this boy's attempts to sabotage the case. Statements had been collected from all the relevant parties and deposited with the Public Prosecutor; the verdict was a foregone conclusion.

'He has something very important to tell you.' Petri was poised to grab the officer by the collar of his white shirt and headbutt him. He spoke through gritted teeth, trying to suppress his rising anger. 'Something I'm sure you'll be interested to hear.'

Sergeant Georgiou turned to Socrates with the characteristic indolence of a Government employee averse to extra work, especially on a hot and humid day. He was due to clock off in twenty minutes, to meet his friends for coffee, and refused to delay his departure from the station. 'Come back tomorrow. I'm busy right now.'

'But the trial starts tomorrow,' Petri said.

'Then come back in an hour.'

'I want to speak to your superior.'

'I'm the only person here right now, and as I told you before I'm busy.'

'Damn you!' Petri shouted, slamming his fist down on the desk. 'Why don't you listen? My brother knows who did it. Who attacked Michali.'

The doubting apostle at the front desk appeared unimpressed by this revelation. He folded his arms across his chest and stared down at Socrates. 'Go on then. Tell me who did it.'

Socrates' cheeks flushed. The room felt stiflingly hot. He fought the urge to run out of the door and keep running until he had exhausted all his nervous energy. His brother's hand was pressing down hard on his shoulder, anchoring him to the spot. His throat felt tight. Socrates had no idea where to begin. What words to use. He feared the sergeant's reaction. Would he be ridiculed or even worse pitied? And what did he really know about Poli? Only his first name and where he liked to fish.

'Come on. I haven't got all day.'

'Tell him about the fisherman, Socrates. About what happened on the rocks.'

The sergeant glanced impatiently at his watch.

'I met a fisherman on the beach.'

'And . . .'

'And he taught me how to fish.'

'Bravo. Did you catch anything?'

'You're a real wanker,' Petri said, incensed by the policeman's mocking tone. 'The kid's trying to tell you something really serious and you stand there laughing.'

'Don't forget to whom you're talking, my friend. Carry on insulting me and I'll throw you both into a cell for the night to cool off. Now . . . tell me all about this fisherman.'

'Well, his name's Poli . . . and . . . he did something to me.'

Socrates stared down at his feet. He could not go on, could not tell this scornful, mocking, disrespectful man his most shameful secret. He had to leave, to get away before he started to cry and made an even bigger fool of himself.

'What are you waiting for . . . Red Thursday?' The sergeant started drumming his fingers irritably on the laminated counter.

'Come on, Socrates. Tell him.'

'I can't. I have to go.'

Petri knew from the distraught look in his brother's eyes

that he could not be pressured into making a statement. 'OK. Let's go now, but we have to come back later.'

'Don't bother coming back and wasting my time,' the sergeant called out, feeling vindicated, pursing his lips and shaking his head. 'I don't have time to waste on silly kids.'

Socrates was only half aware of the boy who brushed past him as he turned to leave. But the voice he heard was unmistakable and stopped him in his tracks. He looked up and saw Michali standing at the front desk, cowering before the stocky sergeant.

'I wonder what he's come in for,' Petri whispered.

The brothers waited by the door.

'I have to speak to someone in private,' Michali said, glancing apprehensively over his shoulder at Socrates.

'Come back later. My shift ends in ten minutes. Sergeant Papadakis will be taking over from me then. Talk to him.' He began straightening a pile of papers on the desk.

'Please, I need to speak to you in private. This can't wait.'

'Surely just for ten minutes?'

'But you've arrested the wrong man.'

The sergeant looked up, suddenly more interested. 'Really?'

'I know who attacked me.' The desperation in Michali's voice was palpable.

'And you've suddenly remembered after all this time? Have you been suffering from amnesia?'

'The wanker,' Petri muttered under his breath, wanting to strike out with his fists. 'I'm going to punch him in the mouth.'

330

'Wait!' Socrates grabbed his brother by the arm. 'You'll scare Michali away.'

'I know who attacked me,' the other boy repeated.

'Then why didn't you tell us before?'

'Because I was too scared to tell the truth.' Michali began shaking, his soft voice fading as he spoke.

'Well, save the truth for my colleague who takes over in . . .' the officer glanced at his watch '. . . about eight minutes from now.'

Petri rushed forward and lunged across the counter, scattering the neat pile of papers, grabbing the policeman by his shirt front. 'Don't you have a heart, man? Listen to the boy.'

The sergeant pulled himself free. 'Attacking a policeman is a criminal offence,' he barked, smoothing down his clothes.

Socrates stepped forward and took hold of Michali's arm, looking him straight in the eye. 'Was it Poli?'

Michali nodded, looking surprised and grateful.

'I know where he is.'

Petri turned to his brother. 'Where the hell is he?'

'At Andrico's house.'

'Then let's go and get him.'

Petri ran out of the station, grabbing his brother's hand. Sergeant Georgiou, suddenly spurred into action and forgetting the end of his shift, leaped over the counter and followed them. All three jumped into the Mazda and Petri sped away from the kerb, car wheels spinning and kicking up dust, the policeman sitting in the front passenger seat.

Poli was still standing where Socrates had left him,

beside the blackened window frame, sweeping the debris into a pile. He viewed the Mazda hurtling towards him with resignation, making no attempt to run away when Petri leaped out and flew at him, sending him toppling backwards on to the broken glass. He did not fight back but simply lay on the ground and covered his face with his hands, flinching and whimpering when Petri threw a punch that bloodied his nose, then kicked him in the stomach.

Socrates wondered if Poli was a coward or simply accepting the thrashing that he knew was inevitable and long overdue. He felt strangely sorry for the man squirming and moaning on the floor and was shocked by the look of violent fury on his brother's face. He had never seen Petri lose control before; never seen him hit a man or spit in his face without compunction. Socrates wondered if he were avenging the crime committed on the rocks or making Poli pay for every pervert who sat in a cinema waiting for a child to fondle.

Sergeant Georgiou was not a fast runner but he was burly and strong and managed to yank the enraged Petri back by the shoulders and fling him against the fence before pulling Poli to his feet.

'Is this the man Michali was referring to?' he asked Socrates.

'Yes.'

'The man he says attacked him?'

Socrates nodded.

'Your name, sir?' he asked, addressing Poli.

'Polycarpo Michaelides.'

'Well, a very serious accusation has been made against

you, Mr Michaelides, and I would like you to accompany me to the police station.'

Poli nodded.

'And what the hell has happened to this house?'

'I don't know. I only came here to feed Andrico's animals,' Poli replied.

'What's your relationship to Andrico?'

'I'm his half-brother.'

Socrates was taken aback by this revelation. How could this be? Was the fisherman's the face at Andrico's window? The man who'd left him money? Was Andrico the estranged relative the fisherman had referred to on several occasions?

'Right, let's take you back to the police station for questioning. And if you want, you can press charges against this clown for attacking you.'

'You walk home, Socrates,' Petri said, struggling to his feet, sensing his brother's need to escape. 'I'll take them back and see you at home.'

Poli climbed into the back of the car, clutching a bloody handkerchief to his nose. He turned to Socrates with a last look of hurt and defiance as the car drove away, and the boy knew in his heart that the fisherman would never feel any remorse for the actions he had committed.

True enough, the fisherman saw no real wrong in anything he had done, though he later admitted to a string of sexual offences against underage boys and hung his head in court – not out of shame but to mediate his sentence. He felt no need to repent when he had never forced himself upon any boy, but only given of himself, educated and loved. The fisherman would always prefer to believe he was unjustly demonised, the true victim of a misguided society that did not understand the real needs and desires of children.

36

The village was racked by its collective conscience and set about making amends. The carpenter who had threatened to slit Andrico's throat if he were ever released from prison offered to fit a new window free of charge. With the help of his apprentice and several other guilt-ridden volunteers he fixed the glass pane in place with putty and nails while the village plasterer repaired the exterior damage. No one knew who had set fire to the house or why, though many speculated that vigilantes were to blame. Inside the house, the pious women of the church philanthropic committee, who had referred to Andrico as cursed and/or possessed by the devil, were painstakingly cleaning, fumigating and restocking the fridge. New net curtains, handmade by Eleni, were ready to be hung once the window had been fitted and painted. Men, women and children who had slandered Andrico mercilessly now slapped paint on his smoke-damaged walls. They were as vociferous in their support of 'poor Andrico' as they had previously been damning of 'the beast'. His uncle, feeling obliged to show his face, arrived with a basket of fruit and a forced smile to welcome his nephew home. No sooner had he walked through the door than he was handed a brush and told to paint the outside toilet. Everyone had heard that Andrico's half-brother was the true villain, a paedophile, bad seed of Patroclos Michaelides and grandson of his namesake Polycarpo Michaelides. The sinner Patroclos had abandoned four children, including Andrico, to their fates and gone to England to start a new life.

A rumour began to circulate, causing ripples of excitement. The carpenter had heard from a friend of a friend that a big shot Hollywood director had heard about Andrico's story and was planning to make a film about it. Everyone agreed that the tragic tale had the makings of a hit movie. Some hoped they might even be cast in the film and imagined their names on advertising billboards and their pockets lined with US dollars. There was in fact no truth at all in the rumour that began life as a throwaway remark made by Kyriaco. 'Andrico's story has the makings of a film,' he had said to one of his customers, who repeated the comment to a friend, adding a pinch of verbal seasoning. Each time the remark was passed on a word was added or subtracted and the intonation subtly altered until it reached the ears of the carpenter, not as a passing comment but as a definitive statement. And the carpenter, a fan of *The Godfather*, added his own spin, telling his friends that the director in question was Francis Ford Coppola.

Kyriaco was unaware of the snowball he had unwittingly set in motion and the incredible stories doing the rounds of Andrico's house. He was in the front yard manning the *foukou*, the barbecue, on which cubes of lamb donated by the butcher were turning on battery-powered skewers.

Offering to feed the workers and cook Andrico's welcome home meal, he had closed up shop for the morning, bringing Barbara with him. They worked as a team, filling pitta breads with meat, hummus and salad, the tomatoes and cucumbers supplied by the grocer who was now planting small lemon trees in terracotta pots at the front of the house. Hector came back for a second filled pitta, lured not by the sweet smell of barbecuing lamb but by the sight of Barbara's shapely legs in a short skirt. He hung around until Kyriaco realised where his gaze was focused and chased him away. There were more than a few raised eyebrows when the arcade owner announced at midday that he was taking Barbara as his wife. Members of the women's philanthropic committee huddled in a corner querying the Filipina's religious denomination, agreeing with slow shakes of their cynical heads that the girl was a gold-digger who was marrying for money and a permanent visa. Meanwhile the menfolk glanced admiringly at Barbara, thinking Kyriaco a lucky man, wondering if the sexual prowess of oriental women lived up to its reputation.

Raphael snoozed beneath the shade of a carob tree, out of sight. He had helped early in the morning to build a new coop for the hens, but after he'd eaten his lamb *souvlaki* lethargy had taken hold and compelled him to lie down. Marco was at the top of a ladder, helping to whitewash the house. Physical work was a comfort to him, keeping his mind off recent events. He was still coming to terms with his loss and with feelings of guilt and regret for having attacked his father, voicing his hatred and wishing him dead. If only he could turn back the clock and erase his words and deeds on the day that blind fury overtook him. The memory of striking his father repeatedly with a broom haunted him, and he feared that he too might have inherited the Kabraras temper.

Fate had taken its tragic course and now Marco would never find out if his papa would have mellowed with age and become a better husband and father. Mingled with this sadness, however, were other, more positive emotions, ones he had not expected. At times Marco felt incredibly strong and confident and more than ready to take on his new responsibility as man of the house, his mother's rock. He climbed down the ladder to refill his bucket and glanced at her through the window, his chest swelling with pride at the dignified way with which she carried herself and the selfless love she lavished on her children.

Dressed in widow's garb, Irini was tending to the plants. Grateful to the benevolent force that had given her back her life, she now felt compelled to help others and in particular Andrico, though she had never slandered him. She pulled the dry leaves off a geranium and cut away the dead part of the stalk, leaving a live stump that would soon grow shoots and branch out. At times she felt euphoric but continued to act in public with all the dolefulness expected of a grief-stricken widow. Joy was a novel sensation for Irini and one that exploded inside her intermittently, bringing that irrepressible smile to her face. Occasionally she forgot Laki was dead and nervously waited for him to walk through the front door, smelling of whisky and menace. Then, coming to her senses, she'd remember with a surge of relief that he was gone for ever, that he would never make her tremble with fear again.

Time was slowly freeing her spirit of the phantom shackles she had worn for fifteen years.

Inner contentment seemed to be radiating through her flesh and bones, seeping out of her very pores and healing like a balm the damage the taxi driver had wrought. The lines around her mouth were becoming less pronounced, her hair was looking healthier, the bags beneath her eyes had begun to deflate and the frown that had rumpled her forehead for over a decade had all but vanished. That morning Eleni had called round to pluck and shape her bushy eyebrows, pruning the dark clouds that had cast a shadow for so long over her bright, nutmeg-coloured eyes. Such a small thing, such a minor act of vanity, yet Irini had felt incredibly uplifted to see her own face lighten. At Eleni's insistence Irini had bought herself a new dress and a pair of high-heeled shoes. Putting them on from time to time in the privacy of her bedroom, she felt like a real woman for the first time in fifteen years and realised with heart-wrenching sadness that she had spent her whole married life denying herself pleasure, pretending she did not need the fripperies demanded by other wives. One day soon she would venture outside wearing her new dress and shoes, and walk through the village square with her head held high. Standing in front of the mirror every morning she dared herself to smile and what she saw then surprised and excited her. She saw the smile of the lost girl, the carefree soul she had once been.

Irini looked up and caught the grocer staring at her through the newly installed window. He flushed and turned away and Irini felt her own cheeks burn. During her married life she had given up on the romantic idyll of loving and being loved, believing this dream had by-passed her. Now, she dared to hope that maybe one day, if her luck had truly turned, she might meet a man she could adore, who might return her feelings, a man like the gentle, self-deprecating grocer. She glanced back at the window and felt a wave of pleasurable heat surge through her body.

Socrates watched Marco's mother at work with interest, amazed that the desiccated plants were slowly rising from their deathbeds. His own crushed spirit was also healing, though he had feared he would never be able to feel un-reserved happiness again, that he would always feel tainted and guilty for what had happened to him. Poli's shadow lingered in the periphery of his consciousness but it was fading, growing less oppressive by the day. His brother had helped to ease his conscience by repeating time and time again that he had been sinned against and was blameless, that the fisherman was a dangerous predator. The two brothers had gone fishing together several times on the rocky outcrop and Socrates had begun to associate the place with good memories now, of happy days spent there with Petri.

Wandering through the house he stopped to stare at Victora who was holding a brush and palette, painting a mural on Andrico's bedroom wall. It was a copy of the forest that hung over his own bed, a vibrant landscape thick with trees and brightly coloured birds with round eyes, sparkling with life. Socrates had purposely kept his distance from the puppet master, feeling guilty for breaking into his house, for doubting an innocent man and allowing irrational fears to get the better of him. How

340

easy it was to malign a man, to blacken his name and turn him into a monster, to misinterpret his kindness. As if sensing the boy's eyes upon him, Victora turned suddenly and beckoned Socrates over.

'I would like my belongings returned,' he said matter-of-factly, turning back to the mural, loading the tip of his brush with brown paint and filling in the outline of a branch. 'You broke into my house, did you not?'

'How do you know?'

Victora sighed and looked down at Socrates. 'I'm surprised you ask.'

'Of course. You know because you can read people's minds.'

'*Non, mon petit garçon avec les yeux coupables.*' Victora smiled. He put a hand in his trouser pocket and pulled out a marble. 'I know because I found this in my wardrobe and I distinctly remember giving it to you as a gift. You must have dropped it when you were going through the contents of my bedroom.'

Socrates felt his cheeks burn. 'I'm sorry. Very sorry. Please don't say anything to my parents. They'll kill me.'

'I won't, though I probably should. I can only assume your curiosity got the better of you. Why else would you break into my house? Now, where is the photograph you took? I only have one copy and it is very precious to me.'

'It's at home. I took your penknife too.'

'And the golden apple?'

'I'll go home right now and bring back all your belong-ings.'

'First, come with me.'

Victora set down his tools and led Socrates by the arm

out of the bedroom and into the lounge, stopping in front of the round table covered with an embroidered cloth on which Andrico paid homage to his mother. He picked up the framed photograph on the table and handed it to Socrates. 'Take a close look. Do you recognise this woman?'

'That's Andrico's mother.'

'Yes. Who looks like . . . ?'

Socrates studied the photograph, those bright eyes jolting his memory. 'She looks like the woman in the picture I took from your pocket.'

'And?'

'My God! *She's* the woman you fell in love with?'

'Bravo. You're a clever boy. And I have something else to tell you, and only you – my deepest, darkest secret. If this gets out I will be forced to tell your parents about your criminal tendencies.'

'I won't tell a soul, I promise. What is it?'

'Andrico is not the son of that sinner Patroclos who fled to England. He's *my* son. My flesh and blood.'

'What!' Puzzlement quickly remodelled itself into anger. 'Why did you abandon him then? Why did you leave his mother? You're as bad a man as Patroclos.'

'No, don't say that. You don't know what happened. I didn't even know I had a son. When I heard his mother was dying, I came back to the village to say my goodbyes and that's when she told me.'

'But why didn't she tell you if she was having a baby?'

'For reasons a young boy doesn't need to know.'

'I'm not as young as I look. Not in here.' Socrates patted his right temple with his index finger. 'Tell me, please.'

'OK. In spite of my better judgement and because you have been a true friend to Andrico, I will tell you. Because, my young friend . . . she was already married. When she heard I was leaving the village, she came to find me and we allowed our passion to get the better of us. You're too young to understand about these things, to understand about emotions too powerful to control. I left without knowing she was pregnant, and she pretended the baby was her husband's to avoid causing a scandal in the village. That woman fought her whole life to uphold her reputation and I must preserve it now she's dead. That's why no one must ever find out about my relationship to Andrico. If I had known she was carrying my child, I would have come back and taken her and the baby away with me.'

'So why did she tell you at all?'

'Because she didn't want to leave our son alone in the world. She made me promise to look out for him, to protect and love and provide for him.'

'So you're the one gives him money?'

'Yes. I am no longer a poor man, Socrates, and everything I have now belongs to Andrico.'

'But how can you love him from a distance? Why don't you tell him?'

'His mother told me not to. She said I would only confuse him. But I know he can feel the love I have for him, he knows someone's looking out for him. And as long as I live, he won't be alone. When I'm gone he'll have my house and everything I own and friends like you to look out for him.' Victora's eyes watered and he swallowed hard. 'The woman I love left me the gift of a son and I bless her for that, every second of the day. I only wish

I could have been a real father to Andrico. I wish I could have raised him and watched him grow and taught him to paint and been a strong shoulder for him to lean on. I would never have left him, never turned my back on him because of his problems, would only have loved him all the more. He really is marvellous, isn't he? You think the world of him, don't you?'

Socrates nodded. 'Yes, he's marvellous, kind-hearted and a good friend.'

'And you're a good boy, whatever anyone in the village might say about you.'

'Are you the one who's been following him and staring through his window?'

'No, I wouldn't do that. I wouldn't want to scare him. That must have been the unfortunate fisherman who thought he'd found a brother.'

'But you paid for the lawyer – right?'

'Of course. I knew all along he wasn't guilty. I hired the best lawyer I could afford. Now, look over there.' Victora motioned towards the side window. 'You see that apricot tree, planted the year my son was born? I gave it to his mother before I left, along with the golden apple you stole. She cherished that apple all her life and gave it back to me on her deathbed.'

'Why did you give her an apple?'

'The golden apple, my young friend, has been a symbol of love since antiquity, and will be for time immemorial.'

'And the apricot tree?'

'The closest thing to a living symbol of my love, the closest I could get to giving Andrico's mother a tree bearing golden apples. Don't look perplexed, just think about it. Work out my riddle. What do we call the fruit that grows on that tree, *mon petit*?'

'*Chrysomila.*'

'Which means, in its literal sense?'

'Golden apples.'

'*Exactement!* In Cyprus we call apricots *chrysomila*, golden apples. In Greece they call the fruit *verikoko*, but then only on our island did Aphrodite's love tree bearing golden apples grow.' Victora smiled and embraced Socrates.

'Andrico's coming,' the carpenter shouted from his ladder and the assembled workers cheered.

'He's arrived,' the puppeteer said excitedly, taking the photograph out of Socrates' hand and putting it back down on the table. 'My son is back where he belongs.'

'False alarm! It's only Niko,' the carpenter called out again, inducing a communal sigh as Niko's car pulled up outside the house.

'I have to go,' Socrates said, heading for the front door, wondering why his father had not come earlier to help as he had promised, his mind swimming with the revelations he had just heard.

Niko climbed out of the driver's seat, greeted his son and unloaded a cage from the back of the car. 'Sorry I'm late, but I had to pick up a passenger. I went into town to buy a present for Andrico – a parrot to keep him company. He's tame and he can talk.'

'What a lovely bird,' Socrates said, tapping the cage. The bird eyed him distrustfully before trying to bite his finger. 'He's not very friendly.'

'He doesn't like being in a cage, that's all. The man at the shop said he usually sits on a perch.'

A police car approached slowly along the unmade road and pulled up outside the house. Andrico had finally arrived and would soon see his welcoming party, his freshly whitewashed house and the parrot. Socrates wanted him to know he was loved and had been missed. Villagers began piling out of the house and followed Socrates along the front path, gathering excitedly round the police car. Sergeant Stelios Georgiou climbed out of the driver's seat and pulled open the back door, waving the villagers aside. A dishevelled-looking man in creased clothing emerged, his shoulders hunched, his eyes fearful of the crowd that had come to welcome him. Socrates took him by the arm and led him through the press of bodies, feeling him flinch every time someone reached out to pat his arm or his back, as if every hand were the point of a blade.

'It's OK, Andrico. Don't worry. Everyone here has come to welcome you back. We've all missed you,' he said, unsettled by his friend's dishevelled appearance, leading him straight to the parrot.

Andrico walked with his head lowered, avoiding eye contact with his estranged uncle, with the women who brought food parcels at Easter time, with the old man wearing black pantaloons, with the arcade owner standing beside a smoking barbecue. He wanted to go back to his cell, to huddle in a corner away from prying eyes and cover his ears. He did not fully understand why they had taken him away in the first place. They told him he had hurt a boy. What boy? he had asked, knocking his fists against his head in desperation. He was depraved, they said, a menace to society who would be locked up for the

346

rest of his life. They had moved him from the holding cell at the police station to Nicosia's central prison, where he had lost all hope of ever being released. Until one day, out of the blue, they unlocked his cell, led him through the prison gates into bright sunlight that hurt his eyes, and drove him home. Just like that. With no word of explanation or apology. And now here he was, as if he had never left, with a crowd of people buzzing around him like mosquitoes, their animated hum vibrating irritatingly in his ears and growing louder. One minute he was locked up in a cell facing a life sentence, the next he was a free man. What guarantee was there that the policeman would not change his mind again, take him by the shoulders and march him back to the car and a life behind bars? People were not to be trusted, their smiles were deceptive, their favours came at a price.

'We've fixed up the house,' Socrates said. 'And built a new pen for the chickens, and Kyriaco has made you something to eat.'

'I want everyone to go away,' Andrico whispered, hands held up to his eyes like blinkers. 'Tell them to leave. I want to be alone.'

This was not the joyous homecoming Socrates had imagined for his friend. Andrico looked terrified, like a man about to be lynched. Socrates feared he might have a panic attack like the one he had had on the day that Koko died. Suddenly, the parrot screeched, arresting Andrico's attention. Slowly he lowered his hands. Niko held up the cage and Andrico brought his face close to the bird.

'Hello, my friend. How are you?' he said gently.

The bird scampered at the bottom of the cage, peeled

a striped sunflower seed and nibbled it before climbing the bars and drawing close to Andrico, making a gurgling noise that sounded like contentment.

'He seems to like you. He tried to bite me,' Socrates said. 'Anyway, he's yours. Papa bought him for you from a pet shop in town.'

Andrico smiled momentarily before anxiety creased his face again and he shook his head. 'I can't keep him. Take him away, Socrates. I don't want him.' His tone was harsh and decisive and he looked to be on the verge of tears.

'But why?'

'Because I cannot keep an animal locked up in a cage. Even my chickens are free to roam, you know that, and the goat comes and goes as it pleases. So take it away, please.'

'But you don't have to keep the parrot locked up. You can take him out of the cage and put him on a perch. That's what the shopkeeper said, isn't that right, Papa?'

Niko nodded.

Swayed by Socrates' assurances, Andrico drew close to the cage and his tired face came alive as he marvelled at the bird's colourful plumage and bright, sensitive eyes. He wanted to stroke the bird, to feel its warmth against his chest, to feed it from his hand and prop it on his shoulder. Captivated by the parrot, he no longer felt afraid of the crowd that slowly closed in on him. They were unimportant, an annoyance, but no threat. He took hold of the cage from the handle at the top and headed for his front door, talking gently to the bird, ignoring the villagers who waited for their individual efforts to be acknowledged and appreciated. Andrico failed to notice the new window, the fresh coat of whitewash and the lemon trees lined up in his yard. He walked into the house and closed the door behind him, shutting out the world, chatting only to the clever bird that would become his trusted companion, that would learn to say 'good morning', that would follow him from room to room and bring him joy, that would outlive the puppeteer and be a comfort to Andrico in his old age.

'Let's collect up our stuff and go,' the carpenter said. 'Let the poor man get some rest.'

'What a waste of good meat,' Hector said, eyeing up the barbecue and Barbara's legs.

Kyriaco clapped his hands together. 'Don't forget we have another happy event to celebrate today. My betrothal! Let's go back to the arcade and have a party. There is plenty of food and the fridge is well stocked with Keo and *zivania*.'

Hector rolled the corners of his moustache between his fingers and smiled in anticipation of the strong spirit that would soon hit the back of his throat and enliven his senses.

'Kyria Irini,' the grocer said, putting down his secateurs. 'Perhaps you would permit me to give you a lift to the arcade?'

When Irini nodded the bumptious woman standing beside her could barely contain her indignation. 'Her husband is still warm in his grave and she agrees to go to a party with another man. Disgraceful!' she whispered to her neighbour.

Socrates watched Victora walk slowly away, a leather satchel hanging from his shoulder. He knew where the puppet master was headed, that his first stop would be the cemetery where he would share the good news of Andrico's return with the woman he loved as much in death as he had loved her in life.

'Come on. Let's go and enjoy ourselves,' Niko said to his son. 'You can come back later and see Andrico.'

'I don't want to go to the arcade, Papa. I have something else to do.'

Niko raised his eyebrows. 'Nothing too perilous, I hope!'

'No, of course not!' Socrates protested, not meeting his father's eye.

In fact, he had spent the previous evening hatching plans to blow up an old car discarded on a piece of wasteland on the outskirts of the village. The white Subaru, dumped by its owners on a field several miles from their home, sat in a bed of dry nettles slowly rusting away. It had become home to several nesting birds and had provided temporary shelter from the rain in winter for a litter of feral cats. Socrates had filled the tank with petrol and managed, after consulting the village mechanic, to start the engine by cutting and manually connecting the ignition wires. He had driven the car round the field several times, jerkily careering over the rocky ground with Marco, Raphael and an old bird's nest as his passengers. After considering then dismissing the idea of driving the car on the open road, he had devised a way to ignite the petrol tank from a distance using a length of rope, a screwdriver and a small piece of wood. His friends had agreed to help and Socrates now itched to put his plan into action, to satisfy his curiosity and quench his thirst for danger.

THE END

EAT, DRINK AND BE MARRIED
Eve Makis

Anna's head reels with plans to escape life behind the counter of the family chip shop on a run-down Nottingham council estate. Her mother Tina wants nothing but the best for her daughter: a lavish wedding and a fully furnished four-bedroom house with a BMW parked in the driveway. She thinks Anna should forget the silly notion of going to college and focus on finding a suitable husband. Mother and daughter are at loggerheads and neither will give way.

Anna's ally and mentor is her grandmother Yiayia Annoulla. She tells Anna stories about the family's turbulent past in Cyprus, the island home they were forced to abandon. Yiayia practices kitchen magic, predicts the future from coffee grains and fills the house with an abundance of Greek-Cypriot delicacies.

Anna longs for the freedom enjoyed by her brother Andy but spends time appeasing her parents, dodging insults from drunken customers or going on ill-fated forays with her petulant cousin – the beautiful Athena. It is only when family fortunes begin to sour that Anna starts to take control of her own destiny . . .

'HEART-WARMING, FUNNY, TRAGIC AND UPLIFTING . . . THE STORY HAS A FEELGOOD FACTOR TO EQUAL *MY BIG FAT GREEK WEDDING*'
Narinder Dhami

9780552772167

BLACK SWAN

THE MOTHER-IN-LAW
Eve Makis

Electra and Adam are living proof that opposites attract.

Electra is warm, passionate and creative. She
wants to have a baby.

Adam is calm, reasonable and very English. He doesn't.

Enter the mother-in-law . . .

Cold, critical and snobbish, she disapproves
of her son's marriage.

And then she moves in with them.

Will their relationship survive?

A darkly funny, insightful and cautionary tale that will
make you question where *your* loyalties lie.

'WITH SIZEABLE PINCHES OF LOVE, TRAGEDY AND
HUMOUR, THIS IS DELICIOUSLY SATISFYING'
Cosmopolitan

'ENGAGING, DELICATELY OBSERVED
AND BELIEVABLE'
Good Housekeeping

9780552773249

BLACK SWAN